Dear Reader:

The novels you've enjoyed over the past years by such authors as Kathleen Woodiwiss, Rosemary Rogers, Johanna Lindsey, Laurie McBain, and Shirlee Busbee are accountable to one thing above all others: Avon has never tried to force authors into any particular mold. Rather, Avon is a publisher that encourages individual talent and is always on the lookout for writers who will deliver *real* books, not packaged formulas.

In 1982, we started a program to help readers pick out authors of exceptional promise. Called "The Avon Romance," the books were distinguished by a ribbon motif in the upper left-hand corner of the cover. Although the titles were by new authors, they were quickly discovered and became known as "the ribbon books."

Now "The Avon Romance" is a regular feature on the Avon list. Each month, you will find historical novels with many different settings, each one by an author who is special. You will not find predictable characters, predictable plots, and predictable endings. The only predictable thing about "The Avon Romance" will be the superior quality that Avon has always delivered in the field of romance!

Sincerely,

WALTER MEADE
President & Publisher

Other Avon Books by
Nancy Moulton

DEFIANT DESTINY

CROSSWINDS

NANCY MOULTON

AVON
PUBLISHERS OF BARD, CAMELOT, DISCUS AND FLARE BOOKS

CROSSWINDS is an original publication of Avon Books.
This work has never before appeared in book form. This
work is a novel. Any similarity to actual persons or events
is purely coincidental.

AVON BOOKS
A division of
The Hearst Corporation
1790 Broadway
New York, New York 10019

Copyright © 1985 by Nancy Moulton
Published by arrangement with the author
Library of Congress Catalog Card Number: 84-091764
ISBN: 0-380-89591-9

First Avon Printing, July 1985

AVON TRADEMARK REG. U. S. PAT. OFF. AND IN
OTHER COUNTRIES, MARCA REGISTRADA, HECHO EN
U. S. A.

Printed in the U. S. A.

WFH 10 9 8 7 6 5 4 3 2 1

CROSSWINDS

Chapter 1

Philadelphia, Pennsylvania—1846

"LOGAN . . . LOGAN, DARLING . . ." THE SOFT VOICE barely penetrated Logan Tremaine's troubled dreams. He mumbled something unintelligible and turned away from the sound, trying to block it out.

"Logan, darling . . . Wake up," the voice persisted. Gently caressing lips moved over his bare shoulders and along his back.

Belle Collier loved to slowly awaken Logan like this, anticipating the moment when he would come to full wakefulness and respond to her searching touch. She snuggled close against his back now, feeling the warmth, the strength of him against her naked breasts and down her whole length. Her body still tingled from their joining earlier. She wanted him to touch her again, to feel his passion thrust to the depths within her body.

Yet Belle realized Logan gave his body to her freely enough, but that was all. He would not reveal his inner self to her no matter how she tried to get close to him. Always he held something back. The realization saddened her.

She couldn't arouse him now. He seemed oblivious to her teasing touches and caresses this morning. In a pout, Belle got out of bed, slipped on a flowered wrapper, and went to the window where she pulled back the heavy gold satin drapes. The bright midday sunlight of the warm June day flooded into the room. Logan stirred and moaned.

"Damn, woman! Are you trying to blind me with all that

blasted light?" he cursed as he threw an arm across his eyes.

Belle smiled triumphantly as she opened the second-story window and sat down on the sill to turn her face to the warm rays.

"You said to awaken you by noon," she replied defensively. "It's that now."

From the street below a man's voice called a greeting to her. Belle laughed and waved, returning his "good morning" merrily.

"One of your many admirers?" Logan asked, but with no real interest. He was standing now, stretching one muscular arm behind him, and rubbing the back of his neck with the other. Then he reached for his trousers and pulled them on.

"Yes, he is, as a matter of fact," she answered loftily, studying his handsome face for a reaction. She wished she could have seen a spark of anger or jealousy there, but his face was expressionless as he walked over to the small washstand and splashed water from the white porcelain pitcher into it. Then he leaned over and lowered his head into the water.

Belle watched Logan from across the room as he dried his black wavy hair with a towel. She let her eyes trace a path along the back of his body from his head to the rippling muscles of his wide, bare shoulders, down to his tapered waist ending in the expensively tailored brown trousers. She memorized every inch of his six-foot frame so she would have something to hold onto when he was gone. Every time he left her, Belle never knew when or even if she would see him again. It might be a week, a month, or as long as six months. The only thing she knew for sure was how frustrated and impatient she would become waiting for him to return. Logan Tremaine was her lover. The other men she had when he wasn't around were only customers. None compared to Logan.

"What in heaven's name did you give me to drink last night, Belle?" Logan was frowning as he turned to glare at her. "My head's splitting."

"Don't blame me for your bad head this morning," she replied, bringing her thoughts back to the moment. "You drank my best bourbon as usual. It wasn't *what* you drank, it was *how much* you drank. You had enough for three men. It's a wonder you have any head left on at all."

Logan went over to the upholstered chair where he'd laid the rest of his clothes the night before and reached for his white silk shirt.

Belle had wondered about his mood last night. It still seemed to be with him this morning, too. Logan had seemed tense, brooding about something. Though he had set it aside when he made love to her, afterward it returned. She could sense it. Something was troubling him, but Belle knew better than to ask him about it.

"I'm paying dearly now for my overindulgence, believe me," Logan replied as he sat down on the chair and bent over to pull on his boots. The throbbing in his temples intensified and his frown deepened as he slowly stood up and slipped on his cream-colored satin waistcoat, then his brown suitcoat.

"You're not staying for breakfast?" Belle asked, knowing the answer. She could already feel the distance between them.

"No," he answered coolly. "I have a situation that must be resolved, and time is of the essence. I must go."

Belle caught his arm as he moved past her toward the door. She couldn't match his coolness any longer.

"Logan, please don't go. Tell me what's troubling you. Let me help if I can," she pleaded, concern showing on her face and in her eyes.

His manner softened only a fraction as he gazed at the beautiful red-haired woman before him.

"You did help for a while last night, Belle," he told her, his pale blue eyes holding hers. He tipped her face up and bent to kiss her lips. Then he turned and went out the door without another word or a backward glance.

Chapter 2

AS LOGAN IMPATIENTLY WAITED FOR HIS HORSE to be saddled at the livery stable behind Belle's house he thought again of his meeting with his friend Hugh Tennyson the night before—the meeting that had put such a black cloud of gloom over his head. . . .

"I should have known that conniving brother of mine would try something like this while I've been away these past months. Miles never was one to let an opportunity slip through his greedy fingers," Logan had observed in a low voice after he'd heard what Hugh had to tell him.

He sat back in his chair across from Hugh in the hotel room. Hugh wasn't fooled by the calm demeanor his friend exhibited. They'd been friends since boyhood. He knew Logan Tremaine only too well, but wished Logan would rant and rave his fury like other men. He knew this cool, carefully controlled attitude was far more dangerous.

"You should get back to Fair Oaks, Logan," Hugh tried to convince him. "Your grandfather's health is deteriorating. If he should die before you have a chance to comply with this codicil to his will or can convince him to invalidate it, you'll lose control of your inheritance. Miles will have charge of everything—the plantation, the orchards, the mill, the champion stock, just as he's always wanted."

"Knowing my pigheaded grandsire as well as I do, I'd be wasting my breath trying to get him to change it," Logan countered. "He was no doubt delighted when Miles proposed this damned stipulation to his will. He knows how I would chafe under it. It's just another way to try to bring me to rein, keep me under his control. He'd love to have me try to get him to change his mind, just so he could have the

4

supreme pleasure of refusing, and it'll be a cold day in hell before I'll ever give the old bastard that satisfaction." Logan's voice remained level, almost casual. Only a slight tightening in his jaw hinted at a smoldering undercurrent.

"Then the only other recourse is to comply with the stipulation," Hugh offered tentatively, knowing only too well what Logan's reaction to that would be.

"An equally repulsive idea, counselor," Logan answered coldly as he quickly got to his feet and walked over to the small desk near the door where a decanter of bourbon was set. "You know of my abhorrence for the holy estate of matrimony," he reminded his friend in a bitter voice.

Logan paused to pour himself a substantial amount of the amber liquid from the container. His eyes narrowed to slits as he stared off into space.

"Logan . . ." Hugh tried to reason.

"No, Hugh," Logan cut in sharply. "I want no part of such an arrangement." He downed half of his drink in one gulp.

"Miles knows that's a weapon he can use against you. Foil him in this, Logan," Hugh went on earnestly, ignoring his friend's stubborn declaration. "Pick one from your bevy of paramours and make an honest woman of her before your twenty-seventh birthday. Give your grandfather the heirs he claims to want before Miles gets control of everything!"

"My paramours will remain just that, my friend," Logan said, his tone a little lighter. "There is not one of them I'd relish waking up to each morning on a permanent basis. And brats . . . perish the thought!"

Hugh Tennyson threw up his hands in exasperation. He loved Logan Tremaine like a brother but sometimes he wanted to throttle him!

"Well, at any rate you should at least go back to Fair Oaks as soon as possible. You're just about finished with your business here in Philadelphia, aren't you?"

"Yes, I hadn't expected to be away from the plantation for these three months," Logan explained, glad for the change of subject. "But then you know of the complications that have detained me here."

Hugh nodded, replying, "As usual, you have been able to resolve the problems. You have an instinct for people, my

friend. You can size up a man quickly and be dead right
about him. How I wish I had that talent to use in the courtroom."

"Well let's just hope my 'instinct,' as you call it, doesn't
fail me or we could all be in one hell of a lot of trouble." Logan gave Hugh an amused half smile as his blond friend
stood up and reached for his hat. Logan stood up also and
extended his hand.

"Thanks for the information about Miles, Hugh. Tell
Watkins I owe him one for keeping his eyes open at my
grandfather's barristers. At least now I'll have a chance to
plot some retaliation instead of having Miles spring this
on me at an inopportune moment. I'll be in touch."

Logan Tremaine's night with Belle Collier hadn't eased
the troubled thoughts Hugh's information had caused
him. He decided a hard ride in the open countryside would
do more to clear his head for thinking up a solution.

Astride his big black stallion on the crowded street, Logan towered over the people scurrying in every direction to
get out of the way of the nervous horse's prancing hoofs.
The animal shied and snorted impatiently while Logan
held him in tight rein as a broken-down tinker's wagon
wobbled by in front of them.

"Easy, Baron. Easy, boy," Logan murmured as he patted the stallion's perspiring neck. "A few more blocks, boy,
then we'll be out of this hellish crowd and I'll give you your
head."

With great care Logan guided his prancing mount,
weaving first to one side and then the other to avoid the
carriages, wagons, and pedestrians that were all vying for
a place on the streets.

Chapter 3

RHEA MERRICK LOWERED HER EYES BEHIND HER
spectacles and let her mouth turn down in a contrite expression so that the hateful woman before her wouldn't see
the anger that smoldered in her blue eyes.

"Please, Mrs. Wiggins. I shall pay you on Thursday,"
Rhea promised meekly. "But I must have these things to
finish Mrs. Corrington's order if I am to do so."

"Oh, very well, take them then. No one else would likely
buy these things anyway," Mrs. Wiggins spewed at her
nastily. The older woman leaned forward over the counter
and wagged a bony finger in Rhea's face.

"But mind you, this is the last time you get anything
from me unless you can show hard coin for it. Now away
with you. I have better customers to attend to."

Rhea bit her lip until it bled to keep from lashing out at
the sharp-tongued storekeeper. As quickly as she could,
she gathered up the brown-paper-wrapped packages of material, skeins of yarn, spools of ribbon and thread, and decorative feathers she'd just purchased on account. They
made a precarious pile in Rhea's arms, and she had to use
all her concentration to control her anger as she carefully
made her way to the door and outside.

A sudden cloudburst earlier in the morning had left the
roadways mired in mud in many places. Logan tried to
avoid these slippery areas as he guided Baron down the avenue. A narrow lane opened along the edge of the wooden
sidewalk to his right and Logan saw his chance to gain
some headway to the street he sought. When he turned
Baron at the next corner, it was easier going. Freed at last

from the tight control on his reins, the big horse dug his hoofs into the soft ground and lunged forward.

At the same moment, Rhea Merrick stepped off the sidewalk directly into the path of the charging stallion. Logan barely had time to jerk Baron's head back fiercely with the reins. The powerful horse screamed in protest as he reared high on his hind legs and twisted his head to try to escape the cut of the metal bit. At the terrible sound Rhea glanced up in fright to see the big stallion's thrashing hoofs pawing the air only inches from her head. She instantly screamed and dropped her packages, throwing her arms up instinctively for protection. She jerked to the side, lost her balance, and sprawled backward onto the wooden sidewalk.

Logan had to use all his skill to keep his seat on Baron's back. He eased the big horse down and steadied him a moment before quickly dismounting.

"Easy, Baron. Easy now, boy," he soothed, patting the horse's neck. Then he tossed the reins over the nearest hitching rail and turned his full fury on the woman sprawled on the sidewalk.

"You stupid little fool! Don't you have sense enough not to step in front of a horse like that?" he shouted as he waded to reach her through the parcels scattered in the mud. His eyes glared at her furiously.

Rhea's own smoldering anger and humiliation sparked into flame. She wanted to scream back at this outrageous man yelling at her that *he* was the fool for riding his horse at such a breakneck speed. For a split second the heated words were poised on the tip of her tongue as Rhea glanced up at him. But then her flashing eyes took in the expensive cut of his clothes, the fine stallion he'd been riding. She didn't need trouble.

Using well-practiced willpower, Rhea swallowed both her angry retort and her pride as she got to her feet before him. She knew arguing with him would gain her nothing except more abuse, and she didn't relish that, especially now that a crowd had gathered. So she lowered her eyes meekly and reverted to the docile, contrite personality she had forced herself to learn during the past year. She hated doing it, but it was necessary.

"I'm very sorry, sir. It was careless of me. I'm sorry," she said submissively, standing there with eyes downcast like an errant child.

Logan was taken aback for a moment by the unexpected change in the woman before him. He'd seen the spark of anger in her blue eyes behind those ridiculous spectacles. Now it was either gone or hidden. He couldn't tell since she'd bowed her head so subserviently.

"Damned careless indeed, young woman," Logan accused her, though he was less angry now. He eyed her with a cocked brow for a long moment, taking in her drab brown hair pulled back severely into a tight bun behind her head, her plain gray dress. Her manner reminded Logan of the defeated demeanor of a reprimanded slave—downcast eyes, slumped shoulders. He'd never liked the attitude in a slave and he liked it even less in this woman. She should be standing up to him, telling him in no uncertain terms that *he* was the cause of Baron's near trampling of her! But before Logan could say anything more, a gloating voice cut in.

"Well now, dearie, don't you have a royal mess here. And them things not even paid for yet." Agnes Wiggins had come to the door of her shop to see what all the commotion was about. She smiled snidely now as she leaned against the door frame to view Rhea's predicament.

"Oh, do be quiet, Mrs. Wiggins," Rhea said wearily as she surveyed the merchandise scattered around her. The brown paper on most of her packages was quickly darkening as the muddy water of the street puddles soaked through. Rhea came close to tears as she realized her last chance to save her small shop now lay ruined in the mud. She couldn't keep a small moan of despair from escaping her lips as she bent to pick up the closest package and tried in vain to brush off the damaging wetness.

Logan was growing increasingly impatient with this whole situation. He didn't like being the center of a spectacle.

"Those things are likely unsalvageable," he decided with obvious annoyance. "Leave them. There is a matter to be settled here. Step inside and we'll discuss this." He didn't give Rhea a chance to protest as he took hold of her elbow firmly and, frowning, propelled her toward Mrs. Wiggins's store.

"You, you two there," he called over his shoulder at the door. He paused a moment to reach into his waistcoat pocket. "See to cleaning up this mess."

"Yes, sir!" the two boys he'd addressed shouted eagerly as they caught the silver dollars Logan tossed their way.

Rhea's surprise kept her from saying anything as Logan escorted her past Mrs. Wiggins and into the shop. The disappointed crowd outside began to disperse.

"Now, Miss . . . Miss?"

"Merrick, Rhea Merrick," Rhea managed to answer him as she raised her eyes to meet his.

"Miss Merrick," Logan began, still frowning at her. "I trust this mishap will teach you to have more care when stepping into the street in the future."

For a moment a spark lighted Rhea's eyes, but she clamped her teeth tightly and forced herself to say nothing. She knew his type well. Wealthy, spoiled, arrogant. He was used to being obeyed, thinking nothing of berating, even humiliating those he considered beneath him. In fact he probably enjoyed doing it. She'd detected a southern drawl in his speech. He was likely one of those rich plantation owners with hundreds of slaves to rule over like a dictator. Yet his next words surprised her.

"However, since I was involved in this incident which resulted in the damage to your merchandise, I feel obligated by simple courtesy to make some sort of restitution. Madam Storekeeper," he continued, turning to address Agnes Wiggins, who had come to stand behind the counter to watch them. The proprietess hadn't missed the authoritative bearing of this handsome man nor the fine cut of his clothes. She immediately came forward at his bidding.

"Sir?"

"See to replacing Miss Merrick's purchases and send the bill to Logan Tremaine at the Amboye Hotel. I trust that will be satisfactory, Miss Merrick?" He turned toward her as he spoke. The set of his mouth was still stern, but his tone seemed less severe.

"Yes, uh, yes, thank you very much, Mr. Tremaine." Rhea was too surprised and unnerved by his intense gaze to say anything more. She'd been expecting a good tongue-lashing and had been close to giving him the same in return no matter what the consequences. Now she was very glad she'd kept still.

He continued to watch her, then seemed to realize she was growing uncomfortable under his scrutiny.

"Very well then, I consider the matter closed," Logan stated abruptly. Then he gave a curt nod, turned, and walked from the store.

Chapter 4

LOGAN'S THOUGHTS WERE BLACK WHEN HE LEFT
his hotel room that evening to go to dinner. He wanted no
company tonight for he had to figure out a way to thwart
his older brother's plan to have the lion's share of control
over their inheritance. Miles was the eldest Tremaine
brother, but having all of an estate go to the firstborn son
was not so strictly observed these days. Logan knew he
would have his share of the inheritance when his grandfather died simply because he was a Tremaine. But it would
do him little good if Miles held the power to run everything, to make all the decisions. Silas Tremaine, Logan's
grandfather, still ruled over all of Fair Oaks, though his
poor health in recent years had forced him to pass on most
of the responsibilities to Miles, whom he had always favored. Besides, Logan didn't doubt Miles's intent to cut
him out of the will entirely. The recent codicil was proof of
that.

Miles . . . Logan's black brows knit into a menacing
scowl at the mere thought of his brother. His square jaw
clenched into a hard line. Always Miles. Forever his
brother was the cloud darkening Logan's horizon.

They'd been rivals for as long as he could remember. At
twenty-six, Logan was two years younger than Miles, and
that span of time had constantly given his older brother
the upper hand. He had been taller, stronger, smarter than
Logan while they were growing up, and he'd used that advantage to best Logan whenever he could.

Even though Logan had caught up with Miles in man-
hood, there was still continued conflict between them. At
times they were barely even civil to one another.

But Logan would think of some way to oppose his brother. He was well practiced in that art. And if not only for himself, he had to do it for Camille and Drew. Logan couldn't help wondering what trickery Miles was up to to try to steal their shares as well.

At seventeen, Andrew was the youngest Tremaine, with all the impatience and exuberance of his youth. His mind was on wine, women, and good times. He'd be an easy mark for the cunning Miles. As would Camille, their sister. Frail in health as a child, she was still often ill and took frequently to her bed. She was six years younger than Logan.

At the thought of Camille, Logan smiled now and remembered that he'd promised to bring her a gift when he returned home. The blue shawl and bonnet he'd seen in that little millinery shop window a couple of days ago would please her. The shop wasn't too far away. Perhaps it would still be open.

The walk did Logan good. The early June air was warm and pleasant. He thought further about Hugh's suggestion about complying with the codicil. The idea he'd been mulling over wasn't exactly what Hugh had had in mind, but the utter audacity of Logan's plan held a certain appeal.

Taking a wife back with him to Fair Oaks was the best immediate solution to the problem presented by old Silas's stipulation. But Logan had no proclivity for a real wife to tie him down. No, he wanted no matrimonial shackles on him. A woman served only one purpose to Logan—as a pleasant diversion, one that he indulged himself in often and enjoyed exceedingly—but he never took any woman or affair seriously. There were so many all-too-willing females that he planned yet to sample.

What he needed was a sporting woman who would wholeheartedly join in this ruse and act the part of his wife for a short time only. He was sure Belle would do it in a minute. Unfortunately, her talents and reputation were too well known. Silas would have a conniption if Logan brought Belle home. He didn't want to push the old man too far, though he would have relished seeing the look on his grandsire's face if he walked into Tremaine Hall with Belle Collier, the notorious and much-sought-after madam of Philadelphia, on his arm!

But even worse, Belle would more than likely plague him to death about *really* getting married. She already had been dropping hints here and there the last few times he'd been with her. No, Belle would never do.

The small millinery and accessory shop looked closed as Logan approached it. Dusk was beginning to settle lazily over the city as he strolled to the front window and saw that the shawl and bonnet set was still displayed there. He peered through the glass into the shop. All was dark except for a small crack of light coming from under a door at the back. Perhaps the owner wouldn't mind opening up if Logan made it worthwhile. He went to the front door and knocked.

Chapter 5

RHEA MERRICK HEARD THE HARD KNOCKING AT
the door to her shop but she decided to ignore it. She was in
no humor to face another demanding creditor, and that
was very likely who it was at this hour. She sniffed and
wiped her red-rimmed eyes in her soggy handkerchief,
then started to gather the dishes from her meager supper
to put in the basin to wash. The pounding continued at the
shop door.

"All right, I'm coming!" Rhea finally called out in annoyance as she yanked open the door leading to the shop.
She was frowning as she pulled her shawl about her shoulders and briskly walked across the room to the front door.
She drew back the locking bolt and opened the door only
wide enough to be seen.

"I'm sorry, but the shop is closed—," she began tersely
before she stopped in surprise when she saw who was
standing before her.

"Why, this is a surprise. Miss Merrick, wasn't it?" Logan asked as he removed his tall black evening hat. "Is
this your shop?"

"Mr. Tremaine—yes, yes, it is," Rhea answered, her anger now replaced by trepidation. What did Logan Tremaine want with her? Had he reconsidered and decided
not to be so generous? It wouldn't surprise her. Rhea
braced herself for what might be coming.

"I'm sorry to disturb you at this hour," he began to explain in a tone that didn't sound at all contrite, "but I had
admired that blue shawl and bonnet set in the window and
would like to purchase it for my sister. I'm planning to

leave the city tomorrow so this will be my only chance to
obtain it."

Again Logan Tremaine surprised Rhea by not doing
what she expected.

"Miss Merrick?"

"Oh, I beg your pardon," Rhea stammered, recovering
her senses. "Yes, of course, please do come in."

She opened the door wider for Logan to pass, then went
to the counter and lit the lamp. When she finally turned to
face him, Rhea found him looking at her intently. She lowered her eyes uncomfortably under his penetrating gaze
and walked over to the window.

"Was this the shawl you meant, Mr. Tremaine?" she
asked as she lifted up the displayed piece.

"Yes, that and the bonnet."

Rhea picked up the two items and brought them to the
counter for Logan to examine.

"Very nice work," he commented after a few moments.
"Did you make them?"

He was looking directly at her again. Rhea felt a warm
flush move up her neck and face as she noticed for the first
time how handsome Logan Tremaine was. Her seamstress's eye took in the superb cut of his clothes and how
the expensive fabric of his dark blue coat and gray trousers
molded to his tall, well-built frame.

"Yes," she finally managed to stammer, forcing her eyes
away from him. "The shawl is hand-knitted with imported
angora yarn and the satin bonnet is my design and handmade also," she continued too quickly. Why was she feeling so nervous around him?

"I'll take them both. I think my sister will be pleased to
have them," Logan announced as he reached into the
breast pocket of his coat and brought out a black leather
wallet.

Rhea regained her composure as she busied herself box-
ing up the pieces for him. Sister indeed, she thought to herself derisively. More likely she'd see them on some doxy
from Kender Street sometime. A man as handsome and so
obviously wealthy as this one would have a number of such
women at his beck and call.

It had crossed Rhea's mind to give Logan Tremaine the
shawl and bonnet as a gift for his gesture earlier that af-

ternoon. But the thought of his mistresses suddenly annoyed her so that she abruptly told him the price as she handed the box to him.

"I trust you were able to work out a viable solution with that storekeeper this afternoon," Logan said casually as he counted out the amount.

"Yes. Yes, I was," Rhea told him, trying to sound convincing. No use in telling him the ruined items had been ordered from a special store in Vermont, and Mrs. Wiggins had nothing else that could serve as replacements. There was no time to send for more, and as a result Rhea couldn't fill Mrs. Corrington's order. Wealthy Althea Corrington had been her last chance to hold her creditors at bay a little while longer. The bank would be foreclosing on Rhea's loan for the shop. She would be out of business and forced to do something else. What that might be, Rhea had not the slightest idea right now. She only knew she could not go back home to live with her mother and stepfather. That was out of the question.

But it was no use telling a stranger all this. He wouldn't care at all.

Logan was watching the play of the lamplight over Rhea's face. She wasn't wearing those unbecoming wire-rimmed glasses, and he was aware suddenly of the delicate shape of her face, the black lashes framing her large blue eyes, the lids reddened, as though from weeping. Logan had an artist's talent for seeing dimension, line, detail. Her figure was trim and nicely curved, although the plain lines of her green gown tended to downplay those attractive features. Here was a beautiful woman trying hard to camouflage it. Logan found himself curious about this Rhea Merrick.

"Will there be anything else, Mr. Tremaine?" Rhea asked uncomfortably, noticing his scrutiny of her.

"I think not for now, Miss Merrick," he answered as he returned his wallet to his pocket and picked up the box. "However, I get to Philadelphia often and I'm certain my sister will send an order with me the next time I come."

"I'm afraid you shall have to look elsewhere to fill it, sir," Rhea replied, trying to keep the bitterness out of her voice. "As of Thursday, I shall no longer be in business."

Logan caught the bite in her tone and sensed her anger

before Rhea masked it with the same downcast eyes and docile demeanor she'd exhibited during their encounter earlier in the day. He wondered with some annoyance why she did that.

"Are you casting into a new business venture then?"

"No, at the moment I am at loose ends," and at the mercy of Grayson Sawyer, she added in her thoughts, thinking bitterly of her mother's husband. "But something will turn up," she continued aloud. "Thank you for your help this afternoon, Mr. Tremaine, and for coming tonight," Rhea went on with an air of dismissal. She really didn't feel like being sociable any longer. "I hope your sister likes the bonnet and shawl."

Rhea picked up the lamp and lighted their way to the front door of the shop. In the doorway Logan put on his hat and turned toward her. His gaze held hers in the lamplight and she could feel herself warming under it. She swallowed and wanted to look away, but couldn't. There was so much magnetism in his eyes, his manner. An unusual sensation started in Rhea's stomach and spread over her. She was still wondering at it as Logan finally spoke again, his voice somewhat less formal.

"Somehow I feel you are not one to be kept down for long, Miss Merrick. Good luck and good evening." Then with a nod of his head and a slight smile, Logan turned and hailed a passing carriage for hire.

The driver jumped down from his seat to open the door for his passenger. Logan was about to tell him to drive to the Willshire Inn as he'd planned earlier. But then he paused with one foot on the step-up and glanced back at the shop he'd just left. Rhea Merrick still stood in the doorway holding the oil lamp. When she saw him look at her, she quickly stepped back into the shadows and closed the door.

Logan was thoughtful. His knack for judging people caused an idea to flick through his mind. He climbed into the carriage and settled into the leather-upholstered seat.

"Quinby Street, driver," he directed as the man closed the door of the carriage behind him. "Number thirty-seven." That was Hugh Tennyson's house. Suddenly he had some confidential business to discuss with his old friend.

Chapter 6

THE AFTERNOON OF THE FOLLOWING DAY FOUND Logan again with Hugh Tennyson, this time at Hugh's law office.

"I managed to iron out the last problems with Frazer this morning. The details are enclosed," Logan told his friend as he handed him a large, thick envelope. Hugh took the envelope and put it in the bottom drawer of his desk, locking it securely afterward.

"Were you able to get that other information I asked you for last night?" Logan asked, changing the subject.

"Yes, I came up with some things, though you didn't give me much time to do it. But I can't for the life of me figure out why you'd be interested in knowing about this woman."

"The less you know, the better for now, my friend," Logan told him as he sat down in the leather chair Hugh had gestured toward. "What have you learned?"

"Rhea Marie Merrick, age twenty-four, only child of Matilda and Joseph Merrick." Hugh read from a handwritten sheet before him. This he handed now to Logan as he continued from memory.

"Joseph Merrick had some family money which he managed to multiply into a sizeable fortune by shrewd business investments and just plain hard work. He built Merrick Iron into a notable manufacturing operation, became one of the main suppliers of rails for the railroads. Unfortunately, he died suddenly of a condition of the heart some five years ago, at age fifty.

"Word has it Matilda Merrick has never quite recovered from his death. She was an easy mark for the likes of a man named Grayson Sawyer, who is twelve years her junior. She married him three years ago."

"Sawyer?" Logan asked, looking up from the sheet of paper. He knew the man slightly from a business transaction he'd once had with him, and he didn't like him. Grayson Sawyer was ruthless and greedy, and an arrogant bastard as well.

"Yes. Sawyer quickly took control of Merrick Iron and made it a part of his own growing business empire.

"But to get back to Miss Merrick. There's a partial list there of her educational background, including the name of the very proper girl's finishing school she attended in New York—I believe it was Kensington. She has never married, though she once had a rather serious relationship with a Philip Winslow of Boston. For some reason their engagement was broken two years ago and Miss Merrick went traveling in New England for quite a while after that. When she returned to Philadelphia she stayed only a short time at her mother's home, then moved out to open a small ladies' millinery and accessories shop. She's made some other investments which have proved to be unsuccessful and have put her rather deeply in debt. Her shop has not done well, and, in fact, the bank is about to foreclose. Apparently there are no other blood family members around upon whom she could call in these dire straits. But I wonder why she has not relied on her stepfather for help. Sawyer has considerable influence in many areas, though I can't say I care for the man personally. That's about all I was able to find out on such short notice. Now would you mind telling me why in blazes you wanted to know about this Rhea Merrick?" Tennyson glanced at Logan, a puzzled expression marking his austere features.

"As usual, a thorough job, Hugh. My thanks," Logan complimented his friend, ignoring his last question as he got to his feet. Folding the sheet of paper, Logan put it in the breast pocket of his coat, then reached across the big mahogany desk to a pile of plain paper.

"May I use a sheet of this?"

Hugh Tennyson nodded and continued to watch Logan with one eyebrow cocked.

"What are you up to, Logan?" he asked suspiciously.

"You'll find out in due time, counselor," Logan answered

nonchalantly without looking up. He quickly wrote a few lines on the paper with the desk quill pen, waited a moment for the ink to dry, then folded it and put it in the envelope Hugh held out to him.

"Have one of your messengers deliver this to Miss Merrick's shop on Third Street, will you, old man?" He put on his hat and headed toward the door. But before leaving he turned once more to Hugh Tennyson.

"One more favor—do you know the whereabouts of Willy-Nilly Scarsdale? I may have need of his artistic talents."

"Willy—? Now you *must* tell me what this is all about, Logan. It's starting to sound on the shady side, and I think I should know about it." Hugh's expression changed to worry now as he eyed Logan.

"Relax, Hugh," Logan admonished him, a small smile of amusement curling up the corners of his mouth. "You're used to that from me by now. I'm just acting on one of your wise counselings. Nothing may come of it. But just in case, do you know where Willy is or not?"

"No, but I know someone who does," Hugh answered reluctantly. He was frowning.

"Good. Tell him I'd like Willy to come to my room at the Amboye about eleven o'clock tonight."

"Logan—"

"My thanks, Hugh," Logan cut in before his friend could say more. "I'll be in Philadelphia a day or two longer yet. I'll see you again before I leave."

And he walked out the door before Hugh Tennyson could protest further.

Chapter 7

RHEA HAD OPENED HER SHOP AS USUAL THIS morning but her heart wasn't in it. She knew she had to admit defeat now. Subtly but systematically over the past nine months or so, Grayson Sawyer had exerted his considerable influence to discourage her patrons and then even her friends from coming to her shop to buy from her. He was obsessed with her downfall, and his persistence had succeeded; the bank would be foreclosing this week.

Though she had thought long and hard about it all last night, Rhea still had not been able to come up with a viable plan for where she would go or what she would do next. She knew her mother would want her to come back home to live. But how could Rhea tell that sweet and trusting soul she couldn't possibly do that. Not as long as Grayson Sawyer remained her mother's husband and shared her house.

Poor Mama. She was completely deceived by Sawyer, depending on his strong and confident manner to run Papa's business and everything else for her. Matilda had been only too glad to hand over control of everything to Grayson. Then she could retreat into the little world she had created for herself to escape from life's harsh realities. There, she still grieved for Rhea's father, sometimes even spoke of him as though he were just away at work and would be returning soon.

Sawyer had all but ignored Rhea until after the wedding vows had been spoken with her mother. Then his manner toward Rhea had changed, subtly at first—a hand stroking her arm affectionately while he spoke to her, a light brushing of his arm against her breast as he walked past her.

22

Soon he had looked at Rhea differently, too. His eyes would travel boldly over her whenever they chanced to be in the same room together.

After Philip Winslow had come on the scene, Sawyer seemed to lose interest in Rhea. But when the engagement was broken after Rhea found out how Philip had used her, Sawyer's attention had started again. By the time she'd returned from a holiday in Vermont, Sawyer no longer bothered to be surreptitious in his advances toward her. He was brazen enough to even try to rape Rhea. That was when she left her mother's house forever, intent on an independent life and as much distance from Grayson Sawyer as possible.

He hadn't bothered her much at the shop, preferring instead to play his vicious game of destroying her business. Now the small inheritance from her grandmother that Rhea had used to start the shop was gone; plus she was badly in debt from some other poor dealings she'd made. Creditors were demanding payment, threatening court action and even prison terms if she didn't pay them. How Sawyer would relish her defeat. She could see the ugly smirk on his face already.

Rhea shook her head to clear her mind of that unpleasant thought and glanced around her. She had to decide on her future before Sawyer had any more hand in it. This little shop had been her labor and her salvation for the past year, her home, just the two small rooms in the back where she could finish her work after hours and sleep exhaustedly but peacefully, knowing the vile creature who had married her mother would not try to force himself on her here.

Rhea's glance fell on the brief letter a messenger had brought earlier. She frowned slightly as she took it up and read it through again. Logan Tremaine was being presumptuous in his bold invitation to dinner. After all, they were barely acquainted. But his mention of a business proposition piqued her interest. Perhaps he wanted to buy the shop for that so-called sister he'd mentioned. That possibility would offer Rhea a reprieve on the most pressing debt, and perhaps even give her some money to get away from Philadelphia. Yes, she would have to accept this invitation, improper though it might be.

Logan Tremaine . . . His handsome face swam before Rhea in her mind's eye, just as it had in her troubled dreams last night. Strange how he affected her. She'd decided yesterday that she didn't even like him. Their first encounter was certainly not something she wanted to remember. He was arrogant, too superior in his attitude, and he was a southerner. His and Rhea's worlds were very different. Still, she couldn't stop thinking about him, and had decided that she'd at least listen to any business proposal he might have in mind, as long as it was just that—business. Rhea told herself she was determined to keep any further dealings she might have with Logan Tremaine strictly professional.

That shouldn't be too difficult, she decided. The plainness she'd exhibited in the way she dressed and wore her hair would never appeal to a man like Logan Tremaine. But she was still confused by the way he had looked at her last night. Just the thought of the handsome southerner did unsettling things to Rhea's stomach. Yet she was wary, wondering just what Mr. Tremaine was up to.

Rhea reached over to the other side of the front display window and picked up a wide-brimmed hat covered in pleated pink satin and accented in lighter pink-colored ostrich plumes. She put it on and cocked her head jauntily to one side, looking at her reflection in the large mirror on the side wall. This was one of her favorites. She'd keep it for herself now, though she would be keeping little else when the bank foreclosed. While most of the inventory of her shop would be confiscated, they wouldn't get *this* hat, Rhea decided determinedly.

"Very becoming," a snide voice interrupted her thoughts. Rhea's blood turned to ice as she whirled around to face the man she hated most in the world—Grayson Sawyer. She struggled to keep her composure as she carefully removed the hat and placed it back in the window.

"What do you want, Grayson?" she demanded coldly as she turned to face him, her blue eyes flashing. "Can't you wait a little longer to gloat over what you've taken from me?"

"I see the past months have not dulled the sharpness of your tongue, my dear," Sawyer countered, his dark eyes locking with Rhea's. The sneering smile that al-

ways made her cringe was on his lips now. As usual
he was impeccably dressed and groomed. Every dark
brown hair was brushed into place, his thick moustache
was neatly trimmed. Everything just so. Rhea hated
the way he looked and even more, hated the way he
looked at *her.*

Grayson Sawyer was walking toward her now and Rhea
instinctively backed away from him until a display table
stopped her. Sawyer quickly grabbed hold of her shoulders
in a strong grip before she realized what was happening.
The last time he had touched her nearly a year ago came
rushing back to Rhea's mind all too vividly. She wanted to
recoil in revulsion from this terrible man and the tormenting memory of the night he had tried to rape her in her
own bed. If her mother hadn't arrived home unexpectedly,
Sawyer would have succeeded. She'd promptly left home
and kept silent about his attack, only too glad she'd escaped him.

"You misunderstand my reason for being here, daughter," Sawyer was saying now in a casual tone. "I only wish
to help you." His almost black eyes stared at her and his
smile became leering as he moved closer to Rhea. Her
hands came up to push against his chest.

"I am not your daughter!" she said fiercely, her eyes
drilling into him. "Never call me that. Take your foul
hands off me, Grayson."

Rhea managed to push his arms away and tried to step
past him, but he grabbed her again and spun her around in
front of him. His left arm imprisoned Rhea around the
waist, forcing her back against his chest. His right hand
reached around to the front of her gown and ripped away
the top buttons of the high neckline. Rhea froze as he
plunged his hand inside and under her chemise to grasp
her naked breast roughly, forcing her to submit to his fondling.

"I will touch you whenever and however I wish!" His
voice was low and threatening, but to Rhea it was as
though he shouted his hideous pronouncement at her. She
was frozen with fear and loathing in his grasp.

"This little show of meekness and homeliness you've exhibited these past months hasn't fooled me. It has only
heightened my desire for you. I will have you, Rhea. I've

been very patient, biding my time, planning so carefully, knowing I would win eventually. I will have you at my beck and call, my sweet little Rhea, for I will pay your debts and keep you out of prison for not meeting your obligations. And you will soon repay me, I promise you, with your body and your so-well-concealed passion. You will learn to do my bidding in all things and say nothing or I will go to your stupid mother with a story of how her saintly daughter played the temptress behind her back and tried to seduce me shamelessly. She'll believe me and hate you, be loathe to look upon you. All of this is within my power to do, dear Rhea."

He pinched her breast hard, laughing cruelly when she winced from the pain. His voice was husky with lust, his breath hot against her ear as he held Rhea pinned close against him.

"I have enjoyed this little game these past months but have now decided I cannot wait any longer to taste your sweetness."

Sawyer clamped a hand over Rhea's mouth to stifle her scream. Then he shoved her roughly ahead of him, holding her arms pinned behind her. When they passed the shop door, he kicked it shut with his booted foot and quickly turned the key in the lock so no customers who might happen by could come in. In the few moments Rhea's mouth was free of his hand, she pleaded with him.

"Grayson, no, please! Let me go!"

But Sawyer only laughed and forced her toward the back room. Near the back counter, Rhea spied her large sewing scissors lying near a basket of spools of thread, where she'd left them earlier. Using every ounce of strength she had, she lunged forward in desperation, twisting out of Sawyer's grasp long enough to snatch the long-bladed scissors from the countertop. She whirled on him then, bringing the scissors down with all her might just as Sawyer reached out to grab her again. He yelped and recoiled with pain as the makeshift weapon pierced his right forearm.

"You vicious little bitch!" Sawyer sputtered at Rhea as she ran away from him around to the other side of the counter. His face screwed up in pain as he grabbed at the handle of the scissors and pulled them out. He gasped and

clutched at his coat sleeve where blood from the wound
was gushing down his hand.

In panic Rhea tried to think. She felt for a small drawer
located here on the back side of the enclosed counter. Finding it, she yanked it open and reached in for the small gun
she kept there for protection. She held the two-shot derringer up with both hands, pointing it straight at Sawyer.

"Take one more step and I'll shoot you where you stand,
Grayson!" Rhea threatened menacingly. Her hands were
trembling but she managed to keep the gun aimed at him.
"Now get out of here and don't ever come near me again or
I swear I'll kill you, Grayson. I swear it!" She was shouting
now.

Sawyer eyed her warily as he moved slowly toward the
door, holding his limp right arm.

"You'll pay dearly for this, you little hellcat. Mark my
words," Sawyer hissed at her through gritted teeth. Pain
reflected in his forbidding look. "Don't get any foolish
ideas about trying to escape me. I'm having you watched
constantly. So you see, my dear, you will be mine for as
long as I want to make use of you. And it will happen soon,
I promise you . . . Very soon!"

Sawyer slammed the door behind him and Rhea ran
across the room to lock and bolt it after him. Breathing
hard she quickly pulled down the shades of the door and
display windows. As she did so she caught a glimpse of
Sawyer talking with two brawny men in laborer's clothes
a little way down the sidewalk. One man walked away
with Sawyer when he turned to leave. The other stayed,
leaning against the lamppost, looking in the direction of
Rhea's shop.

Rhea ran to the back rooms and peered out the curtained
rear door window. Another big, burly fellow stood just
across the alley that ran behind the row of businesses. He
also watched Rhea's shop.

Rhea whirled around and pressed her back to the wall.
She closed her eyes and tried to fight down the rising panic
she felt. She was a prisoner! But not for very long. Somehow she had to get away before Sawyer could return and
abuse her further, for she knew he would return. She
would go to the police . . .

No, not the police. With sinking heart she recalled now

that Grayson Sawyer's older brother was a high-ranking officer in the Philadelphia police force. If he were anything like his brother, Rhea would find no help there. Besides, by the look of the two thugs outside, it was doubtful she'd even be allowed to get down the street, let alone to a police precinct.

The young woman sank down on her small bed in the corner. No longer could she hold back the tears that burned at her eyes and the sobs that welled up in her throat. Burying her face in her pillow, Rhea wept in despair.

Chapter 8

AFTER A WHILE, WHEN NO MORE TEARS WOULD come, Rhea dried her reddened eyes and got up from the bed to get a drink of water from the pitcher on the small sink. As she passed the back door window, she stole a glance out to the alley again. The man was still there, watching.

Sighing deeply, Rhea poured the water into a cup and drank it, forcing her mind to think rationally. She felt like a trapped animal. It was a terrible feeling, frightening and angering at the same time. Grayson Sawyer must be insane. He had no right to do this to her. She wouldn't let him! Somehow she'd find a way to get away from him.

Rhea walked out to the main shop area. It was growing dark now. Soon the shops would be closing, merchants and customers going home. She would be even more alone to deal with Sawyer if he returned. What could she do?

Rhea went to the front door and moved the edge of the shade aside enough to look out onto the street. The guard at the lamppost was still there, also. Gloomily she turned away and accidentally stepped on something that crinkled under her shoe. Bending down, Rhea picked up a piece of paper, and suddenly a surge of hope went through her as she recognized Logan Tremaine's letter. In all the commotion of her struggle with Sawyer earlier, it must have been knocked off the counter. Mr. Tremaine would be calling for her at eight o'clock to take her to dinner if she so consented! Rhea remembered the words written there now, though she could barely read them in the fading light.

She hurried to the back room and glanced at the small wall clock over the dresser. Seven-fifteen now. She still had time to collect herself and be ready when Mr. Tremaine arrived. *If* he arrived. A sudden sinking feeling surged over her. What if he had changed his mind or had a change in plans? No other messengers had come, but perhaps her guards outside had prevented it. And if Logan Tremaine were still coming, would the horrible men who were Grayson Sawyer's henchmen *allow* him to call for her?

Rhea didn't want to think of that. She focused her attention on freshening up and dressing for their dinner engagement. She finally chose a beige taffeta gown that she'd made herself but hadn't worn in a long time. It's lines were not elaborate, but rather were tasteful and elegant. She hadn't had any occasion to wear it during the last year.

She donned the three ruffled petticoats needed to fill out the full skirt. And as she slipped the gown over her head and put her arms through the short capped sleeves edged in lace, Rhea thought again about Logan Tremaine.

He seemed like a man of his word. Certainly he would come. And when he did, she would ask for his help in escaping Grayson Sawyer. What other choice did she have?

But as Rhea put the finishing touches to the bun at the back of her dark brown hair, another disturbing thought occurred to her. What if Logan Tremaine were in collusion with Grayson to defeat her? Was it possible that their meeting yesterday was no accident?

Rhea shook her head to clear it of such a disheartening thought. Fear and uncertainty were making her overly suspicious, she told herself. She had to look to Logan Tremaine for help. He had aided her once with Mrs. Wiggins. Somehow Rhea would persuade him to help her now.

But just to be on the cautious side, Rhea decided that when Tremaine did arrive, she would try to act as though everything were normal. She would hear him out as to his business proposition and then determine whether he might have any connection with Sawyer. Perhaps he wasn't planning to take her to dinner, but directly to Sawyer instead!

"Calm down, Rhea. Keep a cool head," she told herself as she finished dressing. "There's no reason to think that."

Rhea smoothed the folds of her beige gown and adjusted

the matching bonnet on her head. And all the while she watched the clock nervously, praying that Logan Tremaine would come before Grayson Sawyer did.

When a loud knock sounded at the front door at five minutes to eight, Rhea jumped in surprise, then froze. She knew she had to answer it, but which man would she find there?

Taking up her derringer from where she'd left it nearby on the table, Rhea went out into the main shop area, holding the small gun down at her side. The determined knock sounded again. Rhea pulled back the corner of the window shade to peek outside. Relief surged through her as she saw Logan Tremaine standing before the door. A quick glance up and down the street revealed no one watching, but the avenue was becoming deeply shadowed now at dusk. Anyone could be lurking there undetected.

Rhea put the derringer in the deep side pocket of her skirt and quickly unlocked and opened the door.

"Good evening, Miss Merrick," Logan Tremaine greeted formally, removing his tall gray dress hat.

"Good evening, Mr. Tremaine," Rhea answered as she held the door open for him. "Do come in, please. I need only fetch my shawl to be ready."

Logan followed her into the shop as Rhea went to get her shawl. As she slipped it over her shoulders she kept her eyes averted shyly from his but managed to snatch glimpses of her escort out of the corner of her eye. He looked quite dapper in his evening clothes. His well-cut gray coat was double-breasted, coming to the waist in front and falling to knee-length tails in back. The white-ruffled shirtfront that showed at his neck was off-set by a black silk tie wound into a fashionable bow. His gray trousers were tight at the waist and trim and straight down his long legs. Rhea felt that strange flutter in her stomach again as she took in his handsome elegance.

"Shall we go, then? I have a carriage waiting." Logan smiled casually as he gestured toward the front door. Rhea nodded as she turned down the wick of the lamp on the counter, then walked outside before Logan.

The main dining area of the Willshire Inn consisted of a large room richly decorated in emerald green and gold.

It was filled almost to capacity. Green velvet draperies tied back by thick gold cords and topped by scrolled wooden cornices adorned the long windows. Green velvet cushioned chairs surrounded each table. The plush gold carpet under their feet muffled their steps as Rhea and Logan followed the maitre d' to a reserved table across the room.

Rhea made a quick scrutiny of those in the room, though she wasn't sure what she was looking for. The two men who had been watching her shop would certainly not be here in this exclusive restaurant. Yet Rhea didn't doubt for a moment that Grayson Sawyer was having her watched at all times.

Rhea felt nervous. She reasoned the uneasiness she felt now stemmed from her horrible encounter with Sawyer that afternoon. Rhea could still feel his hands on her. How evil that man was. Evil and cruel . . . She tried to push these terrible thoughts from her mind and focus on what was occurring now.

"Harland, tell André to wait a few minutes before bringing us the menu," Logan said to the headwaiter after they were seated.

"Very well, sir," Harland said with proper haughtiness, giving a slight bow before he turned away.

How Rhea wished now that she'd worn something more fashionable tonight. While her beige gown was flatteringly cut, it was rather dowdy and out-of-style in the plush surroundings of the Willshire.

Logan was thinking about his companion's appearance at the same time. She looked somewhat better than when he'd last seen her, but there was still much room for improvement. He wondered how she'd look with her dark brown hair down, out of that matronly bun. Blue would certainly be a more becoming color for her to wear, to match her lovely eyes. Too bad those eyes were half hidden behind the detracting spectacles she was wearing.

Rhea sensed his close scrutiny of her and shifted uncomfortably in her chair, keeping her eyes downcast.

"I was rather surprised to receive your invitation," she began, forcing herself to look at Logan and sound casual. "It was my understanding from our conversation last evening that you were leaving the city today."

"My plans changed, Miss Merrick, and you are the reason for it," Logan answered her directly, smiling slightly. He was amused by the surprised look that came to her face.

"I don't understand, Mr. Tremaine," Rhea replied, on her guard. "You barely know me." She frowned slightly.

"Yesterday I knew nothing about you. Today I do," Logan said evasively, enjoying her bewilderment. "I always investigate the people with whom I'm considering doing business."

"Your invitation did mention a business venture, which aroused my curiosity," Rhea replied somewhat annoyed now. "But I must admit I resent being investigated on the sly. You had no right to do that, sir."

Though Rhea tried to keep her countenance demure and unchanged, Logan still caught the flash of fire in her blue eyes before she could conceal it with lowered lashes. He was not surprised. He suspected there was more to Rhea Merrick than appeared on the surface, though she hid it well.

"You are correct, of course, Miss Merrick," Logan admitted, smiling. "I had no right, but I did have a valid reason. Shall we order dinner now? I'll tell you afterward what I have in mind."

Rhea looked up and saw the smile curling his lips above the strong line of his jaw. She was further annoyed by the amusement in his eyes as they surveyed her openly. Something told her she should leave immediately, get away now from this presumptuous, arrogant man while she still could. She was beginning to feel like the fly being lured to an inescapable web by the treacherous spider.

And yet something held her back, made her continue to sit quietly in her chair across from him. Logan Tremaine was very handsome, obviously wealthy. There was a superior attitude about him that put Rhea off and his pale eyes held little warmth as they looked at her now. Yet at the same time there was something about him, a strength and confidence she'd found so lacking in herself of late. She felt drawn to him by it.

She could at least listen to what he had to say. What choice did she have after all?

"Very well, Mr. Tremaine. Yes, by all means, let us have dinner . . . and talk," Rhea finally managed to reply, trying to sound casual as she met his gaze squarely.

Chapter 9

LOGAN ORDERED FOR THEM, AND THE FOOD arrived promptly. Fillet of terrapin in wine sauce, creamed peas, potato slices in parsley and butter, apples baked with cinnamon and brown sugar. A Bordeaux to sip with the superb fare. Logan and Rhea spoke of casual things—the weather, politics, fashions—until the waiter had departed.

"Now, Miss Merrick," Logan began as they started to eat. "Let us get down to business. In order to move forward with this venture, I must ask you two questions. Take your time and answer them carefully and honestly, for your words may have an important influence on your future as well as mine."

Rhea paused with her fork in midair. Did she detect an ominous tone in his voice?

"All right, Mr. Tremaine. Go on."

"My first question is this: How do you feel about the slavery issue that so divides our nation?"

That was hardly the question Rhea had been expecting. She had braced herself for anything, even a sexual proposition. She was on her guard to detect any hint of a conspiracy with Grayson Sawyer. But her views on slavery? That was certainly a surprise.

Rhea was uncertain as to how to answer him. Tremaine was obviously a southerner from his speech and therefore most likely to be pro-slavery. She was a northerner living in Pennsylvania, a state that was outspokenly anti-slavery. All she could think of to do was to take his advice and answer honestly.

"In truth, I have not taken a side on the issue, for it has not touched my life directly. Slavery is legal in the eyes of the law, still sanctioned by many states and territories and the federal government. I have not had occasion to question what remains the law of the land. The issue of slavery is a difficult one, involving many factors. I have not tried to sort out the arguments for or against it, for I have had difficulties of my own on my mind in recent years which have been more pressing to me."

"The National Anti-Slavery Society has a strong following in Philadelphia," Logan interjected almost accusingly.

"I have heard of it, of course, but I have not been involved in any way with that organization or any other group like it," Rhea replied. "However, that does not necessarily mean I sanction the institution of slavery. I'm sorry. I know that sounds rather ambiguous, but I'm afraid that reflects my position."

Logan was displeased by Rhea's answer mainly because it made her unpredictable. She might indeed take sides if the issue of slavery became part of her everyday life. And therein lay the danger—in not knowing which stance she would take. He knew which side he wanted her to take, but he would say nothing now to influence her. At least she had not spoken forth vehemently as an abolitionist. That would have made it impossible for him to even consider taking her to Fair Oaks. Perhaps enough financial incentive would persuade her to remain undecided, or at least undeclared in her opinions for the amount of time he wanted to make use of her.

"Very well, Miss Merrick. Second question. Tell me, if you were called upon to play a part, do you suppose you might be a good enough actress to accomplish it?"

This conversation was becoming more bizarre by the moment, jumping from slavery to the theater, just like that.

"Well . . . I suppose that would depend on the part and the reason necessitating my playing it," Rhea answered. "If you had me investigated, Mr. Tremaine, then you must know I am not and never have been a professional actress."

"Yes, I do know that. And yet I can't help thinking you are a most accomplished actress despite your lack of experience in the theater."

Rhea was becoming more and more annoyed by this Logan Tremaine and the game he seemed to be playing. She felt painfully uncomfortable under his penetrating gaze.

"Could we possibly get to the point of this meeting, Mr. Tremaine?" she asked a little impatiently now. "You have me at a distinct disadvantage here and I don't think I like it. Just what is it that you want of me?"

A slight frown wrinkled her brow as she watched him steadily. Logan knew he was seeing a little of the real Rhea Merrick now. He was pleased that it had taken her some time to finally become annoyed with his evasiveness. His instinct for sizing up people was telling Logan that Rhea could likely do what he wanted of her. But would she? Everyone had a price. Could he find Rhea Merrick's?

"Yes, of course, it's time to stop beating around the bush," Logan replied. "You have been more than patient to indulge me this long. Here is the bargain I propose. I know the extent of your indebtedness to various creditors. I shall pay off all of your obligations, plus deposit the sum of ten thousand dollars in an account in your name at a bank of your choice." Logan stopped and watched Rhea intently for her reaction.

Rhea's jaw dropped open slightly in disbelief. Why would a total stranger want to do that for her? And what in the world would she have to do in return?

Rhea closed her mouth and cleared her throat. She couldn't help thinking that with his next words she might very well be asked to sell her soul to the Devil himself!

"And just what would I have to do to merit such generosity on your part, Mr. Tremaine?" she asked, looking at him with wide eyes and fearing to breathe until he answered.

"Don't look so worried, Miss Merrick," Logan replied with a slight smile, his tone less stern now. "Actually, all I wish to do is purchase your services. For the next six months or so I would like you to pretend to the world—and more specifically, to my family—to be my most loving and dutiful wife."

Rhea began breathing again but she was too stunned to speak. This man across the table from her must be deranged, or at the very least, joking with her. She was not amused. What he proposed was preposterous, not to mention illegal.

"Your wife! You want me to masquerade as your wife?"

Rhea managed to ask finally. "Why? If you need a wife, why don't you just marry someone? I'm certain a man of your obvious attributes would have no difficulty finding a willing—"

"That is entirely out of the question," Logan cut in pointedly. "I have no desire for a real wife. However, I am forced by certain circumstances beyond my control to have a wife for a while. That is all you need to know for the moment."

Rhea was silent as her mind worked, filling with questions.

"But what would happen at the end of the set time-period? How would you explain your wife's sudden departure to your family, your friends?" Rhea couldn't believe she was asking such a question, as though she might even be considering going along with such a scheme.

"That would be easy enough to resolve," Logan answered casually. "At the end of the agreed-upon time, you and I will take a delayed honeymoon abroad. You will not return with me, having met with an unfortunate fictional accident that will make me a widower. At least that is the story I will tell everyone. At that time, I will pay off your creditors and you will be free to pick up your life wherever you wish, using the ten thousand dollars for a new start. The only condition I will ask is that you do so far enough away so that there will be no chance of our paths ever crossing again—the West, perhaps. It is said that is the new land of opportunity, and wagon trains leave daily for it."

Rhea was silent as she drained her wineglass, welcoming its taste and stinging effect. She found it hard to believe what she was hearing. Tremaine sounded so confident and matter-of-fact, as though he did this sort of thing every day. They might have been discussing the loading of cargo in a ship's hold rather than the important human conditions of marriage and death.

"Why are you asking *me?*" she managed to ask finally. "Why would you think I might be willing to perpetrate such a fraud? You don't even know me."

"I am a good judge of people, Miss Merrick. I'm convinced you have the proper family background and upbringing to play this role convincingly. Surely you can see the opportunity this proposal presents to you. Unless of course you have a more viable means of solving your present difficulties, say, through the kind benevolence of your esteemed stepfather, Grayson Sawyer?" Logan watched Rhea closely for her reaction to his statement.

Her head shot up involuntarily, startled at the mention of that hated name. She eyed him suspiciously for a moment.

"That man is hardly esteemed by me, I assure you, Mr. Tremaine," Rhea told him emphatically. "I would never ask anything of him."

Logan knew he had struck the right chord. Though he didn't know the details of Rhea Merrick's relationship with Sawyer, he'd suspected something like this.

Rhea drummed her fingers on the green linen tablecloth and glanced around the crowded dining room, her thoughts racing. Something told her Logan Tremaine was not in connivance with Grayson Sawyer. She couldn't imagine how Grayson's heinous plans for her could be a part of this strange arrangement Tremaine was proposing. She suddenly pictured the look on Grayson's face when he learned of her "marriage." He'd be livid with rage. How she would relish that. This was certainly a way to escape Philadelphia and his evil clutches—but could she do it?

In a few moments Rhea brought her gaze back to Logan.

"Assuming, just for the sake of discussion, that I might agree to go along with what you're proposing, how long would I be required to act as your wife and what exactly would you expect of me?"

Logan took smug satisfaction in knowing he had read this woman so well. She would be easy to control, perfect for his purposes.

"For the next six months, all outward appearances would be that we are happy newlyweds. We will reside at Fair Oaks, my family's tobacco plantation in Virginia, with the rest of my immediate family members—my grandfather, two brothers, a sister-in-law and nephew, and my sister, whom I told you about before. I travel extensively for various reasons, so we would not have to be in each other's company all that much.

"I would expect you to be a quiet and obedient wife, asking no questions about things that are strictly my business. Your main responsibility, besides convincingly pretending we are happily married, will be to remain in the background and get along peacefully with my family."

Rhea was silent a moment, thinking about what he'd just said.

"And our sleeping arrangements . . . What would they be, Mr. Tremaine?" she asked bluntly, never taking her eyes from his face.

One corner of Logan's mouth curled up in the beginning of an amused smile.

"Have no fear, Miss Merrick," he assured her. "They will be most chaste indeed. Your virtue would not be threatened. At Fair Oaks we will have adjoining, but decidedly separate, sleeping quarters. This is a business venture. I make it a rule never to mix business with—anything else."

Rhea did not stop to question Fate why she was being handed all of this on a silver platter. Perhaps she would regret the hasty decision later, but for now, as Logan Tremaine had said, she could see only the opportunity it presented for her future. She had, in any case, precious few other options to consider at the moment.

"Those are my sentiments exactly, Mr. Tremaine." She eyed him thoughtfully a moment longer, then said, "All right then, by all appearances for the next few months—I believe you mentioned six—you shall have yourself a most adoring but nearly invisible wife. We can make the aforementioned financial arrangements tomorrow, if you are in agreement."

With that, Rhea raised her wineglass, which Logan had refilled for her.

"A toast to seal our business association, sir," she exclaimed evenly then, forcing herself to sound casual as she tried to ignore the tiny feeling of foreboding that was tugging at the back of her mind. Yet there was a bit of excitement there, too. She couldn't help wondering what this peculiar arrangement with Logan Tremaine would be like. Or for that matter, what *he* would be like . . .

"To our—association, Miss Merrick," Logan repeated her words, giving a slight nod and smiling as their glasses touched. "If nothing else, it should be most interesting for both of us."

Chapter 10

RHEA WALKED OUT ONTO THE BALCONY OF THEIR suite of rooms. The night was warm and filled with welcome early-summer fragrances. She put her hands on the smooth wooden railing and turned toward the bright moon. She was exhausted. The last three days had been a flurry of changes and activities. She'd hardly had a chance to catch her breath during that time. Yet sleep eluded her now.

True to his word, Logan Tremaine had made arrangements guaranteeing payment to all her creditors at the end of six months. The ten thousand dollars had been transferred to the First Federalist Bank in Rhea's name, where it would be safe and draw considerable interest toward her future need.

Rhea smiled as she recalled the look on Hugh Tennyson's face when Logan had presented her as his wife. She was glad he was young and strong of heart, otherwise the shock might have done him in. He had quickly taken Logan to a back office where Rhea had heard their voices raised in what sounded like a rather heated discussion, though she could not make out what they were saying. What transpired between them, Rhea didn't know. But when the two men returned to her, Logan's confident look and Hugh Tennyson's frowning countenance told her Logan had won the discussion. Though he clearly disapproved of the situation, Hugh had been very gracious the remainder of the afternoon, and most efficient in devising a plan to satisfy her creditors.

Then there had been the whirlwind round of visits to some of the best shops in the city. Rhea had had her hair coiffured in the latest fashion—pulled over to one side and curled into long thick coils held in place with ivory combs. Short, feathery bangs fell delicately over her forehead.

Rhea had been barely out of Logan's sight during these three days. Except for sleeping in separate rooms at the Amboye, during which Rhea kept the door locked and secured by a chair, she and Logan were together almost constantly. She had asked for accommodations the first night after they had struck their strange bargain, explaining only that for personal reasons she didn't want to stay at her shop any longer, and he had returned with her that night so she could quickly pack her things. She had seen no one in particular watching them, but again she'd suspected that someone was surveying their movements and noting all they did.

Rhea was glad to have Logan Tremaine take over making decisions and arrangements for her. It was a welcome relief from responsibility for a while. He accompanied Rhea to the dress shops and jewelry stores, giving his approval or disapproval. It was obvious from the beginning that Rhea was not the first woman with whom he had done this, for all the proprietors of the shops knew him on sight and gave Rhea their undivided attention when Logan introduced her as his wife.

While Rhea had been trying on a gown in one fitting room, she had overheard two young clerks whispering on the other side of the curtain.

"I never thought *he* would chose one and finally settle down. Half the women in Philadelphia will be brokenhearted when word of this gets out."

"Ain't that the truth. Quite a good catch she's got for herself. Wonder how she managed it."

"If they only knew the half of it," Rhea murmured aloud now as she sighed and turned from the balcony to return to the sitting room of the suite.

It was a lovely room at the Camden Hotel, an exclusive inn they'd stopped at on this first night out on their journey by coach to Logan's Virginia home. Rhea appreciated the luxury of such accommodations. It had been a long time since she'd known such lavishness.

She'd wondered why they did not travel by railroad, which would have been faster and more comfortable. But

Logan had said only that he had some business to attend to along the more circuitous route they would be taking, and that had ended the brief discussion. Rhea didn't mind really, for she was glad for the time to get a little better acquainted with Logan before she was thrust into the uncertainty and intrigue of playing her role before his family.

Rhea glanced at the three large trunks in the corner. They were filled to bursting with her new wardrobe. Beautiful, very expensive gowns and accessories. Logan Tremaine certainly had very good taste, and he was not at all stingy with the pursestrings.

Strange, her old trunk containing some of her own favorite clothes that she'd packed at the shop seemed to be missing. At least it was not among the new trunks Logan had purchased for her which were sitting in the corner. Perhaps it had not been unloaded from the coach since they were only stopping overnight. She'd have to ask Logan about it later.

Rhea went over and picked up the small leather case which contained her toiletries and carried it to the dressing room. She sat down at the mirrored vanity table and opened the case. Immediately her eyes went to the white envelope she'd laid atop her powder boxes earlier. Lifting out the elegant vellum envelope, she reached inside to look again at her copy of the document that had changed her life so suddenly.

It certainly looked authentic enough, this certificate attesting to the marriage of one Logan Templeton Tremaine and Rhea Marie Merrick. All duly signed, sealed and witnessed. Though Rhea had never seen such a document before, she was certain it was just like the real thing. Logan Tremaine would see to that most important detail.

Rhea held the thick parchment in her hand now and looked at the beautifully scrolled writing. This document had made it all possible. This forgery was tangible proof of the lie she had agreed to perpetrate.

There was little chance they would be found out if both she and Logan played their roles well. Only one other person knew of their pretense, the well-dressed young man who'd met with them in Logan's room after they'd dined at the Willshire. Willy-Nilly Scarsdale, Logan had called him. It was only on closer scrutiny that Rhea had noticed

Willy's clothes were frayed and threadbare in spots. And he had a terrible cough coming from deep within his chest. He was the forger who had so expertly drawn up this marriage certificate and had it ready so quickly for them the next morning. That was how he'd gotten his nickname of Willy-Nilly, Logan had explained—for his promptness.

Perhaps Hugh Tennyson knew of the false pretenses of their relationship, though he'd said nothing about it in her presence. Logan did not seem worried that he might know, so Rhea didn't let it trouble her.

She glanced one last time at the document, then carefully folded and returned it to the envelope, placing it back in the leather case. Yes, it looked like the genuine article all right. It would likely fool Logan's family. She wondered what kind of relationship he could have with them that prompted him to deceive them like this. Most likely not a good one. Perhaps playing Logan's wife would be a more difficult task than Rhea had first thought. She would be glad to stay in the background, as uninvolved with all of them as possible. She just wanted to get through the next six months as smoothly and easily as she could—as long as she was away from Philadelphia and Grayson Sawyer.

Rhea couldn't resist smiling contemptuously as she removed the combs holding back her hair and began to brush the long brown tresses free of coils. Her thoughts drifted back to the morning and her visit with her mother.

Rhea hated deceiving her mother, the poor, sweet and simple woman. Mentally her mother had not quite focused clearly on the real world since losing Rhea's father five years ago. She had wept with joy when Rhea told her she had eloped and was leaving immediately to live with her new husband at his family home.

"Oh, isn't that wonderful news, Lizzy, Gina?" her mother had exclaimed to the middle-aged maid and her daughter who were her nurses and constant companions. "And it's so romantic!"

"Yes, Miz Matty," Lizzy had replied, smiling widely. "It's fine, just fine."

Rhea went to visit her mother at a time when she knew Grayson Sawyer would be away from the house. She was alone because Logan was attending to some business elsewhere, but he had agreed to come to the house afterward to meet her mother. Careful to come directly to the house by carriage, Rhea hadn't seen anyone following her.

While Lizzy and Gina went to see about preparing brunch and bringing it up, Rhea had gone downstairs to find a book her mother wished to have read to her. As she had descended the stairway to the main hall Grayson Sawyer suddenly stepped out of the parlor and into her path.

"Leaving so soon, my dear, without a word to your loving stepfather?" he clucked as he grabbed her arm and propelled her into the parlor, closing the door after them so the servants wouldn't hear.

Rhea shrugged off his hand on her arm and straightened her shoulders, standing her ground before her tormentor. She had a weapon to use against him now—the marriage certificate.

"Do not come any closer, Grayson, or I'll scream," she warned in an icy tone. "My mother and the servants are in the house today. I will not allow you to put your filthy hands on me again."

The sharp tone of her words stopped him for a moment. He let his lecherous gaze move slowly over her so that Rhea felt undressed before him.

"That is no threat, dear Rhea. Your mother is sequestered away upstairs. She rarely leaves her rooms these days. And you know all the servants are in my employ. They will choose to hear nothing if I demand it." Grayson's reply was accompanied by a smug smile. "I am a very determined man. I have a score to settle with you." He rubbed his right arm gently where Rhea had stabbed him with the scissors. "I always get what I want. And I want you, especially now that you appear to be coming out of your self-imposed drabness."

His eyes moved boldly to the low-cut neckline of her new green gown as he took a step toward her. But Rhea went around a chair, keeping it between them. Her mind was working fast.

"I warn you, Grayson, if you try to force yourself on me again, you will have not only my wrath to deal with, but you will have my husband to account to as well!"

Sawyer stopped in his tracks and frowned.

"What ridiculous drivel is this?" he demanded. "You have no husband."

"But I do, sir," Rhea told him haughtily, holding her head high. "Two days ago I eloped with Mr. Logan Tremaine of Virginia. I only came here today to tell my mother of the happy event and that I am leaving with my husband today for his family home near Richmond. I won't ever have to see the likes of you again, Grayson Sawyer!"

"You're lying. True, my men have told me you've been keeping close company with this Tremaine the last few days, which surprised me. I've done business with him and know of his considerable reputation with women. But you are hardly his type, unless you are freely giving him what you continue to deny *me!*" Sawyer's dark eyes blazed with fury as he advanced toward Rhea again.

"Logan Tremaine is a gentleman, not a vile animal like you," Rhea stated coldly as she moved around the piano to avoid him. "I have proof of my marriage to him."

Sawyer paused again, stopped by her defiant tone.

"Where is this so-called proof?" he demanded as he folded his arms across his chest.

"Right here," Rhea told him contemptuously as she reached into the side pocket of her gown and drew out the envelope containing the forged certificate which she'd brought with her to show to her mother. This would be a true test of the genuine appearance of the document. Grayson Sawyer was a cunning man. He would not be easily fooled.

Sawyer snatched the envelope out of Rhea's hand and pulled out the contents. She feared to breathe as he studied the paper in his hand, saying nothing. Rhea used the few moments while his attention was distracted to inch her way toward the parlor door. But Sawyer saw her movement out of the corner of his eye and he caught her arm in a viselike grip, whirling her around in front of him. Rhea cringed as his fingers bit into her flesh, but she didn't let herself cry out. She wouldn't give him the satisfaction of knowing that he was hurting her, or that she was the least frightened by him.

"Do you take me for a fool?" he growled at her angrily. "While this looks authentic enough, such things can be forged. I can easily check with the Hall of Records—"

"And you will find everything quite in order there also, Sawyer," a deep voice edged in ice cut in ominously.

Grayson Sawyer spun around to come face-to-face with Logan Tremaine.

"I would advise you to unhand my wife, sir," Logan went on in a carefully controlled voice as he walked forward into the room.

Rhea almost fainted with relief. She was never so glad to see anyone in her life. Sawyer released his grip on her arm. She walked quickly across the room, taking the marriage certificate out of Sawyer's hand as she passed him.

"Are you all right?" Logan asked with a slight frown as she came to stand next to him.

"Yes . . ." Rhea answered a little breathlessly.

"Now hear me, Sawyer—" Logan continued in a menacing tone, turning back to the man before him.

"No, please," Rhea entreated, putting a hand lightly on Logan's arm as she looked up at him. "Don't bother with him." She glanced at Grayson Sawyer with disgust. "He isn't worth it."

Then she looked back at Logan, softening her gaze and her tone.

"Come, my mother is waiting to meet you."

"Very well," Logan replied as he followed her out of the room, leaving a stunned Grayson Sawyer standing in the middle of his parlor.

Chapter 11

SOUNDS COMING FROM THE NEXT ROOM INTER-
rupted Rhea's thoughts, bringing her back to the present
in her room at the Camden Hotel. She put the hairbrush
on the vanity table and left the small dressing room,
smoothing the folds of her new dark blue lounging robe as
she walked to the door.

"Forgive me," Logan said as he turned to see her standing in the doorway. "I did not mean to disturb you."

One arched eyebrow, so black like his wavy hair, cocked
at her now, making him look serious and aloof as usual.
Rhea wondered at how little he smiled. She couldn't remember seeing much of that expression on his handsome,
chiseled features during these three days that they'd been
together. Not that it mattered, Rhea told herself now.
They were business partners, nothing more.

After depositing her safely in the private coach he'd
hired for their journey, Logan had ridden on ahead astride
that mighty black stallion of his, taking a pair of dappled
grays along with him—to exercise them, he'd told her. He
was taking them back to Virginia to add to the plantation's champion line of stock. When Rhea arrived at the
inn that evening, Logan had met her there and they'd
dined together. But they'd spoken little, and what had
passed between them was formal and rather strained.
Rhea was not comfortable around him, for something
about Logan Tremaine disturbed her.

After seeing her back to their rooms afterward, Logan
had promptly headed downstairs to the gaming room.

"You did not disturb me," Rhea admitted quietly as she
came further into the room. "I could not sleep."

"Are you ill?" Logan asked, without changing his expression.

"No, just overly tired, I think, and apprehensive. Mr. Tremaine . . . I mean, Logan," she corrected, somewhat embarrassed. "We must talk. I have so many questions to which I must have answers if I am to play my part at all convincingly."

"You are right, of course," Logan agreed as he removed his coat. "But not right now. It is much too late tonight for serious conversation. I shall ride with you in the coach tomorrow and you may ask your questions.

"Is everything to your liking with the rooms?" he asked, changing the subject.

"Yes, quite," Rhea answered reluctantly. She didn't want to end the discussion, but knew by his tone that the matter was closed. Already she was learning his ways. His coolly appraising, always controlled ways.

"So then, what shall our sleeping arrangements be? I regret that we could not get adjoining accommodations at this inn."

"It's all right," Rhea replied, but she lowered her eyes uncomfortably. She was a bit irritated by his indifference. Yet she could find no fault with his behavior. He was keeping their relationship strictly as agreed upon. And that was, of course, the way she wanted it, too. But this situation was rather awkward and unusual. At least he could show some uneasiness, as she was.

"You may have the bed, of course," Logan was continuing. He gestured toward the door to the bedroom.

"Thank you, but as you can see, I have already made up the divan for myself." Rhea half turned to indicate the long, brown, velvet-covered lounge at the other end of the sitting room, where she'd spread a blanket and a pillow earlier. "It is much more suited to my size than yours."

As Rhea spoke she turned back toward Logan again and was surprised to see that he had moved much nearer to her and was in fact standing only an arm's length away.

"You should always wear that color," Logan said suddenly, his voice somewhat softer than before as his look swept over her face. "It matches the blueness of your eyes."

His handsome face hadn't changed its expression. Rhea

searched his features for some change in his aloofness, for just a little warmth, but she could see none.

". . . And your hair is much more becoming down like this."

He put out his hand to touch one of the long, waving tresses that tumbled around her shoulders. Rhea's pulse quickened and she almost drew back with uncertainty, but Logan turned away first and walked to the armchair where he'd laid his coat.

"I noticed you have not been wearing those ridiculous spectacles—that's good. They certainly do nothing for your appearance. I hope they weren't that necessary to your eyesight and have been left behind, along with the rest of those dreadful things you were going to bring."

Rhea's head shot up at the mention of her belongings.

"My missing trunk—you purposely left it behind?" she asked in disbelief, feeling her earlier irritation growing.

"Of course. You will have no need of the likes of those any longer." His tone was condescending now. "I will provide what you need. You must learn to dress the part you are playing. My social position, as well as the reputation I have for my preference in women, dictates that you make yourself as attractive and fashionable as possible in order to succeed at this. And I intend to do everything in my power to see that you do. Good night, madam."

Logan turned then, opened the bedroom door, and, closing it behind him, disappeared into the next room.

Rhea stood in the middle of the room dumbfounded. Yet her anger smoldered very near the surface, overcoming the commotion his nearness had caused inside her only moments ago.

So the party was so soon over. All the beautiful presents were opened and laid out, showing them clearly for what they really were—cold payment for services Rhea had yet to render. Logan Tremaine had kept his part of this devilish bargain they'd made between them, and now it was her turn. She couldn't do otherwise, even though at this moment she wanted very much to back out of this unsavory enterprise, to free herself of this cold and calculating man with whom she was partnered. But there was no turning back now. She had burned her bridges behind her. And Logan Tremaine held her debts as his trump card.

No, Rhea would have to keep her word to him and do whatever was necessary to get through the next six months. But the more Rhea thought about it, the more her stubborn resolve was weakened by an unnerving feeling of foreboding.

Chapter 12

THE SUMMER DAY DAWNED BRIGHT AND CLEAR, lifting Rhea's spirits somewhat as she rose to meet it. She'd slept fitfully but had set aside her anger in the morning, resigning herself to the task at hand. For a brief time she had considered defying Logan out of sheer spitefulness, matching his heartless behavior in leaving her old trunk behind and speaking so nastily to her. She felt like pulling her hair back into the severe bun and donning the drab gown and the spinsterish spectacles she'd used so effectively as a disguise the past year.

But on second thought, Rhea changed her mind. She no longer had any unattractive outfits, but more importantly, she couldn't risk upsetting Logan Tremaine for fear that he would break their agreement and not pay her debts. She would have to put up with his cool detachment and condescending manner, endure being told what to wear, how to do her hair, and how to act until next December 8th—the date their agreement officially ended.

Logan wanted her to be sedate, compliant, and of little notice. Well, she would start today—he would hardly know she was around!

True to her resolve, Rhea was attentive but spoke little as they traveled in the coach together all morning. She asked some questions, but for the most part Rhea just listened carefully to all he told her.

". . . Fair Oaks has been Tremaine land for over a hundred and fifty years," Logan continued explaining, "yet it could fall into the hands of others unless drastic measures are taken. The plantation is heavily in debt, as are many in these dire economic times."

There was a bitter edge to his voice when he went on to speak about his family. His tone explained to Rhea more than his words how Logan was able to justify using this fraudulent marriage against them. There was clearly no love lost between the members of the Tremaine family. In fact, only when he spoke of his sister, Camille, did Logan's eyes soften a little, the tight lines of his square jaw relaxing. However, he didn't speak of her for long.

"Miles is my older brother and has been my constant adversary since we were children. His goal is the complete control of Fair Oaks, forcing me out altogether if possible. My goal is the same for him."

The cold determination in his voice gave Rhea a chill. Somehow she gathered Logan Tremaine would be able to accomplish anything he set out to do, even if it meant destroying his brother.

"I have been away from Fair Oaks for three months," Logan continued explaining. "During that time Miles has managed to persuade our grandfather Silas to make a codicil to his will stating that all Tremaine heirs must be wed by age twenty-seven and producing new heirs within eighteen months thereafter. I will be twenty-seven the end of next month, but I have absolutely no intention of either wedding or breeding. And that is where you come in, Rhea."

He looked at her with smug satisfaction, obviously pleased by his cleverness in obtaining a pretend wife. Rhea shifted uncomfortably in her seat and was glad when Logan looked out the window to watch the passing countryside.

"Miles has been married for several years and already has a son, Tyler," he went on. "So the stipulation does not affect him. If Drew and I, especially, do not comply with it, Miles will have complete control of Fair Oaks, his reward for guaranteeing the continuation of the family. As it stands, he and I have joint control now, although he has the lion's share of responsibility. I need these next six months to stall for time until some investments I've made pay off. After that it will not matter what the old man's will says, I will have control of everything."

Rhea sighed inwardly. The Tremaines must be just one big happy family, she thought derisively, listening to Logan's narrative. Fair Oaks sounded more and more like a battleground than just a plantation. What on earth had she gotten herself into?

"You have not mentioned your parents," she ventured then, hoping to hear something better about other members of the family than what she'd just been told about Miles and Silas Tremaine.

"My parents died in a sea disaster ten years ago," Logan stated flatly. "The ship on which they were sailing went down in a storm. All were lost." His look was hard to decipher.

"I'm sorry," Rhea murmured.

"Don't be," Logan snapped coldly. "I despised them both. It was a deserving end."

Rhea said nothing. She was too depressed by his cruel words. She glanced out the coach window on her side, seeing the greenness of the land grown lush now from the warmth of early summer sunshine. But she felt no warmth here inside the coach, no warmth in this man sitting across from her. If the rest of the Tremaine family were cut of the same cloth, Rhea wondered if she would be able to endure living among such people for even a few days. Six months seemed almost an impossibility.

"We had better go over the story of how we met," Logan was saying, "so no one will catch us up in this circumvention. Here is what I've concocted.

"We met at Georgeanne Tennyson's coming-out ball two months ago. Hugh will verify that if need be. It was love at first sight. Your family, especially your stepfather—," Logan looked directly at Rhea then, but she kept her eyes averted, "objected to our relationship, so we met secretly and finally eloped so you could be with me now."

"Very well," Rhea answered without enthusiasm. The story was not very imaginative but was probably adequate. She could feign new-bride shyness if anyone pressed her for more details.

Chapter 13

LOGAN WAS FEELING ALMOST JOVIAL AS HE RE-
turned with Rhea to their rooms two nights later. She was
displaying exactly the characteristics he'd hoped for. She
followed his instructions to the letter and he was pleased
with her reticence and cooperativeness. Logan still suspected there was more to Rhea than she displayed—more
fire perhaps. There were hints of it in some of her reactions, in a certain look that would quickly cross her face
when she thought he wasn't observing her. He caught himself watching her at times, curious to see what else she
might reveal about herself.

But Logan convinced himself that he didn't care that
much about what Rhea was like underneath. He didn't
plan to have her around longer than these six months to
find out. As long as she presented the quietness and docil-
ity needed to accomplish this deception, that was all he
cared about. And she seemed quite capable of it.

The food and wine he and Rhea had had earlier in the
evening had been excellent. During supper they'd gotten
into a discussion about an editorial that was in a newspaper Logan had bought. He'd been rather impressed by
Rhea's intelligent questions and comments about the opinions expressed in the article. He'd enjoyed their conversation, and couldn't help thinking he'd chosen his
accomplice well.

Logan found himself beginning to anticipate with great
pleasure his family's reaction when they found out he had
not only brought home a wife, but that she was from Philadelphia as well. A northerner at Fair Oaks. What a stir

that was going to cause! Old Silas might go to his grave just from the shock of it.

Rhea was of a different mind as she walked slightly ahead of Logan up the inn's two flights of stairs. She was feeling the double strain of playing her role and avoiding conflicts with him at all costs. While this evening things had been a little more relaxed between them, she was glad they were returning upstairs now and she would be able to leave Logan for the privacy of her own room. She could let down her guard when she was alone. The less time she spent in his presence, the better, she told herself. That way there was no chance of seeing his forbidding frown or hearing his cutting remarks. When they were together her nerves were constantly on edge, because she feared making a mistake and evoking his displeasure. And he made her uneasy for some other reason that she could not explain, a reason that made her heart jump when he walked into the room or spoke to her. It was a strange and confusing sensation.

"Do you ride, Rhea?" Logan asked casually after they'd reached their rooms.

Rhea had sensed his changed mood and she was wary, uncertain as to how to react to it.

"Yes, though I haven't ridden in over a year. I did quite a lot before that," she answered him.

"You may ride with me tomorrow if you wish to escape the confines of the coach," Logan told her in a magnanimous tone. "However, I have only a regular saddle. Can you ride astride?"

"Yes, that will be fine," Rhea said eagerly.

"All right then, tomorrow we will ride horseback to our next destination and the coach will follow. For now I will bid you goodnight." Logan gave her a slight bow before he turned and left the room.

Now Rhea could look forward to tomorrow. To ride again. It had been so long. She hated being cooped up in that jostling, rattling coach hour after hour.

Rhea didn't know what had put Logan in a better humor this evening, but whatever it was, she was grateful for it. She could only hope it would continue.

The next morning Rhea dressed in yet another of her

new outfits, a dark green riding ensemble which included a short jacket, long pantskirt and green suede riding boots. Deciding to leave her hair loose and held back from her face with combs, Rhea took a last glance in the long mirror, then left the room to join Logan at the stables.

"Her name is Jade Wind," Logan told her as he patted the beautiful dappled gray mare's neck. "She'll give you a good ride."

He helped Rhea up into the saddle, then turned to his own mount.

"I'll ride Lord Sagamore here. He's a bit more spirited." He mounted the other gray of the matched pair and led the way out of the stable yard.

Rhea's spirits soared. It had been too long since she'd felt a good horse beneath her, known the freedom of a good ride. She was eager for it.

"Keep her to an easy canter," Logan instructed as they turned onto the main road. "I don't want her winded, just exercised."

Though Logan treated her like a schoolgirl on her first ride, Rhea refused to let him dampen her spirits. She hardly had to concentrate on controlling her mount. Jade Wind was well bred and trained, she noticed as the slightest pressure on the rein or her sides brought an instant response.

They kept to the main roads throughout the day and rode in virtual silence. Logan seemed preoccupied with his thoughts, and Rhea decided to be thankful for small favors and just enjoy the ride.

About noon Logan signaled he wanted to turn off the main road. Rhea guided Jade Wind through an opening in the tree-lined roadside, following Logan as he led the way on Lord Sagamore. They reined in at a small clearing edged by a meandering stream. Logan helped Rhea dismount, and they walked the horses to the water and paused to let them drink.

Rhea longed to pull off her hot riding boots and wade into the inviting water. But while the mood between her and Logan had been relaxed, she doubted whether such an action would be proper, even though they were alone in this secluded place. He would probably give her that chastising look of his, and Rhea had no desire to see it and spoil the tentatively friendly mood that had arisen between them this morning.

Handing her reins to Logan, Rhea walked over to a sprawling maple tree and sat down gratefully in its cool shade. After the horses were watered, Logan tied them to another nearby tree where they could graze on the grass in the shade. He was carrying a bulging saddlebag with him when he came over to where Rhea sat, her back against the tree and her eyes closed.

For a moment Logan stood off a little way watching her. A shaft of sunlight sliced through the branches of the tree and touched her hair, making it shine with reddish highlights. He noticed the delicate line of her face, the flawless smoothness of her skin. Logan was suddenly touched by the beauty of the scene, by the beauty of the woman before him.

Rhea sensed his nearness and opened her eyes.

"Hungry?" Logan asked as he continued to walk toward her as though he hadn't paused at all.

"A little."

Logan lowered himself onto the grass across from Rhea and opened the flap of the saddlebag.

"Luncheon is served," he announced in a mock-formal tone as he took out several bundles wrapped in brown paper. There was a twinkle in his pale blue eyes as he handed one to her.

"A picnic!" Rhea exclaimed with delight before she could catch herself.

But Logan seemed to ignore her outburst as he handed her the bundles and they unwrapped them together, revealing sliced bread and several kinds of cheeses. Logan also brought out four large, shiny red apples, a small bottle of wine, and two stoneware mugs. He leaned over and submerged the bottle in the weeds at the edge of the stream so the cool water covered it.

"Something tells me you've stopped here before," Rhea ventured, feeling a little less on her guard. But she wondered again at the change in him. She thought she liked it better when he was predictably stern and aloof.

Rhea was feeling relaxed and drowsy after they'd eaten, the result of the potent wine and rays of sunlight warming her inside and out. Logan had walked over to the horses to feed them the leftover apples. All was quiet in this pictur-esque meadow save for the gentle movement of the water over the protruding rocks in the stream. The rest of the world seemed far away and that was just fine with Rhea. It could stay that way.

Her eyes were half closed when a movement at her side caught Rhea's attention. Not five feet away a large brown rabbit stood poised on its hind legs. Its nose twitched curi-ously as it studied her for any sign of danger. Rhea stared back at it, unmoving.

"We should think about continuing our journey," Logan was saying as he walked up from behind the tree. The rab-bit turned tail and hopped away in an instant.

"Oh!" Rhea exclaimed, getting to her feet. "You've frightened it away!" She was frowning slightly as she shaded her eyes with her hand and tried to see where the rabbit was off to.

"What?" Logan stopped short with surprise at her outburst.

"No! There it goes!" Rhea shouted suddenly as she spot-ted the rabbit and went after it toward a clump of low bushes. When she reached the shrubbery where it had dis-appeared, she bent over to move some of it carefully aside so she could peer in.

"What, may I ask, are you doing?" Logan inquired with some annoyance as he came up behind her.

Rhea felt giddy and light-headed and, at the moment, not at all concerned about proper behavior.

"I'm trying to catch a rabbit," she stated simply.

"Such foolishness," Logan said, a slight frown express-ing his irritation. "You'll never catch it and why would you want to anyway?"

"Oh, there it goes!" Rhea cried, ignoring Logan's com-ments, as the elusive rabbit suddenly shot out of the bushes past her and out across the clearing. Rhea moved quickly in hot pursuit.

Logan's frown deepened as he watched Rhea go running across the thick grass.

The rabbit circled around and finally came to a quick stop behind a nearby tree. Rhea couldn't see him from her angle of approach. Logan could.

"This is ridiculous," he muttered to himself. Perhaps the wine and the fine summer day had gotten to him, too, for he suddenly moved to one side and cautiously came up behind the big rabbit.

Logan motioned for Rhea to stop and she did, for she now saw the rabbit, too. Logan had almost gotten to within lunging range when the ever-alert rabbit lit out again and disappeared down a large hole in the ground. Rhea and Logan burst out laughing and sat down on the grass next to it.

"See, you silly wench, I told you it couldn't be done," Logan said, looking over at her and letting a slight smile turn up one corner of his mouth.

"Yes, you were right. I shall listen to you the next time, sir," she told him, nodding and pretending seriousness.

"See that you do," he replied. His blue eyes studied Rhea, as though he was seeing something about her that he hadn't seen before. Rhea felt a slight uneasiness under his stare.

She lowered her eyes and suddenly busied herself picking several small purple blossoms of a wild violet.

"We should be continuing on our journey. It's getting late," Logan declared after a few moments. He got to his feet and brushed the grass from his riding breeches. Then, as he offered a hand to help Rhea get up, she lost her footing for a second on the uneven ground and Logan had to quickly put his hands on her waist to steady her.

They were standing very close. Rhea instantly became aware of the heat of Logan's body, and she felt a strange sensation where his hands touched her waist. Their eyes met and held for a long moment. Rhea's lips parted slightly as she hardly dared to breathe. There was only Logan filling her consciousness. Logan with those piercing light blue eyes and overpowering presence. She could not resist—didn't want to resist—when he gently pulled her to him and covered her lips with his.

A warning signal went off inside Rhea's head, but her body made her ignore it. Her heart was pounding frantically as her arms stole up around Logan's neck almost of their own volition, and she pressed against his length. His kiss intensified and he seemed to draw all her energy from

her, leaving Rhea with an exciting kind of weakness. She
was breathless when Logan finally freed her.

Logan's own breathing was jagged and he found himself
surprised at the effect Rhea was having on him, by the
heat she had ignited inside him with just one kiss. But he
quickly cloaked his reaction as Rhea slowly opened her
eyes to look at him.

The excitement she'd felt just a moment before came to a
crashing halt as she saw the smug smile on Logan's lips,
the look of amused self-assurance on his face. Rhea stiff-
ened and immediately drew back from him, struggling for
composure. Her anger flared, giving her the strength to recover and look at him directly.

"That was most amusing, sir, but shouldn't we be getting on our way?" she asked aloofly. And then with as
much dignity as she could muster—after romping in the
grass chasing a rabbit and being soundly and disturbingly
kissed by a man she had only known for a few days and
didn't even like—Rhea turned on her heel and walked
briskly away from Logan toward the horses.

Chapter 14

TWO DAYS LATER LOGAN INFORMED RHEA SHE could ride horseback with him again if she so wished. The day before he'd ridden on ahead with Baron, leaving her to travel alone in the bumpy, dusty coach. She'd caught up with him at the inn that night.

Now Rhea was delighted by the prospect of being freed from the uncomfortable coach and riding Jade Wind again, though she was careful to simply thank Logan and accept his invitation politely. She'd shown entirely too much lack of control back at the meadow the other day and didn't plan to have it happen again. Nothing more had been said between them about the incident and Rhea was glad of it. She wanted to forget Logan's kiss, forget its branding effect on her senses. And Logan gave little indication that he cared one way or the other whether she rode with him or not, except to say Jade Wind needed the exercise.

It was another warm and sunny summer day, though gray stormclouds seemed to be gathering in the distance as Logan and Rhea rode in that direction. In the early afternoon they stopped in the little town of Deacon's Bluff and took luncheon at the Oxtail Tavern. The small eating place and inn was not fancy but it was clean and homey and the proprietor was friendly.

He seemed to know Logan. Rhea learned that Logan stopped at the Oxtail several times a year during his numerous trips north, even though Deacon's Bluff wasn't on the main route to or from Richmond.

Rhea spoke little, answering only when conversation was directed at her. When she and Logan conversed, it was

only in short exchanges about incidental topics—local
scenery, the food, the weather.

There was considerable speculation among the patrons
of the tavern concerning the weather. Would it be wors-
ening or passing over?

"Been cloudin' up like this for days now," Gideon Murphy, the tavernkeeper offered finally. "And we ain't seen
nary a drop of rain yet. Sure do need it, too. Land's parched
as a desert. Crops is in sorry shape. I reckon you can make
it to Johnstowne without gettin' wet," he added to Logan
as he cleared away the dishes from their meal.

"We'll be on our way, then. Thanks, Gideon," Logan
said as he stood, shook hands with Murphy, then nodded
toward Rhea.

Outside, the sky did seem to be clearer as they mounted
Lord Sagamore and Jade Wind and left Deacon's Bluff.
They rode for the remainder of the afternoon, stopping
only occasionally to rest and water the horses. Rhea was
getting tired. She wasn't used to such a long ride. But she
said nothing to Logan. She really didn't want the ride to
end. The scenery was beautiful. They were not on a main
road, so they met no other travelers. And Jade Wind was
an excellent mount. She hardly ever shied when rabbits
and squirrels darted out of the surrounding woods onto the
road in her path.

Toward late afternoon the weather began to worsen.
What had been only sparse dottings of billowy, gray-white
clouds now gathered threateningly, darkening the sky.
The breeze picked up, and Rhea could hear the distant
rumbling of thunder. Both horses were agitated by the approaching storm. Logan reined in Lord Sagamore. Jade
Wind pranced and snorted nervously when Rhea reined
her in, too.

"We are less than an hour's ride from Johnstowne and
Farley House where we'll be staying the night," Logan
shouted to be heard above the rising wind. "There is no
shelter that I know of between here and there, so we must
try to make it. I do know a shortcut through those trees."
He gestured to their right. "Follow me."

"All right," Rhea answered, nodding as she turned Jade
Wind off to the side of the road in the direction Logan had
indicated.

They were able to ride abreast part of the way along the wooded path, but when it narrowed, Logan went on just ahead of Rhea. She had to use all her concentration to control Jade Wind now and guide her along the rough trail.

Suddenly out of the corner of her eye, Rhea caught a quick movement to her left. But before Rhea could react, Jade Wind had dug in her hoofs and reared, screaming a frightened neigh as she twisted her powerful head and neck violently to avoid the huge snake that had slithered into their path. The rider was caught completely off-guard. She tried desperately to grasp at Jade Wind's mane as she felt herself beginning to tumble backward out of the saddle, but she could not grab anything. Because Jade Wind's thrashing twist had turned them, Rhea landed on the rocky ground with a hard thud, not four feet from where the deadly cooperhead was poised to strike.

The fall had knocked the wind out of her. She could only lie perfectly still, gasping for breath, and watch terrified as the slithering creature began to move slowly toward her. Jade Wind's thrashing hoofs deterred it for a moment before the frightened mare galloped off wildly through the underbrush.

Logan had heard the commotion and turned back in time to see Rhea thrown off Jade Wind. He quickly dug his boot heels into Lord Sagamore's powerful sides and lunged with the animal as he turned and rode back to Rhea. But Logan yanked hard on Lord Sagamore's reins, causing the horse to rear suddenly, when his darting look took in the copperhead and Rhea's horrified expression. In a fluid motion Logan swung off the big gray's tilted back, snatching his pistol out of its saddle holster as he landed on the ground. He dropped to one knee and fired the gun two times. Rhea screamed as the explosion from the weapon shattered the air so close to her. The copperhead jerked and recoiled twice, then lay still almost at Rhea's feet.

Logan came swiftly toward her, his gun cocked back and ready to fire again if the snake showed any sign of life. He poked at it with the toe of his boot but it remained still. Then he knelt to gently help Rhea up. She rose to a sitting position and clung to Logan. Rhea was trembling all over and couldn't stop the sobs of relief that escaped her lips.

"Were you bitten?" Logan asked quickly, holding her a little away to see how she answered. He was frowning.

"No . . . No, I don't think so," Rhea managed to say, shaking her head and lowering her eyes from his angry look.

"Are you hurt anywhere? Is anything broken?" Logan's voice was stern, his look one of annoyance. He helped her to her feet when Rhea shook her head. She winced when she tried to straighten, for the movement caused a sharp pain in her back, but she waved Logan away from helping her further.

"No, nothing's broken, only bruised, I think." She glossed over her injuries even while the pain began to spread along her side where she'd landed so hard on the ground. She wouldn't let Logan know that, though. She didn't want his sympathy, or more accurately, knew she wouldn't get any from him. It was obvious from his expression that Logan blamed her for this incident and not the snake!

The distant thunder cracked louder at that moment. Logan glanced at the threatening sky where black clouds were churning in the increasing wind. Then he looked toward the dense stand of trees and undergrowth where Jade Wind had disappeared. With what seemed like great reluctance, he turned back to Rhea then.

"Can you ride?" he asked, still frowning.

"Yes, of course," Rhea replied with more conviction than she felt. She wanted to thank him for killing that horrible snake, but the words wouldn't come when he treated her like this. She was certain he would have preferred leaving her here and going after his runaway horse.

Logan walked to where Lord Sagamore waited nervously nearby. Leading the big gray back to Rhea, Logan lifted her into the saddle, then mounted behind her. Rhea bit her lip to keep from making a sound when the movement sent a spasm of pain washing over her. Logan's arm came around her as he grasped the leather reins and spurred Lord Sagamore to a gallop.

Rhea was wet, stiff, and miserable by the time they arrived at Johnstowne and turned into the courtyard of a large white clapboard house. Without meaning to, she had succumbed to the exhaustion she felt and dozed off, slumping back against Logan's broad chest as they rode. The rain had begun just before they reached their destination. Rhea was awakened then by the feel of cold droplets of water on her face, and quickly she and Logan were soaked to the skin.

Logan helped her dismount, but instead of putting her on her feet on the ground, he carried her up the eight stone steps to the front door, which had been thrown open so they could enter.

"Well done, Rufus," Logan greeted the Negro butler, who closed the door behind them, shutting out the crashing thunder of the storm.

Logan walked quickly to the closest room, a study, where he put Rhea down on a large brown leather sofa. Rufus followed them in.

"The lady will need a hot bath and a dressing gown immediately," Logan told him. "Have Hazel see to it at once."

"Yes, Mr. Tremaine," the butler answered in a voice that marked him as educated.

"Is Mr. Farlington at home?" Logan asked as Rufus turned to leave.

"No, sir, he's not expected until next week."

"All right. Thank you, Rufus. Have my usual room made up for madam here. I'll take the room adjoining it later. Bring me some dry riding clothes. I'll be leaving as soon as possible."

"Yes, Mr. Tremaine."

"Where are you going in this storm?" Rhea asked meekly from the sofa.

"To search for Jade Wind, of course," Logan answered curtly as he wiped the dripping rainwater from his face with the wet sleeve of his shirt. "Your poor horsemanship has made such an unsavory task necessary."

"My poor horsemanship—," Rhea repeated in disbelief as she sat up on the sofa. "My God, Logan, there was the thunder and the snake. Anyone would have been hard put to handle—"

"The fact remains," Logan interrupted in an icy tone, "that you told me you were an experienced horsewoman. Yet you were unseated by your mount and now that valuable piece of horseflesh is lost in this foul weather. I shall have to hire some men to help me search her out."

"No doubt you wish it were *I* out in this storm rather than Jade Wind!" Rhea exclaimed, her temper at his unfair attack flaring before she could stop it.

"Those are your words, madam, not mine," Logan replied sarcastically. Then he turned his back to Rhea and strode from the room.

Chapter 15

RHEA TRIED TO STAY AWAKE UNTIL LOGAN RE-
turned, but it was not because she cared if he got back
safely, she told herself. If he were to fall into a bog and be
swallowed up forever, she wouldn't grieve overmuch. She
wouldn't grieve *at all*, Rhea decided wickedly as she let the
steaming water of the tub soak into her bruised and sore
body.

But she did hope he'd find Jade Wind unharmed and
wanted to wait up until Logan returned so she could find
out how the horse fared. Jade Wind was quite beautiful
and very valuable. Rhea had known that even before Logan had made such a point of telling her so.

After her warm bath, Rhea ate a little of the cold meats,
cheeses and bread sent to her. From the young slave girl,
Josie, who was assigned as her maid, Rhea learned that
Farley House belonged to Parker Farlington, apparently a
longtime acquaintance of Logan's. Josie told her Mr. Logan stayed here often, but he'd never brought a lady with
him before. That surprised Rhea.

"Lordy, jus' wait till word o' dis get spread," Josie had
exclaimed with a wide grin as she combed Rhea's hair. "Be
a pack o' women mournin' the loss of *him* here in John'-
towne, that fo' shor'. Marse Logan and Marse Parker, dey's
real pop'lar wid da womenfolk hereabouts."

Rhea didn't find that statement surprising. If Parker
Farlington was as rich and handsome as Logan was,
women would flock around them like bees to honeycomb.
However, she wondered if this Farlington was as cold and
critical and condescending as Logan Tremaine was. *She,*

for one, did not find those qualities attractive in a man. Evidently some women did.

After that, Rhea could not keep her eyes open. The big, canopied bed looked so inviting that she decided to just rest on it for a little while. She would surely hear Logan when he returned and then she could find out about Jade Wind. But the last thing she remembered before sleep overcame her was the sound of rain pelting the bedroom window.

It was after eleven that night when Logan returned. He was exhausted and in a foul mood. After four long hours of combing the countryside in the rain with the livery stableman's three teenage sons, they'd finally found Jade Wind mired in the mud near a small, swollen stream. Once they'd gotten back to the livery stable, Logan had personally seen to washing the mare, feeding and bedding her down with warm blankets to ward off a possible chill. He hated the thought of losing Jade Wind by having her sicken on him.

Then he had come back to Farley House and ordered a hot tub of water to soak out the deep, aching tiredness that had seeped into his own body. Afterward, Rufus brought a cold supper to him, which he'd eaten voraciously, and now he lay naked on his bed covered only by a thin sheet, trying to fall asleep.

As tired as he was, sleep still eluded him. He could not stop thinking as he lay in the dark room. No sounds came from the adjoining room where Rhea was no doubt fast asleep after their fateful trip today.

His thoughts drifted back to late afternoon. She'd had quite a scare with that copperhead. The frightened look on her face flashed into Logan's mind, along with some strange thoughts he remembered for the first time now.

What had he felt when he'd seen Rhea thrown from Jade Wind, lying helpless on the ground with a deadly poisonous snake closing in on her? Of course he felt urged to help her—he'd do that for anyone in such danger. But there had been something else, too. A feeling new to him which Logan couldn't explain. Panic and confusion had come over him. Perhaps that was why he'd been so hard on Rhea, because of that.

Even the best of riders could be thrown from their mounts under circumstances like they'd encountered this afternoon. Rhea might easily have been killed from either the fall or the snake. Then what would have become of their agreement? After all, she was his responsibility for the next six months. He told himself that was the only reason he'd been concerned about her.

She had been rather brave through it all, Logan remembered now. While she'd cried some and held onto him, he knew she'd done so more out of relief rather than hysteria.

Logan thought of how they'd ridden here to Farley House together, how Rhea had leaned back against him and even put her head on his shoulder when she'd dozed off from fatigue. She had made no complaint at all. Now the memory of the scent of her perfumed hair came back to him to disturb his ponderings. What if Rhea had been hurt tonight?

"Damn, it's hot in here," Logan muttered angrily as he sat up in bed. He got up and put on his silk dressing robe, then walked to the window to open it wider. Cross ventilation would help, he thought glancing around the room. His gaze went from the door leading to the hallway to the one separating his from Rhea's room.

Logan went to the hall door and opened it, propping one of his mud-spattered riding boots against it to hold it open. Immediately he could feel the cooler outside air being drawn into the room from the window.

Couldn't hurt to open the other door, too, he speculated, walking to the adjoining door. Rhea was likely asleep, so she wouldn't hear him.

Nonetheless, Logan knocked softly before he tried to open the door. Receiving no answer, Logan tried the knob. It wasn't locked. He opened the door halfway and looked into Rhea's room for something he could use to prop the door open. She'd left the lamp burning on the bedstand next to her. It drew Logan's glance there where he could see Rhea outlined on the large four-poster bed.

Logan stopped short. She looked very beautiful. She'd thrown off the sheet and lay only in a filmy nightgown, but she seemed to be sleeping restlessly for she thrashed about, mumbling incoherently.

* * *

The exhausting day's events had caused Rhea to fall
asleep the moment her head had touched the pillow. Yet
her mind had continued to work subconsciously, filling her
with disturbing dreams.

She was in her room back home, the room that had been
hers since childhood and held so many wonderful memories of happy times spent with her mother and father. But
now something was coming toward her. She'd heard the
footfall of the intruder in her room. Suddenly a hand was
roughly clamped over her mouth and another powerful
grip pinned her hands helplessly over her head against the
pillow. In horror she recognized her attacker—Grayson
Sawyer!

"Don't bother to scream, my lovely little whore," he
muttered as he brought his face close to hers and covered
her body with his heavy weight.

"You know you want this as much as I do. For months
I've seen you watching me, begging me with those taunt-
ing sapphire eyes of yours. I have longed to possess you."

"Grayson, no, please!" Rhea pleaded, consumed by fear
and panic. But he ignored her and started to grope at the
buttons down the front of her thin nightgown with one
hand, even while she struggled to get away from him.

"We are alone here in the house, dear Rhea. Your stupid
mother is visiting some sick friend overnight, and I gave
the servants the night off. So I can take all the time with
you that I wish."

He tore at the last button of her nightgown as he straddled her and then threw back the thin fabric so that Rhea
lay exposed before him. His ravaging hands began to
stroke and paw at her naked breasts.

Rhea tried desperately to thrash away from Sawyer before he could violate her further, but her effort gained her
nothing except to excite him even more. His hands moved
all over her body, while his mouth sucked and bit at her
flesh.

Logan crossed the room to the bed in three strides. He
tried to grab Rhea for suddenly she had sat up and was
screaming wildly and thrashing at the air.

"Rhea! Rhea! Wake up!" he shouted at her as he tried to

catch her flailing arms. But she was hysterical now and fought him with a strength that surprised him.

"No, Grayson, stop!" she screamed at the attacker she saw trying to hold her. "Please don't do this! No! No!"

"Rhea! It's Logan, not Sawyer! *Rhea!*" Logan tried to get through to her as he caught hold of one of her arms and pulled her hard against his chest. His arms came around her, pinning her to him while he continued to call her name, trying to wake her.

"Logan—," she gasped in recognition finally, slumping against him weakly. Blinking in confusion, Rhea looked around the room and then back up at him.

"You were having a nightmare," Logan explained softly as she looked at him wide-eyed. "But it's over now. Sawyer's far away. He can't hurt you here."

A moan of relief escaped Rhea's lips as she closed her eyes and took a deep breath. Tears spilled down her cheeks. Logan could feel their hot wetness on his bare chest where his robe had opened in the struggle. He still held Rhea close, though he resisted an awkward urge to stroke her hair.

"Sawyer tried to . . . hurt you?" he ventured when Rhea seemed a little calmer.

"Yes . . ." she answered in a voice barely above a whisper. She closed her eyes to try to shut out the terrible memory of that night and the day last week at her shop. But they both still seemed so vivid.

"He is a horrible, cruel, obsessed man, who only wanted to—to—" She couldn't form the words, but Logan knew what she meant. Now he knew what was between Rhea and Grayson Sawyer and why she hadn't wanted Sawyer's help in anything.

"Only my mother's sudden return home that night stopped him before he could . . ." It was too difficult for Rhea to say the ugly words. "My mother is a sweet and trusting woman who lives in her own little world. He told me that if I said anything to her about what he'd tried to do to me, he would convince her it was I who had seduced *him.* He could do it, too, for he is an expert in deceit. My mother's mental condition is already very delicate. To learn about something like that could have been more damaging to her, so I said nothing. But I had to get away."

"So you left home to start the shop," Logan thought aloud. "I take it that did not deter Sawyer."

"It did for a while, but soon he'd grown so bold again I knew I had to leave Philadelphia to get away from him."

"So our bargain proved timely for both of us," Logan noted, running his hand through his dark, wavy hair.

Rhea nodded. She had pulled a little away from Logan, and as they looked at each other now, she felt a strange uneasiness. It wasn't fear, but she felt uncomfortable and she lowered her eyes demurely, suddenly aware that she was in her nightgown in bed with Logan, who obviously had nothing on under his half-open robe.

"I—I'm sorry to be so much trouble," she began haltingly, studying her hands in her lap.

Logan sighed deeply as he released her.

"Are you all right now?"

"Yes. Did you find Jade Wind?" Rhea asked quickly, looking up at him again, glad to be able to change the subject. "Is she all right?"

"Yes, we found her. However, it remains to be seen whether or not she will fall ill from the exposure during the storm," Logan answered, his cool demeanor returning again.

"I'm sorry. I truly hope she'll be all right," Rhea said sincerely. She knew he blamed her for Jade Wind's condition and was sorry now she had asked about the mare for she sensed Logan's pulling away from her, no doubt because of it. Only a few moments ago he had held her close and comforted her. But now he seemed to be changing before her eyes. The cold and cynical Logan was returning, and Rhea felt suddenly saddened. She wished the other Logan would remain longer.

Logan, too, was feeling unnerved now, and he didn't like it one bit. Touching Rhea had been a mistake, but what else could he have done but hold her when she was so distraught? The low décolletage of Rhea's thin nightgown had caught his eye and he had seen the soft shapes of her breasts molded there. Her long, dark brown hair hung in thick waving tresses about her face and shoulders. He wondered if she even realized how appealing she was at this moment.

My God, am I no better than Sawyer with what stirs inside me now? Logan chastised himself.

"Well, if you're certain you're all right," he said, suddenly turning away from her. He started to get up to leave, pulling the sash tighter around his robe before he tried to stand up. At the moment he felt bone-weary, too tired to try to sort out confusing feelings.

"I can call for Josie to come and stay with you if you wish." He stood beside the bed now, looking down at Rhea.

"Logan—," Rhea reached out and took hold of his arm to keep him from turning away. He looked at her questioningly. She swallowed hard, finding it difficult to say the words that needed to be said.

"I—I'm sorry Jade Wind was lost and you had to go out in the storm. I'm grateful for what you did this afternoon—killing the snake, I mean—and for coming in now. It was . . . kind of you. I don't wish to displease you, Logan. I'm only trying to keep my part of our bargain, truly I am."

Rhea lowered her eyes then and let her hand drop from Logan's arm. But he still seemed able to feel the heat of her touch through the silk sleeve of his robe.

Damn her! Why did she have to look so contrite, so sincere, so *tempting!* Logan knew he should leave her, leave the room right now. But instead he continued to watch Rhea, feeling the same ridiculous impulse rise up in him that he'd had in the clearing that day he'd chased a rabbit for the first time since he was ten years old. Putting out his hand, he tilted Rhea's chin up until their eyes met. Then he leaned down and kissed her softly.

Rhea did not pull back or resist in any way. She was simply too surprised to do anything except let it happen. And she was frightened, but it was not the same terrible fear she had known with Grayson Sawyer. This was more of a fear of the unknown, something new and rather exciting. Rhea had been kissed before. She'd had her share of beaus, and then there'd been Philip . . .

But there was something different about this kiss. It was unhurried, almost tentative, and sent startling sensations through Rhea. Her breath caught in her throat where she held it, afraid to breathe and perhaps break the fragile thread that was spinning between them.

Rhea's mind whirled. Why couldn't she stop Logan?

Why didn't she *want* to stop him? Why didn't she hate him, hate the taste of his mouth on hers as she did Grayson Sawyer's?

Logan's kiss changed now to several small, questioning ones as he pressed his lips over and around Rhea's mouth.

"I won't hurt you, Rhea," Logan's voice was barely a whisper against her cheek. "Don't be afraid of me."

Rhea's eyes opened to look at him. Logan knew he could soon become lost in their deep blueness if she would only let him.

"I'm not afraid," she murmured, yet she felt frozen, not knowing what to do next. She only knew she did not want Logan to stop what he was doing to her. She longed for his closeness, his tenderness . . .

Slowly Logan's lips found Rhea's again, then they moved to her cheeks, where he tasted the slight saltiness where her tears had fallen. He touched her eyelids and forehead with those same light tentative kisses.

A soft moan escaped Rhea's lips as his hand began to move also. Gently, caressingly, his fingers touched her bare arm and moved up and across her shoulder. Rhea's pulse raced as he moved his fingers down to trace a line over and around her breast covered only by the silk fabric on her nightgown. Logan's breath was coming jaggedly now as his desire flared and spread to Rhea. She wanted to touch him, run her hands over the hard cords of his muscles. But a kind of shyness held her back. Not until Logan paused and took off his robe was Rhea so moved by the magnificent sight of his naked body that she overcame her timidity and reached out and drew him down beside her on the bed.

Logan removed her nightgown and gently pressed her back against the pillows. For a few moments he just sat looking at Rhea, watching the glow of the lamplight play over her body. There was no lust in his look, no crude animal craving, like Rhea had seen in Grayson Sawyer's. What did she see in his pale blue gaze? Pleasure? Desire?

Logan made no further move to touch her. He seemed to be waiting for Rhea to want him. She wished he hadn't paused. It gave her mind a chance to work and react to what was happening between them.

Logan saw her brow dip in confusion. His own thoughts

were in a turmoil, though his body dictated what he must do now. Hesitating no longer, he leaned down to Rhea and kissed her, gently at first, and then more fervently. The taste of him, the fiery feel of his body pressed against hers overwhelmed Rhea. Her senses screamed for more. She brought her arms up around Logan's neck, working her fingers through his soft, wavy hair. She hardly dared to breathe as his hand began to stroke her ever so lightly and he ran his fingers over her stomach and up the side of her waist. Using only his thumb and finger, Logan began to trace soft, torturing circles around first one breast and then the other. They glided over her nipples until both were taut and tingling. Then his lips followed his fingers in their exploring path. His tongue began to flick and dart around her nipples, teasing and tormenting her until Rhea could stand it no longer. She brought Logan's head down so his mouth closed over the straining tip of her breast, devouring it. Instinctively Rhea began to move beneath him, answering the demands of his mouth and hands. She pressed her body hard against his length and clung to him, longing for more.

While Logan's mouth tortured one breast his hand played over the other, sending wild sensations of pleasure over Rhea. And when his hand moved down and between her legs, Rhea had to release the anguished moan that had welled up in her throat. Gasping, she arched her back to offer up what Logan sought. She cried out with fevered pleasure as rapturous waves of pulsating feeling crashed over her. Then Logan moved his body over hers and sank deeply within her, adding his throbbing tide to hers. Time lay suspended. There was no awareness except for each other and the desire that consumed them both.

Chapter 16

RHEA LAY AWAKE LONG AFTER LOGAN HAD fallen into an exhausted sleep beside her. His arm encircled her possessively and her head was pillowed by his shoulder.

Awe, shame, bewilderment overwhelmed Rhea as she lay unmoving next to the man who had made love to her but who was virtually a stranger to her. How had this happened between them? she wondered in amazement and confusion. Never before had she felt what Logan had just awakened in her.

While Rhea had had many suitors, she had been like this with a man only once before. Philip Winslow loomed into her thoughts now. Handsome, suave, he had told her he wanted to marry her. He had lied and deceived her, professing his undying love and devotion. And Rhea had believed him for she'd thought she was in love. It had been so easy for Philip to get her to surrender to him that late night after the Christmas Ball when they'd become snowbound at that little inn in the country. Only just before they were to be married did Rhea learn he was really in love with Eugenie Montgomery, her best friend. Philip had never intended to go through with the wedding. He only used Rhea to make Eugenie jealous and it had worked. Eugenie had come back to Philip and Rhea had found them together in Philip's hotel room. There had been a terrible scene. Philip had married Eugenie two months later and they'd gone to live in New York, leaving Rhea with the shame of having been used by him.

But now the memory of the night she'd spent with Philip came back to haunt Rhea. Philip hadn't made her feel as

Logan did. He had cared only for his own satisfaction, and their lovemaking had been swift and disappointing for her. But in her inexperience, Rhea had blamed herself for not knowing what to do or how she was supposed to feel.

That had not happened with Logan. She had responded instinctively to him, to what he had kindled within her, and the result had been overpowering. Rhea blushed now as she remembered how he had touched and caressed her. Now she felt miserable. Why Logan Tremaine? Why did *he* have to be the one who made her feel this way?

At last Rhea slept, bothered no longer by nightmares of the past. Now she dreamed only of a man with haunting pale blue eyes.

Logan opened his eyes, then quickly closed them against the glare of sunlight coming through the wide window across the room. When he could finally focus on his surroundings, he recognized his usual room at Farley House. He also realized in the same instant that he wasn't alone in the big bed.

"Damn!" he whispered emphatically as recollection of the night before seeped into his sleep-clogged brain. He glanced to his side where Rhea lay still asleep.

Ordinarily Logan was only too willing to bed any woman as beautiful and tempting as Rhea had been last night. Even now, relaxed in sleep with the sun shining on her face and hair and bare shoulders, Rhea was a sight to behold.

But this certainly complicated things. He had a business deal with this woman, an important one. Much was at stake and it all hinged on his being able to perpetrate this false marriage for the next few months. This was business, not pleasure. The two didn't mix. He'd have to be very careful in handling this delicate situation. He couldn't upset Rhea in any way and have her walk out on him. And what if a child were conceived? *That* he didn't want under any circumstances.

But then another disturbing possibility crept into Logan's mind. Had Rhea planned the whole seduction last night? She'd left the door unlocked, the light burning. She was not a virgin, that he knew now. What if she were pregnant from Sawyer or even someone else and had seen in his offer to play his wife an opportunity to trap him into being named the father!

In his gut Logan already knew Rhea wasn't that kind of woman. He was much experienced in the beguiling ways of women, and Rhea hadn't used any of them on him last night. Yet he found himself wondering for a moment how she had lost her virtue.

Damn! he cursed inwardly, putting that thought aside. All of this possible trouble might have been avoided if he'd just been able to hold himself in check last night. He usually had better control of himself. Whatever had possessed him to make love to Rhea? What had there been about her last night that had made her so irresistible?

Logan was frowning as he moved carefully to the edge of the bed and eased himself off of it. He had just put on his robe and cinched the sash tight at his waist when he heard Rhea stir. He turned to find her awake and looking at him.

"Good morning," Rhea greeted him tentatively. She searched his face and noted the slight scowl still in his expression. Dread welled up inside her. Looking away, she put her hand out and pulled the sheet up higher to cover her nakedness, feeling her face warming from a blush of embarrassment. She hoped he didn't see it. She didn't know what to do or say next. Somehow she had to let Logan know that last night could never be repeated. Perhaps he was of the same mind, for he looked displeased now, though he remained silent, apparently waiting for her to speak again. She took a deep breath to fortify herself.

"Last night never should have happened," she began bluntly, watching Logan intently for his reaction. "In no way was that any part of our bargain, nor will it be," she added firmly.

"I quite agree," Logan replied coolly, meeting her gaze. "The hard traveling we've been doing and the extenuating circumstances which occurred yesterday no doubt rendered us both temporarily—," the word "insane" jumped into his mind but he chose not to use it, "—not ourselves last night. We have a business arrangement which is advantageous to both of us to continue, but only with the strictest understanding that what happened last night will not occur again. It is best forgotten."

"Of course you are right," Rhea agreed evenly, though

inwardly she was hurt by the indifference with which he'd brushed their lovemaking aside. "Except for one thing. While last night's activities were meaningless to both of us, a foolish accident of circumstances, if you will, nonetheless there is one very serious consequence which could result and most certainly cannot be ignored."

With effort Rhea held her eyes firmly locked with Logan's. This was most disconcerting to be discussing. But she had to pursue it no matter how awkward the subject was. She was not going to be left with the burden that might occur because of their one night's folly.

"I presume you are referring to the possible conception of a child," Logan said bluntly with more nonchalance than he felt.

"Yes," Rhea answered, swallowing hard.

"Well, there's nothing to be done about it now, is there? The die is cast, so to speak. We'll just have to wait and see what develops, then deal with it if the time comes."

How could he be so callous and condescending? His tone made Rhea feel like a bothersome child. Logan was so infuriating! How she longed to tell him exactly that, but he had turned away from her to glance at the clock on the mantel.

"I must be at an appointment in half an hour's time, which will keep me occupied most of the morning. The coach should arrive here with Baron and our belongings sometime this afternoon. I will be going on to Burroughs about noon. You are to remain here for tonight. I want to give Jade Wind a rest to be certain she has no ill effects from yesterday. Follow me to Burroughs tomorrow in the coach. I will leave full instructions with Rufus. From Burroughs we'll go on to stay the night with some friends of mine near Richmond. You need not worry about anything. I'll take care of all the details. Good day," he finished, barely glancing back over his shoulder as he walked to the open door connecting their rooms and disappeared through it.

Rhea sighed deeply as she sank back against the pillows. What an exasperating man Logan Tremaine was. Of course he could dismiss last night as trivial, insignificant. He was probably involved with women all the time, used to satisfying his baser needs whenever he so desired. One more woman would mean nothing to him one way or the other. A man as handsome as Logan usually had little trouble attracting willing partners, in fact he probably had any number of bastard children running around. Of what consequence would one more be to him?

Rhea felt heavy-hearted, lost, alone. Nothing to worry about, he'd said. Nothing except whether or not at this very moment his seed was growing within her.

Chapter 17

RHEA MET LOGAN IN THE LITTLE TOWN OF BUR-
roughs, Virginia, just after noon the next day. Jade Wind
appeared to have recovered from her exposure in the
storm. She had eagerly accepted an apple from Rhea as
Rufus tied her to the back of the coach just before they left
Farley House.

Logan rode with Rhea in the hired coach as they set out
for the Laraby plantation. Little conversation took place
between them throughout the long hours of riding together. Logan seemed preoccupied with his thoughts, and
Rhea chose to keep her own troubled ones to herself.

They would be staying the night at the plantation of
Warren and Priscilla Laraby, friends of Logan's. This
would be a real test of their charade as man and wife. Time
to put her acting talents into play.

As the coach drove down the long lane leading to the big,
two-story gray stone house late that afternoon, Rhea noticed many Negroes around the prosperous-looking plantation. Some were tending the yard and vegetable gardens,
others were working in and around the huge red barn and
other outbuildings. She knew now she was in the South.

The front door of the house was flung open almost before
the coach came to a stop. A man and woman in their early
thirties came down the front steps to greet them.

Logan helped Rhea out of the coach. She winced as her
feet touched the ground and she felt an after-effect from
her fall off Jade Wind and from the uncomfortable coach
ride all day.

"Logan, my friend, how good it is to see thee!" their host
said exuberantly as he clasped Logan's hand and pulled

him into a hug of welcome. "Thee hath stayed away much too long."

"It's good to see you, Warren," Logan answered sincerely as he thumped his friend on the back. "And you, too, Priscilla."

Logan disengaged himself from the man to swing the tiny woman standing next to him up off her feet and around in a circle.

"Saints be with us, thee never changeth, Logan Tremaine!" the petite woman gasped breathlessly, smiling widely and blushing a becoming pink.

During all this commotion Rhea had a moment to size up the couple they were visiting. The man, Warren, wore a black suit, simple in lines but well cut, and a white, high-necked linen shirt. His pretty wife wore a dark brown, plainly cut gown with a full white apron covering the front. Her dark hair was pulled back into a bun which was half covered by a starched white cap. Clearly they were Quakers. Rhea was puzzled by the fact that she'd seen Negroes here. Quakers were well known for being against slavery.

"But I am forgetting my manners," Logan's deep voice interrupted her thoughts. He stepped next to Rhea and took her hand, pulling her forward toward his friends.

"Warren, Priscilla, allow me to present Rhea Merrick Tremaine . . . my wife." The lie rolled off his tongue quite easily.

For a moment the two people before them only stared in surprise. Rhea held her breath. Priscilla was the first to find her voice.

"Oh, how wonderful!" she exclaimed happily as she clapped her hands together and came forward to grasp Rhea's other hand. "Thee must forgiveth our apparent surprise, my dear, but to be perfectly honest, never did we expect to see this happen. We were certain our dear friend Logan wouldst be a bachelor forever!"

The smile Priscilla Laraby bestowed on Rhea was warm and friendly. It put Rhea instantly at ease.

"I decided I envied the outrageous happiness you two have," Logan interjected teasingly.

Warren and Priscilla seemed immensely pleased by his remark.

"But come, let us not stand here in the yard talking," Warren told them as he gestured toward the house. "Welcome to our home, Mr. and *Mrs.* Tremaine."

"So Logan swept thee off thy feet. How romantic," Priscilla Laraby remarked after she heard the fictionalized version of how Logan and Rhea had come to meet. They were all seated around the large maple table in the spacious dining room.

"Yes, quite," Rhea answered. She stole a glance at Logan and knew he was thinking the same thing—about how their first meeting had seen her literally knocked off her feet!

"Being from Philadelphia, Mistress Rhea, thee mayst find our way of life here in the southern states rather different," Warren commented in a more serious tone.

"I know it will be a change for me," Rhea managed to answer, averting her eyes shyly. In truth, she could not meet Warren Laraby's concerned gaze for fear he would see through her deception.

True to the role she'd been hired to play, Rhea had spoken little since their arrival. That was the way Logan wanted her to act and there were less chances for slips of the tongue that way. But she was finding this situation was truly a test of her acting ability, for she was becoming fond of this open and friendly couple who were her hosts. She regretted having to deceive them but knew she had to do it.

"But I know my husband will help me adjust," Rhea replied now to Warren's comment. She forced herself to cast a loving look toward Logan, who was sitting across from her. His cool blue gaze met hers and he smiled slightly, but there was no real warmth in it.

"Of course he shalt help you, Mistress Rhea," Priscilla assured her, patting her hand. Then she addressed the young Negro couple who had served them throughout supper.

"Maybelle, thee and Clem mayst clear the table now. And please try not to break any more of my good china pieces, my dear," she chided gently, "or I fear I shalt have to taketh it out of thy wages."

Rhea's earlier curiosity got the better of her.

"May I ask, please, are these people and the others I saw as we came in not slaves, then?" she ventured, hoping she was not being too impolite.

"Oh, my, no," Warren hastened to assure her. "All here on the plantation art free men and women, duly paid and holding papers attesting to that. But they art more than employees only. They art our friends, part of our family. We art Quakers, Mistress Rhea. Slavery is an abomination to us."

"Does that feeling hold true for slave *owners* as well?" Rhea asked before she realized how bold she was being. She saw a look pass between Logan and Warren Laraby but she wasn't sure of the meaning of it.

"It is not our place to judgeth other's actions," Warren answered her indulgently. "We can only pray for them and hope they art enlightened by our example."

Logan cleared his throat.

"No doubt such supplications will one day have their effect. But weren't you going to show me some yield figures for the last three months, Warren?" he went on, changing the subject. He seemed slightly annoyed by the turn of the conversation.

"Yes, I was," Warren answered as he got up from his chair. "If thou wilt excuse us, Logan and I wilt retire to the accounting room."

"Wouldst thee care to meet our children, Mistress Rhea?" Priscilla asked after the men had departed. "It is time for me to see them to bed."

No children had been seen or heard in the house since Rhea and Logan had arrived late that afternoon, but then, it was not the custom for youngsters to be present when guests were being entertained.

"Yes, I would like that," Rhea answered.

A boy of about five and a girl of two came bounding to them, laughing and squealing as Rhea and Priscilla entered the large nursery upstairs.

"Children, children, where art thy manners?" Priscilla scolded. "Come now, I have brought someone for thee to meet. She is going to help me tuck thee in bed this night.

"Please forgiveth their excitement," Priscilla said to Rhea then. "It isn't often we have guests, isolated as we are way out here."

"I understand and I don't mind at all," Rhea assured her, smiling as she stooped to pick up the adorable little girl who came eagerly toward her. Her hair was a mass of blonde ringlets tumbling around her head. She had on a long white nightgown that left only her face, hands, and tiny bare toes showing.

"That is Martha and this is Martin," Priscilla explained, a note of pride in her voice. "Children, this is Mistress Rhea, Mr. Logan's new wife. She is our friend."

Rhea felt a pang of guilt at the sincerity in Priscilla Laraby's voice.

"They are beautiful," Rhea said, hugging little Martha tightly until she giggled and tried to squirm away. "How fortunate you are to have them."

"Yes, we have been greatly blessed," Priscilla agreed. "But thee shalt be, too, I am certain. Our Lord shalt surely bless thy union with Logan with children. Thee hast only to love God and each other for the miracle of creating new life to happen. Our children art our greatest joy. I am certain thee shalt know the same joy in due time, my dear."

Priscilla patted Rhea's arm and turned toward the beds across the room. Rhea was thoughtful, realizing how much she envied Priscilla Laraby. She did long for just this—a home, a loving husband, beautiful children. Not with Logan Tremaine, of course, but with some man she was yet to meet, a man who would love and cherish her, one she could love and trust with all her heart for the rest of her life.

The reality of what she had to do before a new life could even begin for her cast a shadow of gloom over Rhea's thoughts. But after these six months were ended, then she could look to the future.

Chapter 18

LOGAN WAS WALKING IN THE ROSE ARBOR AFTER his talk with Warren Laraby. Warren's report had been good. All was running smoothly here on the plantation. So far there had been no disruptions in the plan of operations he had set up with Warren mònths ago.

The sky was cloudless. The arbor was drenched in a silvery brightness cast by the full moon overhead. Logan stopped, sensing someone else's presence. A woman was bent over a nearby flowering bush at the side of the path. After a moment she plucked a blossom and tucked it in her hair.

Rhea. Logan recognized the delicate lines of her profile in the moonlight. Logan's eyes roamed over her freely, taking in the play of light on her long hair, the sensuous curves of her body. He was surprised to find himself thinking how lovely she looked just now.

"Oh, I didn't hear you approach," Rhea gasped suddenly as she turned toward him.

"I see we had the same thought before retiring," Logan replied as he came to stand beside her.

"Yes, this is a beautiful place, isn't it? I could smell the fragrance of these flowers coming in the window all through supper. There must be nearly a hundred rose bushes here. How glorious they must look in the light of day. Do you think the Larabys will mind if I pick a few of the blossoms?"

"If it is to adorn your lovely hair, I don't think they would deny it," Logan answered as he reached up to touch the flower Rhea had just put in her hair. He let his fingers touch the wispy curls fringing the side of her face before he moved his hand away.

Rhea didn't like it when softness came into Logan's voice. She wished he wouldn't stand so close, for his nearness did strange things to her. He was so handsome, with an almost overpowering presence about him. Against her will Rhea's pulse quickened, her stomach fluttered with excitement. She couldn't explain it for she'd never had anything like this happen to her before she'd met this Logan Tremaine. It was unnerving . . .

"The Larabys have two beautiful children," Rhea blurted quickly, changing the subject. She turned away from Logan and crossed the narrow brick path to sit on a stone bench.

Logan stayed where he was and leaned back against the large maple tree behind him.

"They had three," he continued in a low voice. "There was another son, Lucas. He was three years older than Martin. I sketched him once. I remember he had the most captivating brown eyes I'd ever seen. They lost him to a consumption in the lungs two winters ago."

"Oh, how terrible," Rhea barely whispered the words. Her heart went out to the Larabys in their loss. "She never said anything about it."

"Warren and Priscilla are ones who count their blessings, not their losses. They are good people. Their religion is their way of life. It helps them bear whatever comes to pass."

Rhea felt annoyed. She couldn't understand this man before her.

"You're right. They are fine people. They call you friend and mean it from their hearts." Rhea stood up and looked at Logan levelly. "What kind of friend are you to deceive them with this false marriage of ours?"

Logan hadn't been proud of his actions in that regard and Rhea's sharp words didn't sit any better with him now.

"That is no concern of yours, madam," he retorted coldly, his forehead creasing into a forbidding frown. "You need to think only of keeping your part of our arrangement. You will question neither my actions nor my motives."

Rhea didn't trust herself to speak for a few moments as she struggled to keep her temper. She wouldn't give him the satisfaction of seeing how his cruel words stung her.

"Of course, I understand," she replied finally, though she didn't lower her eyes in her usual contrite attitude but continued to look straight at him. "There is no place in our agreement for a show of conscience. I shall not forget again, I assure you. Good night, sir."

And with that Rhea swung around and walked purposefully back to the house.

Chapter 19

RHEA AND LOGAN SPENT LITTLE TIME TOGETHER during the remaining day of travel to reach Fair Oaks. Logan rode on horseback while Rhea confined herself to the coach to avoid him. He didn't invite her to ride with him that day.

Stopping at one last inn that night, Rhea and Logan dined together, then Logan left her, returning much later in the night. They were civil to each other for appearance's sake, but clearly no friendship would ever spark between them, Rhea was certain of that. Logan was the employer; Rhea, the employee. He never came right out and stated that for a fact, but his manner made it perfectly clear.

Rhea remained just as withdrawn as she was supposed to be. It was easy to act that way when she felt so heavy-hearted. The cloud of gloom that had enveloped her in Philadelphia seemed to be following her to Virginia as well.

On the other hand, Logan acted satisfied with her attitude and performance. Except for the little flare-up at the Laraby's, Rhea was again behaving exactly as he'd said she should—manageable, causing no trouble, making no demands.

Logan wouldn't tell her any more about himself or his family other than the basic information he'd given her their second day out. He insisted her reactions would be more genuine that way, but this reticence on his part only served to put Rhea more on her guard.

Logan ordered the driver of their hired coach to stop.

He was riding inside with Rhea this morning. They'd been traveling on Tremaine land for the last four hours.

Rhea was greatly impressed by the sprawling size of the plantation. Fields of tobacco stretched out as far as the eye could see. And she noticed scores of slaves—men, women, and older children—bent to the tasks of tending the plants, supervised at all times by Negro drivers who carried menacing buckskin whips.

A white man on horseback with a huge bullwhip wound around his saddlehorn paused a short distance away to send a curt salute their way as the coach stopped. Logan returned his gesture, and Rhea noticed a slight tightening in his jaw.

"That is Dreed Jessup, our overseer," Logan explained to her coolly. "Fair Oaks lies just beyond the next bend. Continue on, driver," he called through the open window.

As they'd ridden together today Rhea had sensed a tension—or perhaps it was an excitement—in Logan ever since he'd pointed out the boundary marker of his family's property earlier that morning. What did she read in his look? Was he glad to be home again or was he girding himself for battle? Whatever it was, Rhea sensed a change in him, though his outward expression never wavered.

"I wish to remind you once more of the importance of this first impression you will make on the people you are about to meet."

His words made Rhea feel like a child being reminded of her manners in front of company. It irked her to be treated so, but she swallowed her annoyance and tried to pay attention to his words. She was feeling nervous herself now. Logan need not have reminded her of the impending confrontation. It was all Rhea had thought about for days.

"They are not expecting us so the element of surprise will be on our side, giving you a chance to win them over. Just be shy and retiring as you have been. Let me do all the talking for both of us." His blue eyes looked at her intently.

"Yes, of course," Rhea agreed, only too happy to leave everything to him.

As the coach rounded the bend in the road Rhea had her first glimpse of Fair Oaks. Its splendor took her breath away. The main house was red brick fronted by six large white pillars that reached from the ground level to the roof, three stories above. Long white shutters adorned the many-paned windows on all three floors.

But the truly remarkable sight was the beautifully landscaped garden that made up the sprawling three to four acres of front lawn. Hundreds of flowering plants and bushes were meticulously arranged among carefully manicured shrubbery and hedges so that bursts of color blended together in a kaleidoscope of beauty.

"Oh, how lovely," Rhea murmured without realizing she'd spoken. She continued to stare awestruck out the window of the coach as they pulled to a stop at the front steps.

Two Negro groomsmen dressed in maroon livery immediately appeared to help Rhea and Logan out of the coach. At the bottom of the steps Logan took Rhea's elbow.

"Ready?" he asked softly.

Rhea took a deep breath. "As ready as I'll ever be, I suppose," she replied as she gathered her skirt and started up the steps.

"Good day, Jemson," Logan greeted the gray-haired Negro butler who held the door open for them.

"Good day, Mr. Logan. Welcome home, suh," the old man answered formally.

"Thank you, Jemson. How is my grandfather today?" Logan's tone was equally formal.

"He has not left his bed, suh."

"I see. Inform him of my return if he is awake, and tell him I shall see him shortly. Then call the rest of the family together in the front parlor."

"Very good, suh."

While this exchange had been going on Rhea had a chance to survey her immediate surroundings. This main entrance hall was very large. Two staircases—one at each end of the hall—ascended in a half circle, meeting in the middle at the second floor. Elegant brocade divans and marble-topped tables lined the wall around the area. The heels of Rhea's shoes clicked on the highly polished inlaid wood floor as Logan led her to the parlor.

A pretty young woman, pale and thin, was the first to come into the room after them. She was small in height and delicately featured. Her ash-blonde hair was attractively coiled in curls along the sides of her face.

"Logan, you're home at last!" she exclaimed warmly as she ran into his welcoming arms. "I thought you'd never return.

"And who is this beautiful woman?" she asked boldly then, turning her lovely smile on Rhea.

"This is Rhea, Camille . . . my wife."

For a moment Camille Tremaine just stared, open-mouthed.

"What? Your wife?" she repeated in surprise. Then after seeing Logan's nod of assent, her smile broadened. "I am so glad to meet you. I'm Logan's sister. Welcome to Fair Oaks, Rhea," she said with genuine pleasure as she gave Rhea a hug.

Then she turned to her brother again. "It's just like you to do something like this, Logan, you rascal," she teased with a twinkle in her blue eyes as she kissed his cheek affectionately. "Congratulations to you both."

"What are we congratulating?" a young man of about seventeen or eighteen asked as he meandered into the room at that moment. He was six feet tall and lanky of build and was dressed in riding gear, obviously about to go out. He had Logan's light blue eyes but lacked his rugged handsomeness.

"We are celebrating my nuptials, Drew," Logan replied to his question. "Rhea, this is my younger brother, Andrew. Drew, my wife, Rhea."

"Well, this is a surprise. A pleasure to meet you, I'm sure." Andrew Tremaine's tone was rather pompously aloof as he gave Rhea a bold once-over look with one dark eyebrow cocked at her. "This will certainly liven things up around here. It's always dull when Logan's not about to keep everyone's hackles up. Welcome home, brother, and you, too, madam. Now if you'll excuse me, Edith Haver-sham is waiting with baited breath to go riding with me. Good day." And with that he turned and left the room before anyone could say anything more.

A man and a woman came into the parlor next. A tow-headed boy of about age six followed reluctantly in their wake. The man looked to be about Logan's age. Rhea noticed the similarity in features between him and Logan immediately. The straight nose, the strong jawline, the black hair, the height were almost the same. Clearly, they were related somehow. Was this the older brother, the adversary? Rhea wondered.

The woman was older than Rhea by several years, and while she probably had been quite comely at one time, her figure was rounded to plumpness now. Her hair was stunning, though. Shoulder length and cinnamon colored, it was brushed back into fashionable deep waves that were held away from her face by ivory combs.

Logan and the man exchanged a look that might have shriveled lesser men. Rhea could feel the tension mounting in the room as she watched them.

"Logan, so you have finally returned to us," the woman greeted warmly as she stepped toward Logan with both hands outstretched. "What have you been up to all this time, dear brother-in-law?" She gave Rhea a sweeping look from head to toe.

Ignoring her question, Logan quickly let go of her hands and took a step closer to Rhea, putting his arm around her waist. Rhea was surprised by his sudden gesture.

"Rhea, darling, allow me to introduce my sister-in-law, Sybil, my older brother, Miles, and their son, Tyler."

Logan paused to lend special emphasis to his next words. There was a definite note of triumph in his voice as he said, "And this is Rhea Merrick Tremaine of Philadelphia . . . my wife."

Rhea was glad for Logan's supporting arm around her now for the malice in the looks she received was almost tangible. Tension all but cracked in the air. Miles Tremaine's face reddened and his dark eyes narrowed dangerously as he looked from Rhea to his brother.

Sybil was the first to recover her wits, but instead of a greeting, she only declared with disdain,

"My God, Logan's brought a Yankee to Fair Oaks!"

Chapter 20

"YOU MIGHT HAVE WARNED ME A LITTLE," RHEA said in a low voice as she removed her bonnet. With an effort, she kept her annoyance in check.

Jemson's timely arrival at the parlor door announcing luncheon had given them all an excuse to escape what had quickly developed into an unpleasant scene. Logan had pleaded travel fatigue for himself and Rhea so they had been able to go to their rooms.

They were now in what would be Rhea's bedroom. She glanced around as she laid her green bonnet and matching gloves on a small, ornately carved hickory table. The bed was the central focus of the room and was canopied in pleated yellow velvet. The room was done in pastel yellow and white decor. It was bright but stuffy from being closed up, and had only been given a quick once-over cleaning, since their arrival had not been expected. It was a beautiful room, though, spacious and elegantly furnished with several chairs and a divan upholstered in rich brocade material.

But rather than thoroughly examining her surroundings, Rhea could only think of what had just occurred down in the parlor with Logan's family.

She could still feel the effect of Miles Tremaine's malevolent stare drilling into her. Unlike Logan, Miles's eyes were dark brown, but they held the same cold and sinister glint Rhea had seen in Logan's often enough. Sheer willpower and Logan's restraining arm around her waist had prevented Rhea from stepping back, shrinking away from that hateful look.

"Is it such a crime around here to be from the North?"

Rhea asked pointedly, frowning as she turned to face Logan. "Except for your sister, they all looked at me as though I had the plague or something."

She immediately noticed the smug smile of satisfaction on Logan's lips and realization dawned on her.

"And you knew they would react to me that way. It's some cruel joke you're playing, part of this devious scheme in which I've gotten myself involved." Her eyes were accusing as they held his.

Logan didn't answer right away. He walked to the window and drew back the heavy yellow velvet draperies. Then he opened the double French doors leading out to a small balcony. Fresh air rushed into the room. Rhea felt its welcome coolness on her flushed face.

"Of course I knew," he said finally. "I planned it that way. And it went better than I'd expected. You did very well, all things considered. Miles was stunned speechless. That alone made all of this worth the doing. I always enjoy rankling all of them and I've become quite adept at it over the years."

"Well, I'm not amused," Rhea told him levelly as she folded her arms in front of her. "You will need to keep me more fully apprised of what to expect if you want me to play my part effectively. I can't wait to meet your grandfather. What will be his reaction? To challenge me to bare blades at fifteen paces?"

Logan walked over to stand before Rhea. She was surprised to see that he was smiling!

"You need have no fear of old Silas. Just stiffen that Yankee spine of yours as you did downstairs and say as little as possible, and you'll get through the audience with him just as well. But we'll save that little episode for this afternoon. Rest and refresh yourself now. I'll see to our luggage and send up someone with a luncheon tray for you. There will be some girls to serve you. They'll help you unpack. You need only pull that cord by the bed to summon them.

"You may, of course, make any changes to this room that you wish. Just tell Mrs. Jerome, the housekeeper, what you would like and it will be done."

He gestured toward a door off to his right. "That leads to a sitting room which adjoins another bedroom beyond.

That bedroom will be mine. I'll have my things moved from my normal room in the other wing this afternoon. This wing was meant for the married members of the family. Miles and Sybil have their rooms at the other end of this hall.

"Is there anything else you require for now?"

"No, as usual, you seem to have thought of everything," Rhea answered coolly. She could not match his jovial mood. Not even his compliment that she'd done well made her feel any better.

"Until this afternoon then." He gave her a curt nod and left the room.

"So you're the one everyone is in such an uproar about. Well, *I'm* not impressed!" Silas Tremaine exclaimed as he looked Rhea over from head to toe.

She tolerated his scrutiny with downcast eyes and a shy demeanor, the way she knew Logan wanted her to act. He had told her to answer any questions put to her as simply as possible and not to get upset by the old man's cantankerous manner.

"Step forward, girl, and look at me. I won't bite you!" Silas demanded.

Rhea moved away from Logan's protective side and approached the large four-poster bed where the seventy-five-year-old patriarch of the Tremaine family held court and issued his edicts. Logan had told her his grandfather had been a career officer in the American Navy and was used to issuing orders and having them obeyed.

As instructed, Rhea now looked at him fully, seeing his thinning gray hair, deeply lined face, and lively eyes—light blue eyes, like Logan's.

"So, you've married my grandson," old Silas stated gruffly. "I hope you know what you've gotten yourself into. As usual, he's no doubt chosen you more for your looks and propensity for bedding than for your wits. You're too skinny. You'll need more meat on those bones if you're going to give Logan many fine sons and not sniveling little brats like that monster of Miles's. I doubt if anything good can come out of a Yankee, though. Nothing ever has. Well, can you at least read, girl?"

"Of course, sir," Rhea managed to somehow answer calmly, fighting inwardly for control. The nerve of him!

"Well, that's something. Starting tomorrow, come every afternoon at two o'clock to read to me. I've grown weary of hearing Sybil's whiny tone. Yours at least will be a change. That's all. You are both dismissed."

Only too gladly did Rhea give an abrupt curtsey, turn, and walk briskly to the door with Logan and out of the room.

"What an outrageous man!" Rhea exclaimed with a frown as Logan closed the door behind them.

"Actually he was in one of his better moods, probably because everyone else is so upset," Logan observed with amusement, his eyes twinkling.

"Must I really read to him each day?" Rhea asked with dread.

"Of course. My grandfather's word is still law around here. And besides, it is imperative to my plan that no unnecessary trouble is stirred up. But the readings probably won't last long at any rate. I doubt if old Silas will be able to tolerate listening to that horrible northern accent of yours for very long."

Rhea opened her mouth to answer his insult, but she closed it again and just walked away from him to her room. This whole family was outrageous! Better to keep quiet and stay as inconspicuous as possible, just as she'd been hired to do. And pray that the next few months would go by swiftly.

Chapter 21

"WE MUST HAVE A FORMAL RECEPTION TO CELE-brate Logan and Rhea's wedding and to introduce her to Richmond society." Camille Tremaine's face was alive with excitement as she stated her plan during the evening meal. The whole family except for Silas was gathered around the elegantly set table in the huge wood-paneled dining room. All the dark wood was beautifully grained and shone with a high polish, but it gave an oppressive atmosphere to the room.

"We haven't had a ball at Fair Oaks in over two years," Camille continued eagerly. "It's time we did. I'll plan everything. We can do it as part of our Fourth of July celebration. Rhea and Sybil can help me."

"I suppose we must," Sybil agreed unenthusiastically. "It would be something to break up the boredom around here. There's been very little to gossip about lately. All anyone can talk about is runaway slaves and that ridiculous underground railroad. I'm sick to death of hearing about that dreadful Mr. Exodus person. I shall be delighted when he is caught and hanged."

"All right, Camille, I'll help you some with this reception," she added reluctantly, "along with Rhea." The disdain in her voice was undisguised as she said Rhea's name.

Rhea ignored her. She wanted to ask what an Exodus person was but decided against it when she saw Logan's angry countenance. It was directed at Sybil but she seemed completely oblivious to his annoyed stare. Rhea didn't want to do anything to change the direction of his irritation toward her.

"I hate to dance! I won't do it!" young Tyler Tremaine

proclaimed suddenly, crossing his arms in front of him to emphasize his point.

"You need not worry, Tyler," Camille assured her pouting nephew indulgently. "This ball will be for grown-ups. Your presence will not be required."

"But I can come if I want to, if Papa says so," Tyler threw back belligerently, his lower lip protruding and his chin pointing up in the air toward his aunt.

"Yes, of course you can if your parents allow it," Camille answered with exasperation. "Really, Tyler, must you always be so argumentative?"

"I think a reception ball is an excellent idea," Logan interjected then, drawing attention from his nephew. "July Fourth is still a few weeks away, which should give you ladies enough time to make plans. But now if you will excuse us, my wife and I will retire."

Logan got to his feet and came to stand behind Rhea's chair, pulling it back as she stood to join him. Gratefully, she said good night to everyone and let Logan lead her by the elbow from the room. It was a relief to reach the hall and be out of that oppressive atmosphere. Sighing, Rhea realized she was very tired and rather depressed by the day's events. She only wanted to reach the haven of her room where no one would bother her, or look at her hatefully, or insult her.

"One of the women who helped you unpack this afternoon—Glory—will be your personal maid," Logan stated as they reached the sitting room that separated their sleeping quarters. "She'll be up shortly to attend you. "Glory was born and raised here at Fair Oaks, as was her mother and grandmother before her. And she tends to be on the talkative side. She'll no doubt be an invaluable source of information to you about this family of mine. That will keep you from bothering me with tedious questions all the time. However, I will caution you to temper what she says with a grain of salt. She, like most Negroes, tends to exaggerate.

"I will say good night now. Tomorrow if you like we can go riding and I will show you some of the estate." His tone had a bored note to it, which matched his expression. He barely looked at her.

"Yes, all right," Rhea agreed, though she was frowning.

Why did he always have to spoil things with cruel words? He was continually so unfriendly and distant.

"I really don't like you much at all, Logan Tremaine," she murmured to herself after he'd said a perfunctory, "Good night," and left the room.

Well, at least Camille seemed to be a little different from the rest of this cold-hearted family. She had been genuinely glad to meet Rhea. It might be fun to plan the party with her, that was if sour Sybil didn't interfere too much.

Rhea had taken an instant dislike to Miles Tremaine's wife, as Sybil had to her. She would have to avoid contact with her whenever possible to prevent conflict. Rhea sensed that Sybil thrived on discord and would like nothing better than to cause trouble if possible.

Rhea walked to her bedroom and began undressing for bed. She was thinking back over the dinner conversation when she remembered the unusual name Sybil had mentioned—Mr. Exodus. A curious nomenclature. Tomorrow she'd have to ask Logan or Camille about this "dreadful person" as Sybil had described him. No, she'd better ask Glory, as Logan had instructed.

Meanwhile, Logan had returned downstairs. Carrying a packet of papers, he went into the study. As he'd hoped, his brother Miles was already there, sitting at the wide oak desk, bent over a thick ledger book. Both Logan and Miles used this spacious, wood-paneled room as the office from which they ran the everyday business aspects of the plantation.

Miles, as the eldest Tremaine heir, had taken on the main responsibility for keeping Fair Oaks solvent. But that task was a difficult and time-consuming one. Their grandfather, who still held the power over the whole estate, had forced Miles to mete out part of the management responsibilities to Logan. While Silas had never gotten along with Logan, the continued operation of the plantation was his primary goal. Nothing else mattered to the senior Tremaine. And Miles needed help, so Logan had been called in to take a more active role in the everyday functionings of the estate.

Miles didn't like to admit it but when Logan had taken over seeing to the productivity of the sawmill and the continued breeding of their champion line of race horses, both areas had thrived, making Miles's efforts with the tobacco crops and orchards seem less fruitful by comparison. He had tried to regain control over Logan's portion by getting their grandfather to change his will. But he now knew he had failed in this latest effort to best Logan. He was frowning when he glanced up from the long columns of figures.

"Bad news?" Logan asked with casual indifference, noting his brother's scowl as he walked further into the room. "Have you allowed things to go awry while I've been away?"

His tone was conversational, but Miles didn't miss the sarcasm that touched his brother's words.

"I wouldn't think you cared one way or the other since you haven't bothered to be here these past three months. We'd begun to think you might be gone for good." Miles let his tone take on a note of hopefulness as he locked eyes with his younger brother.

"Sorry to disappoint you," Logan remarked coolly as he sat down in a high-backed leather chair in front of Miles's desk. "But I was not idle by any means while I was away. I've negotiated a lucrative two-year contract with Gibson and Sons for our timber and arranged to have Wilson Latimer's company be our shipper. Those were no simple tasks. Besides, I left Pemberton in charge of the mill. He's quite capable of managing it. I've trained him well. Did the new trees get purchased and planted as I'd instructed?"

Miles lowered his eyes from Logan's scrutiny and pretended to be going over the figures in the book before him.

"No, not yet," he answered in a low voice.

"What? And why haven't they?" Logan demanded, frowning. "We postponed it last fall and the spring before that. You know we can't keep a lumber business going without new timber. We can't keep cutting acres of trees without replacing them for future need. Why weren't my instructions carried out?"

"For a very simple and ongoing reason," Miles shot back defensively, meeting Logan's gaze. "Money—cold, hard cash money. None of the nurserymen would extend our credit and there was no excess cash with which to buy trees. And there probably won't be either. We had deluging rains all spring and couldn't get the tobacco seedbeds set out on time. Now we've had four weeks of drought so we've had to irrigate by hand to save the seedlings, and that's meant hiring more slaves from other plantations just to get that done. The curing barns needed extensive repairs. We'll be lucky if we have any kind of profit from the crop this season. And if we do, it will all have to go toward paying on those promissory notes we had to take out two years ago. We're heavily in debt with those and they come due the first of the year, in case you've forgotten!''

Miles sat back in his own chair, rubbing a hand over his forehead worriedly.

"I haven't forgotten," Logan replied, trying to keep the smug satisfaction out of his voice. He enjoyed watching his brother squirm with worry. No indeed, brother mine, he added in his thoughts, I haven't forgotten about those notes by any means.

"I'll go and talk to Shepherd myself about the trees. I'm sure I can work something out with him." Logan didn't add the words, "even though you couldn't do it," but his condescending tone let Miles finish the sentence himself.

Miles's look of disdain deepened as his eyes followed Logan when he rose from the chair.

"I bought two foals and two three-year-olds, champion stock out of Alec Forrester's stables in Boston. He'll board the foals for us for a year. The pair of dappled grays I brought with me, a mare and a stallion. They should strengthen our line of stock considerably for a future market. Or they could fetch a handsome price should we have to raise cash in a hurry to meet those notes, though I hope that won't be necessary." To himself, he knew it would not be.

"And that isn't all you brought back with you, is it, Logan?" Miles observed coolly as he eyed his brother. With an effort he had controlled his anger, knowing Logan relished putting him in such a temperament.

"All? Ah, you must be referring to my bride, Rhea. Lovely creature, is she not?" Logan smiled as he glanced at Miles.

"Quite. But then you always did have a good eye for horseflesh and women," Miles replied with forced casualness as he stood and closed the leather-bound ledger. "But I am surprised you married this one, for you have made it no secret that matrimony was not to your liking."

"And so it wasn't, until I met Rhea," Logan replied. His pale blue eyes looked into his brother's dark brown ones. "She made me realize it was about time I settled down. Why, I'll see my twenty-seventh birthday the end of next month. High time for a man to be getting a wife and starting a family, I'm sure you'll agree. And after all, it is what Grandfather has been wanting me to do."

This discourse would have seemed only casual conversation to anyone who might have happened to overhear. But to the two men, far more was being said, fueling their continuing rivalry.

"Yes, of course," Miles agreed, clenching his jaw to hide his anger.

"Ah, well, it grows late and Rhea awaits me," Logan said then, smiling inwardly. He hadn't missed the tightening of Miles's jawline.

"Here are copies of the contracts with Gibson and Latimer and the purchase agreement and blood line records for Forrester's stock," Logan went on, gesturing toward the thick packet of papers he'd brought in with him and laid on the desk. "Oh, yes, and a copy of my marriage certificate is here also. Put these things in the safe for me when you lock up the books, won't you, Miles? I'll say good night, then."

With that Logan turned and left the room. He couldn't keep the self-satisfied smile from curling on his lips now as he stood in the wide hallway. Though it had taken quick and drastic measures, he had foiled Miles's plans and won this round in the ongoing competition he had with his older brother. And they both knew it.

Back in the study, Miles pounded a fist down hard on the ledger book. Damn it! How had Logan found out about the codicil to Silas's will? It had taken months of effort to get the old man to add that stipulation. While Miles knew he was well the favorite with his grandfather, he couldn't understand why the senior Tremaine stubbornly refused to just disinherit Logan completely and send him packing. For years Miles had tried to bring this about, but old Silas would never comply, even though he and Logan were constantly at odds with one another. It would be just like the old man to have Logan around to keep the conflicts between his two grandsons going just for the pleasure of it. Miles wouldn't put it past him.

Miles took some satisfaction in knowing he had forced Logan into marrying. For a moment his thoughts drifted to Rhea. She was quite a figure of a woman, even for a Northerner. He'd have to get to know her better.

Miles knew he'd lost in his latest attempt to reach his ultimate goal—having full control of Fair Oaks. But he was by no means ready to give up. Besides, he enjoyed the challenge of trying to best Logan. Perhaps he might have a chance to do so with the beautiful Rhea.

Rhea did not know of the exchange taking place below in the study. She had washed her face and hands and donned a thin, sleeveless nightgown. Then she'd brushed her thick, shoulder-length hair free of tangled curls and walked out onto the balcony that opened off the far end of her room. She welcomed the feel of the warm night breeze on her face and bare arms, and stood for a few moments basking in it. The moon was nearly as full as it had been the first night out on their journey to Virginia. Its reflected brightness lighted the shrub-lined lawn below her almost like daylight.

Rhea was just turning back into her room when a slight sound—like the step of a boot on gravel—caught her attention and made her stop. Without knowing why, she stepped into the shadows to one side of the small balcony and looked through the spindled railing to the lawn below.

Suddenly a figure darted across the small stretch of open lawn that was part of the large landscaped garden. It looked like a man, though Rhea couldn't be certain since she'd only caught a glimpse of the figure before it was hidden from view by the tall bushes that bordered the lawn.

For a moment Rhea feared the person might be an intruder, perhaps a thief. But he was moving away from the house and didn't appear to be carrying anything suspiciously. Maybe he was a slave making a break for freedom. Rhea had heard a few stories about the cruel conditions Negroes faced on many plantations. Many of them risked everything for a chance for freedom in Canada.

She wondered about the conditions here at Fair Oaks, knowing she'd find out what they were soon enough. Meanwhile, if that were a slave down there trying to escape, he wouldn't be betrayed by Rhea. She would not have that on her conscience, being responsible for returning someone to bondage. She decided not to mention a word to anyone about what she'd just seen.

Rhea watched for several minutes longer but she didn't see or hear anything more. In fact she began to doubt that she'd seen anything at all, he'd disappeared so completely. Perhaps her fatigued mind and the night shadows were playing tricks on her.

After a moment she shrugged and started back into the bedroom. Nonetheless, Rhea closed and locked the French doors leading out to the balcony, just as a precaution.

Chapter 22

"TYLER! STOP THAT AT ONCE!" RHEA SHOUTED as she lunged toward the two boys, one of whom was about to tumble down the long, winding staircase. She managed to catch hold of one of the Negro boy's flailing arms in time to keep him from falling. When she'd set him back on his feet again, she turned a frowning countenance on her nephew.

"Just what do you think you were doing, young man?" she demanded angrily. "This boy might have been badly hurt if he'd fallen down these stairs. You deliberately pushed him." Rhea stood with her hands on her hips staring levelly at the boy.

"Who cares?" Tyler shot back defiantly. "He's just a stupid nigger slave. He's supposed to do what I say. I can do whatever I want to him!"

"He is a human being, Tyler, and I won't stand by and allow you to hurt him."

"I'll do whatever I like to him and you can't stop me! You're not my mother. You're not *anybody* around here!" Tyler Tremaine's fists clenched at his sides as he stood his ground before Rhea.

"That's enough, Tyler," a deep voice warned from behind Rhea. She turned her head to see Miles Tremaine coming toward them down the hallway.

"Mistress Rhea is your aunt now and as such she has a position of authority over children in this household. You will listen to what she says and obey her. Is that understood?"

Tyler shrank back from his father's stern look.

"Yes, sir," he mumbled reluctantly, hanging his head.

"Good. In this case she is quite correct. Caleb is your property, but he is also your playmate and is not to be treated badly. You must learn to take better care of what belongs to you."

"Yes, Father."

"Now apologize to your aunt and then run along and play outside, both of you."

Tyler begrudgingly muttered a quick and insincere "I'm sorry," then he and Caleb raced away down the curving staircase. Rhea was momentarily stunned by Miles Tremaine's words. She was grateful that he had supported her position, yet she was unaccustomed to hearing people referred to as property. It shocked her.

"Boys will be boys," Miles commented matter-of-factly. "Please forgive my son's outspokenness. It's a stage he's going through."

He flashed a charming smile at Rhea as he held out his arm to her.

"I see you are going riding. May I walk with you downstairs?" He gestured with his other hand toward the staircase.

"Yes, thank you," Rhea managed to answer as she slipped her hand under his arm. She noticed then his handsomeness. He and Logan looked very much alike, except that Miles had a small, neatly trimmed moustache and was slightly smaller in stature than Logan.

Their eyes met and held for a moment before Rhea lowered hers. What had she seen in his look? Amusement? Interest? Whatever it was, it made her feel uncomfortable and she was glad when they reached the bottom of the stairs and were in the long hallway. Six doors—three on each side—were located along the tapestry-lined walls and led to other rooms that were built off of this main corridor. Rhea felt a sudden impulse to escape into the closest one to get away from Miles. But she resisted the urge and forced herself to walk sedately alongside him.

"Were I not occupied by business this morning, I would enjoy riding with you." There was that disarming smile again. It came easily to his lips.

"Logan is joining me. He's going to show me some of the estate," Rhea replied quickly. She wanted to leave Miles but he now held her hand in his, preventing her escape as he faced her.

"Ah yes, Logan, my dear brother. How fortunate he is to have acquired such a beautiful wife. And at such an opportune time . . .

"But perhaps we can ride together another day. I do look forward to getting to know you better, dear sister-in-law."

Miles bent his head then and kissed her gloved hand. Though his words sounded innocent enough, the look accompanying them left no doubt as to his interest and intent. And had there been a note of suspicion in his voice about her relationship with Logan?

Rhea murmured a hasty good-bye and quickened her step down the remainder of the hallway to the front door. She was glad when the thick oak door closed sturdily behind her, knowing Miles's arrogant gaze could no longer follow her.

Rhea tried to put her disturbing encounter with Miles out of her mind as she walked the short distance to the fenced-in stableyard that ran in front of a huge, red-painted barn. It was a glorious day, sunny and promising to be quite warm. She had dressed casually in only a white ruffled blouse, gray riding skirt, and boots.

As she entered the stable area she saw Logan standing near the horses talking with a Negro groom. She was glad to see that he, too, was informally dressed. A white linen shirt, brown leather vest, tan, tight-fitting breeches, and brown riding boots accentuated his muscular frame, giving him a rakish air.

Logan smiled as he saw Rhea approaching. Her spirits soared. He was really very handsome when he smiled. It really was too bad he didn't do it more often. Perhaps this would be an enjoyable outing after all.

"Ah, here you are, Rhea," Logan greeted her in a friendly voice. I thought you might like to ride Jade Wind again. She needs exercise." Logan's tone was light and his expression was open and relaxed, as though he might also be looking forward to the ride.

"Yes, I'd love to ride her. Hello, my beauty." Rhea patted the gray's nose and neck as she spoke.

"Rhea, this is Amos, our head groom. Amos, my wife, Mistress Rhea."

"Pleased ta meet yo', missus," the big Negro said formally, doffing his battered cap and bowing slightly. He gave Rhea a friendly smile, showing two rows of straight, square teeth.

"Hello, Amos," Rhea replied, extending her gloved hand to him. The old black man seemed surprised by her action but took her hand gently in his for a moment anyway.

"Amos is an expert on horseflesh. If there's anything you want to know about horses, just ask him," Logan told her, his tone a flattering one.

"Aw, now, Marse Logan, don' go on so," Amos protested, but he grinned and was clearly pleased by the compliment as he helped Rhea up into the sidesaddle.

"Should you ever wish to go riding on your own, Rhea, just let Amos know about it. He'll arrange for a groom to accompany you. Do not ride out alone," Logan warned more seriously as he led the way out of the stableyard.

They'd been riding for only about ten minutes when Logan signaled for a stop. They drew their horses up before what looked like a small compound of log cabins built in two long rows and surrounded by a high, solid wood fence topped with metal spikes. Around the yard were a dozen or so scurrying, half-naked Negro children, several pregnant women, and one or two elderly blacks, all of whom stopped their activities when Logan and Rhea approached.

"These are the slave quarters," Logan explained, his tone and expression stern. "You have complete freedom of the estate, Rhea, except for this area. You are not to go near it, is that understood?"

"Yes, all right, Logan, if that is your wish," Rhea agreed, though she didn't like his manner. It reminded her of the one Miles had used to reprimand Tyler earlier.

"This is where the slaves are confined after their work in the fields is finished. Jessup, the overseer, is in charge here also. It would be unwise for any woman other than a slave to come to this compound." Logan looked at Rhea pointedly, then spurred Lord Sagamore to a trot and continued down the road away from the fenced area. Rhea followed on Jade Wind, deep in thought.

What must it be like to be a slave, owned and ordered about in all things, having no freedom of choice or action? Yet perhaps she did have some idea of it. Everyone had some sort of bondage over his or her life—family ties, social conventions, emotional commitments, religious convictions.

Rhea looked at the man riding ahead of her. For Logan it was his hatred for his brother that enslaved him, directed his life. She wondered if he would ever be free of it. Hatred could be a terrible thing. It occurred to Rhea now that her own loathing for Grayson Sawyer had driven her to this strange bargain she had made with Logan Tremaine. She was bound to that bargain, entrapped by it just as surely as any slave. Yet she would see her way free of it in only a few months. Most of the poor Negroes never would. It made her heart heavy to think of it.

Chapter 23

RHEA AND LOGAN RODE FOR TWO HOURS, STOP-
ping here and there as Logan wanted to point out different
things of interest to her. Rhea was again impressed by the
size of the Tremaine estate, the extent of their holdings.
They rode by acres of tobacco fields and apple orchards.
They stopped briefly at the water-powered sawmill where
dozens of Negro men tended the logs and machinery.

Traveling on, they had just turned a bend in the narrow
road when a sharp scream pierced the air. Logan pulled
Lord Sagamore up short. Rhea, following close behind
him, had to do the same to Jade Wind to keep from
bumping into Logan. Another scream accompanied by a
stream of curses reached their ears. Logan quickly swung
around to their right, the direction from which the sounds
were coming. His eyes narrowed and swept the wide tobacco field before him for only a moment before he swore
under his breath and spurred Lord Sagamore toward a
wagon surrounded by several people. Rhea followed.

Logan rode past several slaves standing in the field and
pulled his mount up in time to reach out and grab a
malicious-looking leather whip from a scowling Dreed Jessup. The angry overseer whirled around, ready to confront
whomever had dared to interfere, but he backed down
when he saw it was Logan.

"What's going on here, Jessup?" Logan demanded
sternly, his black brows dipping together.

Without thinking Rhea dismounted and ran to where a
slave girl of about fourteen was huddled against the wagon
wheel, crying. Rhea sucked in her breath when she saw
how the whip had slashed through the girl's thin blouse,

raising ugly red welts on her back. She took the girl in her arms and tried to soothe her with gentle words, while she watched the exchange between Logan and Jessup. Other slaves stood idle now, also watching the scene.

"Well, why were you whipping this girl?" Logan's tone was carefully controlled but there was no doubt that he expected a plausible explanation.

"She was stealin' water," Jessup replied belligerently, gesturing toward the big barrels on the wagon. "It weren't time for a water break yet. These here barrels is meant for the plants."

"Well, there's no use in watering the plants if your workers are on the verge of collapse from thirst and heat prostration. You know they're not to be worked at this time of the day when it's so hot. Why are they still in the fields?" Logan demanded, his look forbidding as he stared down at Jessup accusingly.

"Mr. Miles says for me to have this south eighty acres watered today, on account of we ain't had no rain in quite a spell now. Doin' that don't leave no time for these here niggers to be sittin' in the shade." Jessup's stance exuded insolence but Logan was not cowed.

"I'll take this up with Mr. Miles myself later. Meanwhile, since I am here to see this inexcusable situation and he is not, you'll answer to me and do as I say, or you'll be off this plantation before the day is out."

The two men scowled at each other, one sitting straight and authoritatively astride his horse, the other standing his ground hostilely before him. Logan wasn't as heavy as Dreed Jessup, but he was taller and well built, a sure match for any man. Jessup seemed to consider this and Logan's threat of dismissal before he finally mumbled something to himself and lowered his defiant gaze.

"I want these people rested for the next two hours and given water," Logan ordered.

"Otis," he called then to one of the Negro drivers who carried out Jessup's orders to the slaves, "get your people in here out of the fields and under shade over there for a while." He gestured toward a small grove of trees about a half mile away. "You heard what I said about the water, so see to it."

"Yes, Marse Logan," the Negro answered with a wide grin. "It'll be done, suh, and thank yo', suh."

Logan seemed to remember Rhea and the slave girl then. He was still angry as his gaze swept over them. The girl had stopped crying but she still clung to Rhea for protection.

"Can you walk, girl?" he asked brusquely, his tone only a little less harsh than the one he'd used with Jessup.

"Yes, suh. Ah thinks so, suh," the black girl answered meekly as she nodded.

"Take more care to obey my overseer in the future," he rebuked her sternly. "If you are caught stealing again, I will administer the whipping myself. Is that clear?"

"Yes, suh, Massa," the girl replied, hanging her head contritely.

Rhea was stunned to think that Logan might even consider doing such a horrible thing, and to a child. She glared at him but he had turned his attention back to the driver.

"Otis, make sure that this girl gets back to the compound and is seen to. She's not to return to the fields for a week."

Dreed Jessup's head shot up at hearing Logan's leniency with the girl. Hatred flared in his dark eyes, but he hid it by turning away toward the wagon. Meanwhile, Logan had coiled Jessup's whip in his hand.

"Don't be so quick to use this, Jessup," he warned menacingly as he threw the whip to the overseer, who turned in time to catch it. "You may find yourself on the receiving end of it one day."

His cold tone didn't change as he turned his attention toward Rhea.

"Rhea, remount your horse. We're finished here." He gestured with his hand toward Otis and the Negro quickly stepped forward presenting his clasped hands for Rhea to use to step up into Jade Wind's sidesaddle.

As she mounted Rhea realized that Logan was displeased with her for some reason. She touched her heel to Jade Wind's side to follow Logan as he headed back toward the road, wondering how she had managed to annoy him.

When they reached the dirt roadway, Logan reined in, looking back to make sure his orders were being carried out. He watched a few minutes as the slaves started moving out of the field.

"Why do you keep such a man as Jessup as overseer?" Rhea asked as she watched the man mount his horse and ride out.

"Good overseers are hard to find," Logan answered curtly. "We are forced to hire white trash like Jessup who can't make a living doing anything else. The methods he uses on the slaves are his business. As long as he gets them to get the work done, we don't usually interfere. It undermines his position of authority over the Negroes. But sometimes Jessup goes too far. He has a heavy hand with that whip and Miles knew that when he hired him. I never would've had that man anywhere near Fair Oaks. You can't accomplish anything if the slaves are treated so badly they aren't able to work."

Rhea couldn't help wondering if Logan's concern for the Negroes was for humanitarian reasons or economic ones. Given what she had come to know about Logan Tremaine thus far, she concluded it must be the latter. Profit was far more important to men like him than human misery. Slaveowners must have hearts of stone and no conscience.

As if to substantiate the negative opinion Rhea had of him, Logan turned his cool gaze fully on her then.

"There is something you must learn about our ways, Rhea." His tone was reprimanding. "What you did just now with that slave girl was undignified and unwise for a woman in the social position you hold now. Should you ever find yourself in such circumstances with me or anyone else again, you must refrain from dismounting and approaching a slave. Not only is it beneath your station to act in such a manner, lowering yourself to their level, but what is more important, if what just happened over there had taken a different turn, you may have found yourself in the thick of a very dangerous situation. I would have been hard put to regain control and protect you at the same time."

Rhea's jaw dropped open slightly in astonishment, but Logan didn't see it for he had swung Lord Sagamore's head around, touched his heels to the big gray's sides, and cantered off up the narrow road. Rhea blew out her breath in exasperation. How was she supposed to know it was wrong to help a weeping child who'd been cruelly beaten! These southern people had strange customs, customs she didn't want to learn!

Logan Tremaine made it very difficult for her to maintain the meek demeanor he expected her to exhibit. Never had a man caused her temper to flare so repeatedly. All she wanted to do at the moment was to tell him in no uncertain terms just what she thought of him and his southern ways!

If Rhea had known how to get back to Fair Oaks alone, she would have galloped away from Logan in an instant. But she didn't, so she was forced to swallow her indignation and guide Jade Wind to follow the man she was coming to dislike with a vengeance.

Chapter 24

AT LAST RHEA AND LOGAN RODE INTO A WIDE grassy meadow near a beautiful lake. With an effort, Rhea had decided to dismiss Logan's criticism of her earlier actions. She refused to let it spoil this lovely day for her. She told herself that Logan had become so unpleasant and critical from long years of practice. He apparently liked being that way. She couldn't change him. It would take far too much time and effort and, thank God, she didn't have that much time to be around him. Her task was to try to tolerate him as much as possible and not cause friction. It was taking extreme restraint on Rhea's part to accomplish that, but that was what Logan was paying her for. It was only for a few months, she reminded herself. Somehow she'd get through them. She had to, for her future depended on it. But if the past few weeks were any indication, she would have her work cut out for her.

A high hill rose up at one end of the meadow they'd just ridden into, and at the base of it were the ruins of a log cabin.

"We'll water the horses at the lake over there," Logan told her as he turned Lord Sagamore in that direction.

"What a lovely place," Rhea remarked appreciatively as she rode beside Logan and let her gaze sweep over the lush valley.

"Yes, it is. I come here often to enjoy the quiet and to sketch. It's an ideal setting," Logan answered as they rode slowly along toward the water.

"Sketch? You've mentioned that before. Are you an artist then?" Rhea asked with growing interest.

"Oil painting is a hobby of mine," Logan answered matter-of-factly. "I find it relaxing."

Rhea wondered about this new aspect of Logan Tremaine. He didn't seem the artistic type. The few she'd known back in Philadelphia had been expressive, passionate men, whose moods reflected every emotion and changed as often as their subjects. The Logan she had come to know hardly fit that description by any stretch of the imagination.

"My great-grandfather five generations back, Samuel Tremaine, built that cabin over there when he first came to this territory," Logan went on to explain. There was a note of pride in his voice as he spoke. "He and Sarah, his wife, came here from England when this country was still mostly wild and unsettled. They cleared this meadow of many of the trees by hand so they could see to the lake. But they left these great oaks." He gestured toward several large trees edging the lake. "Samuel loved oaks. He had the acorns from these trees planted all over the plantation. That's how it got the name of Fair Oaks."

Rhea looked up at the tall tree before her and followed the line of one of its massive black-barked branches, full with the bright green leaves of June. They reached high into the clear azure sky.

"You must be proud to have such a long family heritage," Rhea commented, bringing her gaze back to Logan. "I am only a second-generation American," she went on casually, only to make conversation. "My father's parents came here from England also. My mother met my father while she was traveling here with friends. After they married, she never returned to her home in Wales and over the years lost touch with her family there."

The thought of her dear mother suddenly saddened Rhea. Such unhappiness had befallen Matilda Merrick in these last years. The effect of it had changed her mother so drastically. Rhea wondered if her own life would have the same fate. It wouldn't if she could help it!

"But I don't wish to bore you with my history," she said a little sharply to Logan, now because of her determination. He had reined in Lord Sagamore, dismounted, and just come around to help Rhea down from Jade Wind. "You likely know all of it anyway, from Mr. Tennyson's report on me, the one that determined that I would be suited for your marriage scheme."

Logan's dark brows dipped but he said nothing as he reached up to grasp Rhea's waist and lower her to the ground. He kept his hands on her waist even after she was standing firmly on the grass. He was looking at her strangely.

What was it Rhea saw in those piercing pale blue eyes? Uncertainty? Uneasiness? From Logan Tremaine? He seemed to be debating whether or not to say something. This was new for Rhea to see in him. She suddenly felt uncomfortable, almost wanting his now-familiar look of arrogant disapproval to return. She wished he would let go of her, but he didn't. She didn't like being so close to him. It did something to her deep inside.

"Why—why are you looking at me so?" Rhea ventured hesitantly.

As if he'd suddenly become aware that he was still holding on to her, Logan dropped his hands to his sides and turned away from Rhea. He was feeling ill at ease and most reluctant to broach the subject that was on his mind. And standing so close to Rhea was not helping his composure. Inwardly, he cursed himself for getting into such a situation. It was not what he'd planned, that was certain. But he knew some things had to be settled between them. So now he covered his vexation with an irritated air as he swung around to face Rhea again.

"Since you have brought up the matter of our agreement, this is as good a time as any to discuss it." Damn, those blue eyes of hers, Logan cursed to himself. They seemed to drill into his soul as they focused levelly on him. He averted his own eyes so he'd be able to continue.

"I want you to know that I am a man who takes responsibility for his actions, no matter how rash they may be. The—uh—intimacy that occurred between us at Farley House was quite unplanned, I'm certain you will agree. I never intended to violate the terms of our arrangement nor compromise either you or myself in such a way. However, mysteriously that has happened. I've been giving it some thought and admit to my equal responsibility in it."

Rhea's anger flared at his words. Responsibility and rashness, he'd said. What about the caring or kindness?

That had been present, too, that night. But, of course, she couldn't expect much of that from a man like Logan Tremaine. As she thought about it Rhea convinced herself she didn't *want* those things from him.

But Rhea was surprised to hear that he admitted his responsibility. What had happened between them was obviously meaningless to Logan, except as a possible bother. So should it be to her, too—just a few stolen moments of physical pleasure, ones she only wanted to drive from her memory, where they still lingered all too vividly.

She decided to hear him out, wondering where this strange and disturbing conversation might be heading.

"I want you to know," Logan continued, "that I have come to consider you a woman of some integrity and not one of easy virtue, as was perhaps my first reaction upon discovering that you were not a virgin. So, should you find that a child had been conceived as a result of our—intimacy—I shall, of course, do the honorable thing and really wed you. As a Tremaine and an heir to Fair Oaks, the child would have to remain here with me. You, however, would be free to leave. I know you must find our way of life here quite foreign to that to which you are accustomed. I will add an additional ten thousand dollars to what has already been agreed to in our business arrangement, stipulating only that you never return to Fair Oaks or try to exercise any rights to the child."

Logan met Rhea's astonished gaze and waited for what he felt must be her certain compliance to his most generous offer. Rhea fought for control, but no longer could she maintain her composure. Logan's attitude was so outrageous and so self-righteous that she wanted to scream!

She took several deep breaths and struggled to keep her voice level as she answered him.

"How magnanimous of you, Logan. You, of course, expect me to be overwhelmed that a man of your stature and social position would even stoop to acknowledge what has happened between us." Contempt touched her words as she continued. "The terms of our agreement certainly have been violated, and I am as much at a loss as to how it happened as you are. A moment of insanity perhaps explains it."

Now it was Logan's turn to frown.

"But whatever may have been the cause is of no consequence now, for you will be glad to learn that there will be no child. I thank God that the time to conceive was not then right for me.

"But regardless of that, let me make this clear to you. I also consider myself responsible for my actions, no matter how foolish and irrational they may be. Had a child been conceived between us, I would acknowledge *my* accountability for it and would never stoop to forcing you into an 'honorable' marriage to me. I wouldn't want to marry a man like you. Neither would I allow you to *buy* a child of mine. And *never* would I leave a child born of my body to be raised by a man I find cold and heartless, in a place filled with hate and deception, cynicism and cruelty! I loathe you and everything you stand for, Logan Tremaine. Were you to try to touch me again that way, I would be sickened just as I was that night at Farley House!"

Logan's icy blue eyes clashed with Rhea's in silent combat as the sharp thrust of her words stabbed at him. He looked thunderous as he suddenly grabbed Rhea by the arms. She winced as his fingers bit into her flesh, but she still looked up at him defiantly.

"So the meek little kitten has claws after all. Sickened by my touch, were you? That was *not* my impression when I held you in my arms. I think you are lying, Rhea. Shall I test your words and see exactly what my touch causes you to do?"

Logan pulled Rhea roughly against him then and brought his mouth down hard on hers. Rhea struggled to free herself, trying to twist her head and body away from his ravaging assault. But Logan quickly swept one hard-muscled arm around her waist as he brought his other hand up and roughly caught a fistful of her hair to hold her head still as he continued to plunder her mouth.

In the next moment he had her down on the ground, pinned beneath him. Rhea was not frightened of Logan, only outraged. She knew she was no match for his superior strength. To continue to struggle against him would be useless and likely fire his lust further. Using every ounce of the strong will she'd kept so well hidden, Rhea made herself go limp. She would not respond to him in any way, no matter what he did to her! Clenching her teeth with determination, Rhea mentally commanded her body to remain still.

Logan suddenly stopped his hand's movement over her breast. His momentary look of puzzlement quickly vanished as he righted himself and straddled her on his knees.

"But this will not do, my little tigress," he remarked coldly, with a smug smile. "For I have seen your claws and felt the fire that can erupt within you."

"If you take me, it will be only by rape!" Rhea spat at him, her eyes flashing angrily.

"I've never had to rape a woman to have her," Logan shot back at her as he fought his own fury over her defiance, "though I've come the closest to doing so with *you!* Damn you, woman," he cursed then through gritted teeth, "I'll show you again what it's like to make love." His voice softened some. "I'll have you, Rhea, but I'll have you willingly . . ."

Logan rolled off of her, though he kept one arm around her waist and one leg over her legs to keep her from moving. He lay down beside her and gathered her into his arms.

Still Rhea remained lifeless, determined to resist him in the only way she knew how. Logan started kissing her lips gently. He was suddenly aware of the delicious taste of her mouth, and he wanted more, much more . . .

His right hand started to stroke Rhea's arm, then her back, the side of her waist. And all the while he kissed her, moving his lips caressingly over the softness of her face, then back to her mouth. ·

Rhea's body was not obeying her. Her pulse was racing. Her heart began to pound in her breast. Surely he would feel it against his own chest and know the effect he was having on her!

No, no, I don't want to feel this! she pleaded in her mind, not knowing her lips murmured the words, too, betraying her. She brought her hands up to the sides of Logan's face to try to keep his lips from consuming hers. She felt the slight roughness of his cheek just before her fingers moved up to entangle themselves in the softness of his hair.

Logan's hand moved to her breast then, brushing back and forth over and around it until her responding nipple rose and strained against the revealing silk of her blouse. Another betrayal.

Still Rhea tried to keep control of her body, trying desperately to quell the alarming sensations that were bombarding her consciousness.

The pearl buttons of her blouse and the ribbons of her thin chemise easily gave way to Logan's touch, laying her open to his hungering eyes, his demanding lips. A low moan escaped from Logan as his mouth covered one nipple and his hand gently rubbed over the other. Rhea gasped. Her body arched and strained to press closer against him.

It took all of Logan's control not to rip the rest of Rhea's clothes off of her right then and plunge into the soft depths of her womanhood. With panting breath, he willed down his own body's desire and concentrated again on exploring Rhea's nakedness. He would wait a little longer, wait for her to want him as she had before. He would not let Rhea deny what could be between them.

His lips went back to hers for long, searching moments before his mouth started its searing path down her body again. This time he did not stop at her breasts, though he lingered there, using his tongue tormentingly over and around her taut nipples while his hands removed the rest of her clothes.

Rhea felt like she was helplessly whirling and falling into a deep chasm. She wanted to escape but could not. She was overwhelmed by the barrage of sensations racing through every fiber of her body. The feelings were wonderful and frightening at the same time.

Logan's hands were touching her again now, gently but persistently stroking over her stomach, the sides of her hips, the insides of her thighs. Rhea tried to press her legs together to keep him at bay, but Logan's hands and voice coaxed and lured her.

"Open to me, Rhea." Logan's voice was low and husky with desire. "Remember how it was before. It can be that way again between us. Open to me. Let me come into you."

His touch was more insistent now as his hands moved between her legs to push them apart. Then he was touching the soft, moist folds of her womanhood. Rhea's back arched, sending her hips upward in search of more—more of his tantalizing touch—more of him.

Only one thought now assailed Rhea's mind and commanded her senses—desire. Unleashed and wanton desire for Logan. She must have him, feel his flesh within her, be totally possessed and consumed by him! She could wait no longer.

"Yes, oh, yes, please now, Logan," Rhea begged with gasping breath, clinging to him. The moments of waiting while he hurried out of his own clothes only made her ache even more with impatience for him.

And then he was with her, joining in their tremendous need and passion for each other. Rhea clung to Logan, arching her back to receive his penetrating thrusts, oblivious to all but the wonderful aching fulfillment that overwhelmed her.

For Logan, too, all around him was eclipsed, save for the woman who drove him beyond reason—Rhea. There was only she, beckoning him deeper, soaring with him, surrendering all. His climax came swiftly and gloriously, moving him to a height of ecstasy he had known only once before— and it had been Rhea who had caused it then, too.

Logan's breath came in jagged bursts from deep within his chest as a multitude of magnificent sensations shot through him. He bent down to devour Rhea's lips with his. The long moments of intense, pulsating rapture consumed and enslaved him. He wanted more and more and more of her.

Chapter 25

LOGAN AND RHEA LAY IN EACH OTHER'S ARMS
for some time. Neither of them spoke or moved as their
aroused senses slowly diminished, returning them to the
unsettling reality of what had happened between them
again.

A breeze began to stir. It felt good on Rhea's perspiring
skin. She closed her eyes, trying to block out the thoughts
that troubled her. This was not the way she wanted a joining with a man to be—abrupt, overwhelming, uncon-
trolled, on a meadow ground with a man who only angered
and confused her.

Why couldn't she find a man she could love and trust forever, one she could surrender to with her whole heart and
body without fear of being used or cheated? Logan was
only using her, proving his masculine power over her,
humiliating her so she would know only too well that he
was in control of her life right now.

Why couldn't she find a man she could marry and build
a life with—be truly married to? Not a false husband who
had hired her services and taken more than she had ever
intended to give. She hadn't wanted this to happen with
Logan Tremaine. Whatever had possessed her to let him
do this to her? And not once, but twice now. What had
drawn them together?

Rhea was bewildered, even angry, trying to hide her
shame over being so weak in his arms. She couldn't think
straight when Logan was still so near, while their bodies
were still touching. Her senses were overwhelmed by his
presence. She had to get away from him.

Rhea moved away from Logan then and sat up, reaching

for her clothes. Logan sat up, too. Uncertainty marked his handsome face as he gazed at her. She would not look at him.

"Rhea . . ." he ventured softly as he touched her shoulder to stop her.

"No, please—don't. Don't talk and please don't touch me," she murmured, a note of anguish in her voice. Her forehead was creased slightly by a pained expression as she pulled away from him and started to dress.

Logan reached for his own discarded clothes and put them on. A heavy silence hung between them. His own thoughts were in a turmoil as he went to get Jade Wind and Lord Sagamore from where they had wandered to graze. God, it had happened again! What had come over him? Rhea's body was no different from so many others that he'd made love to. But he'd never been so out of control with a woman before, so driven to possess her until all else was blocked out of his mind. He'd sworn to himself he wouldn't touch Rhea again after that night at Farley House. He wanted no complications like that. His scheme with this false marriage was tenuous at best. A physical relationship, perhaps resulting in a child, did not fit into his plans at all.

A child . . . Damn! If Rhea had told him the truth, there had been no conception the first time they'd come together. But now the threat was there again. They were right back where they'd started, with the same possible dilemma. Only this time he knew Rhea's position if a child did result—she would fight him for it. That would put everything he'd planned in a real fix! Damn! Where was his control? All of this could have been avoided if only he'd been able to resist Rhea!

Logan's anger at himself was apparent in his deep frown as he caught up the dragging reins and turned back toward Rhea, leading the horses behind him. He had just reached Rhea when the sound of approaching hoofbeats drew his attention to the far side of the meadow. A woman on horseback was galloping toward them.

"Logan! I was hoping I might find you here!" the woman exclaimed as she pulled her horse up sharply to a halt. She was stunning, with flowing red-blonde hair and large green eyes fringed by blonde lashes. She turned those cat-like eyes on Rhea now.

"However, I expected to find you alone," she stated coolly as she moved her gaze up and down Rhea, then over to Logan.

"Well, as you can see, I am not." Logan's voice matched her icy tone. He seemed annoyed, but Rhea couldn't be sure whether it was because of her or this woman who had just arrived.

"Vanessa, allow me to present Rhea Tremaine . . . my wife. Rhea, this is Mrs. Vanessa Forsythe."

"Your what? Wife?" Vanessa Forsythe's light eyebrows knit into a deeper frown as she stared at Logan in disbelief. The look on her face spoke volumes. There could be only one reason why a woman suddenly became so angry in a situation involving another woman and one man—when she had a claim on him herself.

"How do you do, Mrs. Forsythe?" Rhea replied frigidly. She was irritated by this scene herself and still unnerved by what had happened before with Logan. She only wanted to get away from here, away from him. She told herself she didn't care that Logan and this woman probably had some kind of illicit relationship, perhaps had even used this secluded meadow as a rendezvous place. A real wife would be upset by such a revelation, but Rhea wasn't—for, of course, she was not really Logan's wife, thank God!

"We'll discuss this at another time, Logan," Vanessa Forsythe retorted sharply. She shot a scathing look from him to Rhea, then dug her heels into her mount and galloped away.

Rhea kept a tight hold on Jade Wind's reins to keep her from following the departing horse. Her ire had risen as the thought occurred to her what this scene might have been like if Vanessa Forsythe had arrived a little earlier!

"Vanessa can be unpleasant at times," Logan said absently, as if he felt he should say something at the moment.

"But quite pleasing at other times, I'll warrant," Rhea commented frigidly as she quickly mounted Jade Wind and spurred her up the path leading out of the meadow. Logan caught up with her, but they didn't speak as they rode back to Fair Oaks together. Rhea tried hard not to think of what had happened between her and Logan at the meadow. It angered her for she didn't like being at the mercy of such an all-consuming, undeniable need for someone. It made her feel helpless, vulnerable. Somehow she would have to find the strength of will to resist Logan. She must keep from being with him as much as possible. That would help. If she just could avoid being near him, having him touch her.

Rhea felt herself blush just thinking about it, and she was glad Logan was riding ahead of her and couldn't see her face. Apparently Logan Tremaine had this disarming effect on other women as well. Women like Vanessa Forsythe, and how many others?

Chapter 26

"I AM SO EXCITED ABOUT THIS PARTY, RHEA!" Camille Tremaine exclaimed as she put down her pen and gathered up the stack of neatly written envelopes she'd just finished addressing. "It's going to be such fun!"

"That's easy for you to say," Rhea teased. "You won't be the one on display—the Yankee intruder. I can feel the dagger looks already!"

Camille laughed and put her head back against the pillows propped behind her.

"Oh, Rhea, I really do love you," she said sincerely. "Everyone around here always seems so glum, but you are like a breath of fresh air coming in and awakening us. I'm so glad you are here."

"I'm glad, too," Rhea lied convincingly. Yet it was not a complete falsehood. She was enjoying being here with Camille. It was the rest of the Tremaine family she didn't care to be with.

Rhea looked at her new friend fondly. Camille seemed almost lost in the big canopied bed. She was so thin and pale. Yet her spirit was bright and lively. Rhea had been grateful for these three mornings spent with Logan's sister making plans for the wedding reception, addressing the invitations, acting like two schoolgirls going to their first party. There were so many decisions to make concerning what to wear, how to do their hair, how to act, whom to talk to.

Logan had been gone for these last few days, off to Richmond buying trees or some such thing. Camille told Rhea he did that often. Running a large plantation like Fair Oaks kept both Miles and Logan quite busy.

Logan had gone the morning after they had been to Meadow Lake. Nothing more was said between them about what had occurred there. Rhea hadn't seen Logan before he'd left on this sudden trip. He'd sent her only a vague message by his Negro valet, Obediah. She told herself she was glad he was gone, for she didn't miss his aloofness and unsmiling countenance at all. And when he was away, Rhea didn't have to fear that he might try to possess her again.

Now with Camille, Rhea could be herself. Camille's zest for life was contagious. Rhea could let down her guard and not feel threatened, though she was careful not to reveal anything about the strange arrangement she had with Logan.

With the others in the Tremaine family, Rhea remained quiet and withdrawn. Except for when it was unavoidable, such as at mealtimes and when she had to read to Silas Tremaine each afternoon, she kept herself apart from the others as much as possible. She especially avoided Miles. He seemed all too interested in her, for all the wrong reasons.

Sybil had quickly grown bored with planning the reception, leaving Rhea and Camille to do most of it. Camille didn't seem to mind this at all and Rhea certainly didn't. Sybil dismissed Rhea as being beneath her consideration, and Rhea returned the feeling.

"That's the last of them, I think," Camille was saying now, drawing Rhea's attention back to her. "Would you have Jemson find some boys to deliver the invitations, Rhea? They should go out today if possible."

"Yes, of course. I'll take them right down," Rhea agreed as she gathered up the envelopes she'd addressed, then went over to the bed and added Camille's to the pile.

"Oh, and please ask Drew if he'll print up a few extra on that machine of his, just in case I think of anyone we may have forgotten."

Andrew Tremaine was a typographer by hobby, Rhea had learned. He had a printshop set up in one of the empty rooms in the west wing of the house. Camille had cajoled him into doing the invitations for the reception in between his many social engagements with the young ladies of the area.

"All right, Camille, I'll ask him," Rhea replied with a smile.

She stopped in her departure to glance again at the portrait of Camille which hung on a wall of the bedroom. It had caught her eye the first time she'd come into Camille's room, and she'd looked at it many times since then.

"This is such a lovely likeness of you, Camille," she commented now as she paused before the gold-framed painting. "The artist captured you perfectly."

It was true. Whoever had painted this had not only caught Camille's outer beauty but also her beauty inside as well, her air of laughter and love of life. It was reflected in her eyes and smile, in the delicate gesture of her hand, in the pose of her body. The artist truly had the gift of empathy with his subject to be able to commune with her spirit and capture it so wonderfully on canvas.

"Logan painted that of me last fall," Camille said with a note of pride in her voice. "He surprised me with it for my birthday. I didn't know he was even doing it. I found out later he was sneaking around making sketches of me the whole summer before. He is a wonderful brother."

Rhea looked at Camille in amazement. Logan had painted this? She couldn't believe it. And it was hard for her to picture Logan as a wonderful brother.

Rhea was thoughtful as she left Camille's bedroom. Logan must be a very complex man. Certainly here was a side of him Rhea had not yet seen. It puzzled her. What other things would she find out about him in the next few months? Had she judged him too hastily?

Chapter 27

LOGAN WALKED OUT OF FRED SHEPHERD'S TREE nursery office on the outskirts of Richmond with a satisfied smile on his face. Shepherd was only too glad to sell his sapling hardwoods when Logan presented him with an affidavit offering his personal stock in the well-known Cornelius Mining Company as collateral. Logan would have his trees and future lumber to cut.

The unexpected trip he'd had to make on the spur of the moment with Saul and Horace had gone without a hitch. It was turning out to be quite successful.

But the smile left Logan's lips as he mounted Baron and turned the big stallion toward the city, thinking about what he had to do next. He wasn't looking forward to it. Usually the thought of the brick townhouse in the exclusive Kenwood Park section of the city filled him with a pleasant feeling of anticipation. For that was where he met Vanessa Forsythe for stolen hours of bliss whenever they could both arrange it. The house was hers, an old family inheritance. Wendall, her husband, never came to it. He was so preoccupied with other things he probably didn't even know of its existence.

But today Logan was not anxious to visit quiet, tree-lined Surrey Lane, though he knew Vanessa was waiting for him. She'd be in a vile temper after what had happened at the lake the other day. He hadn't wanted her to find out about Rhea like that.

Logan recalled the meadow scene now as he skirted the main streets of Richmond. It wasn't Vanessa's untimely arrival that troubled him. It was Rhea who tormented him. Women were usually just a pleasant diversion for him. He was always master of such affairs. But with Rhea he felt out of control, and it was not a feeling he relished at all.

Logan frowned as the picture of Rhea, frightened and weeping from her nightmare at Farley House, flashed through his mind. He'd felt sympathy for her then, much as he often did for his sister Camille when she was ill. Still, that didn't explain how he had ended up making love to Rhea that night nor how it had happened again that day in the meadow. These were unsettling thoughts, to be sure, as was the glimpse of Rhea lying naked in his arms that now appeared in his mind's eye.

Logan shook his head to clear it and forced himself to focus his attention on his meeting with Vanessa in a few minutes. He had to admit the thought of Rhea was a better one.

"Women!" he murmured aloud as he reined Baron to the left down Surrey Lane. "At times they are far more bother than they are worth!"

"Miz Vanessa's waitin' for yo' in the parlor, Mr. Logan," the plump old Negro housekeeper told him, flashing a wide grin as she took his hat. "An', oh my, is she in a state! Ah bin keepin' outta her path all mornin'. Ah hopes yo' kin make her happy agin."

"I hope so, too, Beulah," Logan replied, sighing heavily. "Lead on to the lioness's den."

The big Negress chuckled as she turned and walked ahead of him toward a door on the right.

"Mr. Logan, Miz Vanessa," she announced as she opened the door for him.

As soon as Logan had crossed the threshold, Beulah closed the door behind him and went to sit in a wing-backed chair in the hallway. She had to stay close by because her mistress would likely be calling for refreshments for the two of them before long. And besides, Beulah wanted to be close enough to hear some of the conversation that was about to take place. Her husband, who served as groom and handyman for the house, came into the hall then.

"Come here, Seth," Beulah whispered, motioning him forward with her hand. She grinned at him. "Mr. Logan jus' arrive. Dey's goin' ta be fireworks now, if ah'm any judge of da mistress's bad tempers. She bes' be careful-like, though. We seen a heap o' men come and go through here, but dis one's dif'rent. She bes' take care how she act wid Mr. Logan or he might jus' up an' walk out dat front door and not come back no mo'.''

"So you've come at last," was Vanessa's only greeting. She made no attempt to hide the irritation she felt.

"Good day to you, too, my pet," Logan returned, a note of sarcasm in his voice. He stopped in the middle of the room and made no move to embrace Vanessa as he usually did.

"Good day, indeed! Logan, you owe me some answers. What in heaven's name is the meaning of this marriage of yours to that—that woman?" Vanessa's green eyes flashed angrily at Logan as she faced him, hands on hips.

Though Logan had told himself he would not bristle at any show of temperament Vanessa might display, he found himself doing exactly that right now. With an effort, he kept his cool outward appearance as he looked at her.

"There is an explanation and I shall be happy to tell it to you as soon as you sit down and control that Irish temper of yours, Vanessa. I won't waste words on an outraged woman."

Vanessa's light brows knit into a frown as she pursed her lips, turned, and flounced to the brocade sofa where she sat down and continued to glare at him.

Logan went to the parlor door and opened it. The two Negro servants nearly tumbled into the room from their eavesdropping positions on the other side.

"Ahem," Logan muttered, continuing to look stern. "Since you don't seem to be otherwise occupied, Beulah, bring Mistress Vanessa and me two mint julips. Seth, see to my horse outside."

"Yes, Mr. Logan, suh," the two slaves answered at once. Then they both turned quickly and nearly fell over each other as they bustled away.

Logan closed the door again and turned to face Vanessa. As he walked over and sat down next to her on the sofa he could tell by the slight outjutting of her lower lip that she was changing her tactic. He normally found her coy little pout appealing, but such was not the case now. It only made her seem childish, and again he had to hide his annoyance.

"You don't really love that woman, do you, darling?" Vanessa asked then, leaning toward him. She lowered her eyes with pretended shyness and her lower lip protruded farther.

" 'That woman's' name is Rhea, and our marriage is strictly one of convenience for both of us, for all of us actually," Logan answered, purposely not adding that he and Rhea weren't really married.

"All of us?" Vanessa asked doubtfully.

"Yes. Miles managed to maneuver me into a corner. Having a wife was the only immediate solution. It also will stop the wagging of gossiping tongues about us, and Wendall will no longer suspect the liaison you and I have."

"He never suspects anything anyway," Vanessa remarked derisively. "He's too befuddled with his precious laboratory and the horrible rats and snakes and other despicable creatures he uses there." She shuddered in disgust at the thought. "And gossips' chatter has never bothered you before."

"Well, it never hurts to be cautious, pet," Logan replied with amusement, making his tone lighter now. He put out his hand and touched her bare shoulder, noticing for the first time the provocative low cut of her green gown with the off-the-shoulder sleeves. Its shade matched the color of her eyes exactly. She really is a very beautiful woman, Logan found himself thinking as he let his eyes roam over her freely. Fiery like the red of her hair. A most tempting and worthy prize for any man.

Vanessa bent her head to kiss his hand on her shoulder. She put her hand over his then and looked at him intently.

"You do not love her then . . . this wife of yours? Your heart belongs to only me?" Vanessa asked as she moved closer to him.

"Only to you, my pet," Logan told her, trying to sound sincere. She didn't seem to notice that he had sidestepped her first question, though he knew the answer to it easily enough. Of course he did not love Rhea. He loved no woman. He enjoyed them and the physical pleasure they could give him, but he never took any of them seriously and never intended to. And that included Rhea and Vanessa. No woman would ever reach him completely.

"I was so afraid I'd lost you, my darling," Vanessa said then in a whispery voice as she put her head on Logan's shoulder and leaned against him. "You were away so long and then when you did return, you had that Rhea person with you. I didn't know what to think."

"Well, now you know there is no cause for concern," Logan told her indulgently as he stroked her soft hair with his hand. The scent of her perfume drifted up to him. It was pleasant, but not as intoxicating as usual. It almost seemed too strong, overpowering. Not like a more delicate fragrance worn by another, one that Logan too well remembered.

"Come upstairs with me now, darling," Vanessa said suddenly, getting to her feet. She pulled at his hand still held in hers. "It's been so long since we've been together. How I've yearned for you to make love to me."

Logan looked up at her. For the first time since he and Vanessa had become lovers over a year ago, he had not the slightest desire to make love to her. Yet she seemed to be the same—beautiful, sensuous, eager for him. What could be the reason then?

Nothing, there was nothing wrong, Logan told himself with some perturbation. He just had many things occupying his mind, that was all. Once he got upstairs with Vanessa, his desire would awaken again.

He got to his feet and walked arm-in-arm with her to the doorway just as Beulah stood outside poised to knock.

"We'll take them upstairs, Beulah," Vanessa informed the servant as she took one of the tall, cool-looking glasses of liquid from the tray, while Logan reached for the other one. "And we're not to be disturbed under any circumstances, is that clear?" she addressed Beulah as she turned her green eyes adoringly on Logan.

"Yes, Miz Vanessa. Ah understands," Beulah replied with a knowing smile. Yes, that Mr. Logan knew how to make her mistress happy, that he did, the Negress added in her thoughts as her smile widened to a grin and she turned to go back to the kitchen.

Vanessa felt more confident in her spacious bedroom. She knew how to please a man, how to keep him satisfied but still hungering for more. Now that Logan had assured her that Rhea creature meant nothing to him, she could relax and forget her fears. Just enjoy Logan. Enjoy what he could do to her, make her feel. He was the most exciting and yet mysterious man she had ever known. Other lovers she'd had in the past spent hours talking about nothing except themselves, their wants and ambitions. Logan never bored her with such stupid prattle. He had exactly what she craved—a hard-muscled and so very virile male body and a voracious appetite for making love that matched her own.

"Come, help me undress as you always do, darling," she said now. "And kiss me into oblivion as you know how to do so well." She smiled provocatively as she turned around and presented the back fastenings of her gown to Logan.

He stepped to her and started to undo the row of hooks and eyes almost too eagerly. In a few moments Vanessa's clothing and the bed quilt lay in a disheveled pile on the floor, and she was lying back against the crisp white sheets stretching catlike while Logan hastily undressed, then came into the bed next to her. As they embraced Vanessa clung to Logan, running her hands up and down the rippling muscles of his back and buttocks. She entwined her legs in his and pressed her length fully along him.

"Oh, Logan," she murmured with a happy sigh. "How good you feel, so hard and strong, like a magnificent male animal—a regal, savage lion, stalking me. Make love to me, my darling, for I have ached for you all these three long months. While you were away I had to endure Wendall's absurd fondling and pawing. I could barely stand it." She ran her hand along his side and down to where there should have been a hard swollenness and was surprised to find that there was none. At the same moment Logan pulled his hand away from where it touched her breast and rolled over to the other side of the bed.

"For God's sake, Vanessa," he exclaimed heatedly, "be quiet, can't you? This isn't a safari, and I don't appreciate hearing about the man I'm cuckolding!" He immediately regretted his brusqueness when he saw the stricken look on Vanessa's face.

"Vanessa . . ." He put out his hand to touch her, but

now it was she who avoided his reach as she sat up and frowned at him.

"What is it, Logan?" she demanded, leveling her limpid green eyes squarely at him. "I am doing nothing different from all the other times we've made love. You usually find my words arousing. Just the sight of my naked body is all you have ever needed to awaken your desire. What has happened to change that?"

Her eyes were unwavering as they watched him. Logan had to look away from her intent scrutiny. He turned and sat on the edge of the bed.

"Nothing has changed," he said in a quiet tone. Confusion clouded his thoughts. "You are as beautiful and desirable as always."

"Then what is it, darling?" she asked. She leaned forward and pressed her full, taut breasts against his bare back, bringing her arms around his shoulders to hold him. "Tell your Vanessa what is troubling you," she cooed into his ear.

"It is no fault of yours, pet," he tried to assure her, though he wasn't sure himself why he didn't want to make love to her. "I just have much on my mind here of late," he went on. "Miles is always a threat in his efforts to get the upper hand. There are constant problems at the mill. The drought threatens the tobacco—" Rhea's face suddenly penetrated Logan's thoughts, startling him. But he had to admit, to himself at least, that his "wife" was definitely one of the main problems plaguing him at the moment.

"I understand, darling," Vanessa said tolerantly, hiding her relief. She was surprised and pleased by his sudden openness with her. "I know these things can happen with a man from time to time. And while it's never happened to you before—," she started to kiss his shoulders and run her hand along his arm, "—I am certain I can find a way to get your mind back on me."

"No, Vanessa." Logan got to his feet so quickly that Vanessa was thrown off balance and fell back against the pillows. His own disturbing thoughts annoyed him almost as much as Vanessa's fawning did. He walked briskly to the chair where he'd thrown his clothes and began to dress.

"There is more to this than you are telling me, Logan," Vanessa accused, angry now as she sat up straight in the bed. "This has never occurred between us before, only since that Yankee bitch came into your life! I won't let her have you, Logan. You are mine. You need what only I have to give you."

Logan paused in buttoning his shirt to cast an ice-blue glance at the woman ranting at him from the bed. His carefully controlled voice matched his cold look when he spoke.

"You're being absurd, Vanessa. I've warned you about this jealous possessiveness of yours. You will push me too far. I need nothing from you. No woman owns me or ever will."

Logan looked away from her then, finished buttoning his shirt, and reached for his coat. His words and manner both infuriated Vanessa and frightened her. His arrogance and cool control enraged her. She preferred that he be easier to manipulate, as most men were. She wanted Logan Tremaine. She had not had her fill of him just yet. He had gotten into her blood as no other man had, and Vanessa was not about to give him up without a fight—especially not to any conniving Yankee whore!

Thinking quickly, she changed her tactic.

"You are right, of course, Logan darling," she said contritely as she got up from the bed and came to stand before him, blocking his path to the door. She ran her fingers along the lapels of his coat and let her legs press against his.

"Forgive me for losing my temper, darling," she entreated. She lowered her eyes and pursed her lips in a pout. "Please don't leave like this. Don't leave at all." She ran her finger up the side of Logan's neck and let it play around his ear. With her other hand she took hold of his hand and placed it on her naked breast. "Come back to bed, Logan. I do not wish to own you, only to make love with you. Come back to the bed and take what I so freely want to give you. Please, darling . . ."

She looked up at him with liquid green eyes, eyes that had melted even the most reluctant of men whenever she wished it. Logan gazed back at Vanessa steadily, seeing her flowing red hair, her flawless pale skin, her voluptuous beauty. But he knew the game she was playing and he felt no stirring of desire, no temptation to taste the grand banquet of her body.

"No, not this time, Vanessa," he told her. Then he walked away to the door and left the room.

Vanessa stood seething in the middle of the floor after he'd gone.

"There will be another time, Logan darling," she murmured in a low voice tight with anger. "But it will be on *my* terms, you'll see. And then I will make you beg for the delights of my body." She ran her hands along her naked torso and over her ample breasts. "I will enslave you yet, Logan, for no man can resist what I have to offer for very long."

Chapter 28

AFTER SPENDING THE MORNING PLEASANTLY
with Camille, Rhea had a light luncheon in her own room
and then rested some before facing what had fast become
an ordeal each afternoon at two o'clock. She dreaded her
daily reading sessions with Silas Tremaine. The patriarch
of the Tremaine family was a crabby and dictatorial old
man, outspoken to the point of being unabashedly insulting. Nothing Rhea did pleased him. Her voice was either
too loud, which deafened him, he said, or too soft, causing
him to strain his hearing. He complained she spoke either
too quickly, making her hard to understand, or too slowly,
putting him to sleep. She arrived late or too early, even
though Rhea came precisely at two P.M. each day. He
seemed to enjoy seeing her flustered by his inconsistent
and unreasonable demands.

Well, today she was determined *not* to be upset by him
no matter what he said to her. She only came to read to
him at all because Logan had insisted that she comply
with his grandfather's wishes in order to keep things running as smoothly and normally as possible during these
months of their agreement. She would rely on the well-
practiced control that she had nurtured so carefully all
those months back home in Philadelphia.

Philadelphia . . . Rhea hadn't been gone very long
from the city of her birth, but it already seemed like
forever. Fair Oaks was more than just located in another
state of the Union. To Rhea it was like another world,
foreign and even forbidding to her. She felt an intense
pang of homesickness now as she took a deep breath to

fortify herself and knocked on the door of Silas Tremaine's bedroom.

"Come in!" a gruff voice called from the other side.

Forcing herself to look pleasant, Rhea entered the spacious room. She was surprised to see her antagonist out of bed and sitting in a leather armchair near the open doors leading to the balcony. He wore an elegant man's dressing coat with satin lapels and had a lightweight blanket draped over his knees.

"You're late again!" he snapped before Rhea could even speak a greeting.

The pendulum clock on the fireplace mantel was just striking a second time. Rhea was about to point that out to him but thought better of it. Remembering her resolve to be calm and compliant, Rhea instead chose to make no reply as she crossed the room and stopped next to the chair where she usually sat during these sessions.

"Good afternoon, Mr. Tremaine," she said. She had been unable to call him "grandfather" as the other members of the family did, and he had made no attempt to change the way she addressed him.

"What's good about it?" Silas demanded grouchily. "It's too damned hot and there's not a hint of rain to ease this cursed drought!" His light blue eyes, so like Logan's, swept over her critically as he spoke.

Rhea sighed inwardly and decided that keeping her temper with this man was not going to be an easy task by any means. Her spirit lagged further as she glimpsed the pile of newspapers on the stand next to Silas's chair. With dread she realized she'd have to read the boring financial and crop report pages again.

"Well, sit down, girl, and let's get started," he ordered testily.

Rhea took her seat as he handed her the top paper, pointing to the place where she was to begin.

"And speak up so I can hear you," he added in an impatient tone.

Except for correcting her pronunciation of an industrialist's name and telling her to read more slowly, old Silas quietly listened to Rhea drone out the dull information for nearly an hour. She glanced up from the newspaper then to find his head nodding, his breathing steady. Even he had been put to sleep by the tedious reading.

Rhea put down the paper and got up from her chair quietly, flexing her shoulders back to ease the stiffness. She walked to the doorway to the balcony which looked out over the front courtyard and flower garden of the house. All was quiet outside except for the gentle sounds of twittering birds and the soft, steady drone of insects. The slaves had ceased their work in the garden during this hottest part of the day.

Rhea leaned back against the frame of the door, welcoming the feel of the slight breath of breeze on her. She glanced back at Silas Tremaine, wondering absently about what kind of man he must have been in his youth. Like Logan? She frowned slightly at the thought of her false husband. She didn't want to think about Logan, so she forced him out of her mind. Moving away from the doorway, Rhea thought about leaving. Old Silas was still napping. But the hour and a half she was usually required to spend with him was not up yet. She decided to stay in case he awoke. She didn't want to give him yet another reason for berating her.

Rhea walked slowly around the neatly kept room idly wondering where Jubal was. He was usually not very long out of his master's presence. She wondered how Jubal stood Silas's cantankerous ways. But then he didn't have much choice in the matter. He was a slave with no say in what happened in his life.

She moved to stand before a glass-enclosed display case hanging on the wall. Twelve beribboned medals and various other naval decorations were arranged against black velvet in the case. Leaning closer, she read some of the words stamped on several of them. Valor, honor, distinguished service. Apparently Silas Tremaine's career in the Navy had been marked by outstanding courage and dedication.

Rhea meandered on to a small mahogany bookcase filled with leather-bound volumes that stood in one corner. She let her glance flick over some of the titles. *Maritime Law, Military Strategies of the American Revolution.* She looked down at the second shelf. Shakespeare's *Sonnets,* Dickens' *A Christmas Carol, The Philosophy of Plato, The Raven and Other Poems.* Quite a diversity of subjects, Rhea thought as she carefully took out the newly published Edgar Allan Poe volume and began leafing through the pages.

"Always heard Yankees were a nosey lot."

Rhea jumped, nearly dropping the book, startled by the voice coming from behind her. She whirled around to see Silas Tremaine wide awake and watching her. Her first impulse was to apologize profusely for being caught so red-handedly. But one look at the elderly Tremaine's face told her that was exactly what he expected her to do. He was clearly trying to embarrass her. Well, Rhea wasn't about to be baited.

Smiling and carrying the Poe volume with her, she walked back to the chair she'd been sitting in before and sat down.

"I wasn't being nosey, Mr. Tremaine," she said in a conversational tone. "I was only looking for something more interesting to read." She paused to let her small jibe concerning their reading material sink in before she went on. "Might I read to you from this book?"

"Suit yourself," Silas answered gruffly, pretending disinterest as he looked away, disappointed by her reaction.

Rhea leafed through the pages a few moments before she decided to go back to the main poem of the volume, "The Raven." Silas made no attempt to interrupt her recitation of the woeful and haunting verses; in fact, to Rhea's surprise, he seemed to be listening intently. He was quiet a few minutes after Rhea finished reading the poem, staring off into space. As Rhea followed his gaze, she saw that he was really looking at something—a small oil painting of a beautiful young woman. It was in an ornate gold oval frame on the nearby desk.

Silas suddenly became aware of the silence that had fallen over the room. Clearing his throat, he frowned and looked at Rhea with annoyance.

"Enough of this ridiculous poetry. I don't want to hear any more of it or your irritating voice today. You are dismissed. Go on, get out!"

He was back to his normal disagreeable self again. Rhea felt her anger about to flare at his rude and insulting manner, but she forced it down. She wouldn't give him the satisfaction of seeing her angry.

"As you wish," she replied formally. Then she rose from her chair, walked to the bookcase, replaced the Poe volume, and left the room.

Chapter 29

RHEA WAS GLAD TO REACH THE SOLITUDE OF the lake meadow later that afternoon, pleased with herself that she'd been able to find her way back here again. She hadn't been taking her usual morning rides these last few days while she was working with Camille. Instead, she began to reward herself for enduring Silas Tremaine with an afternoon ride following their reading sessions.

As Logan had instructed, a slave usually accompanied her. But this afternoon there had been some mix-up. Jade Wind had been saddled and left tied to the hitching post with no one around. She probably should have gone to the stables to ask Amos for someone, but instead Rhea had quickly mounted and stolen away like an errant child, glad to be alone and free for a while.

She had hesitated coming to this meadow again for she did not want to be reminded of what had happened with Logan here. Yet it was such a beautiful place, a haven seemingly cut off from the rest of the world and Rhea needed that now, someplace she could go to be out of everyone's scrutiny, especially old Silas's.

Rhea tied Jade Wind to a sprawling oak tree, then spread out the blanket Glory had given her and sat down near the water's edge. She'd been careful to avoid the spot where she and Logan had stopped before. Removing her riding boots, Rhea dangled her toes over the edge of the bank into the cool water. Then she lay back, relishing the feel of the warm sun on her.

The old oak tree lifted its lush green branches to the unending summer sky. Puffs of white, billowy clouds dotted the blueness. The only sound was the chirping of a bird hidden somewhere in the tree above Rhea. Even the blue-green water was silent and still, for there was no breath of breeze to disturb it today.

Rhea dozed peacefully for a while and when she awoke, she felt very warm. The water looked so inviting. A mischievous smile curled on her lips as she glanced around. No one would care or even see her if she took a quick, refreshing swim in Meadow Lake. What better to do on such a hot day?

She gathered her hair on top of her head and secured it there with the combs that had held it away from her face. Then Rhea slipped off her blouse and chemise, her riding skirt and pantaloons, and waded into the water.

She splashed and dived and swam for some time through the cool, deep water of the small lake. The delicious chill felt so good after the humid heat of the summer day. But after a short while, she was tiring from the exertion. The water had cooled her so that when she came up from a deep dive and felt the air on her face and shoulders, a shiver ran through her.

Suddenly Rhea sensed she was no longer alone. She jerked her head around until a movement near the oak tree caught her eye. Baron was standing next to Jade Wind, impatiently pawing the grassy bank and tossing his mighty black head. And Logan stood on the bank looking out at Rhea. His white shirt was opened halfway down the front with the sleeves rolled up above the elbow. His hands were on his hips and there was an unmistakable scowl on his face. At his feet was the pile of Rhea's clothes.

"And just what do you think you are doing?" Logan called out to her sternly.

"I should think that would be rather obvious," Rhea retorted defensively to hide her growing uneasiness. His look made her feel like she'd been caught in some terrible misdeed and she didn't like it one bit. She didn't like having him here invading her privacy, spying on her. But at the moment she didn't know what to do about it. She couldn't very well leave the water now to confront him. Yet she could feel her muscles tightening from the strain of treading water.

"You were instructed never to ride out alone, Rhea," Logan continued, his fury showing now. "It is foolish and dangerous for a woman to be out riding and swimming alone, especially in the state you are obviously in." He glanced meaningfully at her clothes at his feet and then back out to her in the water. "Come out of there at once!"

It was Rhea's turn to frown now. How dare he order her about? He didn't own her!

"I am *not* one of your slaves, sir," she snapped back at him icily. "And I shall do as I please! And it pleases me to remain here!"

Rhea would have said more but at that moment an excruciating pain shot through her right leg, sending it into an agonizing spasm. An anguished cry escaped her lips as she desperately tried to clutch at her cramping limb. Her head went under, and she gulped in mouthfuls of the cold water before she managed to thrash her way to the surface again. She came up with arms flailing, choking, and gasping for air.

"Rhea!" Logan shouted as he saw her start to go under for a second time. Within seconds he had stripped off his shirt and boots and dived into the water, swimming with powerful strokes to the middle of the lake where Rhea was struggling to stay above the surface. She was gasping for breath. The pain in her leg was agonizing. Frightened, she thrashed at the water and struggled against Logan.

"Rhea! Rhea!" Logan shouted as he tried to grasp her arms. She fought him in panic.

"Rhea! Let me help you! Stop fighting!" Logan ordered as he grabbed hold of her.

Something in his tone caught Rhea's attention. She reached out suddenly and grasped his shoulders.

"Logan! Help me!" she cried as she clutched at him.

Logan wrapped an arm around her waist and treaded water with the other to keep them both afloat.

"Rhea, listen to me," he commanded fiercely. "Don't struggle and do *exactly* as I say. I'll get us both to the bank, but you have to let me pull you in."

Rhea couldn't speak. The pain by now was too intense. She only gritted her teeth and nodded. She willed her body to go limp and let Logan wrap his arm around the front of her shoulders. Then he was able to keep her head above water as he struck out with powerful, one-armed strokes for the shore of the small lake.

When he could touch the stony bottom, Logan swept Rhea into his arms and carried her out of the water. He knelt down and sat her gently on the blanket, wrapping it around her. Rhea clutched the cloth to her and reached for her leg.

"A cramp?" Logan asked after he'd had a moment to catch his breath.

Rhea nodded and whispered a hoarse "Yes." Then her teeth clenched against the pain.

"Try to concentrate on relaxing the muscle," Logan told her as he took hold of the calf of her leg and began to gently massage it.

After a few minutes the pain began to subside and Rhea grew calmer.

"Is it better now?" Logan asked with concern.

Rhea glanced at him, then lowered her eyes. "Yes, it's much better. Thank you."

She felt ridiculous, embarrassed to be caught in this awkward situation.

"I'm sorry to be so much trouble," she went on quickly. "I've never had anything like this happen before. Thank you for . . . coming to my aid."

"Are you certain you're all right?" he asked again, his worried eyes resting on hers.

"Yes . . . I think I'd better get dressed now," she said in a low voice, averting her eyes as she started to reach over to where her clothes were lying. But the movement caused a sharp pain to run the length of her calf again. A cry escaped her lips as she pulled back to relieve the strain.

"Here, let me get them for you. Lie still," Logan ordered with irritation. Now that Rhea was safe he could be angry with her, and angry he was. He stood up and retrieved her clothes, tossing them at her.

"I ought to beat you soundly for this little escapade," he began heatedly. He stood over her, hands on hips, his eyes stern beneath his deep frown. "Don't you know what kind of danger you put yourself in? There are often runaway slaves roaming these fields and hills. What if a big buck black had happened on you swimming just now? What do you suppose he might have done to you, a white woman alone and unclothed?

"Or barring that ugly scene, what if no one had been around when that cramp hit your leg? You'd likely be lying at the bottom of the lake at this very moment! Have you no sense at all?"

"Stop, stop it!" Rhea implored him, putting her hands over her ears to try to shut out his harsh words. She was exhausted and in pain. The terrible scenes he described seemed all too real to her now and she felt foolish and frightened and defensive.

Grasping the blanket around her, Rhea struggled to her feet, taking care to put as little weight on her sore leg as possible. She straightened her back and stood her ground before Logan.

"I don't want to hear any more, Logan Tremaine. Perhaps coming here alone was a mistake. But I won't be imprisoned in that house for the next five and a half months. I'm not one of your slaves to be ordered about and threatened and watched constantly!"

One corner of the blanket slipped from her grasp just then, and as Rhea grabbed for it she inadvertently put weight on her right leg. Weakened by the strain of the cramp, it gave way under her and she lost her balance. Logan quickly reached out and caught her just in time to keep her from falling.

For a long moment they stood there glaring at each other. Rhea soon realized her hand was pressed against Logan's bare chest. Her fingers touched the soft dark hair there, felt the wetness and warmth of his skin. She became uncomfortably aware of the hard muscles of his body pressed against hers and her heart began to beat faster. For a moment she was frightened. He looked so thunderous. He seemed about to give her the beating he'd just threatened her with.

And Logan was very close to doing just that. It was a hot day and he'd just returned from a long ride back from Richmond. He'd no more than arrived at Fair Oaks that afternoon when Amos came running to tell him of Rhea's excursion out alone. He'd searched several other places before coming here. He was tired and angry and in no mood for any more argument. He did feel like thrashing some sense into Rhea for being so foolishly headstrong and independent.

The picture of Rhea's nakedness as he'd carried her from the water and the realization that she was clad now in only a haphazardly fixed blanket mixed with Logan's angry thoughts. A sudden savage impulse made him pull her closer to him until her body was molded along his length. Then he brought his head down and roughly covered her lips with his.

Rhea struggled against Logan, trying to push his chest away with her hands. Then the blanket slipped away, leaving her body completely exposed to him. Logan forced her down to the ground and half covered her body with his.

Somehow he managed to get control of himself even though he longed to taste again the honey of her lips, feel once more the tumultuous desire that could erupt in her and carry his own passion to new heights of ecstasy. But strangely, he wanted Rhea to feel the same all-consuming need he did, to want again the rapturous joining of their bodies and spirits. He forced himself to go slower.

"Rhea . . ." he murmured huskily as he brought his head down once more to find her lips.

Rhea sensed the change in him and now a different kind of alarm mounted in her. She tried again to struggle against him, to twist her mouth away from his demanding lips and tongue. But her breath caught in her throat as Logan's hand moved up her side and began to gently stroke over and around the nipple of her naked breast. Rhea tried to resist the insistent stirring that started within her, and a small, agonized moan escaped her lips when she realized she could not keep it from overwhelming her.

"Yes, give in to me, Rhea . . . my beautiful Rhea . . ." Logan whispered. "Let go of your anger and your pride, as I have. Let yourself feel the need inside you . . ."

Rhea began to cry. She couldn't stop herself. She felt confused and lost. She didn't know if her tears were of joy that Logan wanted her, that this magical madness could happen with him, or whether they were tears of anger and frustration that she was so vulnerable to Logan, so powerless to resist him.

Logan gently caressed her breast with his mouth, then moved along her neck to the softness of her face. He felt the wetness of her tears on her cheek and paused, looking at her tenderly. Her liquid blue eyes searched his face intently.

"Are you frightened of me, Rhea?" he asked softly. "I will not hurt you, but neither will I let you deny what is destined between us."

He kissed Rhea then with a deep tenderness that caused a shudder to vibrate to the depths of her soul. Her will was lost to him. She hated her weakness, cursed her longing for him, even while she surrendered totally to him.

Impatiently she waited the few moments it took him to remove his breeches, then she marveled at the magnificence of his nakedness. Her pulse quicked as Logan came to her then and began to move his hands and mouth searchingly over her to accomplish his total conquest of her. Slowly and meticulously he laid siege to Rhea's body, bombarding her senses one by one to cause intense arousal. His lips and tongue plundered her mouth. Expertly he sought out and tortured the most sensitive and intimate places of her body with a touch so exquisitely tantalizing and exciting that Rhea felt herself the victor and not the vanquished in their lovemaking. Her fevered response soon matched his. Locked in each other's arms, Rhea and Logan moved in perfect harmony, she arching and opening to him, he entering the pulsating folds of her womanhood so avidly offered and thrusting again and again to the depths of her being. Together they soared.

At last exhaustion overwhelmed them and they slept in each other's arms on the grassy bank of Meadow Lake.

Baron's agitated neighing awakened Rhea. Logan was already sitting up, all his senses alert. A slight breeze had begun to stir, bringing with it a pungent odor that alarmed the horses and brought both Logan and Rhea quickly to their feet. Logan's eyes narrowed as he squinted in the bright sunlight and searched the surrounding meadow, hills, and sky. In an instant he spotted the billowing black cloud on the horizon.

"Fire. At the Duvall place," he said in a low voice, never taking his eyes off the darkening skyline.

Logan hastily pulled on his clothes and walked to where the horses were tied and prancing nervously. Rhea did the

same and followed in his wake, taking Jade Wind's reins
when Logan held them out to her. Then he swung up on
Baron's back and pulled the reins into a tight grip to control the horse. Still Baron snorted and shied, anxious to get
away from the danger he could smell on the wind.

"Ride back to Fair Oaks, Rhea, and tell them what's
happening at the Duvall plantation. Miles will know what
to do. Stay at the house and do whatever you're told." With
that, Logan swung Baron's head around and dug his heels
into the horse's sides. Instantly man and horse were racing
away toward the low hills and the fire just beyond.

Rhea didn't hesitate. She knew the danger of fire and
wind and the destruction they could wreak on home and
land. And these lands were dry from lack of rain. The
flames would spread wildly unless they could be stopped or
diverted.

Mounting Jade Wind, she held onto the reins tightly, for
as soon as she was seated the nervous mare sprang into
motion, running to full gallop away from the hills to escape the approaching peril. Rhea would have to think later
about Logan and the wonderful and terrible attraction
that had grown between them.

Chapter 30

RHEA RODE HARD FOR FAIR OAKS. AS SOON AS she arrived she had Miles summoned and gave him Logan's message. He immediately put into motion a prearranged plan for fighting any fire and evacuating everyone on the plantation who would not be battling the blaze. From the information Rhea gave, Miles knew the fire was headed toward Fair Oaks. Drew, Rhea, and the household staff were gathered in the front parlor to hear Miles issue their instructions.

"Drew, see to getting messengers sent out to the other plantations to spread the word about what's happening and get more help. Then find Jessup and have him round up all the slaves. Send women and children to the compound, all able-bodied men to the storehouse for buckets, shovels, and any other equipment we might be able to use."

"Right, Miles," Drew replied as he quickly headed for the parlor door.

"Amos, you're in charge of the stock. Have your boys ready to move the horses out on short notice. Cattle and dairy cows second, then if there's time, the rest of the livestock."

"Yes, Marse Miles," the old Negro said as he, too, left the room.

"Mrs. Jerome, you and Jemson are responsible for house servants and important household goods. You are aware of which things must be packed for transportation elsewhere. Get your people started on that immediately."

"Of course, Mr. Miles. I'll see to it at once," the middle-aged housekeeper agreed, turning to leave. Jemson, the Negro butler, followed her.

"Rhea, Sybil and Tyler went to Richmond this morning to visit friends. Therefore, I'm going to put you in charge of seeing to the packing of all our personal belongings. Camille will help you."

He didn't wait for her to agree but turned instead toward Jubal. Rhea heard him giving the old slave orders concerning Silas as she walked out into the hallway and headed toward Camille's room.

It didn't take long for word to come from the Duvall plantation that a revolt by the slaves was the source of the trouble. In the violent uprising, a barn had been torched which ignited several other outbuildings and spread rapidly to the surrounding dry brush and trees. The wind was a willing participant in spreading the destructive flames.

"Do the slaves do this very often?" Rhea asked Camille as they busily packed the many large trunks that had been brought upstairs.

"In the case of Simpson Duvall, often enough," Camille replied as she carefully wrapped an expensive ball gown in large sheets of tissue paper and handed it to Rhea to add to a trunk. "He is a notoriously harsh master, quick with the whip. His slaves live in squalor, are ill-fed, and overworked. Even an animal will resist such treatment when it can take it no longer."

"But why is he allowed to do such cruel things?" Rhea persisted.

"You must understand that a plantation is a world of its own, Rhea. What a man does with his property, on his property, is his business, especially where slaves are concerned. Simpson is the master. He is also a stubborn, stingy, and very mean man. I have never liked him. I don't know how his poor wife, Emma, puts up with him. One of these days his slaves will succeed in murdering him. Miles and Logan have been warning him of that for years, but he will not change. I doubt there is anyone who will mourn Simpson Duvall's demise."

"The Negroes have no rights at all then?" Rhea asked with concern. "Have they no recourse but to endure that kind of treatment?"

"It is very difficult to bring any kind of legal action against a slaveowner. The slaves are not allowed to testify against him and no whites will because they may find themselves in the same situation someday. So they band together and everyone just turns his head to the injustice of it, until something ugly like this revolt happens." Camille paused, then came to stand before her friend, taking Rhea's two hands in her own.

"Rhea," she said in a kind voice, her expression one of fondness and patience as she looked at her. "You will be living here at Fair Oaks for a long time to come, I hope, but I know our ways must seem strange to one who has been raised in the North. Please try to understand. Negroes are not like whites. They are an inferior race with very limited mental faculties. They are like children, or even dumb beasts, who would wander aimlessly and likely die if not directed and controlled and cared for by their masters. Here at Fair Oaks we care about our people, like parents care for their children. They are happy, well provided for, and well treated. We have not had an uprising here in over seventy-five years."

A maid came to the door then, interrupting their conversation, and Rhea and Camille moved on to Sybil and Miles's quarters to continue supervising and helping with the packing of personal belongings.

Rhea was thoughtful as she worked. She found it hard to believe Camille's words, though she knew her friend believed them completely. Negroes were people, not animals. Did anyone have the right to own another human being? Weren't even slaves deserving of some measure of dignity and justice and a chance to have a say in their own destinies?

Rhea had never thought much about such things before, but now that slavery had become a part of her life, she was forced to consider such disturbing questions.

Happy and well treated, Camille had said. Rhea remembered only too well the terrible scene she had witnessed with Dreed Jessup and the slave girl that first day Logan was showing her around the estate. Camille's words hardly described the harsh reality of that ugly episode.

Rhea's thoughts were heavy as she went to Sybil's mirrored vanity table and began to pack the toiletries laid out there into a small traveling case. She and Camille and several of the maids worked long into the night with the packing, until finally Rhea insisted she could finish what little was left.

"Camille, you must go to bed before you collapse," she ordered gently, noticing her friend's pale countenance.

"Perhaps you're right. I do feel tired," Camille admitted wearily, raising the back of her hand to her forehead. "I pray we will not have to move all of these things." A fearful look came suddenly to her lovely face. "Pray the fire will not reach Fair Oaks, Rhea. I cannot bear to think of all of this—my home, all I have ever known—perhaps being destroyed by horrible flames."

"Try not to think about it, Camille," Rhea coaxed as she put her arm around the frail young woman and led her to her bedroom. She gave Camille over to Esta, the old Negress who had cared for Logan's sister since she was born, then went to her own room.

Logan's valet, Obediah, had told her he would see to packing Logan's belongings, so Rhea had only her own things left to pack. She wondered if it could wait until after she'd rested for just a little while. She lay back on the bed intending to close her tired eyes for only a few minutes, but she was instantly fast asleep.

Chapter 31

"MIZ RHEA, MIZ RHEA! WAKE UP!"

Rhea opened her heavy eyes to try to focus on who was shaking her shoulder.

"What is it, Glory?"

"Marse Drew wants yo' down in da front parlor right now!"

"All right, Glory. I'll come immediately." Rhea swung off the bed and shook the skirt of her gown to try to straighten some of the wrinkles. "What time is it? What's the news of the fire?" she asked quickly as she brushed a stray strand of hair away from her face with her hand.

"It seven in da mornin', ma'am, an' da news ain't good. Dat why Marse Drew done come back here."

"Start packing my things, Glory. I'll send someone else up to help you. Use those trunks over there." Rhea gestured a hand toward the corner, then hastily left the bedroom.

When Rhea entered the parlor, she saw that Camille, Mrs. Jerome, Jemson, Jubal, and Amos were already there with Drew Tremaine.

"Ah, Rhea, come in," Drew addressed her as she entered. She saw that his clothes were dirty; his face and arms showing below his rolled-up shirtsleeves were streaked with grime.

"I've just been telling the others that Fair Oaks must be evacuated."

Rhea's glance went to Camille's grave face and she went to stand by her friend, putting her arm around her waist for support.

"The fire's still out of control because of the wind and

157

it's heading this way," Drew continued, his tone very serious. "Mrs. Jerome and Jemson, you will see to the loading of the wagons with the household goods. Amos, start moving the stock out now. Jubal, see to your master's safety. Rhea, I need you and Camille to go to the slave compound and supervise the evacuation there. The women and children are bound to panic when they hear this. Someone in authority will have to direct them and I can't spare any men. Camille, when everything's ready there, you are to go to the Fitzgerald place. It's out of the line of this. You'll all be safe there."

"But I don't want to leave Fair Oaks, Drew!" Camille cried. "Isn't there something more we can do?"

"I know, sis. I don't want this either," Drew told Camille grimly, gently holding her shoulders. "But we have no choice. Unless Miles and Logan and the others can get a backfire started, there's not much chance that Fair Oaks will be spared. They haven't had any success in doing that yet, so we have to be prepared.

"All right, everybody," he said then, turning to the others. "Let's get moving. I'm going back to the fire. We're depending on all of you to take care of things here."

"Be careful, Drew!" Camille called after her brother as he hurried from the parlor.

As Rhea and Camille made their way from the house to the barn for horses they could ride to the slave quarters, Rhea's heart went out to Camille, who was strangely quiet beside her. Rhea had little at stake here at Fair Oaks; a few pretty gowns, some personal items. But this was not her home, her life, her heritage handed down from generations of ancestors. She glanced up at the early morning sky. It looked dark and menacing as billowing clouds of smoke churned across it in the wind. Were there other clouds forming up there? Rhea wondered as she thought she saw something else above her. Rain now would be such a godsend, the miracle they were all hoping for. But rain had been so scarce all these weeks.

Rhea coughed as the acrid air blowing toward her burned her throat and nostrils. She could see a red tinge lining the tops of the trees on the horizon to the north. The destruction was coming closer. As she and Camille quickened their steps the thought of Logan came unbidden into

Rhea's mind and she couldn't help wondering if he were all right.

Logan jumped to the ground even before Baron stopped. He threw the reins to a man nearby and hurried to where Miles was working with several other men trying to dig a wide firebreak trench with shovels and pickaxes.

"How does it look up on the ridge?" Miles asked, stopping work for a few minutes to wipe his brow.

"Damn bad. Worse than we thought," Logan answered gravely as he, too, wiped his grimy sleeve across his forehead to catch the sweat that was dripping into his eyes. It had been nearly sixteen hours since he'd first spied the fire from the meadow with Rhea, and Logan hadn't stopped moving in all that time. He and Miles automatically took on the task of leading the firefighting force of plantation owners, farmers, and slaves who had arrived to help throughout the day and night. And not only had he and Miles directed the men, but they worked elbow-to-elbow with them fighting the hungry flames. For this Logan and his brother put aside their personal conflicts and worked as a determined team against their common enemy—the devastating inferno. They had only one goal: to try to save Fair Oaks and any other lands that might come into the fire's path.

"The wind's shifted somewhat on the north rim," Logan went on now as Miles listened intently. "The widest stretch of flame is headed straight for the timberline just east of the sawmill. If that catches—" His eyes locked with Miles's in wordless understanding.

"So what's your recommendation?" Miles broke in.

"Move as many men as we can up there to the ridge to cut trees and dig trenches for a firebreak." Logan pointed toward the hills to their left. "If the wind shifts again, we may be able to start the backfire we'd planned for down here."

"Right," Miles quickly agreed. "I'll get the men moving here. You head down the line and tell Stokes and Brenner to get their men up there." He let his eyes travel to the blackened sky.

"Can you see anything up there that might help wet all this down?" he asked in a little lighter tone.

"Maybe," Logan answered as he walked quickly back to Baron. "I can't tell if there's really something forming up there or if my imagination sees some clouds because I'm praying so damned hard for it."

Miles nodded, catching his brother's eye again. Logan's words reflected his own thoughts exactly.

Five hours later saw Logan and fifty other men still felling trees at the timberline bordering Fair Oaks land in an effort to create a firebreak that would prevent the flames from spreading to the valuable forestland. It was a long, wide stretch of land stripped of trees and underbrush that hopefully would offer no more fuel for the advancing fire.

Even though it was midday, the thick black smoke blocked out the light so that it seemed like night. The air was barely breathable. The exhausted men worked in somber silence, somehow wielding axes, working two-man crosscut saws, and swinging scythes to take down the trees, brush, and tall grass. Hats were pulled down low to ward off dangerous cinders that rained down from overhead and started small fires all around them. Bandanas covered faces up to the eyes to protect against the pungent, heated air. Teams of horses that were being used to haul away the fallen timber whinnied and shied in fear and were difficult to control.

Logan had stopped brandishing his ax only long enough to direct two men to apply their saw to a big maple tree when Miles came riding up. The heat was tremendous from the main wall of flame only a hundred yards away. Miles dismounted quickly, holding his panicky horse's bridle with a firm hand.

"Logan, you have to get your men and animals out of here!" he shouted above the roar and crackle of the approaching fire. "What's done will have to be enough! We've already pulled out to the west."

Logan glanced down the line of the firebreak. There were at least six more trees he wanted down, but he knew Miles was right. They had to pull back.

"Jergens!" he called to a man working a scythe nearby. "Send word down the line for everyone to evacuate! We can't do any more!"

"Right, Logan!" Jergens acknowledged as he turned away toward two other men working close to him.

"I'll tell the men the other way!" Miles shouted as he grabbed his horse's mane with both hands and tried to remount the terrified, sidestepping roan. Suddenly a dry bush to their right exploded in flame. The roan screamed in fear and managed to twist around and kick Miles full in the chest, sending him sprawling to the ground, where his head struck a protruding rock as he rolled.

Logan dropped his ax and ran to his brother's side. He knelt down and carefully turned Miles over on his back. Miles was conscious but dazed. The right side of his forehead was bleeding profusely from a three-inch gash. Logan quickly pulled off his own bandana and pressed it against the cut.

"Mr. Tremaine, look out!" The warning shout from behind him came at the same moment the cry of "Timber!" reached his ears. Logan's head shot up to see a giant oak crashing down toward him. With pantherlike reflexes he jumped to his feet, grabbed Miles under the arms, and dragged him out of the way just as the huge trunk of the tree smashed into the ground where they'd just been. Logan dragged Miles a little farther until they were clear of the tangled mass of fallen branches, then he knelt beside Miles to catch his breath.

"Damn, but that was close . . ." Miles muttered hoarsely as he pressed his palm against the bandana to try to stop his head from pounding. He staggered as he tried to get to his feet. "I'm surprised you pulled me out."

"I wasn't thinking," Logan replied sarcastically as he, too, got to his feet. Then he pulled Miles's arm across the back of his shoulders to support him. "Come on, let's get the hell out of here.

"Everyone pull back!" he shouted to the men around them. Then with strength he didn't think he had left, Logan half carried his brother into the woods away from the fire.

Chapter 32

AT FAIR OAKS THE WAGONS WERE BEING LOADED with the last of the smaller furnishings the Tremaines wanted to save. Foodstuffs, most of the personal belongings, and many other items had been transferred to the Fitzgerald plantation on earlier loads. Some household packing still remained to be done.

Rhea was exhausted. Since early this morning when Drew had summoned them all to the front parlor, she had been working nonstop. First she and Camille had helped the slave women at the compound load their meager belongings onto several wagons and supervised the evacuation there. Drew had been right; the frightened Negro women and children were running around helter-skelter until Rhea and Camille had arrived to direct them.

The slave quarters were one-story whitewashed wooden dwellings with one or two dirt-floor rooms. They were stark in their plainness and had little else for furnishings beyond a rough-hewn table and chairs and straw-stuffed mattresses, some of which were not even on a bedframe off the ground. On the whole, the ones Rhea entered to help with packing were fairly clean. Camille had told her that the slaves at Fair Oaks were well housed and provided for. Rhea could only wonder at the conditions slaves had to live in on such plantations as Simpson Duvall's.

After that, Rhea and Camille had returned to the main house to help with whatever they could. In the early afternoon Rhea was in the dining room working with Glory and another maid. They were wrapping the silverware in flannel for packing in drawered boxes. Something Glory was saying caught Rhea's attention.

"The white folks is blamin' Mr. Exodus fo' da trouble at Marse Simpson's place, but ah think he got nothin' ta do wid it. It ain't his style."

"It shor' ain't," the other girl, Liddy, agreed.

Rhea was curious. She'd forgotten about the name she'd heard Sybil mention the first night she'd arrived at Fair Oaks.

"Just who is this Mr. Exodus?" she asked now as she carried a teapot over to the table to be packed.

The two Negro women exchanged glances.

"Come, Glory, tell me," Rhea coaxed. She knew from many other conversations with the talkative slave woman that she wouldn't need much persuading. "I've heard him spoken of before in connection with helping slaves escape on the underground railroad."

Glory cautiously glanced toward the hallway door. "We ain't s'posed ta say his name in da house. Ah forgot myself."

"You know I won't tell anyone," Rhea assured her, leaning forward conspiratorially.

Glory could not resist having a chance to tell Rhea about the man she and so many other slaves thought of as their savior. She motioned for Rhea to sit down next to her on the long couch along the wall, then she leaned close and spoke in a low voice, trusting Rhea, whom she knew was from the North.

"Mr. Exodus, he be da one goin' ta lead us outta bondage, jus' like Moses did his people outta Egypt. He were a slave once hisself. 'Scaped to freedom in Canada an' jus' knowed he had ta help others do da same. So he become a conductor on da groun' railroad. He risk his life agin an' agin ta help us colored folk git away a few at a time."

Rhea had heard of the famous underground railroad, made up of people who were so against slavery that they willingly risked life and property to help Negroes escape north to Canada where slavery was forbidden. For more than a decade the network had been in use, with new routes being organized and started all the time. Those who were a part of the underground took on the vestiges of the railroad, using such terminology as depot, conductor, station, and stationmaster to describe the operations and peo-

ple involved. The underground railroad had become an
infuriating thorn in the side of every southern slaveowner.

"But might he have instigated the slaves to revolt at the
Duvall plantation?" Rhea asked.

"No, no," Glory protested, shaking her head. "He don'
do nothin' like dat 'cuz it too dang'rous for the coloreds wid
all da fightin' and shootin' dat sometime go on durin' a
uprisin'. No, ol' Marse Duvall brung dis on all by hisself fo'
treatin' his darkies so poorly."

Just then a loud clap of thunder outside rattled the win-
dowpanes, startling the three women. Rhea quickly led
the way to the window. Huge drops of rain began to pelt
against the glass panes. In a matter of minutes the deluging rain of a severe thunderstorm was drenching the
parched ground outside as lightning flashed and thunder
rumbled across the sky.

"Rhea, oh, Rhea!" Camille called happily as she ran into
the dining room. "Do you see? It's pouring! This will surely
put out the fire!"

The two women hugged each other and laughed with joy.
Rhea saw tears in Camille's eyes, tears of gladness that
Fair Oaks would be saved. After a few minutes of rejoicing,
Camille became serious.

"Oh, my, we must get ready! The men who have been
fighting the fire will be returning. They'll need food, dry
clothing, perhaps medical attention." Her face took on a
worried expression. "And everything's been sent to the
Fitzgeralds'! What shall we do?"

"Now, don't worry, Camille," Rhea told her as they went
out into the hall together. "Not everything's been sent yet,
only the most important items have gone. There is still
food in the kitchenhouse, linens on the beds we can use for
bandages if necessary.

"Oh, Jemson," she called to the old Negro butler as he
came toward them down the hall. He turned to look at
Rhea when she beckoned him. "You'd better send to the
Firtzgerald plantation and have some things brought back
here as quickly as possible," she told him. "Miss Camille
will tell you what we'll need immediately. I'll go find Mrs.
Jerome and have her start the servants preparing food and
setting up the storeroom next to the kitchenhouse for the

men when they arrive. Camille, will you make up a list for Jemson?"

"Yes, Rhea," Camille answered, glad to be told what to do.

Two hours later the first of the exhausted and drenched firefighters began to stagger in through the still-pouring rain. They were met at the door of the storeroom with hot coffee and blankets, and led to the food table laden with breads, cheeses, eggs, sliced meats, and vegetable soup.

It was hard to tell the slaves from the slave owners. All were dirty, coated with mud and smoke. Many were injured—cuts, burns, some broken bones. A young doctor, Evan VanHorn from Richmond, had been tending a patient at a neighboring farm when word of the fire had reached there. He had come to Fair Oaks to offer his services just before the first injured men had arrived.

As Rhea handed out steaming mugs of coffee she wouldn't admit to herself that she was watching for Logan to return, wondering if he was all right. But she felt a surge of relief go through her when she finally saw him stagger into the crowded room helping Miles. She was stunned by how he looked. Wet and filthy, his shirt in shreds, Logan was hardly recognizable. Miles was in no better shape. He had a bloody makeshift bandage tied around his head, and Rhea now noticed blood on Logan, too. His hands were red with it. Blood on Logan's hands—his gifted artist's hands!

Calling to Dr. VanHorn for help, Rhea ran to Logan to lead him to an empty cot. The doctor tended Miles while Rhea cut away Logan's tattered shirtsleeve. She found a nasty burn along the top of his forearm, but no cut. The blood must have been Miles's. Rhea sighed with relief. Logan's hands were not injured.

"Rhea . . ." Logan murmured dazedly as he tried to focus on her. "Miles . . . and Curtis right behind us . . . hurt badly . . . See to them . . ." His voice trailed off as his eyes closed. Rhea was alarmed, fearing he was more seriously hurt someplace she hadn't looked. She checked him over quickly and felt for a pulse at his neck. It was strong and she couldn't see any other injuries on him. He was probably just exhausted from twenty-four hours of battling the blaze.

At Evan VanHorn's direction, Rhea gently cleaned the burn on Logan's arm and applied a salve the doctor gave her. Then she wrapped it in clean strips of torn sheeting and bathed Logan's dirt-and-sweat-streaked face and neck.

Relaxed in deep sleep, Logan's stern expression was gone. The cool light blue eyes were hidden now. He was still very handsome, perhaps more so than Rhea ever had seen before because now a kind of vulnerability came through, something he never allowed to show when he was awake.

Looking at him now, Rhea remembered then their love-making at Farley House and both times in the meadow. The touch of Logan's lips and hands had caused such a strange and yet wonderful thing to happen in her. His intimate possession of her awakened a longing like no other man had ever been able to do. It confused and worried Rhea. She was feeling some shame for what had happened between them, but not as much as she should have. Am I becoming a woman of loose virtue? Rhea wondered in her troubled thoughts. No, she told herself firmly she wasn't. For some reason her strong willpower had betrayed her temporarily, but she was in control again now and would continue to be.

Rhea watched Logan sleep for a few moments longer, deep in thought. She didn't care anything about him, she told herself. She'd only been worried about his return and injuries because her future depended on his being able to keep his part of their bargain, that was all. Someday she would choose the man to whom she would surrender herself, and it would not be to a man like Logan Tremaine!

Chapter 33

THE TOLL IN LIVES AND PROPERTY FROM THE
slave uprising and fire was extensive. Ten slaves escaped
in the confusion, but Simpson Duvall had the revolt under
control even before Logan had first arrived. Duvall lost
half of his house, livestock, and five hundred acres of
prime cropland to the hungry flames. The three slaves who
were the instigators of the uprising were quickly caught
and shot as examples to discourage others from doing like-
wise. Forty more slaves died, mostly helpless women and
children who were trapped by the flames in the run-down,
wooden buildings that housed them. How horrible, Rhea
thought sadly as the story was related to her by Evan Van-
Horn later that night.

They had finished bandaging most of the injured who
had arrived at the makeshift infirmary throughout the
day. Some who weren't hurt and still had the energy to do
so went on to their own homes on neighboring plantations.
Slaves followed their masters doggedly. They were too
weary to even think of doing otherwise.

"Duvall's plantation is nothing like Fair Oaks," Evan
VanHorn told Rhea as she finished helping him tend a
man with a broken arm. "The Tremaines are wealthy and
it has always been a matter of Christian charity and long-
standing family pride for them to treat their slaves well.
Unfortunately, such is not the situation on many plantations, especially in these poor economic times."

While Mr. Exodus was not seen by anyone throughout
the ordeal of the revolt and fire, he was nonetheless adamantly accused of perpetrating the whole thing by the
plantation owners present at Fair Oaks. The reward for

his capture was raised to a tempting ten thousand dollars. Rhea recalled Glory's words in the dining room and Camille's explanation, and she wondered whether they were true and the landowners were just seeking a scapegoat to cover their own guilt in causing the Negroes to revolt.

Police Captain Ross Talmadge arrived from Richmond that night after stopping at Simpson Duvall's first. He eyed Rhea appraisingly when Evan VanHorn introduced her to him and Rhea instantly disliked him. His brown eyes held no warmth, nor did his smile.

"Why don't you go up to the main house and get some rest now, Mrs. Tremaine," Evan said to Rhea in a low voice after Talmadge had walked away to talk to Miles and Logan, who were both now awake. "There's nothing more you can do here. You look exhausted. Thank you for your help."

"I'm glad I could do something," Rhea told him in reply. "But I think I shall do as you suggest, doctor. I am feeling fatigued." It seemed like she'd been on her feet forever. She could barely keep her eyes open.

"We appreciate having you here, Dr. VanHorn," she added, smiling at him. He was about her age and rather handsome, in a boyish kind of way. He seemed to be quiet, competent, and very serious about his work. His eyes were kind and Rhea was glad she'd been able to help him.

"Will you be staying the night?" she asked then. "I'm certain you could use the rest also."

"Yes, I've already claimed a cot over there in the corner," he replied. "I prefer to stay here in case anyone else shows up needing attention."

"All right. I'll come back in the morning to see how things are. Good night," Rhea said. Then she made her way to the back door of the storeroom. She quickly glanced over to where Logan and Miles were deep in conversation with Captain Talmadge. Logan likely didn't even remember that she was there and had tended him. He'd made no effort to seek her out when he'd awakened, and Rhea had avoided him, too. Sighing wearily, Rhea told herself she didn't really care as she walked out into the summer night. The rain had stopped, but she had to pick her way carefully around the mud and puddles to make her way to the main house.

* * *

Though exhausted, Rhea slept fitfully that night. Now that her thoughts were no longer occupied with the crisis of the fire, her mind forced her to focus on her situation here at Fair Oaks. As she lay awake in her wide bed she thought again about the unusual bargain she had entered into with Logan. It had had clearly defined stipulations, a very critical one which had now been violated—that their relationship would be kept strictly business. Rhea realized with trepidation that she could not blame Logan entirely for that. She had been mysteriously drawn to him, had surrendered her body with little protest. Try as she might, Rhea could not deny that. And now she was in danger, the terrible danger that it might happen again between them if she stayed here at Fair Oaks. And a child might be conceived, if that hadn't already happened. That thought depressed Rhea. What should she do next? If she were pregnant, she should leave here as soon as possible, before Logan knew of it and forced her to stay and give him the child.

Why did she have such trouble with men? Rhea wondered wearily. Painful memories of Philip Winslow tormented her still. She had loved him so . . . No, not loved. She realized now that she had never really loved Philip. Admired, yes. Perhaps she had even idolized him. He'd been so charming and devoted, so sure of himself, so sure of her. He had played her along so expertly. What a fool she'd been.

How she had hated Philip afterward. She never wanted to be used like that by a man again. Now that her bargain with Logan Tremaine had gone beyond a strictly business venture, Rhea saw leaving Fair Oaks as the only solution, even if it meant facing a very bleak future without the money Logan had been going to pay her. She would have to plan carefully, so no suspicions would be raised. She'd try to stay away from Logan whenever possible until she could leave. But when that was unavoidable, she'd be calm and collected, matching Logan's aloof indifference with her own. No more would she allow any intimacy between them.

With these decisions made, Rhea was able to fall into a restless slumber for the rest of the night.

Chapter 34

RHEA AWOKE EARLY THE NEXT MORNING. SHE knew there would be much to do today. Everything they had packed and sent to the Fitzgerald plantation would be returning to be unpacked. And she had promised Dr. Van-Horn that she would come to the infirmary this morning.

Rhea washed and dressed quickly. While she was brushing her hair she heard movements coming from the sitting room. Why did her pulse quicken at the thought that Logan might be just on the other side of the door?

"Ridiculous," Rhea chided herself in a low voice. Seeing him would mean nothing to her. She was only feeling nervous because of her plan to try to get away from Fair Oaks, and she'd prove it to herself now!

Setting her chin determinedly, Rhea took a quick look at her reflection in the mirror, then walked to the door leading to the adjoining sitting room and opened it.

"Good morning," she greeted in a formal tone as Logan turned toward her. He was dressed in buff-colored riding breeches, loose-fitting white shirt, and tan leather vest and riding boots. He still looked tired. Dark circles showed under his eyes as they appraised her coolly. The fast pace of Rhea's pulse did not lessen as she'd hoped it would. In fact, a disturbing fluttering in her stomach was added.

"Good morning, Rhea," Logan greeted in an equally punctilious voice.

"Are you going on a journey again?" Rhea managed to ask. She averted her eyes and walked to the Duncan Phyfe table in the middle of the sitting room, pretending to be interested in some of the blossoms in the large vase of flow-

170

ers that had been set there. She began to pick out the wilted blossoms in the two-day-old arrangement.

"Yes, to Williamsburg to meet with the Tobacco Exchange directors," Logan answered as he finished buttoning his vestfront. "I shall be gone two or three days. I should stay and assist with all that needs to be done here at the house, but this meeting was set weeks ago and it is most important that I attend."

"I see," Rhea commented with pretended disinterest. Well, he had told her from the beginning that he traveled often, she reminded herself now. It was just as well. The less time he was around, the less chance there would be that anything could happen again between them.

"I wish to thank you for seeing to my arm yesterday," Logan said then, though his cool tone did not change.

"You are welcome. The dressing should be changed often and the salve applied to prevent infection and aid in healing. If you wish, I could do it for you this morning." Now why had she said that? Rhea wondered as she forced herself to look at him.

"You need not concern yourself. Obediah took care of it earlier, and I assure you I am quite capable of seeing to it myself on my journey."

Rhea started to open her mouth to quickly say that she had not meant to imply otherwise, but Logan cut her off.

"Now if you'll excuse me," he said abruptly as he turned toward the hall door. "I must be on my way. Good day."

Rhea sat down in the armchair nearest her.

"Good day indeed," she murmured with annoyance as she glanced toward the door Logan had just exited by. "It will be just fine now that you won't be around, Logan Tremaine," she added. "And see if I bother to ask you about your arm again!"

Rhea waited a few minutes to be certain Logan had a chance to leave the house, then she decided to go downstairs for some breakfast before plunging into the day's activities. As she descended the stairs to the entrance hall she saw no one. But the sliding double doors leading to the front parlor were open a little and she could hear voices from within as she passed. She would have walked on by to the dining room had not Logan's voice coming from the parlor caught her attention.

"Now what was it you wanted to discuss?" she heard him saying.

"Must you leave so soon again, Logan?" a female voice asked in a pouting tone. Sybil's voice. She must have returned from Richmond sometime last night.

Rhea drew closer to the doors and peered through the narrow opening. She could see Miles's wife and Logan standing very near to each other. Sybil was fingering the collar of Logan's riding shirt.

"We have hardly seen each other as we used to since you returned from up north. And I missed everything that happened at Simpson's and the fire and all. Couldn't you find some time to tell me all the exciting things that took place? Miles told me how you helped him," she added, moving a step closer so that her body touched Logan's. "I am very grateful—"

Rhea couldn't stand to see or hear more. Sybil, too? Logan and his brother's wife? She wouldn't put it past him! She whirled around in anger and disgust and ran toward the dining room before she could hear Logan's reply.

"You should be with your husband now, Sybil," Logan said with a note of contempt in his voice as he drew Sybil's hand away and stepped back from her. "He was also there and can give you all the details. I have more important business to attend to." With that Logan turned away and left the parlor and his glowering sister-in-law.

Chapter 35

"DOES THAT LOOK STRAIGHT, RHEA?" CAMILLE asked as she stood back from her portrait.

Rhea looked up from the trunk of gowns she was helping Camille unpack. "Yes, it's fine," she said as she paused to look again at the beautiful painting of Camille. She still found it hard to believe Logan was the artist who had done it.

"Thank you, Bo. That will be all," Camille was saying to the servant who was perched on the ladder rehanging the portrait. Then she turned back to help Rhea as he left the room.

"Whew, all this work unpacking what we just packed two days ago. But I am so glad to still have a place to put everything. I just shudder when I think how close that terrible fire came to Fair Oaks." She looked up at Rhea, whose attention was still drawn to the painting.

"I declare, Rhea, but you're acting rather peculiar this afternoon. I don't think you've heard a word I've said."

"What?" Rhea blinked and forced her attention back to Camille. "Oh, I'm sorry, I didn't mean to be rude. What were you saying?"

"It wasn't important," Camille answered with an indulgent smile. Then she became serious as she looked at Rhea. "But you have been strangely quiet. Is anything wrong?"

"Wrong? Whatever could be wrong?" Rhea replied quickly, averting her eyes and busying herself shaking out the wrinkles from a yellow satin gown.

"Is everything all right between you and Logan?" Camille asked suddenly. "I saw him ride out alone again this morning. He travels so much. I'd hoped that when he brought you here as his wife he would stay closer to home. Being apart can put a strain on any relationship. Have you two had a lovers' quarrel or something?"

The concern in Camille's blue eyes touched Rhea. But how could she tell her sweet friend that she was disturbed by the scene she'd overheard between Logan and Sybil, and so many other things, too. She couldn't explain it to herself, let alone to Logan's sister . . .

"How easily you read me, Camille," she said finally, deciding to let Camille think she had guessed the problem.

"Well, don't be too concerned about it, Rhea," Camille tried to persuade her. "By the time my brother returns, both of you likely will have forgotten what the disagreement was all about, and you can have a marvelous time making up!" She smiled mischievously and Rhea couldn't resist smiling, too. Camille was so kind and trusting, always looking on the bright side of everything. Rhea found herself wishing she could be more like her friend.

"Please be patient with that big brother of mine," Camille was continuing. The smile slipped from her lips and her voice dropped a little as she stared ahead, apparently thinking about something. "He has not had a happy life. A long time ago I think he decided to raise a protective wall around his heart so he could not be hurt again."

"Would you tell me more of this, Camille?" Rhea asked gently. "I wish to understand Logan better, but it is not easy."

"All right, Rhea," Camille agreed. "If you think it will help, but you must never tell Logan I told you these things."

"I won't," Rhea assured her.

Camille sat down on the edge of the bed and gestured for Rhea to sit beside her.

"Our parents did not love each other. Their marriage was arranged for them. As the story goes from what I've learned from the servants over the years, Grandfather Silas declared that Papa would marry Estelle Fremont, the only daughter of a naval officer friend of his. Papa was not a strong man in personality and Grandfather's word was never questioned. So Papa and Mama were married. But no love ever grew between them. They managed to conceive four children, but it was out of duty that they did it, to please Grandfather in his requirements for Tremaine heirs."

Camille's voice trailed off. She sighed deeply and a sadness showed in her face.

"You do not have to continue, Camille," Rhea told her quickly, her heart going out to her friend.

"No, it's all right. I can speak of it now that I understand. And I've forgiven them—Mama and Papa and Grandfather, too. I did not understand when I was a child. I think Mama loved us the best she could, but she never knew love herself, so how could she show it to us? As the years went on and we grew up, Papa found many women to love—well, I suppose he loved them. But Mama never found anyone that I know of. She became a bitter woman who wanted to hurt people the way she'd been hurt, I think.

"I've always been grateful that I've had Esta and Romey and Dora to love me and take care of me because I've always had poor health. I didn't miss my parents' love and attention so much. Drew was so young when our parents were lost at sea that he never knew very much about how they were, either.

"But such was not the case with Miles and Logan. Miles had Grandfather. He was always Grandfather's favorite, the firstborn male Tremaine heir. And Miles was always at Grandfather's beck and call, doing as he was told, never disobeying. In many ways he is still that way.

"But that was not true with Logan. His spirit was the stubborn and defiant one. He always had to do things his way, no matter what Papa or Grandfather told him to do. I could not begin to count all the times Papa took a strap to him, and Grandfather, too. I remember when we were children I used to cry and beg Logan to obey them so he would not be beaten again. For a while he would do their bidding, just for my sake, I know. But it would never last. Grandfather in particular would constantly rant and rave at Logan, meting out discipline with a heavy hand. Logan could never please him, even on the few occasions when he tried.

"When Logan was twelve years old, he could no longer endure the treatment they gave him. He ran away from Fair Oaks. Papa and Grandfather went out with a dozen men and hunted him for two days. I remember how terribly worried I was about him. But I have often wished since that they had never found him, that he could have gotten away to a city somewhere and made a new life for himself, been taken in by some kindly family or something . . ." Camille's voice broke off and she looked down at her hands in her lap. It was a few moments before she went on.

"But they did find him. He was dragged back here. All the field slaves and house servants were called out to the front yard, and Logan was beaten and humiliated before them. I remember the look on Logan's face. He set his jaw and never cried out once, not even when the whip drew blood on his back.

"Something died in Logan that day. I never again heard him crying in the night. Neither did he argue nor laugh. He just existed, not showing anger or happiness, except perhaps with me. I could always make him smile.

"They broke his spirit, Rhea . . ." Camille went on with tears in her eyes. "After that he kept everything inside, would not let himself feel." She glanced up at the painting on the wall. "Except in his paintings. In those he shows the caring and kind heart I know is still inside him, though it's deeply hidden away and protected.

"Oh, Rhea," Camille pleaded, suddenly turning back to Rhea and taking hold of her hands, "you must help Logan to feel again, to learn to love. Be patient with him, give him your love, so you will both know happiness."

Rhea couldn't say anything. Her throat was tight with emotion, thinking of the unloved boy-child who had grown to be a cold and cynical man. How could she tell dear Camille she was not the one to teach Logan about loving and caring? She knew well about those things, for she had had them amply when she was a child. Her parents had loved her dearly. But she could never give them to Logan. He could not be changed for she doubted that he wanted to change. The die of the man had been cast in childhood. It was too well set, wasn't it? It would take too much time, too much love, and Rhea had neither to give him.

"I hope you can succeed, Rhea," Camille was going on, "for I wonder if the Tremaine men are destined for unhappiness. Miles and Sybil care little for each other now, I think. Oh, they did when they were first married. I remember how they would look at each other in that wonderful way people in love do. But the last few years I've not seen that look pass between them. Is that what happens with married people, Rhea?" She turned a questioning look at her friend.

"I don't know, Camille. I suppose it does once the newness and excitement of first love passes. You get in the routine of married life, day after day with the same person. It would take a tremendous love to keep that first spark alive. I think, though, that love changes with the years and can become even better than that fiery beginning love. My parents were deeply in love. They had that look between them that you spoke about. My mother is still in love with my father even though he's been dead several years."

"Oh, I'm sorry, Rhea. I didn't mean to bring up hurtful memories."

Rhea smiled. "They are happy memories, Camille. Do not be sorry."

"I have never been in love yet," Camille went on with a sigh, "but I know it will come someday. And when it does, when I find the man to whom I shall give my heart, I shall love him always and try with all my might to make him happy."

Dear Camille, Rhea thought. So sweet, gentle, unselfish.

"I wonder if Grandfather was ever in love," Camille speculated. "Grandmother Patricia was a beautiful woman. There used to be a portrait of the two of them, done when they were very young. It was in the music room but was taken down years ago for some reason. I wonder if they were truly in love when they married? Esta told me the story once.

"Grandfather was an officer in the Navy and was often gone away at sea for many months at a time. Grandmother was lonely. She had my father, Edward, but no other children were ever born to them, and she had wanted many. Once while Grandfather was away she met a man named Steven Thorndyke. He was a cousin of a close friend of Grandmother's. They fell in love. Esta was just a young girl then, but she told me she remembered well the long talks she and Grandmother had over the dilemma. Patricia loved Grandfather Silas but she loved Steven in a far different way.

"When Grandfather returned from sea, she asked him to forgive her but she was in love with Steven and wanted to be freed from their marriage to go with him. Grandfather refused to set her free. Steven left the country, for France, I think. Grandmother never saw him again for she died the next winter, supposedly of a fever. But Esta says it was from a broken heart over the love she lost.

"I've often wondered if that was why Grandfather was such an unhappy and embittered man. He never remarried."

"How sad . . ." Rhea murmured, thinking about all Camille had said.

"Well, however did I get off on all that?" Camille exclaimed, suddenly brightening. "Now you know about some of the skeletons in our closets, Rhea. Be warned!"

"I shall, Camille," Rhea told her thoughtfully. "I shall."

Chapter 36

FOR THE NEXT TWO DAYS EVERYONE AT FAIR Oaks was kept very busy putting the household back in order. Sybil made everyone's life unpleasant with her impatience and bossiness, and Rhea, in particular, tried to steer clear of her.

Logan returned on the third day, but he seemed to make himself scarce. Rhea saw him only at meals and a few times in passing in the house. They spoke to each other with only formal politeness and were never alone. Rhea told herself she was glad of it. She thought more and more about getting away from Fair Oaks, but as yet had not devised a plan for a successful escape. She couldn't just leave with no destination and no money.

As if these troubling thoughts were not enough, Rhea could not forget Camille's stories about the Tremaine family, and especially Logan's childhood. Knowing about it only complicated her thinking toward him and made her feel more confused.

"Oh, good, you're ready," Camille remarked with a note of excitement as she approached Rhea in the upstairs hallway one morning. She was smiling as she pulled on short white gloves that matched the ribbon trim on her pink day dress. "It's been quite a while since I've been to Richmond shopping." She gave a schoolgirl-like giggle and grinned mischievously as she added, "We must find a way to get rid of Logan and Drew and sneak off to the shops by ourselves. If we can figure a way to escape from Sybil, too, we can really have fun!"

"There is a streak of devilry in you, Camille Tremaine," Rhea remarked, trying to look reproachful without much success. She had to admit to some excitement herself over the excursion planned for the day—a trip to the city to buy clothes for the Fourth of July ball and festivities. Rhea had had a taste of unbridled buying in Philadelphia with Logan and she was not averse to doing it again.

Drew quickly took his leave of them as soon as they reached Richmond, and Camille was soon able to cajole Logan into letting them shop in several stores that were close together on a main street while he attended to some business with the family barristers.

"Now's our chance!" Camille whispered to Rhea impishly as they waited for Sybil to try on a gown.

"Chance for what?"

"To get away before Sybil comes out. Come on!" Camille struggled to hide a grin as she motioned for Rhea to follow her toward a display of plumed riding hats near the front door. For a few moments they pretended to admire a maroon velvet one with a curled white feather, then they casually slipped out the door.

"There," Camille said quickly, pointing across the street. "Let's hide in that bakery shop!"

"Oh, it's perfect!" Camille exclaimed an hour later as Rhea parted the curtains of the dressing room of the fashionable store they'd found. "It looks divine on you."

The gown with its many layers of dark blue chiffon fabric seemed to float around Rhea as she twirled to show Camille the back.

"Do you think the décolletage is too low-cut?" Rhea asked doubtfully as she turned to face Camille again.

"Scandalously so," Camille answered delightedly, noting the deep vee cut of the neckline edged in delicate scallops of blue lace. "But it is perfect for you. If I had your wonderful figure I would get one just like it for myself, so I could have some of the men looking at me, too. Logan will find you quite tempting in that, I am sure."

Rhea looked away uncomfortably. That was exactly what she *didn't* want. But the gown was so beautiful.

"However do you breathe with your corset pulled so tightly?" Camille went on, noticing the thinness of Rhea's waist where the wide blue satin sash was tied.

"I have no corset on," Rhea whispered, leaning closer to

Camille and speaking behind her head. "I can't abide one in this heat."

"Then I truly hate you for your figure," Camille teased, even though her own small waist rivaled Rhea's.

Rhea laughed, flattered by her friend's comments.

"You think I should get this one, then?" she asked hesitantly. "It's terribly expensive."

"Of course, you must buy it," Camille replied emphatically. "And the long blue lace gloves, the fan, and satin dancing shoes to match. And you must have Logan give you Grandmother Patricia's sapphires to wear with it.

"Madam Beaumont." Turning then, she addressed the proprietress of the dress shop who had been standing close by. "Charge these things and the green gown I had on before to our family account. Can you make the necessary alterations and have everything delivered to Fair Oaks by next week?"

"Yes, Miss Tremaine, whatever you wish," the older woman answered, nodding with pleasure at such an easy sale.

Rhea gave Camille a quick hug of thanks before she returned to the fitting room to have the beautiful blue gown measured for the slightly shorter length she needed. At the moment she wasn't even certain that she'd still be at Fair Oaks for the Fourth of July weekend. She would leave before then if she had a chance, but she had to pretend otherwise for now.

As Rhea gazed in the large, full-length mirror a sudden thought came unbidden to her mind, and she found herself wondering if Logan would indeed approve of her choice in the gown. But what surprised her even more was the realization that she *wanted* him to approve and perhaps even find her appealing. What in the world had come over her?

Later in the day, Rhea and Camille were forced to rejoin Sybil, Logan, and Drew. As they sat in the carriage and pretended to be sorry for venturing off on their own Rhea knew Camille felt as little regret as she did. They'd had a wonderful afternoon together, and Rhea felt a special camaraderie with Camille that she had not found with another person in a long time. Camille looked tired as she juggled a hatbox on her lap, but the sideways glance she cast at Rhea still held the mischievous gleam she'd had earlier.

Rhea avoided Logan's displeased look as the open carriage lurched slowly through the crowded streets of Richmond. Near the slave market an auction was in progress. Logan spotted some men he knew and ordered the carriage to stop. He and Drew got out and went to stand with two men who were among the bidders. The four of them were soon deep in conversation.

Rhea watched with curiosity at first. She'd never experienced anything like this before. In Philadelphia she'd heard about slave auctions where Negroes were bought and sold by their masters, but she hadn't been able to believe the accounts. Yet now as she watched with growing dismay, Rhea found that those descriptions had not been exaggerated.

Over to one side next to the raised auction platform, Negro men, women, and children were being examined like so many cattle. Some were stripped naked and forced to stand and endure having their bodies and even their teeth looked at, felt, and prodded by potential buyers. How heartless and humiliating, Rhea thought, appalled.

"Oh, how can they do that? It's so cruel. Isn't there something we can do?" she asked woefully, looking at Logan who had returned with Drew to the carriage.

Drew answered her, "You obviously don't know much about Negroes, Rhea. They are fit only for manual labor, like animals. They do not think or feel as we do, any more than does a horse or a mule compared to us."

Rhea was stunned to speechlessness. Did they truly believe that? These so-called civilized and genteel southerners?

Only Camille seemed to be touched by the tragic scene, though she said nothing and averted her eyes to avoid meeting Rhea's. Logan smoldered as Rhea looked at him in anger and dismay.

"It is the way of things and no concern of yours," he snapped gruffly. Then he turned away from her. Rhea couldn't see that his jaw had tightened into a hard line and one hand, out of sight at his side, had clenched into a knuckle-whitening fist.

He is just like all the rest of these horrible people, Rhea

thought angrily, preying heartlessly on other human beings, be they those of another race or even those caught up in circumstances beyond their control, like herself.

At that moment Rhea came to a decision. She regretted not having paid more attention to the abolitionists' exposés on slavery. If she had, she wouldn't be in this terrible situation now, for she never would have accepted Logan's offer to come to the South. But she was here, at least for a time, and there must be something she could do. Somehow, in some way, she could help these poor Negro people. Others were doing things. Northern abolitionists, southern Quakers, ex-slaves who had gained their freedom, like this so-called Mr. Exodus. Perhaps she could get in contact with Exodus somehow and find out what she could do to help. Here was something worthwhile for her to do. Perhaps now she could endure her six-month sentence as a Tremaine wife, especially if she and Logan avoided each other the way they had been the last few days . . .

Yes, she would have to act cautiously, but act she *must*.

Chapter 37

"WHAT ARE YOU DOING, CALEB?" RHEA ASKED as she came down the hall and saw the slave boy peering in a partially opened door. Caleb quickly bent down farther and began dusting the baseboard woodwork with the cloth in his hand.

"Caleb?" Rhea stopped beside him.

"Mornin', Miz Rhea," Caleb replied nervously as he continued to polish the wood with great vigor.

Rhea glanced into the room.

"Caleb, were you listening to Master Tyler's school lessons with Mr. Bush?" she asked in a low voice as she squatted down next to him.

Caleb stopped his work and looked down at the floor sheepishly as he nodded.

"I see," she said as she stood, drawing the boy up with her. "Do you want to learn some things, too, Caleb?"

"Oh, yes'm," the boy answered eagerly, looking up at her.

"Is there no one to teach you?"

The Negro boy lowered his eyes again. "No, Miz Rhea. It ain't allowed."

Rhea was thoughtful for a moment. She remembered her resolve of the other day to help the slaves if she could. This was a small thing, but important nonetheless.

"Would you like me to teach you, Caleb?" she asked then.

"Would yo', Miz Rhea?" Eagerness showed in his dark eyes. Then his face fell and disappointment sounded in his voice. "Marse Miles wouldn't like it none if yo' was ta do it."

"Then we won't tell him." Rhea had lowered her voice and smiled. "It can be our secret. You finish your work here, then come to my room this afternoon if you can. Just for a little while so you won't be missed. We'll get started on your ABC's today."

Caleb's face lit up with excitement.

"Yes, Miz Rhea, ah'll shor' nuff be there!"

Rhea smiled again and continued walking down the hallway, feeling a little excitement herself. Even though she enjoyed the many hours she spent doing decorative needlework, especially when she did so with Camille, she'd grown a little tired of it. This would give her something new to do. She had enjoyed the idleness, the lack of responsibility of the first few weeks at Fair Oaks for she had worked long, hard hours at the millinery shop for over a year. But the long daytime hours seemed to weigh heavily on her hands now. Here was something worth doing— teaching a child, opening up to him a whole new world. Perhaps what she could teach Caleb would help him better his life someday.

Caleb managed to spend some time with Rhea for the next three days. He was eager to learn and caught onto things quickly. It did not take Rhea long to become attached to the engaging six-year-old. But their secret was not long kept. Just after everyone had gathered for luncheon one afternoon, Tyler happily exposed them.

"Aunt Rhea's been doing letters and writing with Caleb," he announced triumphantly as soon as they had begun to eat.

Rhea cast him a withering look but said nothing, hoping his remark would be ignored as were most of the things he said. But such would not be the case this time. Miles cocked a brow and looked at her questioningly.

"Is this true, Rhea?"

Rhea had to force herself not to squirm in her seat under his scrutinizing look. "Well, we've just started and we only do it after Caleb finishes his chores." She was talking too fast. Rhea forced herself to be calm, although she resented being put on the spot like this. She didn't dare look at Logan.

"Such activity is strictly forbidden in this household,"

Miles stated sternly, and the tension fairly crackled in the room. "Education is only for the white upper class such as ourselves. Negroes have no capacity for it. There are even laws against it. It can be only damaging to them, making them discontent with their position in life.

"Really, Logan," he continued contemptuously, turning to his brother sitting across the table from him, "you should instruct this northern wife of yours in our customs and practices. If it is beyond your handling, I could undertake the task in your place."

Everything stopped. Rhea glanced sideways at Logan. His eyes had turned to ice as he locked gazes with his older brother. She saw his jaw tense into a hard line but otherwise he showed no other sign of being angered by his brother's cutting words. With deliberate slowness Logan reached for his wine goblet and took a sip from it.

"My wife is my business, Miles," he responded finally with a forced casualness, "and I most certainly do not need any interference or assistance from you regarding her. I should think you would have your hands full controlling your own wife." Logan looked pointedly at Sybil, who gasped in surprise and visibly paled.

"Besides," Logan went on then, looking back at his scowling brother, "I gave Rhea permission to teach Caleb."

Now it was Rhea's turn to be surprised. Logan lying to defend her? She couldn't believe it.

"In view of his parentage," Logan continued with cutting sarcasm, eyeing Miles coldly, "he deserves a better lot in life. Since you refuse to exercise your responsibility in that regard, I am seeing to it."

Rhea's jaw dropped open in shock at the implication of Logan's words. She looked from Logan to Miles, who was obviously struggling to control his anger.

"Caleb is a bright youngster," Logan observed, assuming his usual unreadable expression again as he began cutting his meat. "We've all seen that. If Rhea finds it amusing to teach him a few things, I see no harm in it. It will keep her occupied as well."

Rhea frowned. The nastiness in his tone was directed at her as well as his brother. She should have known he would take her side only if he could somehow use it as an advantage to oppose Miles. Logan cared nothing for Caleb or anyone else except as a means for getting at his brother.

"I will see to Caleb," Miles said sharply. "Occupy your wife some other way."

"If you insist," Logan acquiesced, but no one missed the slight smile of triumph that curled one corner of his mouth.

Somehow they had managed to finish lunch without any further conflicts. But the anger and bitterness hung in the air all through it. Rhea was realizing that such unpleasant scenes were commonplace in this family, especially between the two brothers who so hated each other.

Logan followed Rhea afterward when she went upstairs.

"You will consult me before you take anything upon yourself such as this situation with Caleb," he stated with annoyance when they reached the privacy of their sitting room. "Do you recall that you are *not* to be causing any commotion while you are here?"

"Yes, I know that," Rhea replied calmly, though she dreaded having this confrontation with him. "I didn't bother to mention Caleb to you because I saw no harm in it. The child has such a longing to learn, it is terrible to deny it to him."

"That is not a decision for you to make," Logan told her sternly.

"Who are Caleb's parents?" Rhea changed the subject suddenly. She had to know whether what was insinuated downstairs was true or not.

Logan looked at her, his light blue eyes coolly appraising.

"Is Miles his father?" Rhea added quickly, still finding such a fact unbelievable, though she recalled now that Caleb's skin was much lighter than most of the Negroes she'd seen.

"That was rather obvious from the comments downstairs, wasn't it?" Logan remarked offhandedly, as he looked through a stack of books on the end table.

"But he treats Caleb so badly, like he's a thing of little consequence."

"Miles allows him the run of the house and to be a playmate to Tyler. Most masters sell off such embarrassing evi-

dence of their visits to the slave quarters. It's most likely
Sybil's doing, of course. She enjoys keeping Caleb around
so she can use him to spite Miles and remind him of his
baser weaknesses."

"Is this a common practice among slaveowners?" Rhea
asked pointedly, unable to hide her disgust.

"A slave does a master's bidding no matter what it may
be. Many colored wenches deem it a privilege to be so favored by the master." His tone showed no embarrassment.
He straightened up, evidently satisfied by Rhea's reading
tastes.

"And how many half-breed children do you have running around here?" Rhea demanded bluntly before she
could stop herself. Her tone was scornful. Her gaze locked
with Logan's, but he didn't seem to be at all disturbed by
her question.

"I owe you no answer to such a presumptuous and
unpropitious question," he answered with cool disdain,
"for it is none of your business." And with that he turned
and left the room.

Chapter 38

"GLORY," RHEA ADDRESSED HER MAID A LITTLE while later, "do you know where Caleb is?" She hated to face the child with the news she had to tell him. They'd hardly had a chance to get started with his lessons and already they had to stop. Rhea knew he would be very disappointed. She wasn't happy about it herself. Her dislike of these Tremaines was growing by monumental proportions. Camille was the only one of them worth knowing, Rhea decided. Thank goodness for Camille.

"Miz Jerome done sent him ta da compound ta fetch some women fo' some chores," Glory answered as she helped Rhea into her maroon riding ensemble.

"Well, I must speak with him. I'll go by the compound on my ride, but I may miss him. If you see him later, tell him I want to talk to him this evening."

"Yes, Miz Rhea," Glory replied, handing her her kid riding gloves.

"Glory," Rhea said suddenly then in a lower voice, "I want to ask you something. You must promise to give me a truthful answer and never mention that we spoke of this. Is that clear?"

"Yes, Miz Rhea," Glory agreed, her ears perking up with interest.

Rhea led her over to the yellow and beige brocade divan and sat the slave woman down beside her.

"Now promise, Glory. I want your sacred word."

"Oh, yes'm. Yo' has mah word," Glory vowed solemnly.

Rhea knew Glory tended to stretch the facts when it suited her, so she couldn't be certain her answer would be the truth. But for some reason Rhea felt compelled to ask her anyway. She had to know and this was one thing she couldn't ask Camille about.

"All right, Glory, I have to trust you." Rhea paused for a moment, searching for the right way to word her question. But there was no other way than to ask it outright, she decided. She looked the Negro woman straight in the eye.

"Glory, you know everything that goes on in this family. I found out today that Caleb is Mr. Miles's son. Now tell me the truth. Does Mr. Logan have any slave women he—I mean, does he have any children like Caleb here on the plantation?"

Glory looked relieved that her mistress was asking her something that was easy to answer.

"Oh, now don' yo' worry none, Miz Rhea," she replied, grinning widely. "Ah ain't never heard tell o' Mr. Logan havin' a nigger woman, tho' dey's some what wouldn't mind if'n he did come 'round. But he have plenty o' white ladies he kin have whenever he want. 'Course that were afore he done met yo', ma'am, and brung yo' to Fair Oaks," she added quickly. "Ah don' reckon he look at none o' dem others no mo' now dat he gots yo'all."

Rhea felt relieved for some reason, hoping she could believe Glory, though she told herself she shouldn't even care one way or the other. As Logan had so emphatically pointed out, it wasn't any of her business. And what was worse, it really wasn't very pleasant hearing he had many white women who no doubt serviced him, especially when she knew she was one of them.

Rhea and the Negro groom who usually accompanied her rode toward the slave quarters. Although she remembered Logan had told her expressly not to go there, she had a legitimate reason for going, to talk to Caleb. She'd find him quickly, tell him they couldn't have his lessons anymore, and leave before anyone even noticed she'd been there. She didn't want Caleb to hear the bad news from someone else.

As Rhea entered the slave yard of the main cabin area she immediately heard some commotion and saw a horrible sight. A slave girl of about seventeen was tied to a post in the center of the yard. She was being whipped by Dreed Jessup, who seemed to be enjoying this terrible task immensely. Her coarse cotton blouse had been ripped open down the back and hung in shreds around her waist, leaving most of her upper body and ample breasts exposed. With slow and deliberate precision the overseer wielded the flesh-tearing leather whip across the girl's back, leaving large raised red welts, some of which were already bleeding. The girl screamed and sobbed, begging him to stop. But he only smiled and drew his arm back to strike her with the whip again.

Rhea pulled up Jade Wind sharply and jumped to the ground.

"Stop, Mr. Jessup! Stop this!" she shouted as she ran toward the overseer.

Jessup was so intent on his task that he didn't see or hear Rhea until she grabbed hold of his arm as it swung back to strike again. He whirled around in rage, ready to lash out with the whip at whoever had dared to try to stop him. Rhea stood before him defiantly, gaining courage from her own fury. It was then she noticed the deep scratch marks on the side of his face.

"Jessup! Stop this at once! I order you to cease this horrible whipping!"

For long moments the scene hung suspended. No one moved or spoke. The group of slaves who had been gathered to watch the punishment seemed to hold its breath now. Jessup's half-crazed look disappeared, replaced by an ugly, rage-filled one. But somehow he managed to control his fury. Lowering his arm, he began to wind the whip into a coil in his hand, his cold black eyes never leaving Rhea. Then without a word, he turned and left the yard.

"You there, help me get her down," Rhea ordered two slave women next to her. Two other women stepped forward, too, and an elderly man. They untied the leather straps from around the girl's raw wrists and then carried her to a cabin.

Rhea stood back as the slave women took over tending the girl. When her back had been gently bathed with warm water and a salve applied to the welts, Rhea ordered everyone out so she could talk privately with the girl, whose name she had been told was Ruby.

"Ruby," Rhea said gently to the sobbing girl, "don't be afraid. Let me help you. I'm Rhea, Mr. Logan's wife." The lie rolled easily off her tongue, and in this instance Rhea was glad for the authority it gave her. Otherwise, Dreed Jessup never would have listened to her.

"You must tell me why Jessup was whipping you."

Ruby looked at Rhea with red-ringed eyes. She had beautiful features and her skin color was several shades lighter than the women who had tended her. Rhea thought again of Caleb and wondered if this girl's ancestral line also had a white master's illicit influence in it.

"Is yo' da lady from up north?" Ruby whispered hesitatingly as she turned on her side toward Rhea.

"Yes. I haven't been here very long," Rhea answered. Just long enough to see all this ugliness around me, she added in her thoughts.

"Oh, Miz Rhea, yo' has got ta help me!" Ruby cried suddenly, grabbing for Rhea's hand. "Help me get away from dis place! Please, Miz Rhea, please!"

"Calm down, Ruby," Rhea soothed, patting the girl's hand. "Just tell me what happened to make Dreed Jessup whip you."

Ruby lowered her dark eyes and rolled over on her stomach, wincing in pain as her back registered the movement.

"Ah wouldn't lay wid him," she murmured in a voice so low Rhea had to lean closer to hear her.

"What? Jessup tried to force you to—to lie with him?"

"Yes'm," Ruby answered, crying softly again. "He dun' tried it afore when he bin drinkin' corn licker, but ah got away from him dat time. But dis afternoon ah couldn't . . ." She was going on with difficulty. "He done grab me an' pull me into da toolshed out back. Ah fought him, Missus. Ah fought him wid all mah might, but it didn' do no good." She buried her head in the pillow in her arms.

Rhea sighed heavily and touched Ruby's hand. Of course, there was a chance the girl was lying, but somehow Rhea sensed that she wasn't.

"Is that how he got the scratches on his face?" Ruby nodded.

"Dat was when he say he gon' teach me a lesson wid da whip so's ah won' fight him nex' time."

"Oh, Ruby . . ." Rhea murmured sympathetically. She'd have to speak to Logan, report this to him. He'd be angry with her for coming to the slave quarters, but that didn't matter. Surely he would do something about it to make sure this horrible incident wasn't repeated.

"I'll speak to my husband about this, Ruby," she tried to assure the girl. "He'll—"

"No, Missus, no, please!" Ruby pleaded frantically. "He won' do nothin' 'bout it. Ah gots ta get away from here, away from Massa Jessup! Please help me, Miz Rhea, *please!*"

"But what can I do, Ruby? I must get Mr. Logan's help."

"If'n ah could git word ta Mr. Exodus, he'd shor' nuff help me. Ah knows it," Ruby told her, a note of hope in her voice.

"But I don't know who he is, Ruby, or how to contact him," Rhea replied, wishing she did. She wanted so much to help this girl. Rhea knew only too well how desperate Ruby was. Grayson Sawyer had given her terrible lessons in that.

"Ah heared tell a message to dat nice doctor fella in Richmond—the one what were here durin' the fire—sometime git ta Mr. Exodus."

"You mean Dr. VanHorn?" Rhea asked in surprise. She remembered him from the makeshift infirmary after the fire. He seemed like a kind and caring man, but was he involved in the underground railroad? Did he know the ex-slave Mr. Exodus?

Rhea began thinking fast. The timing might be just right. VanHorn likely would be coming to the Fourth of July festivities at Fair Oaks the end of next week. She remembered filling out an invitation for him. Ruby wouldn't be able to travel for a few days anyway. Hopefully Jessup would leave her alone while she was recovering from his brutality, especially if Rhea made her presence known around the compound each day on the pretense of checking on Ruby. Somehow she'd have to get Logan to let her do that. If she could get a message to Mr. Exodus through Evan VanHorn at the ball next week, Ruby might be able to escape soon thereafter. And did she dare to hope that she, too, might escape from Fair Oaks and the Tremaines at the same time? Might this be the chance?

She had to be very careful in this. On top of not causing any suspicions with Logan, she knew she had already made an enemy of Dreed Jessup this day, and that was not something to be taken lightly. She could tell instinctively that he was a very dangerous man.

"All right, Ruby," Rhea told the slave girl then, shrugging off the unpleasant thought of the overseer. "I'll look into this and see what I can do. But listen to me, girl," she added in a stern voice, "you must tell no one—*no one*—about this, do you hear? Or we will both be in terrible trouble and you'll be at Jessup's mercy for years to come."

"Oh, no, Miz Rhea, ah won' say nothin'," Ruby promised adamantly. "An' thank yo', thank yo' so much." She grabbed Rhea's hand again and kissed it gratefully.

"Rest now, Ruby, and leave this to me," Rhea told her as she left the small cabin to return to Fair Oaks.

Chapter 39

THAT EVENING RHEA SAT OUT ON THE SMALL balcony off from her room. She'd pulled an armchair out there so she could relax and escape the heat of her bedroom. Rhea had spoken to Caleb just a little while before, and she could still see the look of disappointment on the little boy's face. A light had quickly gone out in his eyes when she'd had to tell him there would be no more lessons for him.

Rhea sighed as she looked out over the lawn garden. Pleading a headache, she had taken supper in her room. She had no desire to subject herself to another attack by the Tremaines. Word of her confrontation with Dreed Jessup had no doubt spread like wildfire. She felt a little better prepared to withstand Logan's certain displeasure here in the privacy of her room rather than in the dining hall.

But Rhea discovered that Logan hadn't been present at supper, either. Just now she saw him ride into the stableyard on Baron. How she hoped he knew nothing about the incident with Ruby so she could tell him her version first, but that was highly unlikely. Word-of-mouth news seemed to travel faster than even the telegraph, especially around a plantation where there were so many slaves to spread it. And as she feared, Logan lost no time in seeking her out in her bedroom.

"I thought after our discussion earlier today and on other occasions that you would make an effort to curb your impulsiveness and consult me before becoming involved in certain situations around here," Logan began sternly as he stood before Rhea now. "You were instructed to stay away from the slave compound, yet you disobeyed me and went there today, causing considerable trouble, I'm told."

"And probably saved a girl's life," Rhea answered quietly, forcing herself to be calm. "I went there to find Caleb to tell him there would be no more lessons. When I arrived, I found your overseer savagely whipping that young girl."

"Which it is his right to do," Logan added pointedly. There was an edge to his tone that hinted at anger, but he carefully controlled it. "Jessup has complete authority over all the slaves in his charge. It is his responsibility to discipline any of them as he sees fit, by any method he chooses."

"And does his right of authority include raping Ruby?" Rhea accused, finding it hard to keep her anger from rising.

"He did not rape her," Logan countered. "Jessup told me she was causing trouble with some of the young bucks—"

"Ruby tells a different story," Rhea interrupted him, "and I believe her. The scratches on Jessup's face are proof enough for me. She tried to fight him off, but he still raped her, and then he whipped her to teach her to be more compliant the next time. And being the sick and cruel monster he is, he was enjoying the lesson too much. Ruby's back was already in shreds when I arrived. I have not the least doubt that he would have beaten her to death without a qualm. In good conscience I could not turn away from such horror. I would do the same thing again without hesitation if necessary. If you do not approve of my actions, that cannot be helped." Rhea held her shoulders back and head high. She wouldn't back down in this, for she knew she was in the right. Her conscience was clear. She wondered how Logan and the others lived with theirs. She felt like picking up the double-globed oil lamp next to her and throwing it at Logan now to knock some sense of moral decency into his thick skull. But she resisted. It would only be a waste of a beautiful lamp!

Logan took a deep breath to try to keep control of his temper, which threatened to get the best of him. He knew he was seeing the real Rhea Merrick here before him now, not the meek and acquiescing woman he had hired to play a role. He'd seen hints of this spiritedness and defiance but had chosen to ignore them. He realized now that was a mistake. Damn, but how she aggravated him! His long-practiced control was dangerously close to exploding. No other woman—or man, for that matter—had ever driven him to this. And if he didn't need her still for his plans, he'd send her packing right now, for her recklessness was endangering far more than she would ever know.

With an effort Logan managed to contain his wrath as he spoke.

"I would remind you again that we have an agreement which clearly stipulates that you are to be all but invisible around here," he told her with cold disdain. "I'll look further into this matter with Jessup, but *you* shall not involve yourself in it any more. Nor will you do *anything* from now on without consulting me first, is that understood?"

Rhea didn't answer right away. She was too busy fighting her own anger and forcing herself to keep her defiant stance before him. Logan didn't wait for her to answer.

"You *will* comply with my wishes and our bargain, Rhea, or I will lock you in this room for the next five months to see that you do."

"You wouldn't dare!" Rhea exclaimed, frowning at him.

"Of course I would. Do not doubt it. There is far more at stake here than just your petty crusading conscience, and I will not allow you to cause trouble. Have I made myself clear?"

"Perfectly," Rhea replied tersely. At the moment she could think of nothing else to do but comply, but she hated being in Logan's power like this.

Later that night, it was too warm for sleeping. Rhea was too caught up in her thoughts to be sleepy anyway. She went out on her small balcony seeking a cooler place than her stuffy bedroom. The air was still. Not a breath of breeze stirred the trees. The moon was only half full. Its glow was diffused brightly by a wide ring of haze surrounding it.

She would escape from Fair Oaks as she'd decided before, Rhea kept thinking now. But she would have to play along with Logan for a little while longer yet, biding her time. Ruby had provided the one bit of information she needed—a way of contacting Mr. Exodus. How she hoped Evan VanHorn were the link. She would not abandon

Ruby, for she had promised to help the girl and she truly wanted to. They would escape together on the underground network, even if Rhea had to blacken her own face to match Ruby's to get away with it! She could wait a little while longer, endure Logan and this household for another week or two if need be, she told herself, if it meant a better chance for a successful escape.

Chapter 40

RHEA BARELY SAW LOGAN DURING THE REST OF
the week and she told herself that was just the way she
wanted it. She'd be glad if she *never* had to see him again!
There was a problem at the sawmill—something with the
machinery—and reluctantly he and Miles had had to
join forces to resolve the situation. They left the house
early and didn't return until evening, tired and in foul
tempers. Rhea, as well as everyone else with sense,
avoided any confrontations with either of them whenever possible.

Rhea was glad for their separate bedrooms, for she was
able to keep out of Logan's path more easily that way. At
night she heard him stirring about in his room and wondered
apprehensively whether he would seek her out, for whatever
reason. She told herself that this incertitude was why he
occupied her thoughts so much, and sometimes even her
dreams. But derisively she told herself she probably didn't
have to worry in that regard. Logan was likely too busy with
all of his other women to give her a second thought!

Nothing more had been mentioned between them concerning the intimacy they'd known. Try as she might,
Rhea could not put it out of her mind. With growing anxi-
ety she waited each day, hoping her body would give her
the sign she longed to see that would reveal she was not
pregnant.

What a fool you were, Rhea cursed herself inwardly, to
let yourself get into this predicament.

Rhea continued to spend time with Camille. She did not
go to see Ruby at the compound, for she did not want to anger Logan further and bring his attention and wrath down

upon herself again, not when she might be close to finding a way to escape him. Instead she sent Glory to see how Ruby was every day. And as she'd hoped, Dreed Jessup was leaving the slave girl alone. Rhea wondered if Logan had anything to do with that, but she dared not ask him about it.

Rhea still did her duty of reading to Silas Tremaine in his room each afternoon. She didn't like doing it, but it was expected of her and was one point Logan could not slight her on. In this, she had obeyed him.

But it was difficult enduring old Silas's tyrannical attitude and out-and-out rudeness. So as not to give him the satisfaction of knowing she was vulnerable to his meanness, Rhea set her mind to treat him with extreme patience, much as an overly indulgent mother treats a temperamental child. This attitude had worked during most of this week's sessions, though it exasperated Silas Tremaine greatly. Perhaps that was why today he was particularly cross and seemed to be trying harder than usual to rankle her.

"Are you pregnant, girl?" he demanded suddenly while Rhea was reading a business feature to him from the newspaper.

"Wha—What?" Rhea stammered in surprise. She had come to expect Silas to say just about anything to goad her, but this . . .

"Well, speak up, girl," Silas demanded when she hesitated. "You must have trapped my grandson somehow. Not only would he never willingly marry a Yankee, but he'd never fall in love with one, either. He's not capable of that emotion."

"In that he has had an excellent teacher in *you.*" The sharp words were out of Rhea's mouth before she could stop herself. She'd had enough of this, enough of Silas Tremaine and his foul temper and verbal abuse. She rose to her feet, throwing the newspaper to the floor. What Logan had told her about his grandfather's will gave her a retort.

"Do not accuse me of what *you* are guilty of doing, sir. *You* did the entrapping, the manipulating. You and Miles, his own flesh and blood." Her blue eyes flashed angrily as they leveled on Silas Tremaine.

He returned her drilling gaze for a moment before a sly smile of satisfaction curled on his lips.

"So the mousy little bride is a she-cat with claws after all."

"Only when I am provoked, sir," Rhea returned defensively, eyes blazing as she stood her ground before him.

"Well, that's a relief to hear," he remarked, his tone a little less gruff now. "It took long enough to light your fuse. Sit down, girl, and unruffle your feathers. I'm not through with this discussion yet. There is more I want to know about you and my grandson."

Rhea suddenly understood his tactics now. He enjoyed being argumentative, instigating retaliation from his victims, battling with his wits when his bent and aged body had confined him to an appearance of weakness. She realized that she must match his ways if she was going to have his respect, or just to survive these sessions.

"I have a name," she told him pointedly then as she sat down again on the chair. "It is Rhea. Kindly use it."

One of Silas's bushy gray eyebrows cocked at her but he only snorted a "humph" and made no other immediate comment. After a moment he went on.

"As I asked before, has a child been conceived between you and Logan?"

Even if Rhea had been inclined to answer such a presumptuous question, she could not truly give him an answer, for she did not know it herself. She had been certain there was no conception after the first time she and Logan had been together at Farley House. But after that . . . She was yet unsure and very much worried indeed that such a consequence would be her fate.

"That is none of your business, sir," she answered finally, looking at the older man steadily. "It is a matter strictly between Logan and myself."

"Rubbish! Of course it's my business," Silas exclaimed impatiently. *"Everything* that happens in this family is my business!"

"Why? So you can use it to manipulate them or hurt them?" she accused, her own anger sparking again. "You would enjoy having any information you could use against Logan especially, wouldn't you? Even use an innocent child to somehow score a victory over him, bend him to your will. Why do you do that?" Rhea stopped then to calm herself. She sighed and spoke less vehemently as she went on. "Logan is your grandson. Why do you hate him so? He and your other grandchildren bring you immortality. As long as they live and prosper, so does that part of you that is in each of them live on also."

"There is nothing of me in Logan!" Silas cut in sharply. His light blue eyes were half hidden by the deep frown that further wrinkled his wizened brow. "Nothing that I have ever seen! He has always chosen any course that was contrary to my wishes. He is disobedient, impudent, and ungrateful!"

"Meaning he would not give in to your tyrannical will," Rhea remarked calmly, watching him.

"Meaning he has been a constant source of irritation and displeasure to me all his life!" Silas pounded his fist on the arm of his chair, then leaned his head against its high back, his breathing coming jaggedly.

Rhea was alarmed for a moment that Silas's agitated state might have brought on an attack of some kind, but he waved her away when she got up from her chair and started toward him. They didn't speak for a few moments while he recovered.

"Why didn't you simply disinherit Logan and banish him from Fair Oaks long before now if you found his presence so offensive?" Rhea asked, puzzled.

"Believe me, I've contemplated doing just that on many occasions," Silas snapped in return. Then he looked away from her saying no more.

"Well, then, why haven't you done it?" Rhea persisted.

The old man's head whipped around and his look was contemptuous.

"Because you are not from the South, you cannot understand how it is here with family ties and loyalties. Logan is a *Tremaine.* Our blood runs deep, and even though there may be dissension among us, we are stronger for it. In the face of all others, we stand together and present a united front. You will come to realize that better as the time you spend in this family increases, if in fact you can be tolerated that long! Now go. I am weary of you. You are dismissed."

Rhea was only too glad to leave before she lost her temper with him completely. Without another word, she stood up and walked purposefully from the room.

Chapter 41

THE NEXT DAY RHEA DID NOT GO TO SILAS TRE-
maine's bedchamber at the appointed time. She decided to
let him vent his unpleasantness on someone else for a
while. He could stew over her absence for she would not be
bullied by him. She decided she would return to their regular sessions if and when *she* chose to do so.

Rhea wondered if old Silas would report her actions to
Logan, but she thought not. This was between her and the
patriarch of the Tremaine family. Somehow she felt Logan's grandfather would keep it that way.

To pass the time, Rhea went to the music room. She enjoyed coming to this room. Decorated in yellows and
greens, it had such a light and airy atmosphere about it.
Ten tall, narrow windows located along the one outside
wall flooded the room in sunlight. Rhea opened them now
to air the warm room before she went over to the black
grand piano that took up one whole corner. A dozen plush
armchairs covered in light green velvet were situated in a
half circle facing the piano.

Pretending that an appreciative audience occupied
those chairs now, Rhea smiled and made an elaborate
curtsey to them, then sat down before the keyboard. She
played several simple melodies from memory, humming or
singing softly along with the music she had not played in
years. Each time she came to the music room to play, a
little more would come back to her. Encouraged, she decided to try a more difficult piece now, a Bach sonata, but
her memory failed her.

"No, that doesn't sound right," she murmured aloud,
frowning slightly as she ran her fingers again over the

ivory keys in a difficult arpeggio. What she needed was the printed music, any sheet music, for that matter, that would jog her memory and bring back what she had spent so many hours learning as a child.

Glancing around the room, Rhea spied a door to her left. Walking to it, she found that it led to a large walk-in closet. She lit a lamp that had been left on a small stand, holding it shoulder high, then went in. The light revealed shelves with several instrument cases of various sizes and shapes on them. A number of music stands were stored in one corner.

Rhea opened a cupboard on her right and found a set of small narrow wooden drawers. Opening one, she saw it contained just what she'd been looking for—printed sheet music. Rummaging through three of the drawers, she found pieces by Mozart, Beethoven, and Schubert. As Rhea turned to leave, the lamplight fell on several large gold-framed portraits stacked against each other on the floor. She stopped short as a familiar face looked back at her from the painting facing her. Leaning down, she brought the lamp closer to see better.

"Logan . . ." she murmured as she recognized the pale blue eyes and handsome face of the man in the picture. "In a military uniform?" And who was the beautiful woman posed with him?

Rhea brushed at the cobwebs draping the frame before she stepped back to survey the portrait better. The man certainly looked like Logan, yet there was something different about him. Perhaps it was the set of the mouth. This man was smiling, something Logan seldom did.

The woman looked vaguely familiar. Rhea knew she had never met her, yet she had seen her lovely face somewhere, and recently.

She looked at the clothes Logan was wearing. Clearly a formal dress uniform, with gold buttons and shoulder braid. Rhea leaned closer to try to make out the letters of the insignia buttons on the collar. "USN," she murmured aloud as she squinted to read them. A naval uniform?

And then Rhea knew. Her jaw dropped open a little in surprise as her glance swept from the man to the woman. Now she remembered where she'd seen this beautiful face before—in Silas Tremaine's room, the picture in the small oval frame on his desk, the one he'd looked at so sadly the day Rhea had read Poe's "The Raven."

She looked at the man again. This was not a painting of Logan. It was Silas Tremaine depicted before her. Silas with someone he had once cared deeply about. His wife, Patricia? Was this the painting Camille had spoken of that day in her bedroom?

Silas. So Logan was his reincarnation. Was that part of the reason such an animosity had grown between grandfather and grandson? Did Silas see in Logan the reflection of himself as he had been in his long-passed youth? Did he see more than just the exact physical resemblance in Logan? Was the strong will, the need to be master of himself and others, there, too? And perhaps even the sadness?

Rhea was thoughtful as she looked at the painting a few moments longer, then turned to leave the closet. Taking up the sheet music again, she extinguished the lamp and walked back out to the piano, thinking she would have to ask Glory about that portrait, or perhaps Camille. She found herself curious to know more about Silas Tremaine.

Rhea practiced playing the pieces she'd found for some time, enjoying the satisfying feeling the music gave as it surrounded her and seemed to reach deep within her. As she opened another printed folder she found a tune by the popular young American composer Stephen Foster. Rhea loved Foster's beautiful melodies. She placed the sheet before her and began picking out the chords. Soon she was singing the nostalgic lyrics, so caught up in the song that she was unaware she was no longer alone in the room.

Logan had returned early to the house from the sawmill, and on his way upstairs had heard playing and soft singing in the music room. They were sounds not often heard at Fair Oaks. Surprise registered on his face as he'd come to the open hallway door and seen Rhea at the piano. Now he stood off to one side in the shadows watching and listening as her fingers moved effortlessly over the ivory keys, revealing her to be a gifted musician. And her delicate voice seemed like a caress as it touched him.

This was a side of Rhea he had not seen before. There was a softness, a gentleness in her manner that she did not let show, at least not when she was around him. Or was it that he never gave her a chance to show this side of herself?

Logan found himself wishing he had his sketchbook with him. He was moved by the serenity of the scene before him, with Rhea looking so lovely and natural at the piano. All that might be needed to complete this picture of domesticity would be an angelic-faced child looking adoringly up at his mother seated there.

Logan frowned, a little stunned by the drift his thoughts had taken. The thought of a child sobered his contemplations, yet the picture of Rhea with a child—his child—was not quite as forbidding as it once had been for him.

Logan couldn't take his eyes off Rhea now. He felt something welling up inside him that went beyond only physical desire. He was amazed that she could make him feel this way. He realized he had no need to set charcoal to paper to capture Rhea like this. Here before him was the woman who invaded his dreams and unexpectedly filled his mind during idle moments. No, his sketchbook would not be needed. The vision of Rhea like this would remain etched in his memory to trouble him for a good while to come.

After a few more minutes, Logan pulled his eyes away and forced himself to overcome the urge to go further into the room and let Rhea see him. He suddenly didn't know what he'd say or do if she turned those blue eyes of hers on him.

Shaking his head to try to dispel these disturbing thoughts, Logan turned away and quietly left the music room to continue upstairs.

Chapter 42

A SHORT TIME LATER RHEA ENDED HER PLAYING and stood up to gather the numerous pieces of sheet music together into a small pile. Opening the hinged top of the piano bench, she found it was empty, so she laid the music inside so she'd know where to find it easily the next time she had a chance to play. She was just about to close the bench when a voice coming from the doorway to the hall made her jump.

"So this is where you are hiding!" a gravelly voice shattered the stillness of the room.

Rhea sighed and turned toward where Silas Tremaine was being wheeled into the room by the ever-present, stoic-faced Jubal.

"Good afternoon, Mr. Tremaine," Rhea greeted with forced casualness. She felt some resentment welling up in her because she knew he was probably about to spoil the pleasant time she'd just spent here in the music room.

"You forgot our appointment at two o'clock. That was very irresponsible," Silas accused, ignoring her greeting.

His light blue eyes narrowed under his bushy gray brows as they glared at Rhea. But she was not going to let him intimidate her again.

"I did not forget," she stated simply, then turned away to busy herself folding down the wooden rack that held the music on the piano and closing the bench.

"Then why didn't you come? Look at me when I'm talking to you, young woman," Silas demanded, his tone heated.

Rhea moved from where she'd been standing at the piano and walked a few steps closer to the elderly, round-shouldered man in the wheelchair. She held her hands down, folded together in front of her, and kept her head high as she looked directly at Logan's grandfather.

"I didn't come because I did not wish to do so," she answered in a conversational voice, resisting the urge to use just as spiteful a tone. Her gaze never wavered from his frowning one. "I decided to enjoy myself here in the music room instead of being bullied by you today, sir." Rhea smiled pleasantly as though she had just made a casual comment about the weather instead of leveling an insult at the patriarch of the Tremaine family. Then she braced herself for the explosion of temper she fully expected the elderly man to retaliate with. But Silas Tremaine's lips only twitched slightly and one corner of his mouth actually turned up in a kind of a smile.

"There are few people in this family who would dare to make such a statement to me," he remarked without his usual rancor. "You're a feisty one, all right. Not weak-spined like most of the members of this household. Up to now only Logan has dared to continually stand up to me all these years. He doesn't realize it but he gives me some sport with which to keep my wits sharpened. And now I see that you will, too. At least you'll help keep things interesting around here. And that's saying a lot for a Yankee."

Rhea could hardly believe what she was hearing. Old Silas's tone was almost complimentary! At any rate, she had the feeling that what he'd just said was as close as he was going to come to a favorable comment about her. And had she detected a note of regard in the old man's reference to Logan? That was puzzling.

"Well, stop standing there with your mouth hanging open," Silas's terse voice interrupted Rhea's reflections. She hadn't realized her lower jaw had dropped open slightly. She clamped it shut now in response to his commanding tone.

"I want to go out to the front garden. Jubal—" he turned a little to address the big slave, "—Mistress Rhea will be taking me outside. Fetch some lemonade for us."

"Yes, suh, Marse Silas," Jubal replied, his staid expression never wavering as he turned and walked out of the music room.

"Well, wheel me out of here," Silas snapped at Rhea

then. "I'll show you where the ramp is located that accommodates this confounded chair of mine."

Rhea started to bristle and was about to refuse to do Silas's bidding when she caught herself. Instead she only sighed and did as she was told, deciding she might as well try to get along with the old man. She had to admit she found Logan's grandfather interesting, though she had to add exasperating and infuriating to his description, as well. Funny, those words could apply to Logan also. At any rate, perhaps it wouldn't kill her to humor old Silas. Dealing with him would keep her own wits sharpened for when she had to face his grandson.

Rhea was surprised at how light Silas was to push in the bulky wooden wheelchair. But then he was so thin and wizened. And pale. He really did need to get outdoors more, Rhea promptly decided. Perhaps they could have their reading sessions in the garden instead of in his stuffy room upstairs. She might as well continue her sessions with the Tremaine patriarch if he wanted her to; she had little else to occupy her around here. And doing this for his grandfather would please Logan. Why did the thought of pleasing him appeal to her for some reason?

"Very well, Grandfather Silas," she spoke over the elder Tremaine's shoulder, putting aside that discomforting thought. She made her tone lighter as she pushed him through the wide main hall. It was the first time she had used that form of addressing him, and Rhea wondered a little impishly if using that title irked him. She thought she heard him snort derisively, and she smiled to herself as she continued to say, "I'll take you out to the garden, but I insist that you speak to me civilly, or I promise I shall come back to the house, leaving you out there to stew in your own bad temper."

She saw Silas's shoulders straighten some in indignation, but he only gave an unintelligible mumble, then said nothing more until they were outside.

Summer birds and insects had their various songs and sounds carried along on the gentle breeze. It was blowing through the wide array of trees and shrubbery and flowers planted in geometric patterns throughout the large expanse of garden and lawn in front of the main house. Rhea steered Silas's chair along the smoothly laid-out brick path to a shady spot beneath a tall oak.

No one else was in sight, not even any of the many slaves who regularly cared for this picturesque acreage of the estate. Everyone was likely inside still partaking of the afternoon rest, Rhea decided as she sat down on a stone bench in front of Silas Tremaine. Rhea did the same herself on very hot days, but this afternoon she found it pleasant to be outside, for it wasn't nearly as warm as it had been the last few days.

"This seems like a nice spot. Shall I get a book from the library and read to you now?" Rhea asked then, looking at Silas.

"No, I'm not in the mood to listen," Silas retorted, but his tone wasn't quite as churlish as usual. He seemed to be occupied with looking at the oak tree that towered straight and tall overhead. Its branches were lushly covered with dark green leaves and reached out in every direction around them, intertwining with the boughs of the other three oaks nearby. They lent welcome shade to a wide area of the garden.

"Why did you choose this tree to stop under?" Silas asked suddenly, his tone somewhat testy again. He cocked one eyebrow at her and scowled slightly as he brought his pale blue eyes to level on Rhea.

"Why . . . I don't know," she stammered, a little surprised by his question. "It was the closest one offering shade, I suppose."

"It's Logan's tree," Silas stated snappishly, glancing up the gray-black bark of the trunk of the oak again, then back to Rhea.

"Logan's? I don't understand. What do you mean?" Rhea kept her tone conversational as she posed the question. She ignored his surly ways. She understood old Silas a little better now and was no longer intimidated by him. And she found herself curious about this statement.

"I had an oak sapling planted in this semicircle," Silas gestured a gnarled hand at the four trees near them, "for each of my grandchildren on the day he or she was born. This one is Logan's. See, his name is carved there in the trunk." He pointed a bony finger about halfway up the tree, and Rhea walked closer to see better. She could just

make out the large letters spelling out "LOGAN" etched
there. Over the years the trunk's growth had widened and
distorted the slashes, but she could still reach up and put
her finger into the rough black bark and trace the lines of
Logan's name.

"Miles and Camille and Andrew have the same," Silas
went on, pointing to each of the other trees as he said the
names of his grandchildren.

"And what are these?" Rhea asked as she touched several deeply gouged places along the right side of Logan's
oak. She could tell they were not new, for the tree had
rounded the edges of the wedged-shaped indentations in
an attempt to heal its wounds.

"That's where Miles took a double-edged ax to it one
summer." Silas snorted in amusement. "I think he was
about fifteen; Logan, about thirteen. It always irked Miles
that Logan's tree seemed to grow bigger and faster than
his, even though his had been planted two years sooner.
He got the notion in his head to do some pruning on his
own that day."

Rhea looked at old Silas and was surprised to see a slight
smile touching the corners of his mouth. He did not see her
scrutiny of him, for his eyes were still focused on the cuts
in the tree trunk.

"Logan caught Miles before the fourth swing of the ax,
and they had one of the biggest brawls of their lives that
day. Lasted over half an hour. Logan won, but just barely.
Finally knocked Miles out cold just before he keeled over
half-unconscious himself. They both sported double black
eyes and cuts and bruises for weeks afterward."

The note of satisfaction in Silas's voice annoyed Rhea.

"And I suppose you enjoyed watching your grandsons almost beat each other to death," she accused with a sharp
edge to her tone. Silas's head shot around to face her and
he frowned.

"Of course I did," he exclaimed tersely. "They needed
that rivalry with each other to make them hard, give them
the edge they'd need to succeed over other men." His light
eyes narrowed as his gaze pierced Rhea's. "I nurtured and
honed that competition between them very carefully over
the years. Their father, my son, was a constant disappoint-

ment to me. I expected better from my grandsons, and I saw to it that I got it!"

"But the enmity you so ruthlessly fostered may very well destroy both of them, and Fair Oaks, as well," Rhea retaliated angrily. She stood unflinchingly before Silas Tremaine, her hands clenched at her sides and her eyes locked with his. "And then what will you have gained?"

"Bah! What do you know of it?" Silas spat at her heatedly, flicking a hand at her in a gesture of disgust. His gray eyebrows nearly touched the bridge of his nose. "You are only a woman. You know nothing of the grit and cunning it takes to succeed in this world!"

"I know that I must endure what you have molded Logan into," Rhea parried with equal vehemence. "And I know you have pitted him against his brother so fiercely that he would go to any lengths to best Miles! Even to the point of—," she stopped short, biting off her words, realizing suddenly that she'd been about to say, "pretending to be married to me." That would have been a disaster. She dropped her eyes and quickly looked away from Silas Tremaine.

"To the point of what?" Silas demanded.

"Of—of being obsessed with winning every confrontation with Miles," Rhea answered, thinking fast as she forced herself to meet the elder Tremaine's eyes again.

"Good! He should be obsessed, driven!" Silas declared with what could only be termed as satisfaction in his voice. "That lets me know there is still some life left in this family, still some fire in our blood!"

"Oh, you are an infuriating man, Silas Tremaine!" Rhea accused, throwing up her hands in exasperation and turning away again.

"I've been called worse in my day," Silas snapped back quickly, sounding very pleased with himself.

"Jubal!" he shouted then, making Rhea jump. "Where is that damned darkie with my lemonade? All this confounded arguing's parched my throat mightily. *Jubal!*"

"Right here, Marse Silas. Ah hears yo'," Jubal answered in his usual unruffled tone as he stepped out from behind a tall lilac bush, carrying a small tray with two glasses. It was obvious he'd been standing there out of sight to avoid getting in the line of fire of the barrage of words Rhea and Silas were leveling at each other. He was probably used to witnessing such displays involving his master.

"Well, it's about time," Silas exclaimed impatiently as he watched the big black man hand Rhea her cool drink, then received his in turn. He used his free hand to swat at a large horsefly that was buzzing persistently around his head.

"Take me back inside, Jubal," he ordered then testily. "It's too hot and there are too many annoying things out here." He looked at Rhea pointedly. "Besides, I suspect Mistress Rhea needs some time to regroup her forces before we meet again."

Silas's pale blue eyes held Rhea's, and she could have sworn there was a twinkle of pleasure in them. There was definitely the tug of a smile at one corner of the elderly man's mouth, deepening the wrinkles on that side of his face. He had clearly enjoyed their confrontation.

Rhea sighed and acknowledged his challenge by nodding slightly and raising her glass of lemonade toward him in a gesture of salute. Silas raised his to her in return, then allowed Jubal to wheel him around to go back toward the main house.

Chapter 43

OVER TWO HUNDRED MILES AWAY IN PHILADEL-
phia Grayson Sawyer hid his displeasure with the man in
front of him by turning to gaze out the dirty window of the
warehouse at Merrick Iron. Scarsdale was a cool one, all
right, he thought to himself. The petty forger hadn't
blinked an eye when he claimed he knew nothing about
Tremaine and Rhea. He was a good liar, but Sawyer knew
the type. He'd buckle under rougher treatment.

"Come now, Scarsdale," Sawyer said as he turned back
to the gaunt man being held by two of the ironworks' burly
factory men. "I've spent considerable time and money
tracking you down. I'm not about to be deterred from gaining the information I seek from you. You are trying my patience."

He nodded toward his men. One of them yanked Willy's
arms behind him while the other stepped in front of him
and hit him a vicious blow across the jaw. There was a terrible cracking sound as Willy was jerked backward from
the impact. He moaned and slumped forward, firmly held
by the powerful man grasping his arms. Blood spurted
from the deep split in his lip as the thug who hit him
yanked on his hair to raise his head toward Sawyer.

"Please, Mr. Sawyer," Willy gasped, "I don't know anything."

"So you keep telling me, Willy, but I don't believe you.
Now I'll ask you again. Did you forge a marriage certificate for Logan Tremaine and my stepdaughter?"

"No, Mr. Sawyer, I swear I didn't." Willy denied adamantly before a wracking cough took his breath away.

"You really should take better care of your health,

Willy," Sawyer commented sarcastically as he nodded to his men again.

Five minutes later saw Willy-Nilly Scarsdale writhing in pain on the cluttered storeroom floor, barely conscious.

"Now, Willy, about that marriage certificate . . ." Sawyer prompted again. He gestured with one hand and Willy was hauled to his feet and pushed roughly into a broken-down chair.

"I'm hurt . . . real bad, Mr. Sawyer . . ." Willy gasped, bending over and clutching at his middle.

"This unpleasantness was all avoidable, Willy," Sawyer told him. "To prevent more of the same, you need only tell me what I want to know."

When Willy still hesitated, Sawyer frowned angrily and sharply waved his ruffians forward again.

"No, no, please . . ." Willy pleaded. Another deep cough erupted from him and blood came from his mouth. He tried to wipe it away with the back of his hand. "I . . . the certificate was forged . . ." he murmured finally, laboring for breath. "Mr. Tremaine paid me to do it."

"Then he and Rhea are not really married?" Sawyer demanded with gloating pleasure. Willy could only nod his head in reply.

"And the official record, how was that accomplished?" Sawyer persisted.

"I have a friend . . . a clerk at the Hall of Records—Cable Dawes. He was paid, too . . ." Willy managed to say before a terrible pain stabbed at his insides and he pitched forward to the floor.

Grayson Sawyer ignored him. His eyes narrowed cruelly as he reflected on the implications of Scarsdale's words.

So that little whore had thought to make a fool out of him by running off with Tremaine. With seething anger, he could only imagine how Rhea had gained Tremaine's cooperation.

Fair Oaks. That was the name of the Tremaine tobacco plantation outside of Richmond. One of the biggest in Virginia. He hadn't been down south in quite a while. A trip there seemed just the thing to do now.

Chapter 44

AT LAST, SATURDAY THE FOURTH OF JULY AR-
rived. The whole weekend would be filled with activities
celebrating the national holiday that commemorated the
signing of the Declaration of Independence seventy years
before. There would be no work for the field slaves, though
the house slaves would be kept very busy during most of
the time. They would all have special foods, clothes, goods,
and trinkets, the likes of which were only allowed at one
other time of the year—Christmas. Games, singing, dancing, and fireworks would mark the two days.

There was much excitement and a final flurry of activity
as the last-minute preparations were made at Fair Oaks.
Rhea and Camille spent most of the day together, giggling
and fussing as if they were going to their first ball.

"You must stay near me tonight, Camille," Rhea begged
as they were having the last touches made to their
hairstyles. Rhea had her hair parted in the middle and
brushed out full. Mother-of-pearl combs held it back from
her face on both sides. Her bangs were feathered across her
forehead. Camille's style was similar.

"Silly girl, whatever for?" Camille exclaimed, laughing.
"You will have Logan as your companion. Besides, they
are only people. They will come to love you just as I do."

"Dear Camille . . ." Rhea took her friend's hands in
hers. She couldn't tell her that the thought of Logan gave
her little consolation for surviving the reception ball. How
she hated deceiving Camille about her relationship with
Logan.

"If all southerners are like you, then this shall be a wonderful evening," Rhea said then. "If they are like Sybil, then I shall die!"

Camille laughed again. "Well, you shall have nothing but admirers among the menfolk who will be present, I can assure you," Camille replied as she stood back to look at Rhea. "My goodness, Rhea, you are stunning. However did you know that blue is perfect for you?"

"Thank you," Rhea replied with a happy smile. "Logan told me—" The words were out before Rhea realized it, surprising her. She hadn't thought about Logan's comment weeks ago that she should always wear this shade of blue which matched her eyes. Had she unconsciously chosen the gown to try to please him?

"Well, you are positively gorgeous in it," Camille went on, interrupting Rhea's troubling thought. "I hope your shoes are comfortable, for you shall be dancing all night, I am certain. The men will be tripping over themselves to get to you."

Now it was Rhea's turn to laugh. "Well, stay close to me anyway. Together we shall be the two belles of the ball."

"Agreed!" Camille's blue eyes were bright with excitement. "What jewelry are you going to wear? Has Logan given you Grandmother Patricia's sapphires?"

"No," Rhea replied, dropping her eyes. "He hasn't even seen my gown yet. I wanted to surprise him." That at least was true. As she busied herself smoothing a wrinkle out of the blue chiffon of her skirt Rhea didn't add that Logan had expressed no interest whatsoever in knowing what she was going to wear tonight.

"And besides," she added quickly, "I'm certain the jewels are much too valuable for me to wear." He'd never trust me with them, she thought derisively to herself.

"They are valuable," Camille agreed, "but what good are they if they are kept hidden away unseen? They only sparkle and seem to come alive with color and beauty when someone is wearing them. I'll try to catch Logan to tell him. I'm going to wear Mama's diamond necklace and earrings. Do you think they will look all right with my gown?" She glanced down at her rose-colored taffeta gown, a questioning look on her face.

"They will be lovely, just as you are," Rhea told her sincerely. "The perfect touch."

"Thank you, Rhea," Camille smiled. "Oh, this is going to be such fun! I'll meet you downstairs in half an hour!"

Rhea decided to wear a small square diamond pendant that hung from a thin gold chain and had matching diamond earrings. They were some of the few pieces of jewelry she had not been forced to sell to meet the demands of her creditors. Her father had given them to her many years ago on her thirteenth birthday. A moment of sadness touched her thoughts as she fastened the clasp and was reminded of happier times long passed away now.

At precisely seven-thirty there was a knock on the sitting room door leading to Rhea's bedroom. She took a deep breath to fortify herself, put a smile on her lips, and went to answer it. Logan stepped into the room as she opened the door.

"Good evening, Rhea. I see you are ready. Good," he noted with his usual brusque tone.

"Good evening," Rhea managed to answer. She was taken aback by Logan's appearance. He was positively elegant and more handsome than she'd ever seen him before. His double-breasted dark brown coat had wide notched lapels and gold buttons detailing it. It was short, coming only to the waist and falling to two knee-length "tails" in the back over his matching trousers. A brocade vest in shades of brown showed just around the edges of his ruffled white shirtfront. A thin necktie was tied in a perfect bow around the high starched collar.

"Well, let me have a look at you to make sure you are presentable," he said then curtly, motioning with his white dress gloves for her to turn around.

"Oh, yes, of course," Rhea stammered, startled from her examination of him. She felt a blush warm her face, realizing she'd been staring at him.

Logan was glad she'd turned away from him. He was finding it hard to hide his own surprise at how beautiful Rhea was. The thought came to his mind of how she'd looked the first time he'd seen her, in that drab gray dress, spattered with mud, her hair pulled back severely in a bun, and wearing those ridiculous wire-rimmed spectacles. There was little resemblance to that woman in the breathtaking vision of loveliness before him now. He won-

dered if she'd chosen the deep blue gown because he'd once
told her that color was becoming to her.

"Well, do I pass inspection?" Rhea asked with a touch of
sarcasm.

Logan saw the sudden stubborn set of her chin and knew
there was a strength of will reflected there that rivaled his
own. He realized it had given Rhea the plucky determination she was showing in carrying out their unusual bargain. He couldn't help admiring her for it. He found he
liked the challenge, and smiled inwardly now as he
quickly calculated his reply to her question.

He cleared his throat and glanced away with forced disinterest. "Your gown is very becoming," he replied coolly,
busying himself putting on his gloves. "I think the guests
tonight will find you attractive. Let us hope so in order
that you may make a good impression. And let me remind
you—"

"I know, I know . . ." Rhea interrupted, sighing with exasperation at his meager compliment and constant instructions. She reached for her own long blue lace gloves
and matching fan on the table. "Be sweet and demure and
untroublesome. Have no worry. I shall play my part as you
wish it."

"I hope so," Logan quipped, eyeing her doubtfully.
"There is only one thing I would change about your appearance," he added, his glance going to Rhea's throat.

"What is that?" she asked apprehensively.

"That pendant, those earrings. They're pitifully inade-
quate for this occasion and the way you are dressed. Have
you nothing else to wear among the things I bought you before we left Philadelphia?"

Rhea's resentment flared at his words and his tone. He
was so condescending. But she'd just told him she would
play her part as the dutiful wife, so with considerable effort she forced down her feelings and only shook her head
as she fingered the small pendant she wore.

"I had a personal reason for wearing these," she said
quietly, her fingers touching the pendant somewhat nervously.

But Logan wasn't listening. He didn't bother to ask her
what her reason might be. He just told her what to do, as
usual.

"Of course, none of those things I bought you would have been right with that gown. I know just what's needed. Leave those here and come with me down to the library."

Rhea sighed with resignation as she took off the pendant and earrings and put them away in a small jewelry box on her dressing table.

As she went before Logan downstairs Rhea was silent and unhappy. Already he had managed to spoil the festive mood she'd been in all afternoon with Camille. She could only imagine that things would get depressingly worse as the evening wore on and she was surrounded by a ballroom full of snooty and critical Southerners.

In the library, Logan went to an ornate wooden cabinet in one corner. After removing his gloves, he took a key out of his coat pocket and slid it into the lock that opened the two long doors in front. Inside, what looked like drawers turned out to be a false panel that rolled up and away when Logan touched a certain spot. A small safe was revealed there. Logan quickly worked the combination and opened it. Reaching in, he took out a large, flat black-leather case and brought it over to the desk where Rhea was standing. There was still enough early evening sunlight coming in at the window for her to see what he held out to her. Her eyes opened wide with awe as Logan opened the jewelry box and she saw the splendor that sparkled against the black velvet inside. Logan smiled slightly at her reaction, knowing it was justified. Exquisite diamonds and sapphires set in a necklace, bracelet, and earrings glittered up at Rhea. Camille must have somehow persuaded Logan to allow me to wear these gems tonight, Rhea thought as she admired them.

Logan lifted the necklace out of the case. Four large sapphires, each set in a circle of diamonds, hung from the sapphire-and-diamond strand that went around the neck. From these four gems hung a teardrop-shaped pendant, set with a large sapphire and surrounded by diamonds.

Rhea had never seen anything so beautiful in her life, and she had seen many splendid jewelry pieces. Her own mother's collection was enviable.

"You would let me wear these?" she murmured in disbelief as Logan held out the necklace for her to take. "They are magnificent . . ."

"Yes, you may wear them tonight. My grandfather gave these to my grandmother on their wedding day, so it is rather appropriate, wouldn't you say?" His tone was sarcastic as he looked at her.

"Hardly, since that is not the case between us," Rhea replied in a chilly tone, glancing away. He was so adept at ruining what could be lovely moments between them.

"At any rate, wear them tonight. No one's worn them for many years. They will dazzle our guests." As will you, he added in his thoughts as he took the necklace from Rhea. He turned her around so her back was to him and fastened the jewels around her neck.

The two of them were standing very close. Rhea's delicate perfume surrounded Logan and seemed to beckon his hands to remain touching the soft, smooth skin of her neck even after he had finished snapping the clasp.

Rhea's breath caught in her throat, and she was only too aware of Logan's pause and the heat of his hands where they touched her. She felt a twinge of apprehension. Or was it excitement? She wanted to step away from Logan, but she wasn't sure whether her legs would allow her to do so. Unexpectedly, they seemed to have lost their ability to move, forcing her to continue standing so near to Logan.

His hands started to move along the tops of her shoulders, stopping at her arms to turn her around to face him. His light blue eyes moved over Rhea's face slowly, then went down to her bare neckline where the gems sparkled against her white skin. Logan saw that the swell of her breasts showed slightly along the lace edges of the low V-neckline, and he was too much reminded of the beauty hidden underneath the filmy layers of blue chiffon that made up the bodice of her gown.

Logan blinked and swallowed as he brought his eyes back up to meet Rhea's. She was startled by the warmth in his look. Her breath quickened.

"You should always wear sapphires," he murmured softly. "Their brilliance is reflected in your eyes . . ." He brought the fingers of one hand up to touch the pendant, then let them brush lightly over Rhea's skin just above her left breast. He felt her tremble.

"I—I shall remember that," Rhea somehow managed to say rather breathlessly as Logan's gaze held hers.

He seemed about to say more when there was a sudden commotion in the hallway just outside the library door. Logan immediately dropped his hands from where they were resting on Rhea's shoulders again and stepped back as they heard Camille's voice.

"Yes, I'll check in here, Miles.

"There you two are!" Logan's sister exclaimed as she suddenly walked into the room with a flourish of her full-skirted taffeta gown. "Our guests are beginning to arrive. Oh, Logan, you *are* letting Rhea wear Grandmother's jewels even without my suggesting it. I knew they would be perfect for her."

She came over and picked up the bracelet, holding it out to Rhea. "Here, put this on next. Isn't it just beautiful?"

"Yes, it's all exquisite," Rhea agreed quickly, trying to hide her bewilderment and discomposure at Logan's actions. She could still feel his touch on her skin, and it unnerved her. She was also surprised to learn that Logan had wanted her to wear the gems on his own, apparently without Camille's prodding.

Rhea was confused. She avoided looking at Logan as she held out her right wrist to let Camille fasten the bracelet in place. Then Rhea put on the earrings, taking the few moments to wonder at Logan's behavior just now. Why was he letting her wear these beautiful sapphires and diamonds? Out of the goodness of his heart? He'd seemed pleased by how they looked on her. More than pleased.

"Now hurry," Camille urged then, starting for the door. "You must be in the ballroom to greet your guests."

In the silence, Rhea shot Logan a quick look, but he didn't appear to see it. His expression was impassive and he seemed quite occupied with buttoning on his white dress gloves. With a sigh of irritation, Rhea turned and followed Camille's swishing wake out of the library.

Chapter 45

OVER TWO HUNDRED PEOPLE, MOST OF THEM UP-
per-class Richmond society, were in attendance in the
huge grand ballroom of Fair Oaks that night. No expense
had been spared in making this wedding reception ball a
memorable event. After all, Camille had told Rhea earlier,
the Tremaines had a reputation to maintain, suitable for
the social position they held. Their noted guests would be
treated in the grandest style possible. It would give them
something to gossip about for weeks to come, Camille had
remarked with a twinkle of delight in her warm blue eyes.

Every piece of the fine furniture lining the walls of the
spacious ballroom sparkled from the house servants' cleaning labors during the week before the Fourth. The three
big crystal chandeliers that hung suspended from the ceiling of the rectangular-shaped room glittered spectacu-
larly. Each of the hundreds of pieces of dangling cut glass
was moved by the air currents, and reflected the flickering
light of the small lamps that illuminated the chandeliers
from the inside.

Rich maroon wallpaper textured like velvet covered the
walls, accentuating the decorative woodworking that was
gilded in gold paint. It all gave the ballroom a splendor be-
fitting that of the many elegantly costumed guests now
present in it.

The orchestra of thirty-five musicians was situated at
the far end of the ballroom. They were tuning their instruments as Negro men and boys—house slaves recruited
from neighboring plantations for the evening—mingled
among the ten-score of guests. They were dressed in maroon livery and had the busy job of making certain the

guests were well furnished with the wide variety of taste-tempting hors d'oeuvres and beverages.

The people in attendance were indeed a sight to behold. Rhea was able to view them up close as she and Logan greeted nearly all of them in the receiving line. At first she scrutinized with a careful casualness each person who passed before her smiling graciously and speaking a word or two to each. The women especially interested her. With their meticulously done coiffures, splendidly fashionable gowns, and almost cumbersome adornment of costly jewelry, they created a rainbow parade of colors and glitter. Rhea was proud to see that her blue gown and the diamonds and sapphires she was wearing more than compared to the visage presented by most of the other women. No dowdy seamstress in an out-of-fashion plain beige gown was she tonight.

Rhea held her head high and matched their affected politeness measure for measure, hoping with a touch of haughtiness that Logan was listening to the myriad of compliments she was receiving from the gentlemen she greeted. But after a while Rhea stopped looking so closely at each of the guests as they just kept coming down the receiving line in a seemingly unending stream. Her right hand was numb, her smile felt frozen in place, and she had stopped noticing the critical and cattish looks that were cast over her by many of the women guests. A devilish part of her longed to do something that would really set all of them back on their heels, but she had promised Logan she would behave tonight. After all, that was their agreement. She would let Logan and all these other southerners see the dignity and refinement a northern woman could exhibit. She was going to make a good showing of herself this evening if it killed her!

And Camille had been right. Rhea was popular with the men present, both young and old. Once the greeting ended and the dancing began, she was never without a partner. Their looks and compliments were appreciative and sometimes a bit bold, but Rhea enjoyed it. Apparently her Philadelphia origins didn't bother the male guests in the crowd. At least *they* found her attractive and weren't reluctant to say so. Not like the man who was playing her husband!

That thought made Rhea frown slightly and seek out Logan in the crowded room. She had danced with him only once—the obligatory first dance—but she couldn't help but notice he never wanted for a partner, either. Now she spied him making his way through the people with none other than Vanessa Forsythe, who was stunning in a shimmering gold satin gown, her red hair loose and flowing down her back. They reached the double doors leading to the rose garden and exited together. Rhea turned back to her partner, trying to hide the sudden annoyance she felt at seeing Logan and Vanessa sneaking off together.

"I cannot leave the ball now, Vanessa," Logan said in a low voice when they reached the garden. Many couples walked among the fragrant flowering bushes, so his words had to be guarded. "It's much too early."

"But, darling, I am in agony," Vanessa replied, pouting. "I've been dying of frustration since you left me so abruptly at Surrey Lane. You're not still angry with me for that little tiff we had then, are you?" She fingered the wide lapel of his coat as she stepped closer.

"No, of course not," Logan answered, trying to hide the growing impatience he felt.

"Good. Then you must stop torturing me. I cannot stand to have you hold me while we dance and not know I shall have something more of you. Come with me now. We can steal away and go upstairs to an empty room. You do still want me, too, don't you, darling?"

Logan looked at the beautiful woman standing so close to him. Her intent green eyes reminded Logan of a predatory tigress sighting her prey, and he didn't like it. Perhaps it was because she seemed so confident of her charms and so sure of him. She was getting too possessive. That was the reason why he found her less appealing tonight, he told himself.

"Logan?" Vanessa cut into his thoughts insistently. Her smile had lessened with his hesitancy and one brow was cocked in question.

"If I do still want you, Vanessa, it will be on my terms and at the time I choose," Logan replied finally, his tone leaving no doubt that he meant what he said. "May I remind you that along with my wife, I am the guest of honor at this affair. I can hardly leave for an assignation with you. I will not have our relationship flaunted, Vanessa. We will continue to have our meetings only if I choose to have them and only as long as they are kept discreet. Now, if you will excuse me, I must go back inside."

As Logan walked away from her, Vanessa followed him with her eyes, which narrowed in fury. So she had not imagined the change she'd sensed in Logan the other day at Surrey Lane.

With some regret and no little anger, Vanessa knew her affair with Logan was over. She had just been cast aside, and that realization left a bad taste in her mouth. No man had ever left her. She was always the one who ended the liaison first.

Scowling and barely containing her wrath, Vanessa tossed her head back with a flourish of her mass of red hair and stalked back into the ballroom.

Because Logan was so popular with the ladies present, Rhea was surprised when she saw him coming toward her now. She'd been searching the crowd in hopes of seeing Evan VanHorn, but he apparently hadn't arrived yet.

"Excuse me, gentlemen," Logan said to the five men who surrounded Rhea during the break in the music. "I must claim my wife for a little while. The conductor of the orchestra insists that we begin this waltz set."

Complaining moans accompanied Rhea's leaving. She laughed and called back over her shoulder that she would be glad to dance with all of them later. Applause greeted Logan and Rhea as they walked hand-in-hand to the middle of the open dancing area. They smiled, acknowledging the tribute as Logan nodded to the conductor and the music began. The guests stepped back to give them ample room, and the waltz commenced.

"To what do I owe this honor?" Rhea asked with sarcasm, knowing the conductor probably hadn't really wanted them to dance alone. She kept a smile set on her lips for all those watching them.

"I decided I have been a neglectful bridegroom," Logan replied, his tone matching hers though he, too, smiled. He didn't tell her he had an ulterior motive, but his eyes sought Vanessa out in the crowd.

"More likely you saw I was having a good time and decided to spoil it," Rhea retorted. She turned her head to follow his gaze and frowned slightly. "Oh, I see now," she went on through gritted teeth while she kept her mouth smiling. "This has something to do with Mrs. Forsythe. I might have known. I'm surprised you could pull yourself away from her long enough for this one dance, even if you are trying to prove something by it."

Logan looked down at her, a little surprised by the touch of malice in her tone.

"Is that a note of jealousy I detect in your voice, dear wife?" he asked with one brow cocked.

"Hardly," Rhea answered, trying to appear disinterested. "She is welcome to have you, believe me. Only I think the two of you could be a little more discreet in your attention to each other, at least for tonight. These people are your friends, remember. Whatever will they think of you?" She leveled her large blue eyes squarely on him as she delivered her tart statements.

Logan had planned to compliment Rhea on her appearance and her performance thus far tonight. He'd been pleased with both. She'd made an exceptionally good impression. He was the envy of every man in the room. Even the women could not find anything to criticize in the way Rhea looked and conducted herself, though he knew they were trying. But now annoyance rose in him and Logan bit back the flattering remarks he'd been about to say to Rhea.

"Oh, stop frowning, dear husband," Rhea chided him, pleased that her remarks had pricked him. "Or our guests shall think I've stepped on your toes or something. Shall we just dance and not converse?"

"An excellent idea," Logan agreed curtly. "Let us just get through this as quickly as possible."

With that Logan began to step more flourishingly to the music. They whirled in wide, graceful circles around the dance floor. Rhea let herself be caught up in the glorious music as she leaned back slightly against Logan's arm and let herself flow with the melody and the movement. She followed Logan's lead with little effort, even when he did some intricate steps and whirled her around and around until she felt a little dizzy. Rhea relaxed, smiling with pleasure as she closed her eyes, tilted her head back, and began to hum the waltz melody. The many layers of chiffon in the wide shirt of her gown floated and swirled around her. She felt light as a feather in Logan's arms, and suddenly Rhea never wanted this wonderful dance to end.

But at last the music stopped. Logan halted them in perfect time, bending Rhea back over his arm in a last grand flourish. Then, much to Rhea's surprise, he bent and kissed her. And what was more surprising, she unconsciously kissed him back. It was some seconds before Rhea heard anything but the wild pounding of her heart as Logan's lips pressed against hers. She moaned softly and brought her arms up around his neck, wanting only to be lost in this kiss unendingly.

But the applause and cheers from their appreciative audience soon broke the spell that held Logan and Rhea together, and they stepped apart. Rhea blushed as she forced a little laugh and made a low, graceful curtsey to Logan, though she avoided looking into his eyes. Then she turned to their guests and curtseyed again. Logan took her hand and guided her off the dancefloor.

Vanessa Forsythe's green eyes blazed with fury as she watched them. Her mouth straightened into a hard line as she turned away and walked toward the ballroom entrance.

Logan and Rhea were immediately separated when they reached the edge of the crowd and other people claimed each of them for the next dance. Miles was the first to touch Rhea's arm.

"Please, Miles, I really must catch my breath," Rhea said, smiling as she waved her fan before her face. "Could we possibly forego this next dance and go outside where it is cooler?"

"Yes, of course, Rhea," Miles quickly agreed. All the better, he thought to himself as he pressed his hand to the small of her back and guided her to the French doors and out into the garden.

"Ah, that is much better," Rhea sighed as she felt the cooler night air on her warm skin.

"Would you like something to drink? Champagne perhaps?"

"Yes, that would be fine, Miles. Would you mind? I am thirsty."

"Not at all. I shall be right back. Don't let anyone steal you away until I return." He gave her a charming smile.

"No, I won't," Rhea agreed, returning his smile. "I'll wait over there." She pointed to an unoccupied stone bench close by.

Rhea was glad to be alone for a few minutes to collect her thoughts. She still felt flushed and breathless from her dance with Logan, but she wasn't sure whether it was the actual waltz or Logan's ardent kiss afterward that caused it. She was amazed that he had done it, though at that moment it had seemed like the perfect thing for him to do. She hadn't wanted to resist at all.

"Foolish girl," she muttered to herself. "You let the spell of the music overwhelm you." Yes, that was all it was, Rhea convinced herself in her thoughts. It was not Logan's superb dancing or his handsomeness or magnetism. It was the music that made her glad to be held in his arms, whirled around the dancefloor, and kissed profoundly afterward. But there was no music playing out here now, and she could still feel where Logan's arms had held her, where his lips had burned against hers.

Rhea sighed. She knew his dancing with her had something to do with Vanessa Forsythe. Most likely the kiss did, too. How she wished Logan did not have this effect on her. She'd danced with many other men before coming to Fair Oaks, and had had many other partners tonight. But none had touched her inside as Logan did.

Rhea closed her eyes and lifted her face to the starlit sky, humming the waltz melody again. She didn't notice that Miles had returned to the garden with two glasses of champagne and was standing off to the side a little way watching her.

"Damn Logan," Miles cursed his brother under his breath. Now Logan had bested him in marriage, too. Not only had he thwarted Miles's latest plan to gain control of his share of the inheritance, but Logan had also acquired for himself a beautiful and very desirable woman for his wife. Miles shifted uncomfortably as he stared at Rhea and realized he wanted this woman.

Miles envied his brother's good fortune—the same envy

that had made them adversaries since the day Logan had been born. There had always been the conflict between them. It was more than just a game of sibling rivalry they engaged in. It was a fierce battle of wits with the stakes getting higher as the years went by. Still, at times, Miles found himself wishing the discord between them didn't exist, that he could trust Logan, combine abilities with him to meet the world head on instead of always being at loggerheads with each other.

Miles shook his head to clear it. Such nostalgia for what might have been was uncharacteristic of him. Perhaps it was that at nearly twenty-nine years of age, he was growing tired of such ruthless competitions. Victories under those circumstances were beginning to take on a hollow ring, but he knew it would probably always be that way between him and Logan.

You're getting soft, old boy. Enough of this, Miles rebuked himself as he continued to watch Rhea sitting on the stone bench. How tempting she looked, so lovely.

Miles set down the champagne glasses on the wooden veranda railing and moved forward noiselessly until he was standing before Rhea. Then he bent and kissed her. Rhea's eyes flew open in surprise and she jumped to her feet.

"Miles, what do you think you're doing?"

"You looked as though you were waiting for that to happen, and I couldn't resist," he explained as nonchalantly as he could manage. "Please forgive me for being so weak to the temptation." He smiled charmingly at her, but Rhea could tell he wasn't truly sorry he'd been so bold.

From a secluded corner of the veranda someone who had also sought the coolness of the garden watched the little scene being played out before him. Someone whose thoughts and expression now were as black as the shadows in which he stood. With jaw clenched and brow furrowed, Logan descended the three steps to the brick path and walked straight toward the stone bench.

"Do not take liberties with me again, Miles. I do not welcome such attention from you," Rhea was warning Miles under his mocking gaze. She was startled when she caught a glimpse of Logan approaching out of the corner of her eye. How much had he seen? she wondered in sudden panic. One look at his scowling expression told her he had seen too much.

"Go back inside, Rhea," Logan ordered sternly as he walked theateningly toward Miles.

"Logan, stop . . ." Rhea stepped between the two glowering men and put both hands on Logan's chest to prevent him from advancing any farther. His glaring stare moved from Miles to her.

"You defend him?" he accused coldly, his black brows nearly touching. "Did you encourage him to kiss you, then, here where all could see you?" His wrath was threatening very near the surface now.

Rhea felt as though his harsh words had struck her like a blow. Her own anger flared.

"Don't be absurd, Logan," she retorted, her blue eyes flashing at him. "I am not defending Miles. I only wish to keep you from making a fool of yourself. Besides, good lord, who are you to speak to me about what I do in front of everyone? Perhaps I have learned by watching you and Mrs. Forsythe too much." Rhea's tone was scathing, and though she had kept her voice low, some couples still were stopping now at the heated sound of the words being said.

"Go back inside, Rhea," Logan ordered through clenched teeth as he glared at her. Rhea's sharp words had reached their mark. His eyes narrowed and his look was thunderous as it drilled into her.

"Only if you will come in with me," Rhea countered firmly, standing her ground before him. Her anger kept her from fearing his gaze. "This matter is closed. It is of no consequence unless you make it so. Your brother was just being childishly impulsive."

Miles said nothing, slightly pricked by Rhea's words. But he was delighted to learn from this little exchange that all was not as harmonious between Logan and Rhea as they wanted everyone to believe.

For several tense moments Logan and Rhea just stared at each other, their gazes locked in silent combat. It took all of Logan's willpower to keep control of his anger. Rhea could certainly spark it off easily enough! Suddenly he smiled, though there was no warmth in it.

"As you wish, my dear," he acquiesced in a honeyed tone

as he extended his elbow to Rhea. "Then of course, we'll say no more about it. Shall we go back inside?"

Logan cast a dark look at his brother, who only smiled back contemptuously. Rhea tucked her hand in the crook of Logan's arm and propelled him away from the scene.

Chapter 46

RHEA WAS IMMEDIATELY CLAIMED FOR THE NEXT dance as soon as she and Logan reentered the ballroom. Logan watched as she was led away to the dancefloor. He didn't like what had happened to him outside. He should have expected something like that from Miles. Rhea was stunningly beautiful tonight. With his eyes he followed her graceful movements with her partner around the dancefloor. Something stirred inside him, a feeling he didn't relish at all. Logan suddenly realized he had trusted that Rhea would not get involved with anyone else, that she would be loyal to him, to their agreement. Yet she had betrayed him with Miles. Perhaps she even told him of their false marriage. No, Miles would've said something if that were the case. And thinking back now, he had to admit that what he'd seen in the garden just now could hardly be called incriminating. In fact, now that he remembered it less angrily, it was Miles who had kissed Rhea. She had seemed surprised and put off by it.

Why hadn't he realized that then, instead of losing his temper? He rarely allowed that to happen. Or at least he hadn't until Rhea Merrick had come into his life.

Logan frowned now as he suddenly realized what the real reason had been for his anger out in the garden. He'd actually felt jealous when he'd seen Rhea with Miles.

His mind flashed back to the waltz they'd danced together. He'd enjoyed holding Rhea in his arms. He really hadn't had to dance with her. They could have avoided each other quite well in this crowd of people. But Logan knew he'd wanted to, and not just to spite Vanessa. He

wanted to dance with Rhea for himself, because there was
something that drew him to her.

He had to admit it had taken courage and spiritedness
on her part to enter into their agreement and then stick it
out as well as she was doing. He knew his family was difficult to live with and, except for Camille perhaps, they had
made little effort to make Rhea feel welcome here at Fair
Oaks. Even he had to reluctantly confess that he'd been so
caught up in his own activities that he hadn't made it easy
for her. Even though Rhea tended to act impulsively at
times, for the most part she was carrying out her role with
a tenacity and intelligence he couldn't help but admire.

Thoughts of Rhea at Farley House, the meadow, the music room and on the dancefloor in his arms, all jumbled together in Logan's mind now to further complicate his
thinking. What was the matter here? He certainly didn't
care anything for Rhea, did he? She was only an instrument to help him undermine Miles and nothing more. He'd
have no woman complicating his life. Yet Logan reluctantly had to admit that Rhea had done exactly that, in
more ways than one.

A waiter walked by with a tray of filled champagne
glasses. Logan reached out and grabbed one as he passed,
downing the bubbly drink in one gulp.

"What a fortunate man you are to have such a lovely
bride," a voice said from behind him.

"Ah, Captain Talmadge," Logan greeted as he turned
around. "It's kind of you to say so." Logan had quickly reverted to an unreadable expression, hiding the turmoil in
his thinking. He had no liking for the man who was the
head of the Richmond police force. And he knew the feeling
was mutual for Talmadge. There had been a natural dislike between them ever since they'd known each other.
Ross Talmadge had a reputation for his intelligence and
also for his cunning and ruthlessness in pursuing criminals—especially when they were runaway slaves. His
association with Jake Stryker was also well known.
Stryker was the leader of a brutish band of slave hunters
who roamed the countryside tracking down fugitive slaves
for bounty money. It was dangerous to make an enemy of
either Talmadge or Stryker, yet Logan had come close to

doing just that for the last three years that Talmadge had been captain of police.

"I'm surprised you could find the time to join us this evening," Logan said pointedly now as he stood before Talmadge. "I know you've been kept very busy investigating the Duvall rebellion and tracking down his runaways. Have you managed to catch any of them yet?" Logan couldn't resist asking him that, even though he knew the ten slaves who'd gotten away hadn't yet been recaptured.

"The investigation is proceeding," Talmadge answered coolly, on his guard now. His eyes narrowed slightly as he took in Logan. "Several new leads have developed."

"You don't say?" Logan returned, feigning surprise. "Does that mean you are closer to capturing that trouble-making Exodus character? Word is out that he was behind the revolt at Duvall's."

"Of course he was the one. There can be no other explanation for it," Talmadge put in rather sharply. He didn't like this goading he was getting from Logan Tremaine. He had to take enough of it from all the other plantation owners who were constantly on his back to bring in Exodus.

"The reward for his capture has been raised to ten thousand dollars. I'm certain that will flush him out. Even the slaves he seeks to help will be tempted by such a sum, don't you agree, Tremaine?" he stated with a confident smile.

"Oh, to be sure," Logan agreed, brushing aside the lawman's comment as though it was inconsequential. "But it is a pity such a large amount of money needs to be wasted for that. There are many around who feel the reward money wouldn't be necessary if you were doing your job." He paused only a moment to eye the police captain and let his jibe sink in before he went on, adding another dig before Talmadge could reply.

"But at any rate, I'm glad to hear that our days of being plagued by Exodus may be nearing an end. We can't afford to keep losing good slaves because of that menace's interference. And neither can you continue to have dangerous criminals like him and the runaways at large, especially with election time approaching."

Talmadge's jawline had tightened and he was frowning under the cutting barrage of Logan's words. He was just about to answer those insults with some choice comments of his own when Sybil Tremaine came up to them.

"Logan, you promised to dance with me and you have not yet done so," she claimed in a pouting tone as she linked her arm around Logan's. "You will excuse us, won't you, Captain Talmadge, while I force this brother-in-law of mine to oblige me?"

"Of course, Mrs. Tremaine," Talmadge replied, nodding slightly. He watched the two of them walk out onto the dancefloor. Tremaine will overstep himself one of these days and it'll be a great pleasure to come down hard on him, Talmadge thought to himself with cold conviction. Damn, but he wished he could get his hands on Exodus and be rid of that thorn in his side once and for all, so high and mighty landowners like Tremaine would stop hounding him about it. Elections *were* coming up in a few months and he'd be a shoo-in for retaining his post if he had Exodus taken care of by then. He'd have to have Stryker double his patrols. He himself would pursue his own new theory more avidly. He didn't know why it hadn't occurred to him before a few weeks ago that Exodus knew the happenings of the community too well to be someone who came into the area only every few months. The escapes he masterminded were too well planned and coordinated with other events. It was hard to imagine a darky being smart enough to do all that and elude his deputies and Stryker's patrol, too. Exodus would have to be working with some important whites around here. If only he could find out who those whites might be.

But then again, maybe Exodus wasn't an ex-slave at all like everybody thought he was. No one really knew what he looked like. He was like a phantom, always working under the cover of darkness and wearing dark clothes that covered him completely, including a hood over his head. Maybe he was a white man, even a slaveowner himself or one of those bothersome Quakers who were motivated by too-righteous consciences. Someone who could come and go as he pleased without causing suspicion.

Talmadge glanced around the crowded room just as Logan and Sybil danced by him. A thought flicked through his mind. Wouldn't it be a sensation if he could prove some connection between Exodus and, say, someone like Logan Tremaine?

Ross Talmadge shook his head, shrugging off the idea. The champagne must be getting to me, he thought. That idea was utterly preposterous. The Tremaines were all hard-nosed Virginia slaveowners, had been for generations.

"Captain Talmadge," Vanessa Forsythe greeted suddenly from next to him, interrupting his thoughts. She was smiling provocatively. "I seem to be without a dancing partner."

"I would be honored to remedy that, Mrs. Forsythe," Talmadge replied. As he bowed slightly toward her, his glance swept over her appreciatively.

"Thank you, captain." She gave him her hand. "May I call you Ross?"

"Of course," Talmadge agreed, wondering at her sudden friendliness. Usually the haughty Mrs. Forsythe wouldn't give him the time of day.

"And I insist that you call me Vanessa. So come, let us dance and then perhaps we can have a little chat. There is something I'd like to discuss with you that I am certain you will find interesting." She looked away from him and frowned slightly as she spotted Logan and Sybil dancing together. Talmadge followed her gaze and felt his curiosity being piqued even further.

"You are such a marvelous dancer, Logan," Sybil gushed as she and Logan moved to the music. "It is heavenly to be in your arms." She smiled up at him enticingly, hoping for a similar response from him.

"I see Grandfather has decided to join us," Logan replied, ignoring her comments and looking toward the main archway leading to the ballroom. Sybil hid her disappointment and looked to where the elderly Tremaine was just being wheeled into the room.

"We should go over and greet him," Logan added.

"I suppose we must," Sybil agreed reluctantly as Logan whirled her around in that direction.

"Good evening, Grandfather Silas," Sybil exclaimed with forced gaiety when they had stopped in front of him. "How delightful that you decided to come."

"Delightful nothing," the senior Tremaine retorted gruffly. "I'm here only because I wanted to see if Logan's Yankee woman is being eaten alive by these barracuda that are here tonight. Where is she?" His eyes searched the crowd.

Sybil glanced at Logan to see his reaction to his grandfather's snide words and was surprised to see that he was smiling slightly, apparently in amusement.

"Rhea is over there," he answered, pointing across the room to where Rhea stood smiling and talking. She was surrounded by men. "I'm afraid the barracuda can't get to her," Logan added with a note of satisfaction. Rhea was playing her part well. Except for the incident in the garden, Logan could find no reason to slight her behavior. His grandfather wouldn't be able to, either.

"She does appear to be charming them," Silas admitted irascibly. "Although those strutting peacocks would flock around any female who looked as beautiful as that." He glanced up at Logan with a mischievous glint in his eye. "Does she perform that well for you in bed?"

Sybil gasped. "Grandfather Silas, what a question!"

"Oh, go fan yourself or something, Sybil," Silas spouted with annoyance as he gestured her away with a wave of his hand. "I can't abide having you around. Go, *go!*"

"Well!" Sybil declared in a huff as she took hold of her skirts and flounced away.

Logan hid his amusement, making himself look serious. He was used to such bluntness from his belligerent grandsire, though he found the question about his marriage bed unnerving. He didn't like being reminded of that intimacy with Rhea. It was something he never intended to repeat, something best forgotten. But he was having difficulty enough doing that.

"Well, answer my question, boy," Silas was insisting, interrupting Logan's thoughts. His wrinkled brow creased even more as he frowned at Logan.

"A gentleman wouldn't ask that of me, Grandfather," Logan answered indulgently, but he avoided Silas's gaze.

"Well, I have a right to know whether you've done your duty toward furnishing this family with offspring," Silas shot back impatiently.

Unfortunately, I *have* done that, Logan admitted with a

sigh only to himself. And I can only hope nothing comes of it.

"Such matters are between Rhea and myself," he said aloud then, adding pointedly, "and they are none of your business."

The two men—the older and the younger—eyed each other levelly. Their matching light blue eyes locked in a gaze that showed no wavering on either one's part for some moments. Then Silas looked away.

"Bah! As usual you do your best to annoy me," he spat irritably. "Be off with you. Go to your Yankee wench, though I don't know how Rhea can tolerate you! I assume it must be because you are two of a kind, you and she. Both insolent, outspoken, and totally lacking in respect for your elders. I'm cursed to be plagued by *both* of you now!

"Jubal!" he suddenly shouted at his Negro servant who had brought him in and remained standing silently behind his chair. "Wheel me to the dining room so I can get some food."

Logan decided that nothing would please his grandfather more than having sparks continually flying around Fair Oaks. As he watched his grandfather being wheeled away, he knew the old man would never change, nor would their relationship. It had always been this way. Logan told himself he didn't care, that he would never bend to the old man's tyrannical will. But what had that attitude ever gotten either of them all these years? Nothing but anger and estrangement.

Yet there was a kind of begrudging respect between them, as well. Silas's methods for holding the family together and building Fair Oaks over the decades may not have been the best. God knew, he had bullied and browbeaten all of them to the breaking point often enough, Logan remembered well. He still did.

But Logan understood that it was hard for his grandfather to accept the fact that he was now too old and debilitated to be the driving force in the Tremaine family any longer. Yet Silas would not give up those reins easily, and would likely try to hold onto them to his dying breath.

So Logan had learned to tolerate the older man's critical bluster and constant bad temperament. Yet he would only take so much of it. Then he, too, would stand his ground and not back down. For this, he knew he had his grandfather's respect. And Logan was determined to have that, if nothing else from old Silas.

Logan thought back now to what Silas had said about Rhea. He was surprised that the old man's words had been what amounted to complimentary for him! Somehow Rhea had managed to gain his grandfather's regard. That was no little accomplishment, especially in view of the brief time she had been at Fair Oaks.

Logan looked for Rhea in the crowd again. He saw her standing in the midst of four other women, chatting and smiling. She was handling the barracuda quite well, too. Logan was pleased, even proud of her.

As much as I would be if she were really my wife, he went on thinking before he stopped himself short.

Chapter 47

"DR. VANHORN, I AM DELIGHTED THAT YOU could come," Rhea said as she finally got to dance with him. She'd begun to fear he wasn't coming at all, but he had finally arrived halfway through the evening.

"I was delayed by a patient," Evan explained. "I apologize again for my tardiness in getting here."

"No need to. I understand." Rhea smiled charmingly at him. He was probably twenty-five or so and rather good-looking, Rhea decided. He'd be a good catch from what she'd heard about him, except for the disadvantages of doctoring—irregular hours and even more irregular pay. Still, Rhea wondered if Camille had ever seriously noticed him on his many trips to Fair Oaks to care for her. But if he were connected in some way with the underground railroad, it would be better if Camille didn't become involved with him in any way. Was he associated with Mr. Exodus, as Ruby had told her? What if he weren't? Rhea would have to take great care in broaching the subject with him. The first thing to do was to try to get him away from the ballroom where they could talk without fear of being overheard.

The music ended and Evan escorted Rhea off the dancefloor. Near the edge of the crowd Rhea pretended to sway on her feet, catching his arm to steady herself. Actually it didn't require much acting. She'd been on her feet for hours.

"Are you all right, Mrs. Tremaine?" Evan asked with some concern as he brought his arm around Rhea's waist to steady her.

"Oh, forgive me, doctor," she apologized, putting her

hand to her forehead. "I'm just a little dizzy from too much dancing and champagne, I fear. Perhaps I should lie down for a moment. Would you see me to the parlor, please? There is a couch in there where I could rest."

Any man would have been hard put to resist Rhea's appealing, wide-eyed look. Evan VanHorn was an easy conquest.

"Of course, Mrs. Tremaine," he readily agreed. "Here, lean on me."

They were close to the arched hallway doors, so they didn't draw too much attention in leaving the ballroom. A lamp had been left burning low in the front parlor, but no one was in the room. Evan helped Rhea to the couch, then turned up the lamp.

"Close the doors, will you, please?" Rhea beseeched him as she put her head back and shut her eyes. "The music still seems so loud."

After a moment's hesitancy, Evan pulled the two sliding doors together, leaving them open a few inches for propriety's sake. From his inside coat pocket he took out a small vial of smelling salts and walked toward Rhea.

"I always carry this to affairs like this, especially on warm evenings," he explained, feeling a little awkward. "Invariably it comes in handy."

But Rhea waved him away as she sat upright again. "That won't be necessary, doctor. I am quite all right."

Rhea looked steadily at the man before her, knowing she was taking a terrible gamble with her next words. But she had promised Ruby she would help her, and this doctor was her only lead to Ruby's escape and her own.

"Doctor VanHorn—Evan," Rhea began, deciding to plunge right in. "We don't have much time, so I shall be brief and come to the point. There is something of great importance I must discuss with you, and no one else must hear us."

Evan was surprised by her sudden apparent recovery and even more startled by her words. He gave her his undivided attention.

"Go on, Mrs. Tremaine."

"Call me Rhea, please. I am in desperate need of your help, Evan." She wouldn't tell him of her own need now, not until she was certain he was the one to help and she could trust him. "It is a friend of mine. She must get away from Fair Oaks as soon as possible."

At Evan's questioning look, Rhea said the words Ruby had told her would be so important in this exchange.

"The ebony raiment is cast off . . ." Then she held her breath in fearful anticipation.

Evan VanHorn looked at her for a long moment, his expression unreadable. ". . . Never to be worn again," he answered finally in a low voice.

Rhea gasped in relief. "Oh, thank God, you are the one to help us—I mean, her."

"I think you'd better explain all of this from the beginning, Mrs. Tre—Rhea." Evan's tone was deadly serious as he looked at her intently. But before Rhea could go on, he cautioned her with a wave of his hand and went over to the doors to close them all the way. Then he came back over to the sofa.

"This involves a young slave girl here at Fair Oaks. Her name is Ruby." Rhea quickly proceeded to relate the story of Dreed Jessup's cruelty.

"So you see, Evan, I must keep my promise to try to help Ruby. I would like to help others, too. Ruby says Mr. Exodus will help her escape. Can you help us make contact with him? He's an ex-slave, isn't he? Surely he wouldn't let Ruby go on being treated so."

Evan was frowning deeply as he paced a small circle before Rhea. He was uncertain of what to do next.

"You have no idea what you are getting yourself into, Rhea. This is a very dangerous undertaking, to more people than just yourself." He looked at her sternly. "This is not a game we are playing here."

Rhea matched his serious expression as she got to her feet before him.

"I am well aware of that, Evan. I am not playing games. I know people's lives are at stake here. But my conscience dictates my actions. Will you help Ruby?"

Evan had to have time to think. He couldn't let Rhea Tremaine get involved with the underground. Exodus would never allow it, he was almost certain of that. But at the moment he had to stall Rhea until he could get orders from Exodus. And at the same time, he had to help Ruby. He knew Jessup's reputation. He'd been called to try to help another slave girl Jessup had used his whip on, at the last plantation where he'd been employed before coming to Fair Oaks. It hadn't been a pretty sight.

"All right, Rhea," he said finally, coming to a decision. "Ruby will have to get to my house in Richmond by eleven o'clock tomorrow night. It's on Compton Street at the south edge of town."

"She'll go to Mr. Exodus from there?"

"It is better that you know no more than that," Evan continued. "As it is, I'm taking a terrible risk trusting you." He eyed her levelly, his expression severe.

"And I am risking much by trusting you," Rhea countered, returning his look unfalteringly. "But that is the way it must be."

"Very well. Mr. Exodus will be informed of your part in this," Evan went on. "He will give me further instructions. Whatever they are, you must abide by them. On this I must have your solemn promise, for everyone's safety."

"Very well, Evan, I understand," Rhea agreed. She almost told him then that she wanted to use the escape network herself along with Ruby, but she decided against it. Better to just arrive on his doorstep late tomorrow night with Ruby and insist that she be allowed to go along. He would be in no position to argue with her then.

"I'll see to it that Ruby arrives on time. Thank you. Now we had better return to the ballroom."

They had just opened the parlor doors to walk out when Camille approached them.

"Oh, there you are, Rhea. I've found you at last. I've been looking everywhere for you. And you, too, Evan." She smiled shyly at the young doctor as she looked at him.

"I felt faint from the heat and too much dancing," Rhea was quick to explain, "and the good doctor here was kind enough to come to my aid with smelling salts."

"I, too, have felt light-headed," Camille said sympathetically. "Too much excitement, I suppose. Are you all right now?"

"Yes, I feel much better. We were just going to return to the ballroom," Rhea told her.

"I'm afraid Evan cannot do that," Camille said. "Word has come from the Stillwell plantation. Louisa's baby is coming early and there seems to be some difficulty."

Evan frowned. "I was afraid something like this might happen to her. I'll have to go at once. If you will excuse me, ladies . . ." He nodded slightly and quickly walked away down the hall.

"Rhea," Camille announced then, "Logan is looking for you. It is time to start the fireworks, and as the guests of honor, you and my brother must be present."

Chapter 48

RHEA AND CAMILLE JOINED LOGAN ON THE LONG balcony that spanned the length of the second story of the house and overlooked the back lawn. Miles, Sybil, and Drew were already there also.

"Ah, there you are, Rhea," Logan greeted in a stiffly polite tone.

She was glad the light was dim on the balcony and she could not see Logan's expression clearly. She knew what it would be, though, by his cool tone of voice, but she didn't care. She felt nervous but excited, too, by the plan that had been set in motion with Evan VanHorn. Rhea knew she must be very careful. Under no circumstances could Logan learn that she was helping Ruby or, especially, that she planned to escape herself. She hadn't forgotten his threat to force her to stay and comply with their agreement.

"All right, Abel," Logan called down to a servant below them. "Get them started."

The fireworks were spectacular. Everyone had spilled out of the house onto the wide lawn to watch and exclaim over the brilliant lights and sounds of the bright-colored array exploding before them. Even Rhea put aside her concerns to enjoy the display. She felt like a child again. Her laughter and exclamations of pleasure could be heard throughout the show.

None of this was lost on Logan who sat next to Rhea. He found himself watching her more than the fireworks. She looked lovely. Each burst of bright light illuminated her eyes and face, reflecting her animation.

"Oh, Camille, look at the colors!" Rhea exclaimed to her friend, who sat on the other side of her.

"This is my favorite part of the Fourth of July!" Camille
replied excitedly, her smile radiant.

Rhea is good for Camille, Logan thought to himself as he
watched the two women together. That was a pleasant development he hadn't anticipated. He was glad for Camille,
because he knew his sister was often lonely. But he
couldn't help wondering how Camille would react when
Rhea was no longer a part of the family. It would sadden
her greatly and the thought troubled Logan. Never did he
want to hurt his sister in any way. He just hadn't thought
of this possibility developing.

Rhea felt Logan's eyes on her and looked over at him.
Seeing his frown, she was sure it was for her. Sighing, she
decided to be a little more reserved in her behavior.

As Logan watched the fireworks again he couldn't help
thinking that his quickly arranged agreement with Rhea
Merrick was having repercussions he hadn't begun to
imagine.

The hour grew late. Many of the guests had already departed or gone upstairs if they were staying the night at
Fair Oaks. Rhea was exhausted but was in a euphoric
state of mind from the excitement of the evening, not to
mention the influence of the numerous glasses of champagne she'd had. She was standing with three young gentlemen now.

"Rhea, this may be the last dance. Won't you have it
with me?"

"I'm sorry, Christopher," Rhea told him, managing to
smile, "but if I try to dance one more step, I fear I shall collapse."

"As long as you would be in my arms, I would welcome
it."

"Silly boy," Rhea called him, laughing.

"But come, lads, and lady," another one of the fellows
said then, nodding toward Rhea, "let us have one more
toast." He gestured for a waiter with a tray of glasses to
come over to them.

"I will make the toast a patriotic one for this special
day," Christopher Reston announced. They all held their
filled glasses up before them. Reston cleared his throat.

"To these blessed United States of America, which on

this day, July fourth, in the year of our Lord, seventeen hundred and seventy-six, threw off the bonds of British tyranny and declared themselves a free and independent nation. Long may the voice of this nation be raised to the world, telling all that here is a land of freedom and justice and opportunity!"

"Hear, hear!" the other two men chimed in, clinking their glasses together and then raising them to their lips.

Rhea was thoughtful. She had lowered her glass and not saluted the toast, but now she nearly drained her glass, welcoming its mellowing sensation as it spread over her.

"How strange that you would make such a toast, Christopher," she remarked offhandedly, swaying on her feet. "Or any of you, for that matter. You are all slaveowners. How can you declare yourselves champions of freedom and justice and all of that when you hold people in bondage against their will?" She blinked back the blurriness that made each of their faces fuzzy before her.

Their witty conversation stopped as all three men stared at Rhea in surprise.

"Forgive my wife, gentlemen," Logan said quickly as he came up beside Rhea just then and put a steadying arm around her waist. She turned her head to look at him questioningly.

"I fear Rhea has had an exhausting evening, and she is not accountable for what she says after imbibing a quantity of champagne," he continued. "Come, my dear. I think it is time we went upstairs. Excuse us, gentlemen, and good night." His arm propelled Rhea away before she could offer a protest.

"But the party isn't over yet," she finally managed to sputter as they walked toward the arched doorway.

"It is for you, my dear," Logan answered sternly, and his hold tightened.

They had to stop several times to bid people goodnight before they got out into the hall. Rhea had finished her champagne, and before Logan could stop her, she had gotten another glass from a tray on a nearby table when he'd been talking. She was feeling quite good and was blissfully unaware that Logan was perturbed with her.

At the bottom of the staircase, Rhea drank what remained in her champagne glass, lifted her skirts, and started up the stairs. But she missed her footing twice before she had climbed even five steps. Logan sighed with exasperation as he caught her for the second time.

"Here, let me carry you or we'll never make it upstairs," he decided curtly as he swept her up into his arms and proceeded up the stairs.

Rhea didn't protest. She was so tired, she was glad to be carried. She began to hum the song the orchestra was playing now and waved her hand and empty wineglass in the air in time to the music. Logan set her down on her feet in the middle of her bedroom.

"Oh, stop looking so forbidding," Rhea admonished as she finally noticed his frown. She staggered slightly and grabbed for his arm to steady herself. "You're always looking so disagreeable. Don't you ever smile?" Without waiting for an answer, Rhea turned away, weaving perilously.

"Oh, dear. Look, my champagne glass is empty. What a pity." She waved the crystal glass she'd brought with her in the air. "Can't we get some more of this delicious bubbly stuff? It makes me feel so good. Why did we have to leave? The party wasn't over yet." She turned from across the room, wobbling on her feet again. She steadied herself on a nearby chair until the room stopped spinning before her.

"I think you've had quite enough champagne, Rhea," Logan answered her sternly. "And we left because you were making a spectacle of yourself."

"Good heavens, was I?" Rhea asked with pretended surprise. "I was just having fun. They were being such pompous asses. But then again, one isn't allowed to have fun around here, is one?" She turned her large blue eyes fully on him, looking as innocent as a child.

Logan sighed with irritation. "You're in no condition to discuss this further. I'll call for your maid." He moved to the cord hanging against the wall.

"I gave Glory the night off. She's with the other slaves celebrating. It's a holiday for your trusty workhorses, remember? *You'll* have to do it," Rhea announced almost challengingly. She turned her back to him, presenting the long line of small buttons that needed unfastening. With annoyance, Logan stepped forward and began the task. Rhea started to hum again and sway to the tune. The scent of her delicate perfume drifted up to him, reminding Logan of their dances together. It confused his mind and caused a stirring deep inside him.

"Stand still, will you, woman?" he demanded impatiently, "or I'll never get all these ridiculous buttons undone."

Rhea pulled away from him and whirled around. "Stop scolding me!" she exclaimed, stamping her foot. "You're always so displeased with me, ordering me about. And I'm tired of it! I'm tired of your scowling face and being treated like an errant child!"

"Then stop acting like one," Logan snapped at her as he came toward her again. He turned her roughly around by the shoulders and finished unfastening the last of the buttons. "Now get to bed and sleep off all that champagne you drank."

Logan turned on his heel and walked to the door leading to the sitting room that separated their bedrooms. Rhea stamped her foot again and blew out her breath in exasperation as she moved to follow him. Emboldened by the champagne, she decided to finish telling Logan Tremaine what was on her mind. Her loosened gown hampered her so she shrugged it off and stepped out of it and the wide hoop skirt and petticoats. Clad only in her white, lace-trimmed camisole and pantaloons, Rhea stalked after Logan, who was now in his own bedroom.

"Just a minute, you bully. I have more to say to you!" Rhea stopped in the middle of his room, hands on hips. She glared at him, but Logan ignored her completely and began to undress. He removed his coat, then his vest and tie.

His obvious disregard for her tantrum only rankled Rhea more. She was determined to pierce that cool, controlled exterior of his if it took the rest of the night! She wanted to see him lose his temper completely and rant and rave, to prove to herself that he was just as human and vulnerable to emotions as anyone else! So she threw caution to the wind and gave Logan the full lash of her barbed tongue that she'd held in check for so long.

"I have grown weary of playing this role, Logan Tremaine. Always playing a part, and never doing it well enough, according to you. I can never be myself. I have hated doing such acting for the past year and even more so for the past few weeks with you. I certainly didn't know what I was getting myself into when I agreed to this ridiculous bargain of ours. I won't be married to a cold and heartless man like you—not even in pretense! And I won't live in this house full of hate and deceit another day!"

Logan sat down on the bed and removed his black dress shoes. Then he stood up, removed his cufflinks, and unbuttoned his shirt, as though Rhea were not even there.

"Do you hear me, Logan Tremaine?" Rhea demanded shrilly as she stomped toward him. "As of this moment I am declaring our absurd agreement ended—nullified! I would rather rot in jail for not paying my debts than endure you or this household any longer!"

"I assure you prison would be much worse," Logan said finally in a frigid tone, without batting an eyelid or raising his voice. But had the light been better, Rhea might have seen the dangerous tightening of his square jaw.

"And don't forget, you had some other reasons for leaving Philadelphia, such as Grayson Sawyer. But at any rate, the option of going to court and perhaps jail are no longer open to you. We made an agreement. You gave me your word on it. I shall keep my part of it and you shall keep yours. You shall not leave Fair Oaks until I allow it."

Rhea's jaw dropped open slightly. Oh, the audacity of him!

"I shall tell everyone I am not really your wife. I'll tell Miles how you have tricked him!" She stood boldly before Logan as she made her dangerous threats.

"You will do nothing of the kind," Logan shot back in a deadly low voice. He grabbed Rhea's wrist then and pulled her against him, catching her other wrist to imprison her against his bare chest. "I promise you that if you do, you shall regret it very, very much." His eyes were cold and staring as Rhea flinched under the painful pressure of his hold on her.

"I hate you," she hissed at him, trying to pull away. "You are like a block of stone. You feel nothing, care about nothing. You have no heart."

"And just remember that," Logan returned harshly, trying to contain his wrath. "For then you will know that I do not make idle threats. I mean what I say."

Rhea was afraid of him, afraid of his cold, malevolent look. But she was more angry, furious at herself and him.

"Let go of me, Logan," she demanded as she suddenly pushed at him with all her might. It was enough to throw Logan off balance, though he kept his hold on her as they both fell backward on the bed. He pinned Rhea half under him.

"Let go of me! I hate you!" she repeated, struggling against him.

The struggle and the feel of Rhea's body writhing beneath him inflamed Logan's senses. His control was shattered, replaced by a primitive urge that overwhelmed him. He reached up and ripped open the thin ribbon laces holding Rhea's camisole together, exposing her full breasts to his ravaging mouth. Then his hand remained at her breast as his lips moved up Rhea's body, along her neck, and to her mouth, which he plundered savagely.

"No, no!" Rhea cried, pulling her mouth away and struggling futilely against him. But any further protests died in her throat as her body quickened to meet his raging desire. Their hindering clothes were swiftly discarded and they held fast to one another, feeling the fire that had ignited between them grow to an overpowering, all-consuming height.

Rhea pressed her naked body against Logan's as he lay on his side half covering her. She became aware of his small gasps of pleasure as she ran her hands gently over the muscles of his chest and shoulders. She continued up his neck to entwine her fingers in his hair and pull his head down to her mouth that hungered so to taste him. She could feel Logan's desire for her pressing hard against her thigh and was amazed that he held back to explore the depths of her mouth, her neck, her breasts with his tongue. Rhea twisted and moaned, wanting to be totally possessed by him.

Logan could not get his fill of tasting Rhea, of feeling her soft, warm flesh yield so willingly to his touch. But at last he was seized by a passion that swept away the remainder of his control.

"Oh, Logan, yes, now," Rhea murmured breathlessly, welcoming him as he moved over her.

He sank into the hot moist folds between her legs, and her thrusting hips carried him deeper and deeper within her. Their longing for each other became an insatiable demon that had forced them back together again. For long moments of ecstasy Logan and Rhea were one in an awesome explosion of sensations that touched their very souls. They could not refuse to answer the demands of their desire.

Finally exhausted, Rhea and Logan slept. But with the dim light of dawn came a new awakening, one filled with gentleness, contentment. The desperate yearning of the night was quiet now, replaced by a need to lie close, to touch, to kiss, to caress.

Rhea was lying on her stomach, savoring the gentle stroking Logan was giving her back. He leaned down and nibbled the nape of her neck, making her squirm. She turned toward him and smiled impishly.

"And now I suppose I shall have to pay for that massage?" She eyed him with one delicate brown eyebrow arched questioningly, brushing her hair away from her eyes and high cheekbones slowly.

"Most assuredly, wench," Logan replied with mock seriousness. He lay back against the pillows and stroked his beard-shadowed chin. "It will take me a few moments to decide just what method of payment will be required of you." His eyes twinkled as he made no movement toward her.

"Oh, I see," Rhea said as she propped herself up on one elbow and used her finger to make little circles in the dark hair on his chest. Then she ran it up the side of his neck, over his chin, and around his lips. He nipped at her finger, but she quickly pulled it back before he could bite it.

"So it's teasing you want, is it?" he noted, coming up quickly and grabbing her around the waist before she could get away from him. He pushed her back against the pillows where he'd just been and threw a leg over both of hers to pin her there.

"Then that shall be the payment you must give me." His pale blue eyes glinted with mischief as he looked at Rhea. "You must submit to my caresses until at least noon today."

"Oh, no," Rhea protested, shaking her head and trying to suppress a smile. "You ask too much, sir."

"Do I?" Logan asked, his voice a husky whisper now as

he smiled at her in return and brought his head down to gently cover her lips with his.

Rhea moaned softly in surrender and answered his kiss with an even more fervent one of her own. Logan's hands played over her silky skin, softly tormenting her to the peak of arousal. She trembled as his lips embraced the nipples of her breasts. Their sudden tautness testified ever so readily to the effect he was having on her. Every part of Rhea's body responded in kind to his expert touch.

"How beautiful you are, Rhea," Logan murmured as he let his eyes follow his hands over her. Then he could speak no more, for while he had tried to hold back, he was consumed now by her fire, which had spread so quickly to him. His breath came in small catches as he rose up slightly and came to her, gasping as she arched to meet him. The building tempest of their passion burst forth between them, and Logan and Rhea were quickly lost in the magnificent exaltation of their joining.

As the throbbing pleasure began to subside within her, Rhea would not let herself think—only feel, sensing the wonder of Logan's hard-muscled body near her, over her, in her. She sighed deeply, then smiled to herself and reveled in lying close in his protective arms and sleeping again.

Chapter 49

LATE THAT MORNING A LOUD KNOCK AT THE hall door shattered the stillness. Rhea stirred in Logan's arms and reluctantly opened her eyes.

"What is it?" Logan called out in a drowsy and slightly annoyed voice.

"Marse Logan, yo' is ta come quick," Obediah called loudly from the other side of the door. "Marse Miles say dey's trouble down at da compoun'."

Logan sighed heavily as he rubbed his hand over his eyes. "All right, Obediah. Tell Miles I'll be right there."

"Yes, suh!"

They heard Obediah's retreating footsteps down the hallway.

"Good morning," Logan said softly as he glanced over at Rhea. "I'm sorry you were awakened so abruptly."

"Good morning," Rhea replied, warmed by his look and the caressing sound of his voice. "You have to leave?"

"I'm afraid so. Miles wouldn't send for me unless it were something he couldn't handle alone."

He paused to look at Rhea, the woman he'd just spent the better part of the night making love to. This shouldn't be. It was all wrong. And yet he found himself still wanting her. He had not had his fill of her. He wanted her even now as she lay naked in his arms.

Rhea read the puzzlement in Logan's look and understood, for she was feeling much the same disbelief and confusion. She hated for morning to be here and didn't want Logan to leave, because that would mean the enchanting night they'd spent together was over, the magical spell that had taken them to such wondrous heights of passion would be broken. And she would have to think again and face reality.

"I must go," Logan told her softly as he leaned over to kiss her tenderly. Rhea's arms came up around his neck as she kissed him back. She wanted to cling to him, stay in the strong protection of his arms and feel safe and wanted.

"We shall talk later," Logan added quietly when they had parted. Rhea nodded and lowered her eyes so he wouldn't see the uncertainty in them.

In a matter of a few minutes Logan dressed and was gone, leaving Rhea with her tormenting thoughts and only too vivid memories of the night just passed.

What would she and Logan talk about when he returned? Could she mean anything to him other than as a woman who gives a little pleasure to satisfy his masculine needs? Would he let her mean any more to him than that? She'd told herself she hated him. But then how could she want him so desperately, too? Her body betrayed her with its longing for him even now.

Rhea groaned as she realized why she must be feeling this way. Against all logic and reason, she was falling in love with Logan. Oh, why him? Why Logan Tremaine? If she stayed with him any longer, spent any more nights with him like last night, Rhea knew she would fall in love with him completely. She couldn't give him her heart for surely he would crush it with his cruel detachment and indifference. She was almost certain Logan felt nothing for her except physical desire. And once he was satiated in that way, he would be just as critical, cynical, and cold as he always was. He took an obvious pride in being that way. How could she love a man like that? There was no future in such a relationship, no possible happiness that Rhea could see.

There was only one thing to do—what she had planned to do all along. Leave Fair Oaks. Leave Logan before he could completely enslave her with her need for him. She had to leave now, today, even before he returned. She couldn't see him again, for she knew if she did, if he looked at her again with those pale blue eyes or touched her, she would be powerless to resist him and she would be lost.

Rhea's mind raced. Somehow she'd avoid seeing Logan today. Perhaps she'd be lucky and he'd have to stay at the

slave quarters all day. She would take the jewelry Logan
had bought for her in Philadelphia. It wasn't as valuable
as the sapphires and diamonds she'd worn to the ball.
Then tonight she would slip away with Ruby as planned.
Escape to Canada and start a new life there. Try to put all
of this behind her.

Rhea looked over at the bedstand and saw the priceless
necklace, bracelet, and earrings where she'd hastily laid
them last night when . . .

She shook her head to dispel the disturbing memory. No,
she could not take those jewels. She was not a thief. But
the others Logan had given her. True, they were part of
her compensation for playing his wife, but she'd earned
them at least for these weeks of . . . services rendered. She
would sell them somewhere along the way and use the
money for that new start in Canada.

Before her resolve could weaken, Rhea got up out of bed.
For a moment she had to struggle to gain her bearings as
the pain of her champagne hangover made her head pound
mercilessly. She almost knocked over an artist's easel that
was standing next to the bureau as she staggered toward
the door. She hadn't seen it there last night. But then, she
hadn't been able to see anything but Logan last night.

As Rhea grabbed for the wobbling frame and steadied it
on its wooden legs, the thin piece of sheeting that had been
covering the painting slipped to the floor. She was stunned
to see what was being painted on the canvas. Her own
countenance looked back at her, perfectly depicted on the
cloth. And the music room was sketched in around her, yet
to be painted. Her figure was seated at what would be the
black grand piano, suffused in sunlight from the long window behind her.

Could Logan be doing this painting of her? When had he
seen her in the music room? Did he truly see her as beautiful and serene as he was depicting on the canvas? Logan,
the man she had accused of having no feeling, no heart—
could he be painting this?

Suddenly a knock sounded on the door leading to the sitting room. Startled, she quickly covered the painting and
reached for a long satin dressing robe that Logan had left
over a chair, putting it on. Then she realized it wouldn't be

Logan who would come through that door, which led to her bedroom.

"Who is it?" she called out, reminding herself that everyone thought she and Logan were married, so no one would find it unusual that she was in her "husband's" room.

"It's Glory, Miz Rhea."

"What is it, Glory?" Rhea asked as she opened the door.

"Oh, Miz Rhea, yo' gots ta come right now. It be Miz Camille. She done took powerful sick agin an' she callin' fo' yo'."

Chapter 50

RHEA SPENT MUCH OF THE REST OF THE DAY with Camille, who was weak and feverish from exhaustion. The housekeeper, Mrs. Jerome, hovered about, as did Camille's old Negro mammy, Esta. But it was Rhea Camille had called for. And Logan.

Rhea sat with Camille, talking soothingly to her, seeing that she was kept cool and given liquids. Evan VanHorn was summoned, but old Dr. Feldon arrived from Richmond instead, saying the young doctor had no more than returned from delivering a baby when he'd been called out again to the back country to tend an injured child. There was little Dr. Feldon could do. He gave Camille some medication and it seemed to help some, for by midafternoon, Camille had fallen into a restless sleep. They would all just have to wait it out and hope that Camille's strong spirit would see her through.

Finally Rhea was able to leave the room for a little while, leaving Esta with Camille and telling her to let her know immediately if there was any change. Then she had Ruby summoned to the house on the pretext of having some work for the slave girl to do. Ruby had recovered from her beating from Jessup enough to be a help around the house, but not well enough to return to the exhausting toil of the fields. Rhea hoped the girl wouldn't have to be subjected to that again. If their plan for the escape worked, she never would be.

Rhea had asked Logan if she could help train the slave girl to be a house servant. Logan had consented, and Rhea wondered if he'd agreed so readily because his conscience bothered him concerning Ruby. But more than likely he didn't care one way or the other about the girl's fate, she decided; she had probably just caught him in a little better mood than usual that day. She wondered if Dreed Jessup knew what she was up to.

"I must go back to Miss Camille's room in a few minutes, Ruby," Rhea told the slave girl now in a low voice when they had reached the safety of Rhea's bedroom. "But I had to let you know what's happening. Everything is all arranged. You must get away from the slave compound tonight. Do you think you can do it without anyone noticing?"

The Negro girl's face lit up with excitement. "Oh, Lordy, yes, Miz Rhea! Ah shor' will try."

"I'll meet you at the ruins as we planned before, at nine tonight. Now you'd better get busy hemming this gown as I showed you," she gestured toward a beige satin gown lying across the bed, "so you'll have a legitimate excuse for being here. Then go back to your cabin."

"Yes, ma'am."

Logan arrived back at the house with Miles late in the afternoon. They both came immediately to Camille's room when they learned of her illness. Miles stayed only long enough to find out that his sister was somewhat better and there was nothing else to be done now except wait.

"Was there much trouble at the slave quarters?" Rhea ventured carefully, looking askance at Logan.

He pulled his eyes away from his sister to look at Rhea absently.

"A little too much holiday celebrating was all. Some of the bucks got hold of a jug of corn liquor and were drunk and rowdy. Everything's under control now."

Rhea breathed a sigh of relief. If the trouble had been serious at the compound, security might have been tightened so that it would have been impossible for Ruby to get away tonight.

Rhea's thoughts were heavy as she realized she could not get away from Fair Oaks with Ruby tonight. She'd still help the slave girl, but she'd have to stay. She couldn't leave Camille like this, not when her presence seemed to

comfort her friend so much. She'd have to find another
time to flee Fair Oaks herself.

Logan had stayed standing at his sleeping sister's bed-
side watching her intently. Camille looked so pale and
fragile lying there, nearly lost in the big double bed. How
helpless he felt when she was like this, when her laughter
and gaiety were so cruelly silenced. She *must* recover. He
willed her to do so now with all his might.

Rhea sat next to the bed holding Camille's hand. She
watched Logan now, watched the play of emotions pass
over his handsome face before he masked them with his
usual cool countenance. But Rhea had seen his look of
pain. Was he capable of caring? He seemed to be moved
deeply by the illness of this lovely, frail young woman who
was his sister.

"Thank you for caring for Camille. I noticed that the two
of you have become close these past few weeks. She has
needed someone." Logan's tone was somewhat formal, but
his eyes seemed softer as he glanced at Rhea, then back to
his sister. "I feared she was taking on too much in planning this holiday celebration and the reception ball. Her
health has always been delicate. It's her heart. Evan says
some part of it was not formed correctly. Little is known
about the malady or how to cure it. I shouldn't have allowed her to do so much, for she suffers greatly because of
it now."

As do you, Rhea thought sympathetically as she
watched Logan. "She will get better," she tried to assure
him. For some reason she felt the need to say that to Logan, to try to lessen the burden of responsibility for his sister that he'd taken onto his shoulders. "Esta says she has
had these attacks before and always recovers. We shall
take good care of her. You'll see, she'll be better. We'll
hear her happy laughter soon again."

Rhea tried to make her words sound convincing as she
looked affectionately at Camille. She reached out and
brushed a tendril of blonde hair away from her friend's
perspiring face. For a moment she found she wanted to
touch Logan and comfort him, too. But then she was glad
she hadn't reached out to him for his tone was brusque
when he spoke to her the next moment. His face was unreadable.

"I hope you are correct in your diagnosis. Perhaps by the time I return, she will have her strength back."

"Return?" Rhea asked.

"Yes, I am leaving early tomorrow morning on a business trip north to make final arrangements for the sale of our tobacco and to buy supplies and stock for the plantation. I shall be gone five or six days." With that Logan turned to leave. But he paused a moment to look at Rhea.

"When you can get away from here," he murmured in a low voice, "there is a matter we need to discuss before I leave." He lowered his eyes uncomfortably, then turned and left the room.

They both knew to what he referred, and it did indeed need discussing. But Rhea was tired. She felt drained from worrying about Camille's condition and the tension and danger from her plans with Ruby. She didn't feel up to a confrontation with Logan, and that was surely what any discussion between them would become.

It was evening before Camille finally stopped waking up so often and settled into a sound sleep. Rhea slipped away to her own room. Though she knew Logan was waiting to talk to her, she didn't have time to see him now. Ruby was depending on her. If she'd been able to get away from the slave quarters as they'd planned, Ruby would be waiting for Rhea even now at the old ruins at Meadow Lake.

A feeling of trepidation stirred in Rhea as she changed into dark-colored riding clothes. Or was it something else, too? Excitement for this dangerous undertaking?

Just before she left her bedroom, Rhea went to the bedstand drawer where she kept the small derringer she'd brought with her from her shop in Philadelphia. Hopefully she would have no need for the weapon tonight, but it wouldn't hurt to have it along. After stuffing it deep in the side pocket of her riding skirt, Rhea left her room, tiptoed down the back staircase, and left the house by a little-used side door.

Chapter 51

LOGAN QUICKLY BLEW OUT THE CANDLE AND stepped back farther into the horse stall when he heard the door of the big stable creak open. His dark clothes helped him blend in with the shadows. His eyes tried to pierce the darkness to see who had come in at such a late hour.

The door creaked closed again and a moment later a match was struck and touched to a lantern. Logan frowned when he saw who held the light and walked to Jade Wind's stall—Rhea! What could she be up to?

Jade Wind whinnied in recognition and Rhea patted her nose and spoke softly as she quickly reached for a bridle hanging in the stall and slipped it over the mare's head. She didn't take time for a saddle but led the horse from the stall, blew out the lantern, and left the stable.

Logan's jaw was clenched in a hard line as he waited in the darkness a few moments before following Rhea. It was foolhardy and dangerous for a woman to be out riding alone at this hour. Where could she be going? Logan frowned. There could be only one reason for a woman to venture out alone and so surreptitiously at night—a rendezvous. His temper flared. Would she dare? And with whom? Miles?

Hesitating no longer, Logan hastily led the horse he'd just saddled out of the barn. Outside, he paused long enough to listen for the sound of hoofbeats indicating Rhea's direction. Then he swung up into the saddle and spurred his chestnut mount to follow her.

Rhea arrived at the log cabin ruins glad for the bright moonlight to illuminate her way. Her nerves were on edge.

She was only too aware of the danger she might be getting herself into. But she couldn't back out now.

Jade Wind felt her nervousness and pranced and pawed the ground. Rhea dismounted, patting the mare's neck as she tied her to a nearby tree. Then she cautiously tiptoed into the crumbling building.

"Ruby . . ." she whispered as she tried to see in the dimness of the main room. "Ruby!" she called a little louder. Her heart was in her throat as she waited to hear some sound.

A creaking noise suddenly sounded from the corner in front of her. Rhea held her breath, forcing down the panic and impulse to run that threatened to overcome her.

"Miz Rhea?" came a frightened voice from near the floor in the corner. Rhea breathed again in relief as she recognized Ruby's voice.

"Yes, Ruby," she answered as she watched a small door in the floor creak open wider. The slave girl emerged and hurried over to her.

"Where were you hiding, Ruby?"

"A little room under da floor," Ruby answered in a quivering voice, pointing toward the corner. "Lattie done tol' me 'bout it. She tol' me other runaways has used it."

"Lattie?" Rhea asked, worried that others knew of their plans tonight.

"She an ol' slave at da compoun'. She don' work no mo', jus' take care o' da young'uns. She won' tell nothin'. She help me git away tonight."

"All right. We must leave quickly now and get on our way. Time is growing short."

Rhea drew Ruby up behind her on Jade Wind's back, then she guided the horse to the main road, the only route she knew for getting to Richmond and Evan VanHorn's house. Staying in the side shadows as much as possible, they set out for the city.

After they'd been riding a short while, Rhea spied a flicker of light up ahead. She quickly reined in Jade Wind and turned her off the road. Then she and Ruby dismounted and concealed themselves with the horse in the dense trees and underbrush, waiting nervously for whoever might be coming to pass by. Within a minute, a group of five men came riding toward them on horseback. Two were carrying lanterns, the others had rifles. They came to a halt almost abreast of the women's hiding place and started to talk among themselves.

Ruby clutched Rhea's arm. "Slave catchers," she murmured fearfully before she dropped to the ground to hide herself better.

· Rhea feared to breathe as she waited anxiously, praying the men would pass by. She hugged Jade Wind's head against her and patted her neck, trying to keep the mare quiet. But still the mare snorted as she caught the scent of the other horses so close by. Rhea's heart seemed to stop.

"You hear somethin'?" one of the men called out.

The long seconds of waiting seemed like an eternity. Through a small opening in the thick brush, Rhea could see the man who'd spoken standing up in his stirrups, gazing around in their direction. She'd never been so frightened in her entire life. She held Jade Wind's muzzle to keep the excited horse silent and closed her own eyes to try to block the terrifying thoughts that flashed through her mind. If they had dogs with them, she and Ruby would have no chance at all of escaping detection. Was that a hound's yelp she'd just heard?

"Yeah, come on. I heard somethin', too, over there," another voice spoke up.

Rhea pressed her hand over the cold metal of the derringer in her pocket but realized with despair that it would be of little use against an entire posse. How she wished she and Ruby were anywhere but here at this moment!

Logan was watching the scene from a hidden vantage point close by. He'd followed Rhea and Ruby here but hadn't overtaken them because he wanted to find out where they were headed. He swore under his breath now as he saw the slave hunters moving toward the place where the two woman had hidden. Thinking fast, he reached for the hood that he'd tucked into his belt before he had left the stable and pulled it over his head. He wished Baron were under him instead of Gem Boy as he jammed his heels into his mount's sides and plunged noisily with the horse out of the thicket and onto the road. Then he yanked back hard on the reins, causing Gem Boy to rear and neigh loudly.

"Hey, look there! It's *him! Get him!*" The gang of slave catchers swung their horses around toward Logan and set off after him in hot pursuit.

Rhea and Ruby collapsed with relief in each other's arms.

"It were *him*, Miz Rhea!" Ruby gasped excitedly. "Mr. Exodus! He save us, drawin' dem bad men away!"

Rhea held onto Ruby, trying to quell her own shaking. She looked down the road where the horsemen had disappeared in the darkness, astounded by her narrow escape.

"Thank God he came just then," she whispered, wondering at the amazing coincidence that had found them in the same place, at the same time, as Mr. Exodus.

Logan gave Gem Boy his head as they raced away from the men following them. Gem Boy was fast but he didn't have the power and endurance Baron did. He wouldn't be able to hold this breakneck speed for very long. There was only one thing to do. It was a long shot, but he'd have to take it.

Logan reined Gem Boy off toward a narrower side road, grateful for the moonlight to help him see the way. Several shots rang out, one of them whizzing by close to Logan's head. He ducked lower, leaning down near Gem Boy's neck to call encouragement to him.

They broke out into a clearing and Logan reined Gem Boy to the right, letting the horse gallop flat out over the open ground. He glanced back over his shoulder to see that the posse behind him wasn't gaining on him yet, but neither was it falling behind.

Gem Boy sped past the small stand of trees that Logan was looking for. The only way of escape lay just ahead, if they could make it.

"Come on, boy," Logan encouraged. "You know what's coming. We've done it once before. We can do it again. I'm counting on you, boy." He gripped the reins in one hand and grabbed a fistful of mane with the other as they raced toward the dark void just ahead.

"Now, boy! *Jump!*" Logan shouted, willing Gem Boy into the air and across the wide opening that topped the deep ravine. They hung in the air for a long, suspended moment before Gem Boy's front hoofs came down hard on the other side. The ground crumbled away under his back hoofs, but the horse managed to scramble away from the edge of the precipice just in time.

"Good boy!" Logan exclaimed, laughing and thumping the horse's neck as he swung him around to see what his pursuers would do. As he'd hoped, all five men pulled up their mounts on the brink of the other side. Amidst the bullets that came flying at him, Logan reared Gem Boy back, sent a salute toward the slave hunters, then rode away into the night.

Chapter 52

RIDING FAST, RHEA AND RUBY SET OUT FOR RICHmond again, in the opposite direction Exodus and the slave catchers had gone. Keeping to the back streets and shadows, they arrived at Evan VanHorn's house just after eleven o'clock. The young doctor quickly admitted them and hid Ruby in the tiny attic where four other runaways were also waiting to journey to the next station of freedom.

"You took a terrible risk bringing Ruby here yourself," Evan said seriously when he returned to the small parlor where Rhea was waiting.

"Yes, I know, but there was no other way to get her here in time," Rhea answered, matching his tone. "We were almost discovered by slave catchers. If Mr. Exodus hadn't come along and led them away in another direction—"

"Exodus?" Evan interrupted, frowning as he looked at her intently. "You saw him tonight? A patrol was after him?" He shot the questions at her rapidly.

"Yes, five men. He didn't have much of a head start . . ." Rhea's voice trailed off as she realized that Mr. Exodus might well be caught tonight because of her and Ruby. She was certain he had purposely exposed himself to decoy the patrol away from them. She could only wonder what he'd been doing there at just that time.

"Is there anything we can do?" she asked.

"Only wait and see what happens," Evan answered, adding, "and pray that he got away from them. I was expecting him tonight. He was going to start the people in the attic on their way on the network. I need to go and let someone know what's happened in case we have to make alternate plans. You cannot stay here. Is there someone you can stay with here in the city for the rest of the night? Or the Blakely Hotel is just three streets over. I could walk you there before I leave. Return to Fair Oaks in the morning. Don't involve yourself in anything like this again, Rhea. It's too dangerous for you and for the rest of us. I only hope tonight hasn't been too costly already."

Rhea nodded in despair. Evan wasn't trying to be unkind, but his words hurt her because she knew he was right. She had no business taking people's lives into her hands like that, at least not alone. Evan and Exodus and the others worked as a coordinated team. She hadn't thought of how she might be interfering with that.

"I'm sorry, Evan," she said dejectedly. "I only wanted to help Ruby. I—I'll do as you say in the future, but I must go back to Fair Oaks tonight before I am missed. I hope everything will be all right."

Evan took time to give instructions to the fugitives he was hiding before he went to the shed behind his house for his horse. He had just finished saddling the mare when Logan found him there.

"Thank God you're all right!" he exclaimed as he clasped Logan's hand.

"You know what happened?" Logan asked in surprise.

"Yes. Rhea just left here. She brought Ruby and told me Exodus saved them from a patrol."

"And a damned close call it was, too," Logan told him grimly. "So that's what she was up to with Ruby. I had no idea what they were doing or where they were going. I followed Rhea from Fair Oaks but lost her and Ruby when I led the patrol away. How did she know to bring Ruby here to you?"

"Rhea cornered me at the ball last night, saying she wanted to help Ruby get away from Dreed Jessup. I didn't know what to think because she acted like she didn't even know you were Exodus. I was suspicious that she might be setting me up for Talmadge, but she gave me the new passwords. I intended to tell you about it, but I was called away from the ball suddenly to deliver the Stillwell baby. Then all day today I was clear across the county putting Toby Pepperton's leg back together and couldn't even get a message to you."

"Damn her," Logan cursed in a low voice. "I was going to see to Ruby soon enough. Rhea had no business interfering."

"Listen, would you mind filling me in a little about what's going on here?" Evan asked, his tone worried. "Out of the blue you spring this Yankee wife on all of us with no explanation. I figured maybe she'd be joining us, but when you barely mentioned her these past few weeks, I thought you didn't want her involved. But then she cornered me and said she wanted to help the slaves. I didn't know whether to take her seriously or not, until she showed up here tonight with Ruby. What's going on, Logan? Why didn't she work with you on this?"

Logan's frown deepened, narrowing his light eyes. "It's a complicated situation, Evan, and I don't have time to go into it now. Leave Rhea to me. She won't be doing anything reckless like this again to jeopardize our operation, I'll see to that. We've worked too hard, taken too many risks, to have the whole thing endangered now by one headstrong woman who decides to do things on her own. Get Reeves to make the run to Denning's Hollow for me tonight." Logan went to the door of the shed and opened it a crack to check outside. "I'll pick them up from there tomorrow."

"What are you going to do now?" Evan asked as he cinched up the saddle strap on his mount.

"Take care of what's become a thorn in my side," Logan replied coldly. "I'll be in touch."

Chapter 53

LOGAN RODE GEM BOY HARD TO OVERTAKE RHEA. After a half hour, he rounded a bend in the road and found he'd caught up with her. She was stopped just ahead and surrounded by six men on horseback.

Logan swore under his breath. Another slave patrol. They were really out in force tonight. He glanced down to make sure his hood was still safely tucked away inside his shirtfront, then he headed Gem Boy toward the group.

Jade Wind was prancing nervously and Rhea was struggling to control her as the men moved in closer. One of them grabbed the reins out of Rhea's hand and she had to hold on to Jade Wind's mane to keep from falling off. Another had dismounted and was reaching up to pull Rhea off her horse just as Logan rode up.

"There you are, my little vixen!" he exclaimed angrily as he snatched the reins away from the surprised man. "Thank goodness you stopped her, gentlemen. She was quite foolish to ride out alone like this at so outrageous an hour."

"Who're you?" the man demanded, reaching for the gun holstered at his side.

"Take it easy, McCord," a gruff voice ordered from Logan's left. "I know who he is."

Logan turned toward the man who'd spoken. Jake Stryker. He recognized the slave bounty hunter. So these must be some of his cutthroats, though it was a different group from the one he'd escaped from earlier. Stryker was a mean bastard, one to be carefully reckoned with even when he wasn't backed by five of his men. The next few moments would be crucial ones. Logan knew both he and

Rhea would have to be very convincing if they were going to get out of this without causing suspicion. He hoped she would have the presence of mind to play along with him.

"You know this here woman then, Tremaine?" Stryker asked, gesturing a hand toward Rhea.

"I certainly do. She is my wife."

"Oh, yeah, I heard there was some sort of weddin' shindig over at Fair Oaks last night. Your wife, huh? Why's she out ridin' this late like the devil's after her, with no saddle or nothin'?"

Rhea waited anxiously for Logan to answer. She'd been so glad to see him when he'd ridden up, but she knew they were still in serious danger.

"Well, ahem," Logan cleared his throat as if embarrassed. "You see, we had a little quarrel and my bride is rather hot tempered and impetuous." He turned a deeply frowning gaze on Rhea.

"We are taking a little honeymoon excursion in Richmond," Logan continued, "staying with friends. After our argument, my wife dashed out, ran to the stable for her horse, and before anyone could stop her, rode hellbent away. I came after her, of course. A damned foolish thing to do, my dear," he added in a sternly reprimanding tone. "Not knowing the road at night, you might have misguided your mount and caused her to fall, ruining a perfectly good piece of horseflesh."

Rhea had her wits back enough to pick up the cue. "Horse *indeed!*" she spewed at him indignantly. "That's all you ever think about. You don't care a whit that *I* might have been thrown and broken *my* neck! Logan Tremaine, you are heartless!" She crossed her arms in front of her in a pretended pout.

Stryker snorted contemptuously. "Looks like you got a real spirited one on your hands there, Tremaine."

"Nothing that a good leather strap can't tame, Stryker," Logan replied all too convincingly.

"That's the idea, all right," Stryker agreed with a smirk. "Best way to handle a woman. Keep her in line from the beginnin'." There were murmurs of agreement from the others. "Give her a good lesson real soon. Come on, boys. Let's move on. We got runaway slaves to catch."

Stryker turned his horse away and the others did the same.

"Don't say a word, Rhea," Logan whispered threateningly. "I'll deal with you later."

As soon as Stryker and his men were out of sight, Logan touched his heels to Gem Boy's sides. Pulling Jade Wind by the reins behind him, he guided the two horses off the main road and onto a side path. Without another word to Rhea, he led the way as they galloped for Fair Oaks.

An hour later of hard riding over back roads and narrow pathways, Rhea and Logan arrived back at the plantation. Logan woke Amos to take care of the horses, then he all but dragged Rhea into the house and up the back staircase to their rooms.

All the way home, Rhea had tried to figure out how she would explain what she'd been doing tonight, even while she wondered how Logan had come to be on the road from Richmond at the same time.

She knew Logan was very upset with her. And she knew she deserved it. She'd acted foolishly tonight. She never should have undertaken to help Ruby on her own. She couldn't forget the raw fear she'd felt when that first patrol had almost discovered them. And the looks on the faces of Stryker and his men when they'd caught her alone on the road were only too clear in her memory. If Logan hadn't come upon them just then . . .

Rhea had no more time for speculation though, for just then Logan let his wrath descend on her, keeping his voice low so he wouldn't be overheard.

"Are you stupid as well as reckless, woman? Do you know the danger you were in tonight, what kind of trouble you might have caused to yourself, to me, to many others? Not only did you jeopardize your own life, but Ruby's and Evan's and even mine, as well!"

Rhea was stunned by his words. He seemed to know about everything. But how?

"You know I took Ruby to Evan's tonight? You know of his involvement with the underground?" she asked incredulously.

"Of course I do. I was at Evan's after you left," Logan was quick to answer, his anger very apparent now. He didn't know what to expect from Rhea from one minute to the next lately. He couldn't trust her.

"And you have not exposed him?"

"Evan is a good friend," Logan replied curtly. "I owe him much. He's saved Camille's life, breathed life into her when we thought she was gone. He's pulled her from the brink of death three times. I would not deprive my sister or anyone else of his great medical gifts simply because he feels the need to help a few slaves escape from time to time."

"But don't change the subject," Logan continued, bringing the conversation pointedly back to Rhea. His light blue eyes drilled into her. "Will you never stop acting so rashly? You had no business taking Ruby's fate into your own hands like that."

His eyes had taken on a glacial glint and the cold tone of his voice cut into Rhea like a knife. She was suddenly very tired. Fear and the long hours on horseback were taking their toll of her strength. She was exhausted and had no more energy to defend herself further.

"You are right, of course," she admitted dejectedly as she sighed and sank down in the armchair next to her. "Again I didn't think of the consequences of my actions." She looked up at Logan. "But I only wanted to help Ruby. She was so desperate and I have known that feeling only too well myself." Her voice dropped to a whisper as she looked away from him.

For a moment Logan eyed her suspiciously. He'd expected more fight out of her than this, yet he was glad she had acquiesced so readily. Considering his state of mind, he might have given in to his first impulse and beaten her soundly if she had continued to argue with him.

Rhea looked so small huddled there. So vulnerable and full of remorse. He might have been moved to forgive her if he hadn't again thought of the cost her actions might have incurred for him and others. It helped to strengthen his resolve.

"I wish I could trust you not to be so impulsive in the future, but I cannot. I told you before that I would see to it that you kept your part of our agreement. But you have disregarded my instructions again and again. You force me to use sterner measures."

Rhea raised her head again to look at him.

"So as not to raise suspicion about our relationship, I cannot confine you to these rooms while I need your services as my wife. Therefore, during the day you will still be allowed to come and go as you please. Ride, read, use the music room, spend time with my sister, do all the things you have been doing that are acceptable activities for my wife. However, from now on Obediah will be like your shadow. I will instruct him to watch you and follow you at all times while I am gone. And at night he will lock you here in your bedroom so there will be no more midnight venturings."

"That is not necessary," Rhea replied, coming to her feet. Some of the fire sparked again in her eyes. She felt angry and desperate at the same time. He was going too far.

"On the contrary, I feel this is quite necessary in order for us to get through the next months as we agreed."

"I won't be treated like this, Logan. I won't allow you to imprison me here." Rhea stood her ground before him defiantly. Her anger made her unafraid of his threatening look. "I shall tell Miles everything about our false marriage. And if you try to use physical violence to stop me—"

"I have no need of that," Logan cut in as he stared back at her coldly, "though of late you have tempted me greatly to do so." He took a threatening step toward her and Rhea instinctively backed a little away from him.

"Do not forget I have proof of our marriage."

"It is a forgery," Rhea stated levelly.

"You would have a difficult time getting anyone to believe that, especially since there is also an official entry of our union in the Hall of Records in Philadelphia."

"Also counterfeit!"

"And also quite difficult to prove."

Rhea and Logan glared at each other for a long moment in silence.

"But should you attempt to tell your story," Logan went on finally, "I would be forced to bring up the question of your sanity, my dear." His tone dripped with sarcasm.

"What?" Rhea was caught completely off guard by his remark. Her puzzled blue eyes continued to stare at him.

"I believe it is no secret that your mother's mental faculties have been found wanting in recent years. It would not be hard to acquire confirmation of that fact and plant the seed of doubt that her daughter may be afflicted with the same malady and is therefore not responsible for certain things she might say. I'd be looked upon quite favorably for having married you under those circumstances."

"My God, how could you do such a thing?" Rhea murmured, stricken by disbelief. "To bring my mother into this . . ." She turned away from him in despair, freshly wounded by his cruelty.

Logan knew he had won, but he felt no satisfaction in it for some reason. Trying to ignore Rhea's slumped shoulders and beaten look, Logan reminded himself that she had forced his hand tonight by her own actions. He could not let her ruin everything he had worked for, either with Miles or anyone else.

Without saying another word, Logan walked to the door leading to the hallway. He turned the key in the lock and removed it. Rhea watched in stunned silence as he went to the open door leading to the sitting room that adjoined their bedrooms. Without even a backward glance, he walked out, closing the door behind him. The finality of the click of the key in the lock spurred Rhea to run after him.

"Logan, please don't do this," she begged against the unyielding door. Hot tears burned her eyes as she futilely tried to turn the brass doorknob. "Please . . . Logan!"

When there was no response, Rhea sank to the floor and buried her head in her hands, weeping quietly in misery.

Chapter 54

THE SOUND OF A KEY TURNING IN THE LOCK of the sitting room door awakened Rhea from her restless sleep. Getting quickly out of bed, she ran to that door and found the knob now turned easily at her touch. She hoped to find Logan on the other side as she flung the door open. But only Obediah stood in the adjoining room, returning the key he'd just used to his pocket.

"Is Mr. Logan here, Obediah?" she asked, glancing over the Negro's shoulder to see into the sitting room.

"No, missus. He done left early dis mornin'. Ah'll be waitin' outside da hall door fo' when yo' is ready ta go down ta breakfast."

Rhea nodded defeatedly. So Logan had left instructions for Obediah to watch her, just as he said he would. She was virtually a prisoner in this house now.

Rhea dressed slowly, her heart heavy. As she went down the hall Obediah followed, though at such a distance that it was barely noticeable. Still, Rhea hated being guarded like a criminal.

Before going to the dining room, she stopped in to see Camille. Logan's sister was somewhat better but still in a weakened condition. Sybil came in while Rhea was there.

"Oh, you are here, Rhea. I thought you would have gone with Logan on this trip of his. Newlyweds usually hate to be parted for so long a time. Has he tired of you already?"

Rhea bristled at her mocking words. She was in no mood for a confrontation with Sybil, but she managed not to show it. At least Logan had taught her the fine art of feigning indifference.

"On the contrary, Sybil—the situation is quite the reverse," she lied expertly with a smile. "Logan seems never to have enough of me. He wanted me to go with him, but I pleaded a need for rest. And since his days will be taken up almost completely with business, I decided not to accompany him."

"But there are still the nights, and I would worry about those if I were you, dear Rhea," Sybil returned venomously as she eyed her opponent. "Logan's reputation with women has been well earned. I doubt that *you* could appease his ravenous appetite for new . . . encounters."

"Reputation or not," Rhea replied haughtily, though she was seething inside, "I still am not worried, dear sister-in-law, for I am secure in my husband's affections. I know he'll return faithfully to me with his appetite—as you put it—that much more renewed for what only I can give him. Can you say the same of *your* husband?"

Rhea bestowed a honey-sweet smile on her adversary. Sybil's face visibly reddened as her temper flared. Her jaw clenched shut and her eyes glared dangerously before she whirled around and fled from the room without another word. Rhea should have felt elated by her besting of Sybil, but she didn't. If anything, she felt even more depressed; she was becoming more like the Tremaines every day.

While Rhea knew it never would be easy to escape from Logan and Fair Oaks, she realized now it would be harder than ever with Obediah acting as her constant companion. She decided to maintain the routine she'd fallen into these past weeks, but all the while laying very careful plans for getting away. In this she would not be rash. Too much was at stake.

Later in the day, Rhea went to the stables to get Jade Wind for their daily ride. Amos saddled a horse for Obediah, too. Logan's servant had just helped Rhea to mount when Dreed Jessup strode angrily into the stableyard and headed straight for her. He grabbed hold of Jade Wind's bridle and roughly shoved Obediah out of the way as he came to stand next to Rhea. An ugly scowl twisted Jessup's face as he glared at her.

"Headed for the nigger yard where you ain't supposed to be, missus?" he spat at her.

Rhea was stunned by his boldness but managed to keep her composure as she looked down at him disdainfully.

"That is none of your business, Mr. Jessup. Unhand my horse at once and let me pass," she ordered in an authoritative tone, frowning at him.

"It's my business when one of my black bitches lights out—the same one you bin stickin' your nose in about," Jessup growled at her viciously. "Ruby turned up missin' this mornin', but of course you wouldn't know nothin' about that now, would you, missus?" Jessup's tone was becoming more threatening and the malevolent look on his face sent a shiver of fear up Rhea's spine. With great effort she continued to stare him down, trying not to show any reaction to his malicious verbal attack.

"You are impudent, sir! My husband shall hear of this!" she replied evenly.

"That don't bother me none. But what will bother me is if I find out you had anythin' to do with Ruby's escape."

"Are you threatening me, Mr. Jessup?" Rhea demanded as she worked the reins to try to control Jade Wind's nervous prancing.

"Call it whatever you want. Just remember what I said." With that Jessup let go of Jade Wind's bridle and hit the gray's rump hard with his hand. The horse lunged forward in fright, almost unseating Rhea. When she was able to pull Jade Wind up and swing her around back toward the stableyard, Rhea saw that Jessup was no longer in sight. Only Obediah came riding toward her, a worried expression marking his dark face. With feelings of revulsion and anger and just a little fear, Rhea gripped the reins hard and, turning Jade Wind toward the stone driveway, rode away.

Chapter 55

RHEA HAD TROUBLE HIDING HER EXCITEMENT as she sat next to Logan in the big open surrey. She needed this outing after helping to tend Camille so closely for the past week.

Logan's sister was almost completely recovered from her latest bout with illness. Rhea was certain it was Camille's vibrant will to live that had helped her body shrug off its debilitation once more. Camille was still confined to her bed, however, so she had fussed and pouted about not being able to attend the Founder's Day Fair in the nearby town of Huntsville, where Rhea, Logan, Miles, Sybil, and Tyler were going now.

Rhea wished her friend had been well enough to come with them. Then there would have been at least one smiling, friendly face among them. Miles exuded only disdain and impatience at having to serve as Grand Marshal of the celebration. Sybil looked equally annoyed sitting regally beside him opposite Rhea.

Logan maintained an aloof attitude. He had arrived back at Fair Oaks from his buying trip north only last night. He and Rhea had attended the family dinner together, but he had given her little of his attention, preferring to discuss the business details of his trip with Miles. After dinner was over, Rhea had gone up to bed, glad really, she told herself, that Logan had not bothered to pay her any mind. She had said nothing to him about her ugly confrontation with Dreed Jessup, even though it had often been on her mind during the past week. She didn't want to tell Logan anything that would recall her involvement with Ruby and cause him to remember the subsequent

nasty scene that night in Rhea's bedroom. She was glad
when he made no mention of it in the few words they had
exchanged upon his return. She wanted to stay out of Logan's line of attention as much as possible as she waited
and watched for an opportunity to escape from him and
everything else at Fair Oaks.

Rhea had gotten to the point where she hated the sight
of Obediah, who had been overly diligent all week in
obeying his master's instructions. She had hardly been
able to draw an unobserved breath, let alone try to escape.

For today, however, Rhea decided to concentrate on just
enjoying herself at the fair festivities. And she would, that
was, if Logan allowed it. Fearing to rile him, she re-
strained her own excitement now, maintaining the quiet
and demure deportment expected of her. She was convinced Logan would order the surrey back to Fair Oaks immediately if he had the slightest idea that she wanted to
enjoy herself today.

Rhea looked away from Logan and adjusted her yellow
parasol so that it shaded her from the warm rays of the
sun. She was glad she'd chosen to wear a lightweight cotton dress on this hot day. It was pale yellow like her
parasol, with short puffed sleeves and a square-cut, low
neckline that would help her stay somewhat cool. She wondered how Logan and Miles stood the heat in their cut-
away coats and high-necked shirts with wrapped ties. The
price one had to pay to uphold his social image, she decided
a little derisively. After all, they were the guests of honor
at this Founder's Day Fair and they had to dress for the
part.

The Tremaines all sat together on the high-backed
chairs which lined the raised wooden platform in the middle of the town square's small park. They had to appear to
be listening attentively when Miles gave the expected
lengthy Founder's Day speech. Even Drew had joined
them on the platform, bringing along his latest beautiful
young lady.

After that tedious amenity was observed, they were free
to go their separate ways for the rest of the day. How Rhea
wished Logan would find something else with which to occupy himself, but she knew he was not about to let her go

around alone, out of his sight. In the back of her mind, Rhea clung to the hope that she might find a chance to slip away from Logan in the crowd. She'd brought with her what little currency and gold coins she had. They were in a small flat pouch in the side pocket of her dress. If she could get away, she might be able to hire a horse for her hoped-for escape north.

The time passed quickly. Rhea's resolve to remain reserved slowly slipped away as she became caught up in the excitement of the festivities. Even Logan seemed to scowl less as the afternoon went on and they walked the crowded streets, stopping at the merchants' booths, sampling special foods and treats, watching daring acrobats perform their breath-taking stunts. They even took in a puppet show. Rhea realized Logan was taking care not to let her out of his sight. Even when he stopped to talk to acquaintances, he always kept one eye warily on Rhea, drawing her back to his side if she moved even a few steps away. She finally gave up hope of trying to slip away from him.

Near late afternoon to Rhea's surprise, Logan entered the arm-wrestling contest with the local champion, a giant of a man who was the town blacksmith.

"I'm back again, this time to beat you, Hans," Logan taunted as he smiled at the stocky, bushy-bearded man seated at the thick oak contest table. "I've taken enough defeats from you. This time I shall win, I'm certain of it."

"*Ja, ja,* it is goot you come back each time to try, Herr Logan," Hans came back in a booming voice that was thick with a German accent. He laughed loudly as he put his huge arm in place on the table and flexed his thickly calloused hand with anticipation.

A crowd of onlookers quickly gathered around the scene, hemming Rhea and Logan close into the table. People called out taunts and encouragement as they elbowed each other for a better view and laid bets on the winner. Hans was heavily favored.

"Don't put your money on Hans this year, boys. 'Twould be a shame for you lose it," Logan harassed the men around him jovially as he handed his coat to Rhea and slowly rolled up the sleeves of his shirt.

The two men eyed each other with feigned fierceness. Logan stretched his arm back and flexed his fist several times, making an exaggerated ritual out of these preliminary actions. Then he sat down on the sturdy three-legged stool across from the big German and put his right elbow down on the rough-hewn table. His other arm went behind his back, as did his opponent's.

Logan's arms were powerful. The cords of muscle rippled along his right forearm as he flexed his fist one last time before grasping Hans's hand in his. But the German's arm was almost twice as thick as Logan's, the product of years of wielding his blacksmith's heavy iron tools.

"You vill give us das start, Frau Tremaine?" Hans asked hopefully, glancing at Rhea standing near them.

She looked askance at Logan, who nodded his assent.

"Very well, then," she agreed, still wondering at Logan's more relaxed mood and willingness to participate in such a contest. "On the word 'go.' "

The small crowd was hushed now with expectation as they waited for the signal to be given. Logan and Hans stared at each other. Logan's face was set into a mock-serious expression, as though he were going to concentrate hard on beating the blacksmith. The husky German was grinning broadly as his blue eyes twinkled merrily.

"Get ready," Rhea began the count. "Get set—go!"

Immediately the cheering and jeering was renewed as Logan and Hans locked arms in combat. Logan quickly gained a small advantage, tilting the blacksmith's hand over at a slight angle toward his side of the table.

"You see, Hans, I am bound to win this time. You seem weak today," he taunted good-naturedly, eyeing his adversary.

Hans grunted and brought their arms straight up again. A laugh rumbled in his broad chest as he gave the appearance that Logan was no challenge at all. But it was clear to Rhea, who was standing so close to them, that both men were exerting a powerful effort. She could see the beads of perspiration stand out on their foreheads, their knuckles whiten and their forearms shake under the strain of resisting each other's pull.

Now Hans took the advantage, moving Logan's arm a little past center toward his side of the table. Logan managed to bring his arm back again but he was clearly straining now. His teeth were clenched and the thick cords of muscle protruded in his neck and forearm. Without thinking, Rhea began calling her own encouragement to Logan as she became caught up in the tense excitement of the contest.

Now the smile was gone from the big German's face as he, too, set his jaw and bore down with all his might. For long moments the two men's arms remained locked in the straight-up position of matched strength. Then Hans muttered a growling sound deep in his throat and with a final burst of power, forced Logan's arm over and down, defeating him. Loud shouts erupted from the crowd as both men grinned and stood up, embracing each other in a friendly bear hug. The spectators were exuberant in their cheers and back-slapping for both men.

"You vill try again next year, *ja*, Herr Logan?" Hans asked over the uproar around them.

"*Ja*, Hans, if my arm recovers," Logan replied, nodding and returning his grin as he flexed his right arm and fist several times.

Rhea watched this exchange in bewilderment. Was this the same Logan Tremaine she knew? The man who was always so stern-faced and quick to point out her deviations from "proper" behavior? Logan was clearly liked by all those around him now. They were enthusiastic in their praise of his effort and in their encouragement for him to try again next year.

Logan was still smiling as he and Rhea left the contest area. He didn't put his coat back on when she handed it to him. Rhea was surprised to find herself thinking again how handsome he looked when he smiled. It made him seem almost human . . . Almost.

"Do you think it is wise to challenge giants?" she ventured as they walked along toward some display booths.

"Wise, no. But permitted at fair time," Logan answered lightly. "It is expected of me."

Rhea's face fell slightly but Logan didn't notice, for he had turned then to call a greeting to a passerby. Of course, he had only participated in that event out of duty to his social position, Rhea thought with exasperation as she pretended to be admiring some handmade jewelry on a table. How foolish of her to think he might have joined in the activity just for the fun of it!

Chapter 56

TOWARD EVENING THE SOUNDS OF MUSICAL IN-
struments being tuned could be heard coming from the
park in the town square. Logan and Rhea came out of a
shop located close to where the musicians were taking
their seats. A bearded man stood up just then and announced the start of the evening's hoedown.

"Oh, dancing!" Rhea exclaimed enthusiastically, glancing hopefully at Logan. His relaxed mood had continued
through the light supper they'd just had. He wasn't acting
at all like the critical and cynical bully he usually was. At
a festival crowded with merrymakers and exciting events,
it was easy not to think of the threats and harsh words
they had spoken in the middle of the night. Rhea decided
to take a chance on Logan's better humor.

"Could we stay and dance some?" she asked, as a child-
like look of longing touched her face.

Logan cocked one eyebrow in a slight frown. "The hour
is growing late, Rhea. We should be getting back to Fair
Oaks."

"Please, just one or two dances?" Rhea persisted. "It's
expected of us, isn't it?" She looked at Logan with wide-
eyed innocence as she whispered so only he could hear,
"And if you won't be my partner, I'm certain one of these
farmers will be happy to take your place."

Logan's look of annoyance deepened, but before he could
answer, the man with the beard loudly announced a circle
mixer dance. Before they knew what was happening Logan and Rhea were caught up in the gaiety as people began to join hands.

Laughing and breathless, Rhea passed Logan several

times during the dance, which required partners to change often. When their eyes met, Logan's look told her he was slightly annoyed, but Rhea didn't care. She was enjoying herself too much and wasn't about to let him spoil it.

When the dance ended, the small band went immediately into a waltz. As Logan walked toward Rhea she held out her arms to him in dance position, and he could do nothing but take hold of her right hand and waist and begin to waltz. To do otherwise would have drawn attention to them.

"Oh, do smile, Logan," Rhea chided him in a low voice as they moved smoothly around the dancing area. "At least *pretend* to be enjoying yourself, for these good towns-people's sakes."

Logan's lips pursed in exasperation as he whirled Rhea around the other couples. Then he shook his head as though resigning himself to his fate and finally relaxed into the rhythm of the dance. Rhea was light and graceful in his arms. She followed his lead easily, just as she had at the Fourth of July ball, and her smile was radiant. Logan found himself thinking what a beautiful woman Rhea was and how appealing she looked right now. He knew he was the envy of every man around. It was with some reluctance that he relinquished his hold on her when the music ended.

"Grab your partners for a Virginia Reel, folks!" the announcer sang out.

"One of my favorite dances!" Rhea exclaimed. Her blue eyes sparkled with pleasure. "Please, Logan, let's do just this one more and that can be the last. No true Virginian can pass up dancing this reel and keep his self-respect!"

"All right, but this is the *last,*" Logan stated firmly as they walked out to join one of the lines being formed by other couples.

The familiar, fast-moving dance was accomplished with unleashed enthusiasm by all involved. Rhea was so caught up in concentrating on the steps that she took no notice of a man who watched her intently from the edge of the crowd. His black, sinister eyes moved over Rhea as she and Logan whirled past him, his gaze lingering on the swell of her breasts that showed just above the square-cut neckline of her gown.

Grayson Sawyer licked his dry lips, lusting to taste and touch what should belong only to him—*would* belong to him! After spending the afternoon mingling with the huge crowd attending the fair, he'd finally found Rhea. Only the night before had he arrived in Virginia. But a small notice printed in the Richmond *Guardian* had brought him to the Founder's Day celebration today. Miles Tremaine's name had appeared as Grand Marshal. Where there was one Tremaine, there was always a chance to find more, and Rhea along with them.

Rhea looked as lovely as ever. Her face was flushed and animated. What did he see in the look she bestowed on Tremaine? He couldn't really read her expression. In his cold rage, Grayson only knew he hated it.

Chapter 57

"WHEW, MY, BUT IT'S WARM," RHEA EXCLAIMED
laughingly as she fanned herself with her lace handkerchief after the reel had ended.

"I agree. Come on, we'll get something to drink," Logan
replied, a little out of breath himself.

Rhea retrieved her parasol from where she'd laid it on a
nearby table and let Logan guide her at the elbow toward
the waterfront where the James River bordered the town
to the west. They stopped to buy some lemonade from a
booth on the wharf, then stood silently observing several
sailboats maneuvering on the river.

"What are they doing over there?" Rhea finally asked,
noticing some couples venturing out in rowboats near the
shore.

Logan had been watching one skiff try to outrace another near a small island in the middle of the river, but he
turned his attention to where Rhea was now pointing.

"Those boats are for hire for short rides," he told her.
"Just around that bend," he gestured toward an outjutting
of rock a ways off to their right, "is a small lagoon. It has a
sandy beach and hundreds of sea gulls."

"I'd love to see the lagoon and the birds," Rhea remarked impulsively, feeling emboldened by her earlier
success in persuading him to dance. "Could we rent a boat?
Is that permissible during fair time? Or are you too tired to
row us after all that dancing?" She couldn't resist the
taunt but wondered if she'd said too much.

"I think I still have a little strength left," Logan replied
drolly. "I suppose we could hire one."

"Good," Rhea said, relieved by his answer. Then she

quickly turned around before Logan could change his mind, and headed toward the dock where the small boats were moored.

"This be the last one," the old fisherman remarked as he took the coins of payment from Logan. "Lots of them young folks like you has wanted to go out to the lagoon to watch the sunset. Mighty romantic place, that lagoon." He gave them a toothy grin and winked at Rhea, who didn't welcome the old man's remarks. She was glad for Logan's friendlier mood, but romance was the last thing she had on her mind. Besides, she doubted that he was capable of being romantic anyway. A boatride was all she wanted now to round out the day.

"Watch your balance," Logan warned as he helped Rhea into the rocking boat.

Rhea sat down on the stern seat and Logan sat facing her on the middle seat. Dipping the oars in the murky water, Logan propelled them away from the dock and out into the slow-moving current. Rhea watched him for a while, then leaned over the side of the boat a little to let her fingers trail in the cool water. She began to hum one of the tunes she'd heard a minstrel playing earlier in the day.

Unbidden, the picture of Rhea singing in the music room came into Logan's thoughts as he rowed. He saw the special look on her face, the same look he was trying to capture on his canvas. Logan didn't even know why he was doing that painting. He doubted if he'd ever even show it to her. It was just that there was something delicate and vulnerable about the way Rhea could look—the same way she was looking now as the early evening sunlight touched her face and hair and glistened on the water around them. He wanted to catch and keep that look for . . . For what? For the time when Rhea was gone from his life?

"Is it difficult rowing us?" Rhea asked, looking over at him.

"No," Logan answered, amusement touching the corners of his mouth. "The current is carrying us mostly. It will be harder on the way back. I plan for it to be your turn to row then."

"You think I couldn't do it?" she remarked in mock indignation, hiding her surprise that he seemed to be teasing her.

"I think you would give it a damned good try just to prove to me that you *could* do it."

And now a compliment, of sorts! Would wonders never cease? Rhea thought.

"Ah, you are getting to know me then," she observed lightly as she turned back to running her fingers through the water.

Logan seemed to take a long moment before he answered simply, "Yes."

The sun was starting its final descent on the horizon as they rounded the outjutting of rocks and entered the lagoon. Eight or nine rowboats similar to theirs were already beached on the narrow shore, their occupants strolling arm-in-arm along the sandy beach or sitting close together higher up where the sand was edged with grass.

"The beach is so crowded. Let's watch the sunset from over there," Rhea decided suddenly, pointing to the rocks they'd just passed. She had no desire to join the obvious lovers on the beach.

Logan glanced over his shoulder to where she had indicated, then maneuvered the boat around in that direction until the prow bumped lightly against one of the rocks. He swung the oars into the boat and jumped to a low, flat boulder that was protruding out of the water. Pulling the boat close up beside him and holding it in place, he held out his other hand to help Rhea out.

"Take my hand and watch your balance," he instructed as he leaned forward.

Rhea had just put one foot on the boulder when the small boat lurched from the shift in her weight. In an instant she lost her balance, and before Logan could catch hold of her, she fell over the side. The water was only waist deep near the rocks, but still she was soaked before she could gain her footing on the pebble bottom. A moan escaped her as she stood up dripping and looked down at her beautiful yellow dress clinging soggily around her. She didn't mind getting wet as much as she did looking so foolish in front of Logan. When she made herself glance up at him, he was looking at her just the way she knew—and dreaded—he would be, with a critical frown.

"Are you all right?" he asked, the same note of annoyance sounding in his voice as showed on his face.

"Yes," Rhea answered with a sigh of despair as she waded the few steps toward him.

"I told you to be careful of your balance," he reprimanded in his all-too-familiar condescending tone. "These small boats can shift at the slightest movement."

Rhea's embarrassment fueled her temper. As usual she could expect no sympathy from Logan, only irritation. Well, she was irritated herself!

"*You* were supposed to be holding it steady," she accused, hands on hips.

"I *was* holding it steady. *You* were just clumsy."

Oh, he could be so infuriating! Rhea fumed inwardly. Clumsy indeed! Suddenly a wicked thought flashed through her mind. Pretending contriteness, Rhea hid her anger and reached a hand up to him. "I'm sorry. You are right. It was careless of me. Help me out, please?"

With a look of disdain, Logan unsuspectingly leaned forward and took her hand. But before he could pull her up, Rhea yanked backward with all her might. Logan was now the one thrown off balance and he pitched forward head first into the river shallows, almost on top of Rhea, who also fell backward again into the water.

"Now who was being clumsy?" she accused him, laughing as they both scrambled to regain their footing. "I hope this cold water has doused that nasty disposition of yours!"

"It hasn't done much for *yours,*" Logan retorted, wading toward her, a rather menacing look on his face.

"No, now, Logan, what are you going to do?" Rhea held out a hand to stop him while she took several steps backward toward deeper water to put space between them. But in a flash he was lunging toward her, catching her around the waist and pulling her down into the water with him. This time Rhea went under completely and came up sputtering.

"Is revenge so sweet now, wench?" he taunted, holding her by the waist before him.

"You nearly drowned me!" she fumed, trying to twist out of his grasp. But he only tightened his grip and pulled her closer. It was then she saw the mischief in his eyes, the slight smile curling on his lips. Suddenly they both started to laugh, realizing what a comical sight they made for the observers on the beach.

And then they stopped laughing. Logan still held Rhea by the waist. Their eyes met and held, drawing them closer together. In the next moment they were in each other's arms, their lips touching tentatively and then a little more fervently in a kiss. Sudden cheers and clapping coming from the nearby beach caused a quick end to their kiss. Logan waved a hand at the watching couples in a good-natured acknowledgment, then reached down to take Rhea's.

"Come on," he smiled at her, "let's watch the sun go down."

They waded in to the rocks of the peninsula, climbed carefully up to a level spot at the top, and sat down next to each other to watch the day end.

"There is better attire for swimming, you know," Logan said as he helped Rhea wring some of the water out of her sopping skirt.

"Well, I hadn't planned on going swimming," she countered, flicking her skirt at him so he was sprinkled with water.

Rhea caught herself feeling apprehensive then. Would these warm, silly moments between them end as suddenly as they had happened? It would be nice if they could last, she thought as she watched the sky grow red from the sun's fiery contact with the horizon. Cottonlike white clouds blushed crimson, then a deeper magenta as the rays spread over and around them. It was a breathtaking sight. Logan and Rhea watched it in an appreciative silence, each lost in contemplative thought.

Rhea glanced over at Logan sitting next to her to find that he was watching her as well. And for once he wasn't frowning. She smiled at him a little sheepishly and brushed her wet hair out of her eyes. What a sight she must be, but there was nothing to be done about it now. Besides, Logan was just as wet and disheveled as she was. So why did he still look so handsome?

As Rhea looked away to watch the sky again Logan let his thoughts drift. He gave a little laugh to himself when he remembered again how she had pulled him into the water, made him dance, even how she had cheered for him during the contest with Hans. Today had been one of the

most enjoyable he'd spent in a long time, and Rhea had
made it so.

There was something happening between them, Logan
realized. Something he had not expected or ever known before. He wondered about it a few more moments, then got
to his feet.

"We'd better start back while there's still some light,"
he said. The sun had disappeared from view. He helped
Rhea to her feet and led the way over the rocks to the boat.

"Now be careful," he warned, but a slight smile touched
the corners of his mouth as he reached down to steady the
small rowboat so Rhea could climb in.

"Yes, captain," Rhea quipped. "If you can keep this boat
from rocking, I shall be just fine."

They both managed to get in without incident, and Logan rowed them to the wharf. The fair was far from over
when they arrived back. Every house and shop in the town
was ablaze with light. Musicians were playing and people
still crowded the streets.

"I'll see if I can hire a buggy to get us home," Logan told
Rhea after they'd returned the rowboat to the old fisherman. "Miles and Sybil have no doubt taken the surrey
back to Fair Oaks by now. We usually don't stay this late."

"But isn't the livery stable at the other end of town?"
Rhea asked, frowning a little. Logan nodded. "We can't parade through town looking like *this,*" she went on with
concern. "What will people say? You saw how the old man
on the dock looked at us just now." She brushed a stray
lock of hair back from her face and looked down at her
crumpled, still-damp dress. She was nowhere near presentable.

"There is a roundabout route through that woods over
there," Logan offered. "It's a little longer and steeper,
but . . ."

"We'll take it," Rhea finished for him as she gathered
her skirts and started for the path he'd pointed to.

Chapter 58

THE PATH RHEA AND LOGAN FOLLOWED WOUND through a thick woods that bordered the north side of Huntsville. They passed only one other couple as they walked. Most of the fair celebrants were still enjoying the festivities below in the town. But one was not, and he followed Rhea and Logan now, staying in the shadows as he had before, and spying on their journey.

"I have to rest," Rhea said breathlessly as they reached the top of a steep rise. A fallen log offered a convenient seat, and Rhea was quick to take advantage of it. Logan sat down next to her.

"Don't lean back," he warned. "There's about a thirty-foot dropoff behind us. Anyone who can fall out of a rowboat might easily fall off a cliff, too."

"I think you're not going to let me forget that too soon, are you?" Rhea remarked, eyeing him accusingly. But she was not annoyed. She rather liked his teasing.

"These petticoats are so heavy still wet like this," she said then, giving her skirt a shake.

"Well, take them off or we'll never get through these woods. No one will see you here," Logan told her, then added when he saw her questioning look, "I won't look."

It was too dark for Rhea to see his expression before he obediently turned away and waited for her to finish. As quickly as she could, Rhea untied the fastenings of the two layers of ruffled underskirts and tossed them in a pile on the ground. What a relief to get their weight off of her. She was glad she hadn't worn a corset today.

Logan had gone to stand on the small, grassy cliff in front of the log. There was an opening in the trees here, and as Rhea stepped up beside him she could see the bright roundness of the nearly full moon beginning its ascent in the black night sky.

"How lovely . . ." Rhea murmured. It was a warm evening, but when a small gust of breeze swept up and over them from below the cliff, it made Rhea shiver.

"Here, put this over your shoulders." Logan turned her sideways so she was facing him, and wrapped his coat around her. "It didn't get wet before."

Rhea smiled at Logan gratefully. On an impulse, she voiced the thought that had been going through her mind while they'd been walking.

"Why can't you be like this all the time?" she asked softly.

"What do you mean by 'like this'?" he asked in return, smiling slightly.

"Like you've been most of today and tonight. Relaxed, amiable . . . human . . ."

Logan gave a little laugh at her description and didn't reply for a few moments.

"*You* are the one responsible for any rash behavior on my part, Rhea," he said finally, his voice gentle. "You have greatly upset what I've practiced long and hard to control, you know." He took her chin in his hand and raised her face to look at her. "You have unleashed in me continuous exasperation, anger, and unnerving confusion."

Rhea opened her mouth to protest and tell him he had the *same* effect on her, but Logan hushed her with a finger to her lips, then brushed back a scraggle of hair falling over her forehead. In a softer voice he went on speaking, "And also laughter . . . and worry . . . and desire . . ."

"Logan . . ." Rhea stepped closer into his arms and raised her lips to meet his. Their kiss was gentle at first, searching, asking. Then it became more fervent as their shared passion flared to life once more.

Logan held Rhea closely after they'd parted a little to catch their breaths. "My God, Rhea, what is there between us that causes this to happen?" he whispered against her soft hair, his voice husky with desire.

"I don't know . . ." Rhea murmured as she rested her head against his chest and hugged her arms around him.

"I only want to feel the wonder that makes my heart race madly and makes every part of me long for you." She raised her head to look up at him. "Open your heart, Logan. Feel with your heart as I am doing now."

Logan's head came down then to claim her lips again. His strong arms pressed her hard against him. Rhea felt as though she'd been struck by a lightning bolt as the wild sensation of Logan's kiss charged through her body, leaving her breathless and trembling with longing for him.

"I must have you, Rhea. I must . . ." he murmured.

"Yes, oh, yes, my love," was her breathless reply as their lips met again.

Logan lifted Rhea in his arms and carried her away from the moonlit spot deeper into the woods. Then they lay down together, using their hurriedly discarded clothes to blanket them on the pine needles covering the ground. And there Logan and Rhea made love.

In the darkness of the deep woods, the seclusion of the towering trees and dense undergrowth was disturbed for a time as an ancient rite of nature was fulfilled between a man and a woman. Yet they were drawn together by more than just impassioned need. The rest of the world fell away for Rhea and Logan as they clung desperately to each other. They were totally unaware of the night creatures pausing in their flights to watch them. Rhea knew only that Logan wanted her, that his caressing hands on her flesh filled her with feelings she had known with no other man. And she returned his ardor, using her own hands to explore and memorize Logan's magnificent body. His quick intakes of breath and murmured words encouraged her to grow bolder. She matched him touch for touch, kiss for kiss. Her breasts, with the nipples taut in arousal by his tongue and fingers, pressed into his chest. Her limbs began to ache as her need for him grew more and more consuming.

"My God, Rhea . . ." Logan whispered raspily, awestruck by the magnitude of what he was feeling for her.

The dense forest would have hidden them and remained the silent and sole witness to their lovemaking if an evil intruder had not lurked close by, watching with abject hatred. Grayson Sawyer's fists clenched at his sides and his teeth ground together as his face twisted in an ugly grimace. There would be revenge for this carnal betrayal. Rhea would pay dearly for it, he vowed to himself in unspoken rage from the shadows. And Tremaine, too.

Chapter 59

WHEN RHEA AND LOGAN LATER ARRIVED BACK at Fair Oaks, they crept up a back staircase to their rooms like two errant children trying to avoid detection.

"Shhh," Rhea hushed Logan, trying to suppress a giggle when his footfall caused a loud creak on the wooden stair.

Safe finally in their suite of rooms, Logan once more became serious as he took Rhea into his arms.

"What am I going to do with you, woman?" There was a softness in his eyes that warmed Rhea to the depths. "There is so much to discuss. What has happened between us changes many things. We must talk."

While Logan was speaking Rhea unbuttoned his shirt. She pulled the ends of it out of his trousers now and pressed her legs firmly against his as she ran her hands over his naked chest. Smiling to herself, she felt a shudder run through him.

"Rhea . . ."

"There will be time enough for talking in the morning," she interrupted softly. She let her hands move along the sides of his tapered waist and pulled him tightly to her, placing tiny kisses down his chest. Logan's quick catch of breath told her she would have her way.

"Come, my darling, and let us make love again," she coaxed gently. "Let me show you what you have awakened in me."

The time of intense, eruptive passion had been spent in the woods. Now came the time for slow and tantalizing arousal. By the light of a single candle, Rhea took long, unending moments to finish undressing Logan. She rubbed her hands caressingly over the rippling muscles of

299

his back and chest, marveling at the visible response this caused in him, and wondering at her power to elicit such a reaction in a man. She caressed his bare shoulders and back with her lips until Logan stopped her. He would allow her to do no more until he had had his chance to undress her.

When only her lace chemise remained, Logan lay Rhea back against the pillows on his bed. Then he toyed with the four ribbon fastenings down the front, slowly untying each one and moving first his fingers and then his lips over every inch of her soft flesh as it became uncovered to him. His touch was heavenly, making Rhea yearn wantonly for the bold foraging of her body to continue. His lips tasted the sweet warm nectar of her breasts again and again, while his hands stroked her slowly, provocatively.

But Rhea would have her turn. As Logan moved to press his body over hers she somehow found the strength of will to delay their joining.

"No, my love, you must wait yet a little longer . . ." she murmured huskily, trying hard to catch her breath and force her own insistent response to delay. She wanted to prolong this wondrous happening as long as possible.

Rhea rolled with Logan until he lay on his back and she was over him. She used her lips and tongue as he had, to probe his mouth, relishing the taste of him. Then she used her teeth and lips to trace a nibbling, nipping path around his earlobes, along the side of his neck, across his shoulders, and down over his bare chest. When Rhea's hands moved hesitatingly to that part of him which most strained to throb within her, Logan could hold back no longer. The control he'd been forcing himself to maintain to prolong their mutual pleasure was lost to him now just as Rhea's own longing heightened to an unbearable pitch. She gasped and welcomed his penetration, meeting his violently heaving thrusts with wildly arching hips until the throbbing of climax burst from his body to hers.

Rhea awoke the next morning still flushed with the afterflow of their lovemaking. She didn't want to ever move from this spot, snuggled close against Logan's left side with his arm possessively encircling her. This was where she belonged—with this man, wherever he was. God help her. She hadn't meant for this to happen, hadn't wanted to fall in love with Logan Tremaine, but she knew she could not deny it any longer, at least not to herself. Somehow she had to have him care for her in more than just a physical way. She had to make him love her in return or she would be lost.

Logan stirred beside her. Rhea felt her apprehension rise. What would his reaction be this morning to what had happened between them yesterday and last night? Did he feel anything for her beyond physical desire? She couldn't be certain. Would the Logan she'd loved yesterday be there to greet her this morning? Or would he revert back to the aloof and cynical man whose extraordinary bargain had changed her life forever? Rhea feared it would be the latter.

"Good morning," she greeted tentatively, biting off the words "my love" which her heart longed to speak. She would tread ever so carefully now for she was very unsure of her standing with him. Her entire future and her happiness hinged on what took place in the next few minutes. Rhea found herself holding her breath, waiting for him to say something.

For a long minute he was silent. Then he blew out his breath in a heavy sigh and turned his head to look at her. Rhea's heart sank when she saw his expression. His face held a pained look as though he was greatly burdened. It was not what Rhea had hoped to see.

"Are you sorry to find me still here in your bed, Logan?" she ventured timidly, lowering her eyes from his gaze.

He didn't answer her as he sat up in bed and ran a hand through his dark hair. Logan didn't know where to begin. He couldn't have Rhea in his life like this now, couldn't draw her into it any further. Too many things were happening that she wasn't aware of and couldn't be told about because of the danger it could bring to her and many others. She would only distract him, be caught in the middle of the perilous activities he was involved in as Mr. Exodus. He had to be able to think clearly if he were to succeed in what he had set out to do. And he couldn't keep a clear head when Rhea was near, when all he could think about was making love to her, keeping her close so he could protect her, take care of her. He had to separate himself from her, for her sake as well as his own.

"Please don't do this, Logan" Rhea whispered then, interrupting his troubled thoughts. "I can feel you closing yourself off from me. Please don't do it. Talk to me. Please tell me what you are feeling."

She sat up next to him and looked at him with wide blue eyes. Logan had to turn away from her beseeching gaze. He got out of bed then and walked to the tall wooden armoire. Hastily opening one of the lower drawers, he pulled out a pair of black riding breeches and put them on. Then he opened the two upper doors of the large cabinet and drew out a white linen shirt which he quickly slid his arms into, ignoring the buttons down the front. He was thinking hard, thinking of what he had to say to Rhea.

Rhea said nothing as she watched him with growing dismay. She didn't know what to do, what to say to him to stop him from doing this to her, to both of them.

"I'm sorry, Rhea," Logan whispered at last as he came to stand next to the bed, looking down at her. His face still hinted of the pained expression Rhea had seen before. Could he possibly be hurting as much as she was?

"I have no wish to hurt you. I want you to believe that," his deep voice went on, "but I must give very serious thought to what has happened between us, and so must you. This was never to be a part of the bargain we made. You know that. And it cannot be a part of our relationship under any circumstances." His gaze held Rhea's for a long, troubled moment before he lowered his eyes and turned away from the bed. The hurt in her eyes cut him to the quick.

"I am going to Richmond for two days about some horses," he went on suddenly with firm resolve. "That will give us both time to think, unencumbered by the other's presence. When I return, we shall talk of this in depth and make whatever decisions are necessary to resolve this dilemma."

Saying no more, Logan turned and walked toward the door to the hallway, pausing only long enough to pick up a pair of black riding boots from a nearby rack. Then he left the bedroom without even a backward glance.

Rhea stared at the closed door for a long time unable to

move. She knew nothing of the torment Logan had been feeling, for she had seen only his cold resolve, heard his harsh words that told her he would not allow her into his heart. Rhea wished she could scream or throw things or weep hysterically. But she couldn't. She could only sit paralyzed in the middle of Logan's bed, her mind numbed by his seeming indifference.

Finally the deep hurt penetrated to the depths of Rhea's being. A tear escaped down her cheek. She brushed at it with annoyance as her mind slowly began to function again. All right, if that was the way Logan wanted it— she'd been a fool to think he might return what she felt for him. Or rather, what she *had* felt for him, for at that moment, Rhea was determined to erase from her heart completely the love that had begun there. It was still so new to her, budding and fragile. She would extinguish what remained of it no matter how long it took or how hard she had to try.

Rhea knew she had to get away from Fair Oaks before Logan returned from Richmond. She would never again give him a chance to use her, to hurt her so much. Her thoughts were cold and calculating. In that, Logan had taught her well. She would take the jewelry he'd given her as she'd planned to do before. It would buy her way north. She'd go to Evan VanHorn and insist that he help her escape by the underground railroad. If he refused out of loyalty to Logan, she would threaten to expose his abolitionist activities. She would think of nothing else until she had accomplished it, until Logan Templeton Tremaine remained only a bad memory of a terrible mistake she'd once made.

Chapter 60

"I TOLD YOU JUPITER WAS THE ONE FOR THIS task," Vanessa Forsythe announced triumphantly as she burst into Ross Talmadge's office with a flourish. She sat down in the chair in front of his desk without being asked.

"He's gotten some information then?" Talmadge asked eagerly, sitting forward on his own chair behind the desk. It was about time something started happening to put their plan to capture Mr. Exodus into motion. He hated the waiting.

"Word has come to Jupiter and the three others that the escape will be tonight. They're to try to get away from the compound and be at Frenchman's Point by midnight. That's all they've been told for now."

"Are you certain this Jupiter is telling you the truth?" Talmadge asked, looking skeptical. "You know darkies can lie just as easily as not and they're usually very close-lipped about escapes."

"Of course he's telling the truth," Vanessa answered with some impatience. "He's a loner and mean as sin. Jupiter doesn't care about anyone but himself, and he wants his freedom more than anything. That's what made him so perfect for our scheme. The deal we offered him was too sweet for him to turn down. His freedom papers and twenty-five hundred dollars in cash money to make a new start, five thousand if he actually catches Logan for us as Exodus. For that, he'd be glad to expose his own mother without a moment's hesitation, believe me. And that still leaves half of the reward money for you and me to split." Vanessa stared off into space, relishing the thought of Logan's capture. She'd show him for spurning her. No man did that to her.

Ross Talmadge eyed Vanessa Forsythe from across the desk. She was quite a woman. All fire and ice. She'd insisted on helping plan this ambush of Tremaine out of pure revenge. Vanessa was a woman scorned, but her angry determination to bring about Tremaine's downfall had surprised even him. Yet she had calculated the details of it with him with a coldness that made Talmadge want to keep his distance from her. He would use her to pull off this scheme, then he'd get rid of her. He was only too glad that her vengeful fury wasn't directed toward *him!*

"So you'll have your men at Frenchman's Point tonight?" Vanessa's words were more of a statement than a question.

"Yes, a few key men, Stryker, and two of his men. I don't want too big of a crowd for fear of tipping our hand. This may be just a routine rendezvous handled by a minor conductor. Tremaine may not show up there but could join them later somewhere else. I want to be able to follow them easily if that happens." Vanessa nodded, agreeing with his strategy while Talmadge went on. "I just hope you're right about Jupiter and we don't find ourselves on a wild goose chase tonight while Exodus and the slaves give us the slip in another direction."

"Well, if you need more proof, go out to Fair Oaks," Vanessa countered defensively, her Irish ire rising. "I'll wager Logan's not there. They'll tell you he's off on one of his horse-buying trips or getting supplies for the sawmill, or some such thing, just like he's always been whenever a major slave escape has occurred. You'll recall the dates and coincidences you and I compared before."

"Yes, very well, you're probably right. But all that is circumstantial. We have to catch him in the act with witnesses if we're going to make anything stick. As a little insurance toward the success of our plan, I've had a man on surveillance at the Tremaine plantation for the last couple of days. He'll report in if he sees Logan leaving on what could be a journey, or anyone else, for that matter. There's still the possibility that wife of his is involved in this somehow, too."

A wicked smile spread over Vanessa's lips. "Wouldn't it

be delightful if Logan's obnoxious little wife turned out to
be a card-carrying member of that National Anti-Slavery
Society? Are you doing anything to try to find that out?"
Her green eyes leveled on Talmadge.

"I'm making inquiries. I already suspect she may have
been involved in a recent escape. Stryker reported coming
across Tremaine and his wife on the road from Richmond
at an unusually late hour. It was Sunday night, after the
Fourth. Tremaine explained it away by saying they were
having a lovers' quarrel or something and Mrs. Tremaine
had taken a horse and run off. Stryker thought the whole
incident humorous, but the next morning Dreed Jessup,
the Tremaine overseer, reported a female slave missing
from Fair Oaks. Four others turned up missing from two
other plantations that same night. There's a little too
much coincidence in all that."

"Ross, you are a man after my own heart. I like the way
you think." Vanessa's voice was honey-sweet as her eyes
glanced over him appreciatively. Then she stood to leave.
Talmadge came to his feet also.

"I almost wish I were going with you tonight. But that's
your department, isn't it?" Vanessa's voice had turned
cold again. "I've done my part and shall do so again on the
witness stand at Logan's trial. But tonight is up to you.
Don't make any mistakes at Frenchman's Point, Ross.
You may not get another chance to have the elusive Mr.
Exodus laid right in your lap."

Chapter 61

AS LOGAN CAUTIOUSLY APPROACHED FRENCH-man's Point his thoughts were bleak. He had a bad feeling about what he had to do tonight. Not only was his relation-ship with Rhea weighing heavily on his mind, but things were not running as smoothly as usual on this run. Gem Boy, the horse he usually rode for such a night's work as this because of his dark chestnut color and common-looking breed, had gone lame, and he'd had to use Baron at the last minute. The big black was fast, well trained, and difficult to see in the dark, but his very size and bearing distinguished him from other horses. While Logan wore his usual hooded disguise he knew he was running a dan-gerous risk of revealing his identity if anyone other than the slaves he was going to help tonight recognized Baron.

Then to complicate matters more, there had been sev-eral last-minute changes in the timetable and number of "passengers" he'd be conducting tonight. Originally, three had been coming from Vanessa's plantation. How she would rave if she knew he was behind their escape. But now another slave would be coming—Jupiter, a known troublemaker. They'd join up with two women at Den-ning's Hollow, making up a bigger group than Logan liked to work with at one time. He'd have to break them up, leave the women with Warren and Priscilla. Take two of the men on to Peterson's place, the other two to Camp-bell's.

That decided, Logan rode on, keeping off the main paths and staying close to the tall, dense bushes and under-growth leading to Frenchman's Point. But, still, some-

thing about this whole situation didn't sit right with
him . . .

Frenchman's Point was a high hill that on one side
dropped off sharply eighty feet to the James River below.
Logan liked to use it as a rendezvous place because it was
easy for the slaves to find and the heavy covering of brush,
pines, and other trees leading up to its summit offered
good hiding places for the fugitives.

He pulled his watch out of his leather riding vest and
pressed the small button that released the cover. Angling
the timepiece to catch the reflected light of the moon, Logan noted it was just past midnight. He touched his heels
to the stallion's sides and headed for the dead oak where
he was to meet the runaways.

Suddenly Baron dipped his head and snorted. Logan
quickly pulled him up. "Whoa, boy, whoa . . ." he whispered, patting the big horse's neck to calm him. Baron
tossed his head and pranced in place, resisting Logan's
firm hold on the reins.

Logan's senses flashed to alert. Had he heard something? Above the normal sounds of the night, had he heard
a muffled whinny? None of the slaves hiding up ahead would
be on horseback. It could only mean one thing—a trap.

Four crouching figures came toward Logan now from behind the old oak—the slaves he was to meet. But the
sounds of hurried movement through the surrounding
brush told Logan his hunch had been right.

"It's a trap—run for it!" he shouted to the Negroes who
had almost reached him. Drawing his gun from its holster,
he pulled Baron sharply around with his free hand to face
whoever was coming at them now. He'd try to hold them
off to give the runaways a chance to scatter.

A man jumped out at Logan from behind a tree not ten
feet away. Startled, Baron screamed a frightened neigh
and reared as the man ran at him. Logan held his seat on
the big stallion's back but couldn't loose a shot at any of
the figures who now came running into the small clearing
from their hiding places. Logan managed to get Baron's
front hoofs back on the ground and was taking aim at a
man to his right when he was grabbed from behind.
Caught off guard and thrown off balance, Logan went

crashing to the ground with his attacker. Confusion reigned as the slaves panicked and ran in different directions and Baron reared and neighed, thrashing the air with his deadly hoofs. Logan grappled with the powerful man holding him. The two of them rolled away from the melee into the shadowy underbrush. Logan caught a glimpse of his adversary's face and was stunned to see he was fighting for his life with one of the runaways. Jupiter. It was Vanessa's renegade buck, Jupiter!

Logan's momentary shock cost him dearly for the big black man took full advantage of his slight hesitation. Rising up on his knees to straddle Logan, Jupiter landed a bone-jarring blow to his jaw. The pain blurred Logan's senses for an instant before he was able to come back with lightning swiftness, bringing his legs up and locking them around Jupiter's neck to pull the slave backward and off of him. Whipping back his hood so he could see better, Logan went for the powerful Negro and drove his fist deep into his midsection. Gasping, Jupiter toppled forward into Logan, and the two men hit the ground again. This time their struggling took them dangerously close to the edge of the precipice.

Logan punched Jupiter again, this time landing his blow to his foe's jutting chin. In the seconds while Jupiter was dazed, Logan jumped to his feet, ready to swing at any other attackers. Two others came toward him, plus a third on horseback. But before any of them could reach Logan, Jupiter was on his feet again and coming at him.

"Damn it, Jupiter, get the hell out of my line of fire!" Ross Talmadge yelled from horseback then. But the big slave either didn't hear the warning or chose to ignore it, for he lunged at Logan and caught him in a crushing bear hug around the chest. Logan gasped for breath as he struggled to break the Negro's powerful hold.

Logan twisted and threw himself sideways, carrying Jupiter with him. This quick movement put the slave between Logan and Talmadge and the others, just as two guns exploded at once. Logan felt a shattering pain cut into him as one of the bullets hit its mark. In the same instant Jupiter's body jerked violently, hit by the other deadly bullet. His hold on Logan slackened some, but when he pitched forward in death, his heavy weight carried Logan with him, and the two of them toppled over the edge of Frenchman's Point to the swirling depths of the James River below.

Chapter 62

"YOU BLUNDERING IDIOT!" VANESSA FORSYTHE
spat viciously at Ross Talmadge in his office in Richmond
the next morning. "I hand you Logan Tremaine—Mr. Exodus—on a silver platter and you let him get away!"

"I didn't *let* him get away," Talmadge retorted defensively. "I told you what happened. That damned nigger
Jupiter got in my line of fire. I only wanted to wound Tremaine but Jupiter turned just as Stryker and I fired. It was
dark but it looked like Tremaine caught a bullet. We may
never know for certain. Both Jupiter and Tremaine went
over the cliff. I have Stryker and his men out with the
bloodhounds combing the shoreline right now. If Tremaine
is still alive, they'll find him."

"I have my doubts of that!" Vanessa said sarcastically.
"It isn't likely Logan survived that eighty-foot drop, especially if he was shot."

"Perhaps not, but I haven't given up yet. In addition to
Stryker's search, I'm also sending a man to watch Fair
Oaks. If Tremaine somehow did manage to come out of
that water alive, perhaps someone from the plantation—
someone like that sweet little wife of his—will know where
he's hiding and lead us to him. We should know something
in a matter of a few short hours."

"Well, I hope so," Vanessa said coldly as she walked to
the door of his office. With her hand on the knob she
turned. "Because if you have allowed Logan to escape,
Ross, I shall use my influence with certain friends of mine
to see that your career and any political plans you might
have are ruined. Be certain you send word to me the mo-

ment you hear anything." Then she turned and left the office.

"Damn you, Vanessa, and curse the Fates that made everything go wrong last night!" Talmadge muttered to himself as he sat down heavily in his desk chair. Vanessa Forsythe was not making an idle threat, he knew. She had powerful friends in high places. Stryker had better come up with something—and fast!

In another part of Richmond, a messenger was just being dispatched for Fair Oaks. Young Ben Tilson rode hard for his destination. He'd been well paid to run this errand and he wanted to do it well to impress the wealthy man from up north who'd hired him. That could mean more work, which he needed. At any rate, he didn't want to displease his employer. The man from Philadelphia didn't seem the type you would want to cross up.

"I'm Miles Tremaine. You have a message for me?" Miles asked Ben when the messenger had been brought into the library.

"Yes, sir. An urgent letter from Mr. Grayson Sawyer of Philadelphia," Ben announced importantly as he held out the vellum envelope.

The name meant nothing to Miles and he resented the interruption when he was working on the ledgers. But he took the letter, broke the wax seal on the back, and took out the single sheet of elegant stationery.

Dear Mr. Tremaine,

I know we are as yet unacquainted, but I am certain you will be interested in learning of information I have acquired concerning the alleged marriage between your brother Logan Tremaine and one Rhea Merrick of Philadelphia. Said information is most alarming and must be kept in the strictest of confidence. To that end, I should like to meet with you personally to discuss this matter at length. It would be prudent for us to meet at eleven o'clock tomorrow morning at my hotel—The Blakely, Room 210.
Until then I am respectfully yours,

Grayson Sawyer

Miles quickly read the missive over again, then stared off into space for some moments, deep in thought. Alleged marriage. The words had jumped out at him from the paper. Who was this Sawyer? Some criminal element, an extortionist or blackmailer?

Miles glanced at the letter again. The writing was done in a precise script, the wording that of an educated person. Of course, Sawyer could have had someone else write it for him. But if he were an opportunist or blackmailer, wouldn't he have gone to Logan with such information, in hopes of gaining money for his silence? Miles frowned with uncertainty but his curiosity was piqued. If Logan and Rhea were not truly married . . . The thought was a delectable one, certainly worth a ride to Richmond tomorrow to look into.

Chapter 63

RHEA WAS VERY CAREFUL TO DO EVERYTHING as usual this morning, for she was going to make her escape from Fair Oaks today and she didn't want to do anything to jeopardize her chances of succeeding. Logan had gone to Richmond yesterday and was due to return tomorrow. This would be her only chance to get away. She had to leave Logan, leave all of this behind.

Since Rhea had done nothing lately to arouse Obediah's suspicions, the slave had grown a little less diligent in his duty the last few days. Rhea hoped her plan would catch him off guard, though she worried about his punishment if she managed to slip away from him.

Rhea surveyed herself in the mirror. She was wearing one of her usual riding outfits just as if this were another of her regular daily rides. White ruffled silk blouse, brown riding skirt with matching boots, gloves, and ostrich-plumed hat. She patted the side pockets of her skirt. She had to look hard to see where her jewelry caused a little bulge in the line of the skirt. She'd wrapped it in two silk handkerchiefs, but it was barely noticeable. In the other pocket she'd hidden what little money she had. She couldn't safely take anything else except her small derringer, which she now tucked into her riding boot.

Rhea glanced over toward the large walk-in closet on the other side of the room, where the many elegant and expensive outfits Logan had given her hung waiting to be worn. Logan had picked almost all of them out for her. She shook her head and sighed, then took one last look around the room before she went to have breakfast with Camille as she did every morning.

An hour later she was riding Jade Wind toward Meadow Lake with Obediah close behind her. It was another hot summer morning. No hint of clouds touched the clear blue sky. There would be no relief from the blistering heat today.

As she rode Rhea thought back to the time she'd just spent with Logan's sister. About Camille, she felt great regret. It had been so hard to get through their breakfast together today. Camille had chatted and laughed as usual. They had even made plans to be together later this afternoon so Rhea could teach Camille an intricate embroidery stitch she'd been wanting to learn. Plans Rhea could not keep, but she didn't dare arouse a suspicion that today would be different from any other day.

Rhea's heart was heavy. How she'd hated to lie to dear Camille. She was so sweet, so trusting. Rhea loved her like the sister she'd never had. It was hard to believe Camille was part of the Tremaine family. She vowed now that once she was away from Fair Oaks and safe in Canada or wherever she finally ended her running, she would write a long letter to Camille and try to explain everything. She only hoped her friend would understand and forgive her.

"We'll water the horses at the lake," Rhea called back to Obediah as they entered the meadow. But as they turned their horses toward the water their attention was drawn by the whinny of a horse from somewhere close by. Jade Wind answered the neigh, tossing her head. Rhea pulled in the reins to steady her mount and glanced around. Obediah reined in next to her. A black horse stood grazing near the ruins of the old Tremaine homestead. Moving in closer, Rhea saw that the horse was Baron, still saddled but riderless. Neither Logan nor anyone else seemed to be around.

Rhea dismounted and walked over to the big stallion. It was then she spied something on the ground. She stopped to examine the large dark spot. Blood. A fresh trail of it led inside the ruins.

Rhea had Obediah tie the horses out of sight in the trees behind the old cabin. Then they cautiously followed the trail of blood inside and over to the far corner of the main room where it disappeared. This was the same room where

Ruby had hidden while she'd waited for Rhea that night. Was someone down there now? Logan perhaps?

Rhea and Obediah cautiously raised the hinged floorboards of the secret trap door and descended the five steep steps into the dark room below. In the moments it took their eyes to adjust to the dimness, they heard labored breathing and then the deadly click of a gun hammer being pulled back.

"Who's there?" Rhea called softly. "Logan, is that you? Don't shoot. It's Rhea."

There was no sound except the sudden heavy thud of something slumping to the dirt floor. From the light coming through the trapdoor overhead, Rhea could just make out the shape of someone lying on the ground. An oil lamp was on a nearby table. She told Obediah to light it as she hurried to the unconscious figure.

The glow of the lamp flooded the small room. Rhea knelt beside the man and turned him over on his back. Blood seemed to be everywhere. It covered his hands and flowed even now from a bad wound in his right shoulder.

"Logan . . ." she whispered in shock. His face was ashen, his lips colorless. Instinctively Rhea reached for the vein at the base of his neck. A faint pulse was still beating. But he looked terrible. His cheek with its day's growth of beard was cold to the touch.

Rhea lifted away Logan's shirt as gently as possible, revealing a nasty hole in his shoulder. The bullet had gone straight through.

"Obediah, take that bucket over there and fetch some water from the lake quickly," she ordered. When he'd gone she took the moments to remove her ruffled pantaloons from under her riding skirt and began tearing them into makeshift bandages. When Obediah returned, she washed Logan's bleeding wound as best she could, then covered the shredded skin around the two gaping holes with thick wads of cloth held by longer strips tied around his shoulder.

Logan was still unconscious. Perspiration soaked his brow. Rhea was uncertain as to what to do next. What had happened to Logan? Had he been attacked by someone as he traveled? But why would he come here to this hiding place and not back to Fair Oaks? How did he even know about this hidden room that runaway slaves used while escaping?

"Do you know anything about how this might have happened, Obediah?"

"Ah don' know nothin' 'bout how Marse Logan come ta git shot, missus," the black man answered her, never taking his eyes off his beloved master. His face was creased with worry.

Something on the floor next to Logan caught Rhea's eye then. She leaned over and picked it up. It was a piece of black cloth with holes cut in it—some sort of hood. Hood? Her thoughts raced. Again she was stunned. No, it couldn't be. But one look at Obediah's face when she held out the cloth gave Rhea the answer she was looking for. Mr. Exodus! Logan was the notorious Mr. Exodus? How could that be? But she knew there could be no other explanation. Obediah clearly knew who he was. And now Rhea knew.

It was obvious Logan needed a doctor, but he'd lost too much blood to be moved now. Rhea sent Obediah for Evan VanHorn. While she waited the long hours for Evan's arrival from Richmond, Rhea used the time to bathe Logan's face and chest with the cool lake water and tried to make him as comfortable as possible. An old mattress would have to serve as his bed. She pulled it over by him, then gently rolled him onto it to get him off the damp dirt floor of the cellar room. Food had been stored in a small wooden cupboard—beef jerky, salt pork, dried fruits and vegetables, biscuits in a tin, even a jug of corn liquor—for anyone using this room as a hiding place. Rhea kept the jug close by in case Logan awoke and could drink some of it. It would help against the pain.

Rhea used the time to think. It was incredible that Logan could be Mr. Exodus, the man who risked his life again and again to help runaway slaves along the underground network to freedom. Logan, the man she considered to be heartless and selfish and cruel. The man who was Mr. Exodus would have to be anything but those things. Not to mention cunning and courageous as well. How had she been so fooled by him? But then, she hadn't been the only one duped by his double life. Probably very few people knew of his clandestine activities. Obediah, Evan, perhaps a few others in the underground railroad.

Warren and Priscilla Laraby came into Rhea's thoughts then. She remembered the looks that had been exchanged between them and Logan. They had known. They were probably part of the escape routes.

Rhea shook her head in bewilderment. This was all so confusing. Other things came back to her now. That shadowy figure she'd seen in the garden from her balcony that night when she'd first arrived at Fair Oaks. She had thought it was a slave trying to escape. Had it been Logan going out as Mr. Exodus? Had there been a slave escape somewhere around then? Rhea couldn't remember, but the possibility seemed likely now.

No wonder Logan had been so enraged when she'd taken it upon herself to help Ruby escape. If she and Ruby had been caught . . . But why hadn't he told her the truth after that? He must have known then she was sympathetic to his cause and would have helped him.

Rhea sighed heavily, realizing the answer to her own question. Logan didn't trust her. She was nothing to him except a way to thwart Miles. She knew the animosity between Logan and his brother was real enough and no act. She could see that in the looks they gave each other, the tone of voice they used.

Rhea looked down at Logan. So he hadn't gone to Richmond yesterday to buy horses as he'd told her. At least not directly. He'd evidently become Mr. Exodus again to help some slaves in their escape and he'd been shot doing it. She had so many questions she wanted to ask Logan, but he wouldn't be answering them now in this critical condition.

"Hurry, Evan," she murmured in the quiet room. "Logan needs you."

Still watching him, she listened to his labored breathing. He must have had so many distressing things on his mind with his Exodus responsibilities. Perhaps that was part of the reason he had hired her to be a quiet, unobtrusive, noninterfering wife. She'd tried to be that way, really tried. But she realized now that she'd failed dismally in that task, no doubt adding greatly to the heavy burdens already on Logan's shoulders.

Rhea sighed again and busied herself changing the dressing on Logan's wound for the fourth time. She looked at his face.

"Oh, Logan . . ." she murmured wearily. "I love you so. I need you to love me. I want to help you. Dear God, I hope it isn't too late . . ."

Rhea's throat tightened as she watched him. He was so pale, his breathing sounded so jagged. Logan . . . Mr. Exodus . . . Everything was in such a mess.

She was relieved to find the bleeding from his wound had nearly stopped. As she reached for what little remained of her pantaloons and wadded it up to make the last bandage, she found Logan had awakened. His eyes were glazed and darkly circled as he stared at her with what looked like surprise.

"Rhea?" His voice was shallow and hoarse as he tried to speak. "What—?" He tried to raise himself up, but pain and weakness forced him back down on the mattress.

"Please don't try to move, Logan. Lie still and save your strength. You've taken a shot in the shoulder and lost a lot of blood," Rhea told him as she wrapped the bandage in place. She didn't know what to say next. Was he glad she was there to help him? How would he react when he learned that she knew the truth about him?

"How did you find me?"

"Obediah and I were out riding. We saw Baron and the trail of blood you left outside and upstairs. I remembered this room from when Ruby used it. You were lucky it wasn't Stryker or Talmadge who found you first." Rhea looked at him intently, watching his reaction as she held up the black hood.

"You know, then . . ." His clouded eyes tried to focus on her as he made the simple statement.

"Yes."

"I never wanted you to find out about this, Rhea, never wanted you involved." He stopped to catch his breath. "But now that you know, what are you going to do?"

Rhea met his gaze and their eyes held for several long moments before she finally spoke. "I shall keep your secret, Logan, and help you if I can."

Logan closed his eyes and visibly relaxed. "I'll owe you greatly for this," he said with an effort.

"You'll owe me nothing, Logan," she replied softly, looking down at her hands clasped in her lap, "for this is not part of the bargain we made before. I shall do it because it is my choice and because—," Rhea paused, biting her lip to catch the words "I love you" that she'd been about to speak. She was afraid to say them. Instead she only added, "Because I agree with the cause of freedom for the slaves which you've been striving for."

"I see . . ." Logan murmured, his breath coming falteringly. Then he lapsed into unconsciousness again.

Chapter 64

AT LAST OBEDIAH ARRIVED BACK AT THE RUINS with Evan VanHorn.

"Have you found out what happened yet?" Evan asked as he came over to where Logan lay and knelt down next to Rhea. He quickly opened his medical bag and began taking out instruments and bandages. "I couldn't get much out of Obediah except that Logan had been shot and was here. I've been out at a farm with a patient and returned to my office just as Obediah arrived."

"I don't know much more than that, Evan," Rhea answered, taking the wad of rolled-up clean bandages he held out to her. Her words were hesitant as she added, "I do know . . . he's Mr. Exodus."

"That's dangerous information to have." Evan paused to look at her, frowning slightly.

"You need not worry. His secret is safe with me," Rhea answered quietly. "I have no love of slavery. If I did, I never would have taken such a risk to help Ruby. Did she and the others get away all right?"

"Yes, they're well on their way. Logan took them through the first three crucial stations."

"I'm glad of that. I did so want Ruby to be free."

Evan looked at her for a moment longer before he nodded and turned back to tending Logan.

"What can I do to help you with him? He's lost a lot of blood." Rhea leaned forward to lend a hand.

"It looks as though you've done everything correctly so far," Evan said as he cut away her makeshift bandage with scissors and looked closely at Logan's wound.

"The bullet went all the way through," Rhea told him.

"Good thing. Saves a lot of nasty digging." He wiped both sides of the injury with a cloth soaked in a liquid he'd gotten from a bottle in his bag. "That will help keep the infection down. Looks like a clean wound. I don't think the bullet touched any bones. It should heal quickly." He held out his hand and Rhea gave him the wad of bandages. In short order the wound was covered again and secured with a long strip of bandage that wound several times over Logan's shoulder and around his arm, immobilizing it.

Logan stirred and opened his eyes.

"How are you feeling, my friend?" Evan asked as he gently raised one of Logan's eyelids higher so he could look into his eyes.

"Like a wagonload of bricks fell on me," Logan answered. His voice sounded stronger than before. "Evan . . . How did you get here?"

"Rhea sent Obediah for me," Evan replied as he began putting things away in his medical bag. "What happened, Logan?"

"I rode into an ambush at Frenchman's Point last night," Logan began. "Talmadge and his men were waiting for me. Stryker was probably with him, too, though I didn't have time to count heads." He shifted uncomfortably on the dilapidated mattress and winced when the movement sent a searing pain through his arm.

"Easy, Logan," Evan cautioned. "The bullet went straight through your shoulder, but I've seen worse. It will heal all right if you stay as still as possible."

"I can't stay here too much longer. None of you can," Logan said as he glanced from Evan to Rhea and Obediah. "If Talmadge was tipped off about the run last night, he may know about this place, too. I'm hoping he thinks I'm dead, but when my body doesn't show up in the river, he's likely to start a search."

"Start at the beginning, will you?" Evan interrupted. "Tell us everything that happened."

Logan quickly related the details of what had taken place at Frenchman's Point.

"The other three runaways scattered. I can only think Jupiter must have been in on it," Logan speculated then. "There's no way to ask him about it now. He's dead. The current was strong where we went into the river. It carried me downstream quite a ways, so it took me a while to circle around and make it back to here. I found Baron along the way. Somehow he got away from Talmadge's men."

"It was seeing Baron that led Obediah and me to search in here," Rhea put in then.

"Are the horses well hidden now, Obediah?" Evan asked the Negro. "We don't want anyone else stumbling onto us."

"Yes, suh," Obediah answered, nodding quickly. "In da thick bushes out back."

"Any idea who might have betrayed you, Logan?" Evan asked, turning back to his friend.

"If my hunch is right and Jupiter was in on it, then that points to only one person . . ."

"Vanessa . . ." Evan finished for him. "Would she do that to you, Logan, after what you've been to each . . ." Evan caught himself then and glanced uneasily at Rhea. "I mean . . ." he stammered.

"She'd do it," Logan went on. "She had a real fit over Rhea. I wouldn't put it past her at all. This is just the kind of thing she'd do for revenge."

"But did Vanessa know you were Exodus?" Evan asked.

"I didn't think she did. But she may have put two and two together and come up with a strong hunch. She's a very clever woman. There were times when I had to break my plans with her at the last minute or I arrived late because of my activities as Exodus. And a few months ago she walked into the library at Fair Oaks unannounced when Dodd Peterson and I were making plans for a run. At the time I didn't think she heard any of it, but now I wonder."

"So you think she told Talmadge. Could he have any proof he could use in court?" Evan asked, his tone very serious.

"I'd say that's a good assumption, especially now. He's sure to have recognized Baron. Gem Boy came up lame on me so I rode the black. I'm glad he was with me, though. If it hadn't been for the confusion Baron caused, I doubt if I would have gotten away. If Talmadge finds me now with this hole in my shoulder, he won't need much more proof than that." Logan closed his eyes then, weakened by his narrative.

Evan said nothing for some minutes, deep in thought. Rhea, too, was lost in her own contemplation. Indirectly, Logan was hurt and in this dangerous predicament because of her. Vanessa would have had no cause for jealousy if Rhea hadn't agreed to the pretend marriage bargain with Logan in the first place. But if she hadn't, she never would have come to Fair Oaks or known the wonderful intimacy, the passion that had awakened between her and Logan. Her mind whirled in confusion.

Logan opened his eyes then. He glanced first at Rhea, then at Evan.

"I want Rhea out of here, Evan," he said sternly, his expression grim. "Now—as soon as you can get her on a horse. Obediah, too." There was an urgency in his voice.

"Yes, of course, Logan, I understand," Evan readily agreed, his face equally serious. He got to his feet and turned toward her. "Rhea—"

"Now just a minute," Rhea protested, frowning. She couldn't leave Logan like this. "I have a say in this. I—"

"Rhea, please," Evan entreated, taking hold of her arms gently. "Logan's right. It's dangerous enough for the two of us," he gestured with one hand toward first Logan, then himself, "to be hiding here, but we're used to this kind of thing. You're not and neither is Obediah. If we're caught by Stryker or one of Talmadge's patrols, you can't be found with us. That would make you an accessory."

"But, Evan . . ." She stopped when she saw the stern resolve written on the young doctor's face. She turned to Logan. "Logan, perhaps I can—"

"Do as you're told, Rhea," Logan interrupted sharply, but he didn't look at her. He stared at the raftered ceiling above him as he continued. "Evan knows what needs to be done. You'd only be in the way. Even he won't be staying too much longer. And once I get my strength back a little, I'll be pulling out, too, probably tonight. Go back to Fair Oaks at once and do not return here for any reason. I shall send word to you by Evan regarding how I'll resolve our agreement. Do nothing until you hear from him, no matter what happens."

Logan's harsh words were like a slap in the face. Nothing had changed between them. He didn't trust her and didn't want her around anymore. And he wasn't taking any chances on letting her hear the plans he was making with Evan for getting out of this mess. That way, she would never be able to betray him like Vanessa had probably done. Well, all right, if that was the way he wanted it, so be it. Rhea let her anger force down the hurt she felt, telling herself she would be just as glad to be finished with their relationship and rid of him as he seemed to be.

"Come, Obediah," she said then, letting her anger show in her voice. "Your master speaks. Apparently there is nothing more for us to do here." Then she lifted her skirt, walked briskly to the short stairway, and left the cellar room.

The slave didn't follow Rhea up the steps but looked instead to his master.

"Go with her, Obediah," Logan told him tiredly. "Try to keep her out of trouble at Fair Oaks until I can figure out what to do with her."

The Negro nodded and followed Rhea up the stairs.

"You were a little rough on her, don't you think?" Evan asked as he pulled up a three-legged stool to sit by Logan. "That could be dangerous in light of what she knows about you now. Vanessa should have taught you that."

"Yes, I suppose I was," Logan replied wearily. His shoulder was throbbing badly now but a differend kind of pain was bothering him more. This one was inside him, because of Rhea. There was a heavy-heartedness in his voice as he continued. "You know I couldn't let her stay here, Evan. I don't want her in this business anymore than she is already. I don't want her knowing my plans, but it's not because I don't trust her. She isn't anything like Vanessa, believe me. I don't want her to know because she might do something impulsive and get hurt because of it. Damn it, everything is coming down around my head. I can't take her down with me."

Evan was surprised by Logan's words and the note of anguish in his voice. He didn't understand exactly what Logan's relationship was with Rhea and now was not the time to ask about it. He wondered if his friend was sure of it himself. It was not Logan's way to show his feelings. He must care something about Rhea to say these things.

"I could use something to eat, Evan," Logan said suddenly, changing the subject. "See what you can scrounge up in that cupboard over there, will you? Then after we talk of what's to be done next, you're to leave as well."

Evan carried the lamp to the wooden cupboard and looked through the foodstuffs stored there. He didn't want to leave Logan in this condition. He was weak from loss of blood and his wound could become infected. But he knew by Logan's tone that there would be no arguing with him. Better to use his energy to help Logan escape somehow. There had to be a way.

Chapter 65

JUST BEFORE MIDNIGHT RHEA SAT STRAIGHT UP
in bed, breathing hard. For a moment she was disoriented,
unsure of whether she was still dreaming or wide awake.

"Logan . . ." she whispered in the darkness, coming to
her senses. She'd been sleeping fitfully and dreaming of
him. Now she was awake, but a disquieting feeling lingered around her.

Somehow she'd managed to get through the rest of the
day and evening after she and Obediah had left Logan and
Evan at the ruins. No one had questioned her long absence
from Fair Oaks. Apparently she hadn't been missed.

Rhea had kept to her room on the pretext of not feeling
well. She wanted to see as few people as possible for fear
that they might read this dangerous secret about Logan on
her face. She'd stopped in to see Camille for only a few minutes to ask her if they could postpone the embroidery lesson to another day. Camille had been concerned for her
health, but Rhea had assured her she only needed to rest.
Then she had hurried from the room before Camille's sympathetic look could pry anything more from her.

Now as she sat in the middle of her bed Rhea couldn't
dispel the uneasy feeling that gnawed at her. She had to
get to Logan. Something was very wrong. She could sense
it. He needed her. She couldn't explain how she knew that,
she just did. And even though he'd told her not to return to
the ruins, that he wouldn't even be there by tonight, Rhea
still felt strongly drawn there.

She dressed quickly in dark-colored riding clothes so she
would be less likely to be seen in the darkness. She took
the small two-shot derringer from the bedstand drawer

where she kept it and tucked it into the top of her riding boot, then went to her bedroom door leading to the hallway and tried the knob. It wasn't locked. Rhea breathed a sigh of relief as she closed the door silently behind her. Obediah hadn't followed his master's instructions tonight.

Staying in the shadows against the wall, she stole down the long corridor of the east wing to the back staircase. All was quiet in the house and outer grounds as she cut through the large vegetable garden to the stables. The side door into the barn creaked as Rhea opened it and slipped in. Jade Wind snorted as Rhea cautiously approached her stall. The darkness was hampering.

Suddenly a match was struck. Rhea froze as the light from a lantern washed over her. She whirled around in fright to face Amos, who was walking toward her.

"What yo' doin' here now, missus?" he asked, looking at her suspiciously.

Rhea's heart barely started beating again. Her thoughts raced. What should she say? The urgency she felt to get to Logan left no time for making up stories or arguing. She'd have to take a chance and tell Amos the truth, hoping he'd believe her and not give Logan away. Amos was Logan's friend. There was a mutual respect and liking between the old slave and his young master. But could she convince him to let her go to Logan?

"Marse Logan tol' me yesterday mornin' ta be on da lookout in case yo' tried somethin' like dis. Ah ain't ta let yo' go, missus."

"Amos, please listen to me." Rhea's eyes pleaded with him and she tried to put her whole heart into her words to persuade him. "I know what Mr. Logan told you, but something's happened since yesterday to change all that. Please believe me, Amos. I have to trust you. Logan's been shot, but no one must know about it because it could cost him his life. That's all I can tell you. Please, Amos, let me go to him. Logan needs me."

The old slave was silent for a long moment as his black eyes surveyed Rhea. Tense seconds ticked by before he seemed to come to a decision and broke the silence.

"Reckon what ah heared today were true den," Amos stated as he suddenly walked over to Jade Wind's stall and hooked the lantern to a nail on a side post. Then he quickly

saddled the mare. "Word out is Mr. Exodus were almos'
ketched las' night in a ambush. Got shot up some, too."

"You know Logan is Mr. Exodus?" Rhea asked in surprise as she came to stand by him.

"Since da beginnin' a couple a years ago. Ah had ta
know, 'cuz ah's da only one touches Marse Logan's special
horses, 'sides him. Many a night, late-like, ah rubs down
Gem Boy and feeds him after Marse Logan got back from
one o' his conductin' trips. He been doin' somethin' powerful fine fo' mah people fo' over two years now. Ah been
afeared somethin's like dis were gonna happen ta him
sooner or later. He hurt bad?"

"A shot in the shoulder," Rhea answered as he helped
her mount Jade Wind.

"Reckon ah bes' come wid yo', missus. Patrols likely be
heavy lookin' for him. Jus' wait up whilst ah saddles me a
mount."

"No, Amos. I have to go alone," Rhea told him firmly. "I
don't want to put you in danger. One rider has a better
chance of slipping by a patrol than two. I'll see that Logan
knows what you've done tonight, Amos. He'll be grateful,
as I am." She gave the Negro a small smile, then turned
Jade Wind out of the barn.

At the edge of the stableyard Rhea halted in the shadows. Here was her chance to get away. She could ride away
now from Logan and Fair Oaks and never look back. She
could even betray Logan to Ross Talmadge or Jake Stryker
to ensure that he would never come after her or be a part of
her life again.

But Rhea knew she could not do any of those things. Her
heart wouldn't let her. Even now it decided her action for
her, and without another moment's hesitation, Rhea
turned Jade Wind south toward Meadow Lake.

In the secret cellar room at the old cabin, Rhea found
that not only was Logan still there, but he was delirious
with fever as well. He must have been too weak to leave as
he'd planned.

"Logan, it's Rhea. Please, you must lie still. Your wound
is bleeding again," she told him anxiously as she pressed
against his chest to try to stop his thrashing movements.

At the sound of her voice, Logan's eyes half opened and seemed to strain to focus on her.

"Rhea . . ." he murmured hoarsely. Then his eyes closed again but he quieted some.

His body seemed to be on fire. Glancing around the room, Rhea saw the bucket of water Obediah had gotten from the lake earlier. Using some of the fresh bandages Evan had left, Rhea changed the dressing on Logan's wound, then bathed his face and upper body with the cool water over and over again. All the while she spoke quiet, soothing words to him. And under her breath Rhea prayed that Logan would be all right. That was all she wanted. Her anger was gone now. Her heart ached, seeing him like this. She wanted him well and whole again and safe from those who hunted him. She'd even welcome his stern displeasure if his pale blue eyes would just look at her clearly again. More than anything, she wanted to feel Logan's strong arms around her, taste his lips on hers, wanted to love him and be loved by him.

After what seemed like a long time, Logan's fever broke. Rhea went to the lake for more water and returned to find him sleeping quietly. She sat down wearily on the floor next to him and gently touched his brow again. It was cool.

"Why did you come?" Logan's low voice suddenly broke the stillness, making Rhea jump. He was awake and looking at her now, his eyes once more clear and sharply scrutinizing.

"I—I had to come. Somehow I knew you needed me," she replied haltingly, lowering her eyes under his steady gaze.

"I'm glad you came," he simply said, breathing out a heavy sigh. "I did need you, Rhea. I need you now. Come, lie beside me. I need you close." There was a softness in Logan's voice that Rhea had never heard before. Her heart filled with joy as she lay down beside Logan, resting her head against his uninjured left shoulder.

No words passed between them, but their touching bodies spoke more than words could convey. Rhea's hand rested on Logan's bare chest. She could feel the strong beating of his heart. She closed her eyes and smiled, sending thankful thoughts heavenward for prayers that had been answered.

After a long while, Logan spoke. "It feels right having

you beside me like this, Rhea." He turned his head to look at her. "What has happened between us, my make-believe wife?"

"Something neither one of us could ever have imagined, my love," Rhea answered softly. "I've fallen in love with you, Logan Tremaine. God knows, I've fought against it, but I've lost the battle." Rhea rose up on one elbow to look at him. "Will you let me love you, Logan? Let me into your heart just a little? That's all I ask."

He didn't answer for a moment, then whispered, "You have vexed my thoughts and my life sorely, Rhea Merrick." A shudder of weariness washed over him. When he was able to go on his look and voice had turned gentle. "You've made me feel things I didn't want to feel, wouldn't let myself feel. While I was alone here today, I had a lot of time for thinking. Thinking of how things were before I met you, how you've thrown my precisely planned life into a turmoil. And how my life would be without you now. When I awoke tonight and you were here, I knew I couldn't deny what I felt any longer. I do love you, Rhea . . ."

Logan's left hand came up to gently touch the side of Rhea's face. "I think I fell in love with you the day I saw you in the music room. You were sitting at the piano, playing and singing, unaware that I was there. You looked so lovely with the sunlight touching you. At that moment you were not the Rhea Merrick who was running away from Grayson Sawyer, nor the woman who so calculatingly bargained her services to a stranger. Yes, I think it was then that I fell under your bewitching spell."

Rhea smiled at his confession, feeling a happiness fill her whole being. She leaned down then until their lips met. It was a tender yet searing kiss of love, and Rhea felt the heat of it reach to the depths of her soul. How she loved Logan. She had never known any feeling like this before. The joy, the longing. How she wanted him, all of him, in every way. Wanted to be a part of his life always. Yet in that longing was also a great need to give, to offer every part of herself to this man, to hold nothing back.

Rhea and Logan lay in each other's arms for a long time, communicating by quiet touch and all the whispered words that filled their hearts, reveling in just being together. Logan's wound would allow only that for now, but it was enough. If the Fates smiled on them, there would be time for more loving later.

Chapter 66

RHEA AND LOGAN SPOKE OF MANY THINGS IN the hours they lay together in the hidden room of the ruins.

"How did you ever become Mr. Exodus, Logan?" Rhea asked, still finding it a little hard to believe. Everything had changed so quickly. It was difficult to absorb it all.

"When I was a boy, I had a friend named Joshua." Logan's eyes took on a distant look, remembering. "He was a slave, but we were the same age and had been raised together. That's not uncommon in the South. His mother was a house slave, a cook in our kitchen. So he was always around, too. He lived in the servants' quarters in the main house. Miles and I never got along, but Josh and I always did. He was like a brother to me. We had wonderful adventures together, climbing trees, swimming in the lake, conquering all the make-believe worlds boys can create." Logan was quiet a moment before his expression changed and his tone became cold.

"But when we were both twelve, my father decided it was long past time for Josh to be put to work in the fields. I rarely saw him after that, or when I did, he was too exhausted by the hard work to do the things we'd done before. I remember the look in his eyes, the emptiness, the hopelessness where there had once been mischief and laughter.

"It was then I started realizing how wrong slavery was, what a terrible injustice it was that one boy had a life of leisure and freedom and the other a life of toil and bondage. And all because one was born with white skin and the other with black.

"Josh's mother died suddenly that autumn—a fever that struck quickly and claimed several lives. Camille became very ill, I remember, but she survived it. Josh went wild after that. He was uncontrollable, causing trouble at every turn, and Father decided to get rid of him.

" 'He has bad blood in him.' I remember my father saying that when I pleaded with him not to sell Josh. But he sold him just like that, just as though he were a horse or a piece of merchandise with no feelings, no intellect, and little worth. I never saw him again after that, nor was I ever able to find out what became of him, even though I tried when I was older. What happened changed me. I knew I couldn't free all the slaves in the South, but I vowed to do whatever I could to free as many as possible. When I was old enough, I began to work secretly with some abolitionists around here. That was when I met Warren Laraby. He and the others were deeply involved with the underground railroad.

"My devotion to the cause to free the slaves wasn't entirely unselfish," Logan admitted then, his tone lightening some. "I was attracted to the danger and adventure of it, too. I enjoyed the chance to dupe men like my father and grandfather.

"Two years ago, the man who was the chief conductor for the Richmond network was shot and killed when he had a run-in with Jake Stryker and his men while helping three runaways escape. I took his place and disguised myself as Mr. Exodus to try to keep my identity secret."

Rhea had been quiet during the narrative, deep in thought as she listened.

"Were you behind the revolt at Simpson Duvall's then?" she asked, voicing the question she'd wondered about since the days of that fire.

"No," Logan replied, shaking his head. "I tried to stop it, but Jonias wouldn't listen. He was one of Duvall's slaves and led the uprising. Duvall brought it on himself for treating his slaves so badly. All I could do was help fight the fire and see that the ten slaves who managed to get away got north safely. But Jonias was killed."

Rhea shook her head in wonder. Logan had fooled everyone all this time.

"Having me here has complicated things greatly for you, hasn't it?" she asked, looking at him intently.

"A little more than I planned," Logan remarked, giving her a little smile. "I couldn't let Miles get control of Fair Oaks. I owed it to Camille and Drew to try to protect their shares of our home. And I also needed Fair Oaks as a base of operations to work out of as Mr. Exodus. Our false marriage provided the way for me to hinder Miles's plans because I needed until December to be able to ruin him financially and gain major control of the plantation.

"But all that has changed since last night. My conflicts with Miles don't seem so important any longer. I'll have to leave Fair Oaks now and he will remain. He's won and he isn't even aware of it. I should feel bitter about that, but I don't. Perhaps in the back of my mind I always knew he was the one who fit in at Fair Oaks, while I never quite seemed to. Perhaps that was at the root of our clashes."

Logan turned a little and a stabbing pain shot through his injured shoulder. He clenched his jaw until the throbbing subsided some. Rhea sat up next to him, a worried look on her face. At last he released his held-in breath in a long sigh.

"Are you all right, Logan?" Rhea's eyes were wide and bright in the flickering lamplight.

"Yes. It's passed now," he assured her, taking her hand in his as he looked at her. "Rhea, listen to me. You cannot stay here any longer. It's too dangerous."

"Logan, please. I can't leave you here like this. I want to be with you. I *need* to be with you." Rhea leaned toward him as she spoke, putting her hand on his chest. Her very touch seemed to brand him. The look on her lovely face wrenched at his heart, but he forced himself to go on.

"I'm a hunted man, Rhea. The wolves are snapping at my heels. I can be caught at any moment, and if I am, it'll mean a rope around my neck." At Rhea's sudden horrified look, Logan added quickly, "Don't worry, my love. I intend to do everything in my power to prevent that from happening, but I won't take a chance on having you drawn into this with me any more than you already are. You must leave me now and leave Fair Oaks as well, as soon as possi-

ble. Once you are away, I will rest easier and be better able
to follow a plan I have for getting out of all this. But I must
know you are safe. Evan was going to tell you to go to Warren Laraby's on the pretext of a visit. He'll know what to
do."

"But I want to be with you no matter what happens,"
Rhea protested again. "I love you, Logan. Now that we've
found each other, let us have some time together, no matter how brief. Don't send me away, my darling. Please, not
that."

But Logan only shook his head. "No, Rhea, in this you
must listen to me. Warren will see that you get back to
Philadelphia by the underground. I should be strong
enough to leave here by morning. I'll be taking a different
route, but my destination will be the same as yours. Go to
Hugh Tennyson when you get there. Evan will wire him
my instructions. Hugh will give you the money we agreed
upon. If I haven't joined you in Philadelphia in two weeks'
time, take the money and go to Canada. Hugh knows
where I have friends there. I'll join you as soon as I can."

A tear spilled down Rhea's cheek. Her heart was weeping as well. She couldn't look at Logan. Though his words
were spoken with his usual self-assurance, Rhea was not
fooled. She knew only too well how terrible the situation
was here. The chance that Logan would be able to escape
was a slim one at best. That he would think of her safety
and future before his own only made her want to stay with
him more.

Yet Rhea knew she would only be a burden to him by remaining. Alone, Logan would at least better his chances of
getting away, too.

Logan raised her chin with his finger until their eyes
met. Then he gently touched her cheek where it was wet
with tears.

"You know I do not want to be parted from you," he murmured softly. "If there were any other way, I would choose
it so we could be together."

Rhea nodded. She didn't trust herself to speak. The
tightening in her throat wouldn't let her. She put her head
down on Logan's chest then and pressed her body close
against his. Was this the last time she would lie in his
arms, feel his warmth, his strength?

They didn't speak again until it was time for Rhea to leave.

"Go to Warren and Priscilla today, Rhea, as soon as you can," Logan told her with a gentle firmness as she moved away from his side. "I'll be all right."

Rhea reluctantly nodded agreement. Her heart was heavy as she leaned over to touch her lips to Logan's one last time. She tried to put everything she felt into her kiss. The moment burned into her memory as she concentrated on the feel, the taste of him. She would never forget these last hours with Logan, the man who possessed her heart, her body, her very soul.

"I love you, my darling," she whispered against his ear just before she drew away.

"I love you, my Rhea . . ."

When she could force herself to turn away from Logan, Rhea lowered the wick of the lamp on the small table next to the bed to lessen its glow. She met Logan's gaze one last time before she went up the cellar steps to the dark room above.

Rhea had barely come up through the trapdoor when she was suddenly grabbed from behind. A hand clamped roughly over her mouth before she could even cry out in surprise. The click of a gun hammer being pulled back sounded next to Rhea's ear, paralyzing her reflexes. The strong arm holding her around the waist threatened to crush the breath out of her. A match was struck then and touched to a piece of candle. In the flickering light, Rhea was horrified to see Ross Talmadge, Jake Stryker, and several others surrounding her.

"Tremaine! We know you're down there," Ross Talmadge called down into the darkness left by the open trapdoor. With a wave of his pistol, he directed his men to point their guns toward the hole. "Come out now with your hands up and no one will get hurt, especially this pretty little wife of yours."

No sound came from the cellar room. Rhea struggled to be free of her captor, to no avail. The tension mounted. Talmadge pointed his gun at Rhea and calmly cocked it. The sound was loud in the deadly quiet.

"This is your last chance, Tremaine. My gun is pointed at your wife. She's already guilty of aiding and abetting a wanted criminal. It would be a shame if she were to be shot, say, trying to escape."

Just then Rhea managed to twist her head free of the deputy's restraining hand.

"He's wounded, captain, and very weak!" she exclaimed quickly. "He may even be unconscious again. Please give him a chance," she pleaded desperately. "Let me go down ahead of you."

Talmadge hesitated a moment, glancing at Stryker, who only shrugged. Then Talmadge roughly grabbed Rhea away from his deputy and thrust her in front of him.

"We're coming down, Tremaine. Your wife is in front of me with a gun in her back. Don't try anything foolish or she'll be shot." Talmadge's deadly tone left no room for doubt that he'd do exactly what he said. He handed Rhea the candle to light their way, then pushed her ahead of him down the stairs. His men followed.

Logan was half-standing, leaning heavily on the rickety wooden table for support. Rhea's eyes flashed to him. Even in the dim light she could tell his jaw was clenched against the pain and weakness that threatened to topple him. She tried to go to him to help him, but Talmadge's iron grip around her waist stopped her short.

"Don't hurt her, Talmadge," Logan warned in a cold voice as he saw Rhea jerked back. "I'm not armed. I won't try anything. You have my word." He weaved dangerously on his feet. Talmadge gestured to Stryker and another man to go to him.

"Be careful of his shoulder," Rhea begged, straining against Talmadge's arm. But Stryker only smiled as he viciously yanked Logan's arms behind him to tie his hands. Logan fought to stay conscious as waves of excruciating pain shot through him. He fiercely ground his teeth together to keep from uttering a sound.

Talmadge pushed Rhea toward one of his deputies, who tied her hands behind her also. One of Jake Stryker's men turned up the lamp wick, illuminating the room more. Rhea could see the beads of perspiration coursing down Logan's face. Redness slowly spread on the white bandage over his wound. How she longed to go to him, but she was tied and held securely by the deputy. She could only stand

and watch, blinking back hot tears of fear and anger over what was happening.

Talmadge found the cloth hood. He held it up in his fingers and smiled. Why hadn't she hidden the hood or destroyed it? Rhea cursed herself for not thinking of it.

One of Stryker's men discovered the jug of whiskey.

"Take whatever you want out of this hole, boys," Talmadge directed. "Then I want it torched. I don't want anyone else using this place for illegal purposes."

He turned to Rhea then as his men wrecked havoc with the room. His voice was tinged with sarcasm when he spoke. "I want to thank you, my dear, for making Tremaine's capture so easy for us, not only just now, but when you led my man here earlier. He rode hard for Richmond and showed us the way to this place." Talmadge delighted in the horrified look that came to Rhea's face.

"But I didn't—" she protested in alarm.

"Oh, not knowingly, but you did nevertheless." Talmadge gloated over his own cleverness as he shifted his gaze to Logan. "You see, I've had you and all the other Tremaine's under surveillance for several days now. It was all part of my plan, my carefully calculated plan to capture the troublesome Mr. Exodus. I almost had you at Frenchman's Point, Tremaine. Jupiter was good enough to provide us with that information about the rendezvous, just as Vanessa said he would. A pity such a useful nigger was killed in the commotion. Does it surprise you to learn that Vanessa Forsythe was in on this little intrigue?" He gave a cruel laugh. "She was. She's quite a woman, that one."

Logan didn't take his eyes off Rhea for a moment. He saw the stricken look on her face as she silently stood across the small room from him.

Rhea's mind reeled with the terrible realization of what she had caused to happen. She had not listened to Logan and instead had come back here tonight. Because of that, Logan was captured.

Chapter 67

ROSS TALMADGE WAS GREATLY PLEASED WITH himself. He'd have no election worries this year, that was for sure. Likely wouldn't even have to campaign. The idea appealed to him as he sat in his office at police headquarters in Richmond. Capturing Exodus was prize enough, but having him turn out to be high and mighty Logan Tremaine was really a crowning touch.

Talmadge felt a little regret, though. Exodus had certainly kept things lively around Richmond the last two years. He had to admire Tremaine's shrewdness and audacity, though all he'd have to show for it now would be a meeting with the hangman. At least when this was all over, Talmadge would have those damned complaining landowners off his back.

Talmadge picked up the newspaper as he ate his lunch at his desk. Nothing too exciting in the headlines today, but tomorrow would be another matter. Babcock down at *The Guardian* office would have himself a real blockbuster of a story for his next edition. Talmadge hoped to have more than just Logan Tremaine to expose as an abolitionist. After this afternoon, he planned to have the names and locations of Tremaine's whole underground railroad network.

Talmadge smiled to himself as he thought of the interrogation session ahead. Tremaine had been weak after the long two-hour ride to Richmond. He had to delay their little talk until Logan could rest up and get his strength back. To be able to knock this uppity landowner down a few pegs in the interest of gaining vital information about criminal elements was not an unpleasant thought at all to

Ross Talmadge. He needed those facts on the underground to present to the city council and the prosecutor, to build a case quickly to bring to trial. Word was already out that Mr. Exodus had been captured. While the plantation owners would certainly be clamoring for Tremaine's head in a noose, Talmadge wanted everything to proceed by due process. That way he could draw the whole affair out as long as possible, milk plenty of publicity from it. He wanted to get as much out of this, popularly and politically, as he could.

Talmadge doubted that he'd have much trouble getting Tremaine convicted. The evidence was stacking up against him. Vanessa Forsythe would testify against him, presenting incriminating dates and incidences. She'd have to present them very carefully so as not to reveal that she and Tremaine had been lovers. But he had little doubt that Vanessa could pull it off, for she was a very clever woman.

True, most of the evidence against Tremaine was circumstantial, except for the hood they'd found at the old cabin ruins. But Talmadge was certain public sentiment would be running so high against Tremaine that even circumstantial evidence would be enough to get a conviction.

In order to destroy the troublesome underground railroad located in his jurisdiction, he needed names, locations. And he'd get them from Tremaine this afternoon. If he proved to be uncooperative even after a certain amount of "persuasion" was applied, Talmadge had an ace up his sleeve—that nice little woman of Tremaine's, his wife. He hadn't missed the looks that had passed between the two of them. He had Rhea Tremaine isolated in an old basement cell where Tremaine couldn't see her or know what was happening to her. Let him worry about her for a while. If Tremaine proved to be reluctant to talk, a little rough treatment with his wife should loosen his tongue.

Talmadge wished he knew more about Rhea Tremaine. He hadn't gotten any response yet from a friend of his in Philadelphia who owed him a favor. He'd wired him to find out what he could about Logan Tremaine's wife, especially if she had any connections with the National Anti-Slavery Society. If he could get proof she was involved with that group, he'd have a good chance of getting *two* sensational trials out of all this.

* * *

At the Blakely Hotel several blocks away, Miles Tremaine had met with Grayson Sawyer at the appointed time that morning. In the ensuing conversation, Miles learned of Logan's deception.

"My stepdaughter Rhea tends to be a rather rebellious young woman, prone to rash behavior that has caused her mother and me great anguish and worry in the past. But this has been by far the most unexpected and serious," Sawyer said after he'd shown Miles his credentials and given him a brief explanation regarding his relationship with Rhea. The lies had rolled effortlessly off his tongue.

"I have no idea why she would choose to pretend to be married to your brother, nor why he would want her to do so. But as you can see by this affidavit, duly signed by one William Scarsdale and witnessed by my barrister, the marriage certificate Rhea produced to convince me she was wed to Logan Tremaine was a forgery." He handed Miles the executed document and a letter of verification from Granfield and Turner, Barristers. He didn't tell Miles that Graham Turner of that firm was heavily indebted to him and had agreed to produce these papers to eliminate those obligations.

Miles examined the documents carefully. They looked authentic enough, signed, sealed, and stamped according to due process, from what Miles knew of such things. Of course, *they* could be the forgeries, perpetrated by Sawyer for some yet unrevealed reason.

Miles eyed the impeccably dressed man across from him. Sawyer's clothes were well cut and expensively made. He carried himself with the bearing of a man of position. This room was one of the best the Blakely had to offer its guests. It seemed likely Sawyer was telling him the truth. Besides, Miles wanted to believe this incriminating information about Logan and Rhea. His own suspicions about his brother's sudden plunge into matrimony were verified now. Old Silas would be livid with rage when he found out how Logan had made fools out of all of them with this trick. He might just cut Logan out of his will for good, without any further need of manipulation by Miles. He would have the final victory over Logan in this latest battle of wits between them and it would be a decisive one—in Miles's favor. But still he had to be cautious.

"You checked this information at the proper Hall of Records?" he asked then.

"Of course," Sawyer answered confidently. "There was an official recording of the marriage at the Hall of Records but an unscrupulous clerk there was bribed by your brother to make the entry. Your brother paid Scarsdale and the clerk for their services."

"So it would seem," Miles replied, glancing again at the papers in his hand. Then he looked at Sawyer again, searching his face for any sign of duplicity. "Why didn't you take this information directly to my brother?"

"I intend to do just that, but I decided to consult with you first." Grayson chose his words carefully now. "This is a delicate matter, Mr. Tremaine. It is obvious to me that your brother is likely involved in some illegal venture. And he has drawn my stepdaughter into it with him, whether by her own misguided choice or by some treachery. I would like to have more facts before I confront him on this matter. I hoped you might be able to help me in that and perhaps become my ally."

Grayson was beginning to have doubts as to the wisdom of this plan. Perhaps he had been wrong to approach Miles Tremaine in the hope of having him on his side. He often traveled and did business with the larger plantations in Virginia and other parts of the South. It was no secret that the Tremaine family, and especially the two older brothers, were often at odds with each other, to put it mildly. But perhaps the two brothers were in some scheme together involving Rhea.

But Miles's next words allayed his growing apprehension.

"I should like to be present when you do confront Logan with these findings, Sawyer. I believe I can enlighten you as to my brother's motive for having a counterfeit wife. I'll tell you of it as we ride to Fair Oaks. Logan is expected back from a brief journey sometime today. If what you've shown me here is the truth, I shall do all I can to help you expose Logan's treachery."

"While I shall be glad to assist you in that," Grayson continued, "I would ask one condition—that no legal action be taken against my stepdaughter. It would be most embarrassing to a man in my position. But you can be assured that if Rhea is turned over to me, she will be properly punished for her part in this scheme." He didn't add how much he was looking forward to that.

"I understand and readily agree," Miles replied curtly. "Rhea is of little consequence to me in this matter. Logan is my main concern. This will be his undoing. Shall we depart?"

"As you wish," Sawyer said as he took the documents from Miles's outstretched hand and turned away to hide his sinister smile of satisfaction as he deposited the papers in a leather portfolio. His plan had been set in motion. His revenge would be sweet.

Out on the sidewalk in front of the hotel, Sawyer found the enterprising Ben Tilson waiting to be of assistance.

"Have Mr. Tremaine's horse brought around at once, Tilson. And hire one for me also."

"Yes, sir, Mr. Sawyer! I can show you a shortcut to police headquarters if you like. I know some back streets that ain't so crowded."

"What in heaven's name are you talking about? Why would we want to go to police headquarters?" Sawyer asked with annoyance.

Tilson looked confused. "Well, after what I just heard, I reckoned Mr. Tremaine would be goin' there."

"Don't talk in riddles, Tilson," Miles cut in impatiently. "Explain yourself. What did you just hear?"

"Why, that Mr. Logan Tremaine was arrested this morning and charged with bein' none other than Mr. Exodus."

"What?" Miles looked incredulous. "What nonsense is this?" he demanded, grabbing young Ben by the shirtfront and glaring at him.

"Honest, Mr. Tremaine. It's what I heard. Everybody's talkin' about it," Ben answered quickly, a worried expression on his face.

Miles released Ben and turned to the Negro hotel door-man. "Hail a coach immediately!"

"Police headquarters as fast as possible!" Miles ordered the driver a few moments later as he and Sawyer hastily got in, leaving a bewildered Ben Tilson standing on the sidewalk.

Chapter 68

ROSS TALMADGE GOT TO HIS FEET WHEN MILES
Tremaine burst into his office, followed closely by another
man.

"Mr. Tremaine. The message I sent to Fair Oaks concerning your brother must have reached you sooner than I
expected."

"I received no message there. I was in the city this morning and heard a most disturbing piece of information about
Logan from a common street person," Miles told him indignantly. "Just what is going on here, Talmadge?"

"I am sorry you received word of this matter in such a
manner, but that does not change the facts. I have arrested
your brother Logan on the very serious charges of conspiracy and aiding and abetting runaway slaves. I have evidence and witnesses to prove that he is none other than the
notorious criminal, Mr. Exodus."

"That is absurd, of course," Miles replied contemptuously. "If this is some sort of ludicrous joke—"

"I assure you it is not," Talmadge cut in levelly. "Your
brother was apprehended at dawn this morning with an
accomplice at a runaway hideout on Tremaine land, as a
matter of fact. He was still dressed in his Exodus disguise
and had a shoulder wound which he acquired in a confrontation with me and my men involving four runaways at
Frenchman's Point the night before last."

"But this is unbelievable!" Miles was stunned by what
he'd just heard. Yet he knew Ross Talmadge was too
shrewd to make such a serious accusation unless he could
back it up.

"Perhaps you should sit down, Tremaine."

As Miles went to the chair across from the desk that Talmadge indicated, Grayson Sawyer stepped forward, extending his hand to the police captain.

"I'm Grayson Sawyer from Philadelphia. Logan Tremaine's . . . wife . . . Rhea, is my stepdaughter. This is most distressing news to hear. Has Rhea been informed?" He was anxious to get to the bottom of this startling development. It could have quite a bearing on his own plans.

"I regret to tell you, Sawyer, that she is only too aware of these happenings, as she was arrested with Tremaine and is charged with complicity."

"What? Now I know all of this is some ridiculous mistake," Miles exclaimed angrily. "Rhea has been at Fair Oaks for only a month—"

"Yet apparently that was long enough for her to become involved in her husband's criminal activities, if she wasn't already involved in them somehow in Philadelphia," Talmadge countered, growing annoyed now himself. He resented Tremaine's superior tone. "As a matter of fact, I will need for *you* to answer a few questions for me as well."

"You suspect *me* of being somehow connected with Logan in this?" Miles looked stunned.

"You are his brother," Talmadge stated flatly, enjoying putting Miles on the defensive. "Surely he could not have masqueraded as Mr. Exodus for over two years without your knowledge, and perhaps even your assistance."

Miles came to his feet, frowning deeply. "You're insane, man! If Logan has been Exodus all this time, I indeed had no knowledge of it and certainly had no part in it!"

Talmadge knew Miles was probably telling the truth. Miles Tremaine was rarely away from Fair Oaks. But Logan traveled often, supposedly on business. And he always managed to be away when there was slave trouble. No, knowing the animosity the two brothers had for each other, it wasn't likely that they had worked together in Exodus's escapades. And Andrew Tremaine was too young and irresponsible to have been a part of any of it, either. But it had been worth the try, to see Tremaine squirm just now.

"I demand to see Logan at once, to get to the bottom of this. I would like to hear what he has to say to these absurd charges."

"Of course, Mr. Tremaine. That can be arranged," Talmadge agreed with a note of triumph in his voice.

"And I should like to meet with my stepdaughter, if possible," Grayson Sawyer added. "I have reason to know that she was not acquainted with Logan Tremaine until shortly before she allegedly married him." He glanced meaningfully toward Miles.

" 'Allegedly'?" Talmadge asked, cocking one dark eyebrow. His interest was sparked.

"Yes, it would seem that Logan Tremaine and Rhea are really not married. So I may be able to persuade her to give you her fullest cooperation, as I am certain she was somehow duped into participating in this shocking situation."

"I'll want to hear more about this later, Sawyer," Talmadge replied, barely able to contain his delight at this newest development. The newspaper headlines would be even better than he'd imagined when all this got out. "Follow me, gentlemen. I shall take you to the prisoners."

Rhea jumped as the noise of the key being turned in the lock of the heavy iron door broke the stillness of her dingy basement cell. Her nerves were raw and she was distraught from hours of worry and fear, not for herself, but for Logan. How she longed to see him. Talmadge was cruel to leave her imprisoned alone down here like this, cut off from everything. She hoped it was Ross Talmadge coming now.

Perhaps she'd still have a chance to use the small derringer that was hidden in her riding boot. The guard who'd searched her when they were captured had been too occupied in running his hands over other parts of her body to bother to check her boots. Rhea knew she had to make herself bide her time and wait for just the right opportunity to use the small gun, an opportunity that would help Logan above all.

But Rhea's hope for information or escape died and her heart nearly stopped as the door swung open and Grayson Sawyer stepped into the cell. She gasped and instinctively took a step backward. Sawyer motioned for the guard to leave them, and Rhea felt panic well up inside her as the door was closed and locked, leaving her alone with the man she hated most in the world.

"Well, see what trying to escape me has brought you to, my dear," Sawyer said in an ugly tone as he looked around the gloomy room.

"What are you doing here, Grayson?"

"Seeing to my parental responsibilities. You have been quite naughty, pretending to be married when you really weren't, among other things. Your punishment will be quite severe for making a fool of me." He eyed Rhea. She tried not to cringe under his hate-filled look, but it wasn't easy.

"How did you find out?" she asked, trying to keep him talking as she moved a step away for every step Sawyer took toward her. She could only imagine with horror what kind of "punishment" he would inflict on her if he got the chance. At this moment she was glad she was imprisoned, although she feared what he might do next. Would the guard come in if she screamed? Could he hear her through the thick door?

"I am a suspicious man by nature. It took me some time and a considerable amount of money, but I made a thorough investigation which led me to finally uncover your expert forger, Willy-Nilly Scarsdale. Willy was . . . persuaded . . . to tell what he knew. A pity about him, though. His health was very poor, and I fear my men were a little overly zealous in their dealings with Mr. Scarsdale. He died quite suddenly."

Rhea sucked in her breath in shock over his cruel words. Sawyer quickly closed the gap between them and grabbed both her wrists, pulling her hard against him.

"I don't like to lose, my dear," he told her coldly, his dark eyes drilling into her. "I told you that you would be mine one day for as long as I want to make use of you."

"And how will you do that, Grayson?" Rhea shot back at him, forcing herself to face him defiantly. She recognized the lustful look in his eyes as their bodies touched, and her anger and revulsion overcame her fear of him.

"Do not forget I am a prisoner here, and Captain Talmadge is not about to release me. Unless you intend to rape me now and have everyone here learn of your terrible perversion, you'd better let go of me *now*, Grayson." Her angry gaze held his unflinchingly.

Rhea tried to twist her wrists out of his rough grasp and

pull away from his hold, but her struggling only aroused
Sawyer further. His breath started coming jaggedly as he
pinned her against him. He had planned to wait a little
longer to have Rhea, to try to persuade Talmadge to let her
go in exchange for his promise to use his important government and business contacts to further the police captain's
political career. Then when he had Rhea away from here
and in his power completely, he would teach her obedience
and absolute submission. But touching Rhea now, having
her defy him so, ignited his demented lust and he was
blinded to all but that and his outraged memory of her
with Logan Tremaine in the woods.

"You will give me now what you give *him* on the ground
like some wanton whore!" He pushed Rhea away from him
with such violence that she fell to the floor. In panic she
tried to avoid his reach, knowing he was out of his mind
with rage and lust. She tried to scream, but Sawyer lunged
for her and struck her viciously across the face before she
could utter a sound. The blow made Rhea's senses swim,
but instinctively she rallied her strength to fight off his attack. With all her might she wrenched her wrist out of his
grasp and pushed him away. Then she scrambled to her
feet, fleeing to the other side of the room with Sawyer close
behind her. He grabbed for her again, catching hold of her
riding blouse and ripping the sleeve and part of the shoulder. Though Rhea tried to twist away from him, he still
managed to get hold of her and strike her again. She fell
backward, crashing into the small table in the corner of
the room. The sharp pain cleared her mind for a few seconds, leaving it open for the sudden thought that flashed
through it. Her gun! The derringer hidden in her riding
boot!

Rolling to one side out of Sawyer's reach, Rhea dug in
the top of her boot for the small gun. But Sawyer saw what
she was doing and lunged for the weapon before she could
take aim. He and Rhea rolled together across the floor,
struggling for possession of the pistol. Rhea still held it but
Sawyer's big hand closed over it, squeezing Rhea's hand
excruciatingly. In a spasm of pain her finger yanked back
the trigger and the gun exploded between them. Sawyer
reeled backward, a startled look on his face. Then he

clutched at his stomach and crumpled over sideways. Rhea sat in the middle of the floor unable to move. Stunned, she looked from the smoking pistol to Sawyer's limp body. Two guards rushed into the room then and while one of them grabbed the derringer from Rhea before her senses could react, the other ran over to Sawyer.

Chapter 69

IN LOGAN'S CELL, THE TWO BROTHERS FACED
each other. Ross Talmadge watched intently from the
other side of the bars.

"So you do not deny these charges?" Miles glared at Logan.

"No," Logan answered simply. "It would be a waste of
effort. Our good Captain Talmadge there has outsmarted
me at last." He spoke for Talmadge's benefit, knowing the
police captain could hear all they were saying. "This
shoulder wound will offer the most damaging testimony,
I'm afraid."

"I can't believe this. You, Exodus? A nigger lover and
abolitionist." Miles spat the words out like they were
poison.

"I've been called worse," Logan returned with feigned
indifference.

"Don't be sarcastic. This is serious. The family will be
ruined by this disgrace!" Miles snapped.

"The family survived the hanging of Endicott Tremaine
as a British spy during the Revolution. It will survive this
one as well," Logan replied.

"How can you be so glib about this? What you've
done—"

"I did because I had to, Miles," Logan cut in, frowning angrily now as he stood his ground confronting his
brother. "My conscience demanded it. Can you understand
that? I would do it all again if I could. I have no regrets except that I was caught before I had a chance to help every
slave in Virginia escape to freedom!"

The two brothers stood barely an arm's length apart,

glaring at each other. Ross Talmadge watched the exchange with obvious enjoyment from outside the cell, though he would prevent the situation from becoming too heated if necessary; he didn't want the two brothers at each other's throats with anything stronger than words.

At that moment another guard entered the cellblock and came directly over to Talmadge. "There's trouble downstairs, sir," the guard said in a low voice.

Talmadge frowned. "What is it?"

"Mrs. Tremaine, sir. She's shot the man who was seeing her."

"What?" Talmadge's surprised exclamation resounded through the quiet corridor. "How in the hell—?

"You, Fenton," he suddenly directed his words to the guard who'd been standing with him. "Keep your eye on those two." He gestured toward Miles and Logan. "Don't let them kill each other. Let Miles Tremaine out whenever he's ready."

"Yes, sir."

"You, come along with me." Talmadge waved the guard who'd come with the message to follow him as he hurriedly left the cell area. The remaining guard stood by the heavy iron door that separated the corridor from the next one.

Miles sighed heavily and walked to the far side of Logan's cell. He put his arm on the brick sill of the barred window, pretending to look out.

"My God, Logan, you've really gotten yourself into it this time," he muttered in a low voice that only Logan could hear. "You're right. They'll want to hang you for certain."

Logan was surprised by the sudden change in his brother, but he managed to keep his guard up and his tone aloof as he spoke. "Except for the embarrassment this will cause to the sacred Tremaine name, I should think you'd be glad as hell to finally be rid of me. No one will ever stand in your way again for anything you want."

Miles looked directly at his brother, his expression serious. "You're wrong, Logan. True, you've caused me a damned considerable amount of trouble all these years of our lives, right up to your latest little trickery with Rhea."

A puzzled look crossed Logan's face, but Miles went on. "We were always so different, you and I. But for all our

conflicts, I've never wanted you dead. You are still my
brother and a Tremaine. The same blood runs through our
veins. I won't see you hang for any reason if I can possibly
prevent it." His mouth curved up at one corner as he
added, "Besides, things would be damned dull around here
without you. There's not a man around for two hundred
miles who can match wits with me as well as you can. And
I owe you for that tree you saved me from during Duvall's
fire."

Logan was speechless. He couldn't believe what he was
hearing. Had all of Miles's shouting before been only for
Talmadge's benefit? To have Miles say these things to him
was a shock . . . and a relief. He looked at his older brother
intently. Somehow Logan knew Miles was speaking the
truth.

"We have had some interesting times together, haven't
we?" he said finally, as he came to stand by the window
next to Miles. "I've never thought about it before, but if
the tables were turned, I'd feel the same about you. Too
bad this situation seems to be a bit out of our hands."

"You're not swinging from the noose yet," Miles replied.

Logan suddenly remembered something else Miles had
said. "How did you find out Rhea and I weren't really married?"

"Grayson Sawyer, her stepfather, sought me out with
proof of the forgery of your marriage certificate."

"Sawyer?" Logan's brow creased into a frown. "Sawyer's here?"

"Right here in these headquarters, in fact. He came with
me. He's with Rhea now, I think. He was pretty upset
when he heard she was charged as an accessory. Insisted
on seeing her."

Logan began pacing a small circle in the cell. "You have
to keep him away from her, Miles. Do whatever you can.
She didn't know anything about my being Mr. Exodus until yesterday. She helped Ruby escape, but that's all she's
been involved in. She hasn't been a part of this with me
and shouldn't be punished for it. Sawyer's no good and he's
no friend to Rhea. He'll harm her if he can. You have to—"

"First things first, Logan," Miles put in, stopping him.
"We haven't much time. I'll do what I can for Rhea. Nothing's likely to happen while she's here in Talmadge's cus-

tody. The immediate issue is you. Talmadge will no doubt be returning soon. We have to think fast. How can we get you out of here? I assume you'd be able to escape by that underground of yours if you were able to get out of this place."

"Yes, of course, to Canada. That's no problem. I have many friends there. But I wouldn't go without Rhea."

The two men's eyes met for an instant.

"So that's how it is. I was afraid you'd say something like that," Miles said as he saw the determined look on Logan's face. "There is something between you two, then. Damn, but that complicates things even more. This could very well be our greatest challenge, brother mine."

"And our last," Logan said quietly. "For no matter what happens, whether I hang or escape to Canada, I'll be gone from Fair Oaks . . . for good." He stared out the high, barred window of his cell for a long moment.

"Logan—"

"No, it's all right, Miles," Logan said quickly, turning back to face his brother. "Fair Oaks never was big enough for both of us. We were always scheming to wrest control of it from one another. That's how Rhea became involved in all this, when I hired her to play my wife until I could—" He broke off his words as he thought better of finishing his sentence.

"Could what?"

"It doesn't matter. It hardly seems important now. I'll tell you of it another time." The plan Logan had nurtured so carefully to ruin Miles seemed to be only a childish game now, like so many contests he'd had with his brother for so long. He found that he was suddenly weary of them.

"It would be ideal," Miles went on then, "if we could figure a way out of this for both you and Rhea so that you would be free to start a new life together and not be hunted down. But I'm afraid that's asking for a miracle. I don't think there's much chance of your being absolved of this in court. Even if we could manufacture evidence to try to prove your innocence, our good friends and neighbors aren't likely to be in the mood to listen to it. When word of this spreads that you were Exodus, they'll be talking lynching instead of trial. So we have to act fast, Logan, break you out of here or something before that can happen.

That won't be easy because Talmadge has a virtual army around this place. You're a prize package and he's not about to let you slip through his fingers."

Logan's mind was working fast. He certainly hadn't foreseen this godsend of finding a friend in Miles, but now that he had, there was a spark of hope on the horizon. A thread of a plan ran through his thoughts.

"There may be a way . . ." he said in a low voice, thinking aloud now. "I'll need your help, Miles. I'll have to put my life in your hands, and Rhea's, too." Logan looked steadily at his brother, searching his face for any hesitancy. He saw none.

"I'll do whatever I can, Logan. Trust me."

What Logan was thinking of was tenuous at best and extremely dangerous. It would require precise planning, perfect timing . . . and absolute trust in his brother. He'd have to rely on his gut feeling and hope it didn't fail him. Right now it was telling him to believe in Miles. It was the only way.

"You'll need Evan VanHorn, Tucker Corey, and several others in this. I'm sure they'll help," Logan began then, wasting no more time. "Here's what I have in mind . . .

"Remember that summer when we were boys . . ." Logan went on, relating the daring plan that just might save his life.

Chapter 70

LOGAN WAS SECURELY TIED HAND AND FOOT TO the bars of the isolated interrogation cell that Talmadge had had him brought to. His shoulder was killing him, throbbing constantly. But Logan only gritted his teeth against the pain and steeled himself for what was next in store for him. He knew what Talmadge wanted from him. He also knew he could take whatever Talmadge had planned to get that information on the underground network out of him. He would never betray the friends who had risked their lives with him to help slaves to freedom, no matter what Talmadge did to him.

But one thought ate at his insides more than any physical threat. The one person he cared most about in the world—his beautiful Rhea—was being pulled down into all this with him. He couldn't stop thinking about her, hoping she was all right. How he hated himself for ever involving her in his life, drawing her into this whole bad situation. Yet on the other hand, he was grateful that Rhea had touched his life. He loved her so much.

Ross Talmadge, Jake Stryker, and two guards entered the cell then. Talmadge came to stand before Logan.

"You are aware of the charges and evidence against you, are you not?" the police captain asked. Logan didn't answer. Talmadge frowned slightly and went on. "You know their seriousness and the consequences of your actions as Mr. Exodus over these last two years. There is no doubt in my mind that you will be found guilty by a jury of your peers and hanged." He paused for a moment to let his words sink in. He was annoyed by Tremaine's attitude. Though he had said nothing, Logan's look was one of disdain, even arrogance. Well, so much the better. It would make Stryker's work more pleasant, knocking Tremaine down a few pegs. Talmadge rather relished the thought of watching it. He motioned Jake Stryker forward.

Stryker was a big man, thick in body to the point of obesity, but powerful. He had a well-known reputation for meanness and brutality. There was an ugly smirk on his face as he came toward Logan now.

"All right, Tremaine," Talmadge continued in a conversational tone. "I'm going to ask you some questions about your activities as Exodus. I'm especially interested in hearing names and locations of your cohorts."

"Save your breath, Talmadge," Logan replied, breaking his silence and eyeing the lawman levelly. "I won't tell you anything."

"I advise cooperation on your part, Tremaine, for I assure you, lack of it will be very—shall we say—unpleasant for you. My friend Stryker here has a nasty punch, which he seems very eager to use." He took a small pad of paper out of the inside pocket of his coat and went to the table in the middle of the room. There he sat down in the one chair in the cell and picked up the quill pen lying next to the inkwell.

"Now then, to begin the list. Give me names and locations of your criminal colleagues in the underground."

Logan said nothing, bracing himself for the blow he knew would be coming.

"It would seem our prisoner has had a temporary lapse of memory, Jake," Talmadge went on. "See if you can jog it for him a bit. But take care. Nothing that shows. I want no visable marks on him that might draw sympathy for him at his trial."

Jake Stryker smiled and he brought his big fist back and swung it forward twice into Logan's stomach. Logan felt the breath gush out of his lungs as his body pitched forward in reflex. But his arms bound against the bars held him securely. Excruciating pain bit through him from the sharp jerk on his shoulder and the blow to his midsection. Logan gasped for air and tried to right himself.

"Now, let's try it again, shall we?" Talmadge said with a satisfied sneer. "Let's start with the names of your contacts here in Richmond."

When Logan only glared at him making no reply, Talmadge again motioned to Stryker and the hulking man hit Logan another paralyzing blow to his stomach, then gave him a hard punch to the kidney. Logan lurched again, his senses reeling from the brutal pain and lack of air. He shook his head to try to clear his senses as he gasped for air and used his anger to fortify himself against the next blow. His fists clenched white below the ropes that held his wrists.

"Come, Tremaine," Talmadge admonished, "why put yourself through this? It's quite distasteful to me really. We are both gentlemen and can conduct this session in a civilized manner if you will only choose to cooperate."

"Go to hell, Talmadge," Logan spat through gritted teeth before a spasm of coughing consumed him.

Ross Talmadge frowned and nodded to Stryker. This time Stryker applied his powerful fist to Logan's wounded shoulder, landing first one terrrible blow on it, then another. His shoulder bled profusely as Logan lost consciousness and slumped forward against his bonds.

"You idiot!" Talmadge fumed at Stryker, coming quickly to his feet. "Get him off those bars. I didn't want him unconscious. He can't talk then. And look, he's bleeding all over the floor! Dodge, go get something to clean it up."

While the man called Dodge left the cell, Stryker and the other guard untied Logan and eased him to the floor.

"This isn't getting us anywhere," Talmadge went on, still annoyed. "Tremaine's not going to talk this way. He's a tough bastard. You, Crothers, get some water to throw on him to wake him up. And something to bandage him with," he ordered the other guard. "Stryker, go get Mrs. Tremaine and bring her here."

When they'd gone, Talmadge came to stand over Logan's unconscious form. "As much as I was enjoying this little session, I'll have to try a different approach. I need you in one piece. We'll see if we can loosen that tongue of yours with your pretend wife's help."

Logan was just starting to revive from the bucket of cold water that had been thrown on him when Rhea was brought to the cell. She walked in a daze, letting Jake Stryker lead her by the arm, for she still hadn't recovered from what had happened with Grayson Sawyer. But when she saw Logan's condition, she came to life again.

"My God, what have you done to him?" She wrenched free of Stryker's hold and ran to Logan, falling on her knees next to him on the floor. She took his head gently into her lap and brushed the wet hair away from his face. The blue prison shirt he'd been given to wear was soaked with blood.

"Logan, darling . . ." she murmured his name tenderly, touching his ashen face and lips with her fingers. Then she turned blazing eyes on Ross Talmadge.

"You animal! Why have you hurt him like this? He lost so much blood before. Much more and you'll have a corpse on your hands. Get a doctor for him!"

"He'll have a doctor when I'm finished with him," Talmadge answered coldly.

Rhea eyed him furiously for a moment before she turned to look at the guard who'd just entered the cell. "Give me those!" she ordered angrily, reaching a hand out for the clean bandages he held.

"Rhea . . ." Logan whispered her name hoarsely as he opened his eyes and looked at her. He couldn't focus clearly yet but he knew it was Rhea.

"Yes, darling, I'm here. Please try to lie still. You're bleeding badly."

Rhea took the next twenty minutes to redress Logan's shoulder for she worked as slowly and gently as possible. She saw that his teeth were gritted against the pain and he flinched when she touched the blood-soaked old bandages and applied the clean ones. But no sound came from him. She tenderly wiped the perspiration from his face.

"Are you all right?" Logan asked then, looking at her. He raised his good arm and touched the side of her face where a dark bruise showed. "Has Stryker hurt you?"

"No, darling, it wasn't Stryker," Rhea stammered, clasping his outstretched hand. "It was Grayson Sawyer. He . . . I . . . I shot him, Logan. He's dead. I didn't mean to do it, but he attacked me. We struggled and the gun—I had a gun in my boot . . . It went off . . ."

"So you say, Mrs. Tremaine," Ross Talmadge interrupted then. He motioned to Stryker who stepped forward and grabbed Rhea roughly by the arm, yanking her to her feet so she was wrenched away from holding Logan's head.

"Tie Tremaine to the chair," Talmadge ordered Dodge and Crothers.

As the two guards dragged Logan to his feet he blanched white and gasped slightly under his breath at the movement.

"Be careful with him!" Rhea shouted, trying to free herself from Stryker's hold, to no avail.

The guards tied Logan's wrists to the wooden arms of the chair Talmadge had occupied before.

"Now, shall we get back down to business," Talmadge said then. "You were about to give me certain names and locations pertaining to your illegal activities as Mr. Exodus."

Logan made no reply. Rhea watched him in anguish. She longed to go to him and hold him. *Tell them what they want to know so they won't hurt you anymore,* she pleaded in her thoughts as she strained against Stryker's hold. She bit her lip hard to keep from speaking the actual words, for she knew Logan wouldn't want her to show weakness. Neither would he heed her words. She knew he would never betray his friends to save himself, no matter what barbaric treatment Talamadge inflicted on him.

Rhea felt hot tears of anger and frustration well up in her eyes, but she blinked them back and willed herself to be strong. If Logan could be strong during all this horror, she could be, too . . . she hoped.

Logan had his senses back now, sharpened to the extreme by the constant stabbing ache in his shoulder. He ignored Talmadge and looked steadily at Rhea, taking in her torn blouse, disheveled hair, and bruised cheek. He felt a cold and deadly anger that forced all else out of his mind. His hands clenched the wooden chair arms in a knuckle-whitening grip.

"You are trying my patience, Tremaine," Talmadge said then with irritation.

Logan looked away with feigned disinterest. Talmadge frowned and nodded curtly toward Jake Stryker, who immediately pulled Rhea's arm behind her, giving it a hard twist. Caught off guard, Rhea couldn't stop herself from gasping at the sudden pain that shot through her. Logan's head whipped around toward her. His eyes were a glacial blue and narrowed to dangerous slits as they drilled into Stryker.

"Let me put it in another way, Tremaine," Talmadge continued, in control of his own temper again because he knew he would win now. "Miss Merrick here is not legally your wife but has pretended to be, which constitutes criminal fraud. She was caught aiding and abetting a known and wanted criminal, namely you. As if these charges were not enough, I can now add murder to the list, the cold-blooded killing of one Grayson Sawyer, her very own stepfather, right here in this jail."

"That's not true!" Rhea exclaimed, then she winced as Stryker's hold tightened. "It was self-defense. He attacked me!"

"So you claimed before, Miss Merrick," Talmadge came back with. "But my guards, men who are loyal to me, will testify otherwise if I order them to do so." He shifted his gaze from Rhea to Logan. "Do you get my point, Tremaine?"

"I'm listening," Logan replied coldly, a feeling of dread eating into his gut for he knew the tactic Talmadge was going to use on him now. He would be forced to tell Talmadge what he wanted to know. He couldn't see Rhea sacrificed.

"Good," Talmadge went on with a note of triumph in his voice, "because the point I wish to make is that I might be persuaded to, shall we say, reassess the circumstances surrounding Miss Merrick's crimes so that lesser charges could be brought against her. I might be persuaded, that is, if I were to receive information that I considered to be more valuable and useful."

"No, Logan!" Rhea cried in a panic as she, too, saw Talmadge's ploy. Where only moments before she had wanted Logan to speak out to save himself, now she wanted only the opposite. "Please don't tell him anything! I'm not important. It doesn't matter what happens to me. What matters is what you have done as Exodus, what you've built. Don't let him destroy that. Please, Logan, don't tell him anything!"

"It matters to me what happens to you, Rhea," Logan replied in a softer tone, "and Talmadge knows that." He reluctantly pulled his gaze from Rhea's to meet Ross Talmadge's look of satisfaction. Logan's mind worked fast, searching for a way to somehow placate Talmadge and save Rhea, without revealing too much about the network.

"All right, Talmadge," he said at last, his voice stern again. "I'll tell you what you want to know, but on one condition. I don't want Rhea here. She knows nothing about all this and that's the way I want it. I hired her to play my wife for an entirely different reason. She didn't know I was Exodus until she accidently found me at the ruins two days ago. As to Sawyer, Rhea's telling the truth about shooting him in self-defense, I'm certain of that. Let her go, Talmadge."

"Logan, no, please don't . . ." Rhea echoed in a tortured whisper as she hung her head in despair.

"You are hardly in a position to bargain, Tremaine," Talmadge retorted sharply. "It is out of the question that I let her go. She is still useful to me. But if you talk, I don't care whether she's here in this room or not. Though Jake will probably be disappointed," he added wickedly. "He was looking forward to roughing her up a bit, I think." He smiled and winked at Stryker, who sneered back at him. "Sorry to disappoint you, Jake. Take Miss Merrick back to her cell. She's served her purpose for now. And try to be careful not to damage the goods on the way."

Stryker yanked Rhea around toward the cell door, but she managed to look at Logan one last time. The distraught expression on her face tore at Logan's insides. He hated putting her through this, but he had no choice now; Talmadge held all the cards at the moment. Logan could only hope something would happen to change that before it was too late.

Rhea let Jake Stryker push her ahead of him down the corridor to the outer door. Her spirit was too devastated to offer any resistance to his rough handling. It didn't matter anyway. Nothing Stryker could do to her would make her feel any worse than she did right now. For not only did she have to live with the fact that she had been responsible for Logan's capture, but now many other noble and courageous people would be sacrificed because of her.

When Rhea was left alone in her solitary cell, she could no longer hold back her tears of anguish.

Chapter 71

THE CITY OF RICHMOND BECAME EVEN MORE stirred up by Mr. Exodus's capture than Ross Talmadge had anticipated. The tide of the slavery issue was turning against the South. The outcry of powerful abolitionists was spreading far and wide in many northern states. Mr. Exodus was an all-too-real reminder of that fact. He had defied and outwitted their time-honored traditions and laws for over two years, and that didn't sit well with Exodus's southern victims who had been made to look so foolish. Then, to find out that this long-sought-after nemesis was in fact Logan Tremaine, one of their city's own wealthy gentry, was even more incensing. The good citizens of Richmond were soon making loud demands for revenge, and murmurs of taking matters into their own hands could be heard everywhere.

Somewhat nervous over the frenzied degree of the furor, Talmadge decided to expedite Logan's trial sooner than he'd first planned. He was riding the crest of public favor now over all this and didn't want to do anything to change that sentiment. And neither did Pacer McGill, the fiery prosecutor who, along with Talmadge, clearly saw the political ramifications such a sensational issue would afford him. He worked closely with Talmadge to push Logan's trial to court only five days after his capture.

Rhea was kept in solitary confinement in her basement cell and saw only the guards who brought her meals twice a day. Talmadge would allow her no visitors, a precaution against having anything else happen like the Sawyer shooting.

The guards spoke to her only in perfunctory remarks,

save for one man who seemed somewhat sympathetic to her plight. At her repeated pleas, he finally brought her news of Logan, but only that a doctor had seen to his wound with successful results. Logan seemed to be recovering well. It was so little to hear, but all that Rhea had to cling to. She'd been so afraid Logan's shoulder might become infected after his brutal treatment that day in the interrogation cell. It was a small relief to learn he was better.

Rhea wondered absently if Ross Talmadge would keep his word to charge her with lesser offenses in exchange for the vital information Logan had given him about the underground. But she didn't really care whether he did or not. Her spirit and hope were all but extinguished from the long, lonely days in solitary, when she had nothing to do but mourn for what might have been between Logan and her. How she wished there were some way she could change all the terrible things that had happened. But she knew she couldn't. If he died, then she wanted that fate also, for she knew she would never be able to endure any kind of life without Logan.

Logan's trial was merely a formality, a farce really. The jury and almost everyone else in the courtroom was clearly of a hanging temperament.

Talmadge made Rhea attend, but she was kept separated from Logan. Logan looked far better than he had when she'd last seen him five days ago. He was still somewhat pale and looked tired, though he sat straight and proud in his chair at the defense table.

Talmadge had seen to it that Logan and Rhea had suitable clothes to wear. He didn't want either of them drawing any sympathy from the spectators by having them appear in court unkempt. Rhea's cheek was only slightly discolored now where Grayson Sawyer had struck her. By the time her own trial came on the docket, there would be no sign evidencing Sawyer's assault on her.

As the trial progressed, Vanessa Forsythe's appearance on the witness stand proved to be the most spellbinding. She was stunningly beautiful in a demure, pale green dress that accented her good figure, though in a tasteful fashion. Few sounds were made in the crowded courtroom as she spoke her testimony in a clear and confident voice, telling the details of the information she had given Ross Talmadge concerning her suspicions about Logan. Then she went on to tell of the plans she'd made with Talmadge to try to trap Mr. Exodus.

"Mrs. Forsythe's courageous actions, along with Captain Talmadge's, have rid this community of a great and dangerous menace, one who is a traitor to the very sacred, grass-roots traditions of the South!" the young prosecutor expounded forcefully after Vanessa's dramatic testimony.

Murmurs of assent rose to a considerable din throughout the courtroom. Rhea watched in horror as even the old judge nodded his agreement.

Logan's attorney didn't even bother to cross-examine Vanessa. He was an elderly man, a long-standing friend and attorney to the Tremaine family. Yet it was apparent by his disdainful expression that he did not relish his task as Logan's defense attorney. The defense he'd finally decided to plead was that of not guilty by reason of mental instability. But this defense he offered only half-heartedly, either because he recognized the futility of such a plea in view of the jury's state of mind or because he didn't believe it himself.

This was no impartial court of law. It was a kangaroo court only going through the formal steps of a trial. With sinking heart, Rhea realized Logan had already been tried and condemned by everyone in the room save only herself. And there was nothing she could do about it.

In desperation, Rhea looked around the room hoping to spy an ally who might speak on Logan's behalf. She visibly recoiled when her eyes locked with a malevolent gaze directed at her. Dreed Jessup watched her now from his seat near the back of the room. A nasty smirk curled on his mouth, revealing how greatly he was enjoying her plight right now. Rhea forced herself to look away from him.

She saw Vanessa Forsythe sitting regally in her chair near the prosecutor's table, basking in the attention she was receiving. Her smile was cold, her look steeped in malicious satisfaction as she cast her green eyes on Logan. He acknowledged her gaze with a slight nod of his head, but his expression of bored indifference never wavered.

Rhea wanted to scream at Logan to stand up and defend

himself. Somehow he had to make these people see that what he had done in helping slaves to be free was noble and just and right. But he did nothing, said nothing as the evidence was presented against him piece by piece. Rhea could hardly endure it. With a heavy sadness in her heart, she sank back in her chair. Perhaps she did know why Logan remained silent. Two centuries of thinking regarding slavery couldn't be changed in one afternoon and he knew it.

Rhea looked over at Logan's family sitting together on the other side of the room. Camille was pale and drawn. A stricken look marred her lovely face and Rhea's heart went out to her.

Miles's jaw was set in a grim line. He watched the proceedings with rapt attention, but Rhea could not read his expression.

Silas Tremaine sat straight-backed and frowning in his wheelchair, moving little else but his light blue eyes, which were so like Logan's. They flicked and darted around the room, taking in all that was happening. He had told Rhea once that the Tremaines stood together against all others. If only they would stand with Logan now.

Rhea's eyes caught Silas's for a moment, and she thought his gaze softened some as it met hers. But he said nothing to anyone and made no effort to stop the proceedings.

Only Drew Tremaine showed a sign of any real emotion. He was clearly uncomfortable, fidgeting in his chair and leaning over several times to whisper something to a young man of the same age who sat next to him. Rhea wondered if his apparent anger was directed toward a vindication of his older brother or as a condemnation. She feared there would be no help from any of Logan's family.

Rhea longed to take the stand herself to plead for the man she loved, but she was not called. Besides, no one here present would listen to her now. Pacer McGill had seen to it that her fraudulent arrangement with Logan was brought out as part of his condemnation of Logan's character and proof of his criminal tendencies. He also had been quick to point out that Rhea would soon be on trial herself for treachery and complicity and perhaps even more serious crimes.

Miles was the last to be called to the witness stand for
the prosecution. He spoke on behalf of himself and the rest
of the Tremaine family. He forcefully and repeatedly denied any knowlege of or participation in Logan's illegal
and clandestine activities as Mr. Exodus.

"We are as shocked and outraged as the rest of you in
discovering that one who calls himself a Tremaine could do
these despicable deeds." Miles sat forward on the witness
seat, his tone growing more heated and emotion charged
with each condemnation he spoke.

"We were as deceived by him as you were. I should have
suspected something when he brought that contemptible
woman into our home." He pointed an accusing finger at
Rhea and all eyes in the courtroom turned toward her.

"His only purpose was to trick the trusting members of
his family and further his own selfish and conniving ambitions! It is a great shame to us that he bears the name of
Tremaine, for he is a disgrace to us and dishonors all we
hold proud and dear. He is a disgrace to the South!"

Cheers resounded through the crowded room as Miles
was dismissed from the witness stand and walked back to
his place with the rest of the Tremaines. When he passed
Logan, he kept his eyes straight ahead and didn't even
venture a glance toward the man who was his brother.
Rhea simply couldn't believe his heartlessness.

When called as a witness in his own defense, Logan was
brief.

"I acted on the dictates of my conscience and did what I
knew to be right. All of you must do the same." Then he
stepped down from the witness stand, saying no more.

Rhea's heart was leaden with despair. Had he given up?
Why didn't he even try to defend himself? But she knew
what he must be feeling because she was feeling the same
way herself. Everything was against them. It looked so
hopeless.

The mockery of a trial didn't take long. In less than two
hours the condemning testimony had been spoken, the
incriminating evidence presented. The jury didn't even
bother to leave the box. The men put their heads together
for only a few minutes before announcing they were ready
to give the verdict. Twelve times the terrible pronounce-

ment of "guilty" rang out loudly and clearly through the courtroom.

Logan stood tall and proud before Judge Bentley to hear the verdict and the sentencing. Murmurs of excitement spread through the crowd until the old judge pounded his gavel for quiet. Then everyone became hushed with anticipation as he cleared his throat and his deep voice resounded through the room.

"Logan Tremaine, you have been tried by a jury of your peers and found quilty of malicious crimes against your neighbors and the honorable State of Virginia. Do you have anything to say before sentence is passed against you?"

Logan took a long moment to look slowly around the sea of faces in the room. His eyes paused on Rhea before he turned back to face Judge Bentley again and said, "No, your honor."

"Then hear the sentence pronounced. Logan Tremaine, you are condemned to death by hanging. Said hanging shall take place four days hence. Use those days to reflect on the futility of your crimes and make peace with your Maker. And may God have mercy on your soul."

Judge Bentley banged the gavel on the bench and rose to leave. Two bailiffs stepped forward to lead Logan away. Everyone in the room seemed to be talking at once. Some exited quickly to spread the news of the trial's outcome to the waiting throng outside.

Logan's and Rhea's eyes met as he was being taken from the courtroom. Logan smiled slightly, his pale blue gaze lingering on her as he walked between the guards. She drew strength from that momentary touching of their spirits. Logan hadn't lost any of his dignity and strength of will, she could see that. Rhea determined that she wouldn't either, not even when her time came to go to trial. She would show these southerners the dignity and fortitude a northern woman would have.

Yet it would be so hard. How could she possibly endure Logan's death? She would never have the strength to keep from falling to pieces if she were forced to witness his hanging. Logan, Logan . . . To have found his love, then only to lose him like this. She wished she had been condemned to die with him. Life could be so heartlessly cruel.

Chapter 72

RHEA STOOD FROZEN WITH FEAR AT THE BARRED window of her cell. After the trial had ended the day before, she'd been moved from her basement isolation cell to this regular one in the east cellblock located in the back of the large headquarters away from the main street. She was again kept separated from Logan, who was in the other cellblock, isolated from other prisoners.

Now it was night, likely after midnight. Rhea could catch only a glimpse of the main street from her cell window that looked out over a dark alley. But that glimpse caused her great alarm as she saw people walking by the alley entrance. Men carrying torches and guns. The noise of their angry shouts and murmurings increased even while she strained to see them. Rhea slowly realized with a terrible fear that a lynch mob was forming with only one intent in mind—to take the law into its own hands. Apparently these people couldn't wait for Logan's formal execution in just a few days. They wanted to do the dirty job themselves—now.

With growing panic, Rhea paced her dark cell. Only the dim glow from a lamp hanging from the ceiling in the corridor gave her some light. Could Talmadge handle this mob? Would he even try to stop them from killing Logan?

"Please, God, save him somehow . . ." she whispered in the darkness.

Rhea involuntarily gasped with fear as several shots suddenly shattered the night. She ran to the window again, standing on tiptoe on the cot to try to see down the alley. Long moments passed. It was quiet, too quiet . . . Rhea's nerves were on edge as she waited for something else to happen. And then she saw them, men walking away up the street. They passed the alley entrance in pairs and groups of three and four. She could hear their angry grumblings but couldn't make out their words.

Rhea felt weak with relief. She climbed down from the cot and sat down on it, hugging her arms around her. Talmadge had been able to turn back the mob. Logan was safe . . . for now.

Ross Talmadge hadn't stood with his men against the hostile crowd out of any noble sense of duty or for any humane reason such as wanting to prevent bloodshed. He would be glad to see Tremaine dead and out of his way now. Only the hanging remained and then Tremaine would be of no more use to him. He would have served his purpose for furthering the lawman's political ambitions.

But he'd received a telegram that afternoon which had spurred him to do his duty in seeing that Logan Tremaine went to the gallows legally and at the appointed time. The governor had wired that he'd be coming through Richmond on his campaign swing for re-election, and he intended to witness the hanging of the notorious Mr. Exodus. Talmadge couldn't allow such an opportunity to be taken from him by a lynch mob.

The next morning Rhea tried to sing to give herself courage and also to drown out the relentless sound of hammering she could hear through her barred window. She put her hands over her ears but still could hear the death-tolling pounding. She knew that with each passing moment, another nail had been added to the gallows that would bring Logan's death.

As she stood at her window Rhea noticed many more guards were patrolling around the jail than she had seen before. Ross Talmadge must not be taking any chances on having a mob descend on his headquarters again. While she was glad Logan would be protected for these last remaining days, at the same time she saw all hope dashed that Evan VanHorn or some of Logan's other abolitionist friends would be able to break into the jail and help him escape before his doom could be sealed.

* * *

Logan's execution day dawned rainy and dreary. It matched the deep gloom shrouding Rhea's heart. It had been four days since she'd seen Logan. Though she'd pleaded with the guards who brought her food to let her see him just once, they'd paid no heed to her.

The morning crept by. The execution was set for twelve o'clock. Would she not even get to see Logan one last time before he was made to walk those last terrible steps to his death? Rhea wept in misery and despair.

It was nearing noon, and looking out of her cell window, Rhea could see hoards of people milling about on the street that ran by the front of police headquarters. The gallows was out of her line of view, and for that Rhea was grateful.

Footsteps approached. A key sounded in the heavy iron door leading to Rhea's cellblock. The door swung open and four men came through—Captain Talmadge and Logan, flanked on either side by a guard with gun drawn. Rhea's pulse quickened at the sight of Logan. Her heart raced as she watched Talmadge turn the key in the lock of her cell door, then remove the manacles securing Logan's hands behind his back.

"Ten minutes, Tremaine," he barked gruffly as he locked Logan in the cell with Rhea. Then he smiled smugly as he added, "We don't want to keep the hangman waiting."

Talmadge stationed one guard at the iron door, then he and the other deputy left.

"Logan . . ." Rhea's voice was barely a whisper as she hurried into the circle of his arms. She couldn't keep the hot tears from welling up in her eyes, though she blinked hard trying to hold them back so she could see him clearly. "Oh, my darling . . ." she murmured as she wrapped her arms around Logan's waist to hold him close. They kissed long and lingeringly.

"Are you all right, Rhea?" Logan asked softly when they finally parted a little. "Has anyone hurt you?"

"No, I haven't been harmed. Are *you* all right, my darling? Your shoulder?" Rhea turned liquid blue eyes up to look at him. How wonderful to be near Logan again. Clean-shaven, in gray trousers, open-necked white shirt, and gray vest, he looked so very handsome.

"It's mending well," Logan replied. "Evan's been tending me. Talmadge doesn't know of our association."

"I'm so glad," Rhea whispered as she laid her head against his uninjured shoulder and ran her hands along his back, relishing the feel of him. Suddenly her hands stopped and she looked up at Logan puzzled. He put a finger to her lips and made a slight gesture toward the guard with his head before she could question him about the strange feeling under his shirt and vest. What was it? Something rough, with some slightly raised places . . . Straps? Or buckles?

Logan's voice was low as he spoke. "Don't ask any questions, my love, just listen very carefully to me, for we haven't much time." He took her two hands in his and raised them to his lips before he went on.

"How can I tell you how sorry I am that you've been involved in all of this?" Logan's heart was in his eyes as he gazed at her.

"It is I who am sorry, Logan. I caused you to be captured and forced to betray your friends. Can you ever forgive me?" Rhea asked, weeping openly now.

"Shhh, I'll hear no more of this," Logan told her gently as he reached up to brush a tear from her cheek. "I had been tempting fate for too long. You are not to blame. Do not shed your precious tears for that. This certainly wasn't part of our bargain, was it, my love?" A slight smile touched the corners of Logan's mouth for a moment.

"Nor was falling in love with you," Rhea replied. "But that happened, too. I have no regrets, except about now." She reached up to run her hand through his dark hair.

"All is not lost yet," Logan went on seriously. "Trust me. You must be very brave today, Rhea, and for the next few days. Show them that stubborn Yankee tenacity of yours. If my luck holds out and Miles comes through, we'll be together again, I promise you." He sounded more confident than he felt, but he wouldn't let Rhea know that.

Rhea's heart leapt at his words. "Miles? . . . Together? Miles has always been against you. Will he help you now? Logan, what—"

Logan shook his head to stop her. "I don't have time to explain," he said quickly, keeping his voice low. "But he will help if he can. There is a plan afoot for me to cheat the hangman today. All hinges on Miles and Evan and some others. And you, Rhea. Especially you. You must play the bereaved wife as convincingly as possible. Just when the noose is being put around my neck, you must cause a distraction. Become hysterical, scream, cry, anything to draw everyone's attention to you for a few moments."

"Oh, no, Logan! That will be dangerous for you!" Rhea cried in alarm. "Isn't there some other way? What if I'm not permitted to be there? What if something goes wrong?" Her face creased with worry.

"Knowing Talmadge, he'll have you there, to add to the spectacle," Logan told her. "This is the only way it can be done. Try not to worry, my love. Everything will work out."

"But how? What will be happening?" Rhea asked desperately. "Logan, I must know if you will be all right!"

"It is better that you know no more than that. Only trust me, Rhea. I've gotten you into this and I'm doing my damnedest to get you out of it—get us *both* out of it! Just remember this. If for some reason something does go wrong and the hangman has his way today, you must rely on Miles to help you. He and the others will try to get you out of here and away to Canada on the underground network. Do whatever they want you to do, Rhea. Rely on your inner strength to get you through this, my love. Be strong, for me. And no matter what happens, remember that I love you with all my heart. I want to live, Rhea, live for you . . . for us."

Logan kissed Rhea then, long and lingeringly. Pressing her close against him, he memorized all about her that he could gather with his senses—her softness, her beauty, the taste of her lips on his, the feel of her body against him. Yes, he wanted to live. He could only hope he'd have a chance to spend the rest of his life with this woman in his arms—Rhea, who held his heart as no other woman ever had or ever would.

"It's time, Tremaine." Ross Talmadge's brusque voice shattered the stillness.

Rhea felt as though her heart had stopped. She and Logan still stood close together. She could feel the warmth of his body. His hands seemed to burn into her where they touched her. How she needed his strength, his courage now. Rhea clung to Logan one last moment, hoping to gain some of it from him, praying that all would go well and Logan would somehow remain alive and be free.

"I can't lose you now, my darling," she whispered.

"You won't," Logan assured her in a voice only Rhea could hear. As he turned away from Rhea to leave the cell he couldn't help wondering if he'd used up his share of good luck. He hoped not, for he was going to need a mighty big share of it now to pull off this plan.

Talmadge waited until Logan's hands had been manacled behind his back again and the two armed guards were holding him before he turned to speak to Rhea.

"You'll be joining us, too, Miss Merrick."

"You bastard! You'd make her go through that?" Logan shouted angrily as he tried to lunge at Talmadge. Even though his outburst was a pretense, Logan would have liked to have reached the police captain even for the briefest moment, to settle a score. But the two brawny guards quickly pulled him back, stopping him with their drawn and cocked guns jammed into his ribs.

"Of course," Talmadge answered matter-of-factly. "It will make this event just that much more memorable for our distinguished audience. Did I tell you the governor arrived last night to witness this historic event? I intend to see that he gets the full exhibition."

"You dirty—"

"No, Logan, don't," Rhea only half pretended to plead. She feared he might be shot right then and there if he said any more. Quickly stepping between the two glowering deputies, she put a hand on Logan's chest to stop him. "Please, I'll do as he says. I want to be with you to the last." Logan finally nodded and stood quietly between the guards again.

Chapter 73

THE HUGE CROWD GATHERED AROUND THE GAL-
lows suddenly hushed as Logan was brought out and taken
up the steps by the guards. Another deputy stood with
Rhea, holding on to her arm securely. But she was glad for
his forced restraint. Otherwise she might have given in to
the weakness in her knees and collapsed right there.

Could this really be happening? Was Logan about to be
hanged? Could she do what he needed at precisely the
right moment to save him? Rhea's mind had trouble ac-
cepting the harsh reality of what was taking place before
her. It was all a dream, a terrible, paralyzing nightmare.
At any moment now she would wake up and find herself
safe in Logan's arms back at Fair Oaks. Why couldn't she
wake up?

Rhea saw Vanessa Forsythe sitting straight and proud
on a chair on the special raised platform that had been
built just for the hanging. A distinguished elderly gentleman sat next to her. Rhea heard the murmurs of the word
"governor" ripple through the crowd. Vanessa looked
beautiful. She was elegantly dressed, every shining red
hair was in place. She smiled charmingly as she spoke, and
might have been attending a party rather than . . .

Rhea couldn't finish the thought. She made her eyes
scan the crowd until she found the Tremaine family a
small distance across from her in the mass of people. Miles
was standing next to Camille, supporting her weeping figure with one arm. Sybil stood on the other side, and then
there was Drew. Young Tyler was missing from the group,
and Rhea was grateful he at least would not be subjected to
this horrible spectacle.

Even old Silas Tremaine was there in his wheeled chair. He looked straight at Rhea now, his gaze one of grim sympathy, as though he, too, were feeling the same anguish as she.

Rhea looked hopefully at Miles then. His face was solemn, lacking expression. Why was he standing there so calmly? Rhea's mind raced in alarm. Wasn't he supposed to be about to rescue Logan somehow? Why wouldn't he meet her gaze now? Had something gone wrong? Was he going to betray Logan after all and allow him to die?

Rhea felt panic welling up inside her, but she forced herself to remain standing with head held high for the moment. She would not have to fake the hysteria Logan had asked of her. She was on the verge of it right now. She only hoped she could keep herself in control until the moment Logan had told her.

Logan had reached the platform at the top of the steps. He turned and searched the crowd with his eyes, looking at each member of his family in turn. He paused the longest at his grandfather, who stared back solemnly in return. Then Logan looked away to seek out Rhea. His gaze held hers all the while his sentence was being read aloud by the bailiff. His look of assurance calmed Rhea some.

A man with a clerical collar stepped forward next and administered a prayer for the soul of the condemned man, offering the hope that Logan's death would not be in vain but would serve as an example to discourage unholy abolitionist activities.

Logan was permitted to say his last words. He spoke in a strong voice and with sincere conviction.

"My only regret is that my personal battle against slavery is about to end. But the war will go on against this terrible injustice. Slavery is wrong, my friends. Others will rise to take my place, to try to right that wrong. Men and women who are governed by heart and conscience will put an end to the abominable practice of owning human beings. It may not come tomorrow, but it will come, because we are in the right, in the eyes of God and moral justice. America can never call itself a land of freedom as long as one Negro wears the shackles of bondage. Remember someday that I told you this."

Rhea could almost feel the anger and hostility of the

crowd as the people reacted to Logan's words. Many began murmuring their condemnation of him. Suddenly someone raised his voice in a shout.

"We've heard enough! Carry out the sentence! Hang him! Hang him!" Other angry shouts joined the outcry.

Rhea stood frozen as she watched the hooded hangman slip the deadly noose over Logan's head. In panic she locked gazes with Logan one last time and prayed that she could do what was needed right now. She took a deep breath.

"NO!" she screamed at the top of her voice. Heads turned in her direction. *"No, no! You can't do this!"* she shouted while half twisting her body to get away from the deputy holding her. Catching him off guard, she was able to wrench her arm free of his grip and push her way through the confused spectators nearest her. Shoving people out of her way with a strength she didn't know she was capable of, Rhea tried to make her way to where the governor was, but too many people surrounded him. She turned toward Miles instead.

"You must stop this horrible execution!" she kept shouting loudly. "You cannot kill Logan! Someone stop it, please!"

Rhea now let go the hysteria that had lurked in her so near the surface. She was crying and flailed out with her fists at hands that were reaching out and trying to stop her. Two men finally grabbed each of her arms, but she managed to drag them both with her the few more steps it took to reach Miles and Silas Tremaine. Miles's emotionless expression did not change as he looked at her.

"How can you let this happen?" she demanded, straining against the hands that held her. "He is your *brother!* Your *grandson!*" She swung her gaze to the elder Tremaine, then back to Miles. "For God's sake, can't you do something? Do you hate him so much that you would allow him to be murdered here today because he offended your pride, your stupid, stubborn, southern pride?" Rhea struggled against the men holding her, twisting her head around so she could look at others.

"Murderers! You are all murderers for doing this! This is not justice! This is revenge! I curse all of you! May your consciences torment you for the rest of your miserable

lives!" She swayed against one of the men next to her and wept uncontrollably. Camille rushed to her then, gathering her in her arms.

"Proceed with the execution!" the governor called out suddenly, rising to his feet.

Rhea's outburst had taken only moments, but it had caused such a distraction that no one noticed the hangman had taken longer than necessary to cover Logan's head with the usual solid black cloth hood. He'd first stood in front of Logan to pull it down over his face, then he'd stepped behind Logan again, putting to use those precious moments Rhea had gained for them. To anyone who was not watching Rhea's performance, it might have looked as though the hangman was just making some last-minute adjustments to the noose.

The crowd was hushed again now. Rhea turned and looked with dread at Logan's hooded figure standing on the gallows platform. She held her breath in agony, for she did not know if what she'd done had been enough.

The hangman had walked to the edge of the platform where the fatal release lever awaited. A somber drum roll was sounded. The whole assemblage seemed to be standing frozen at that suspended moment when the lever was thrown. The trap door under Logan's feet instantly fell away, but his body was held in place, suspended over the opening by the strangling noose. Logan's body jerked in a last spasm of movement for several moments, then was still. His hooded head was wrenched over awkwardly to one side at a sharp angle.

Someone was screaming. Again and again the piercing cries shattered the air. At the moment Rhea realized it was her own voice making the anguished sounds, she collapsed to the ground, unconscious.

Chapter 74

THE PUNGENT ODOR OF SMELLING SALTS FORCED
Rhea back to wakefulness. The gloomy grayness of her jail
cell met her eyes as she tried to focus and regain her
thoughts. She felt worse when she did . . .

Evan VanHorn stood over her, recapping the small bottle. Rhea started to speak. She had to ask him about Logan. Did he live or was he lost to her by death forever?

But a quick warning frown from Evan cautioned Rhea to
silence so that she only moaned and turned her head to
survey the cell. Ross Talmadge stepped into view then and
she knew why Evan had stopped her.

"Come now, doctor," he said somewhat impatiently.
"She is revived. You have other matters to attend to. Tremaine will be brought in shortly. You'll have to make the
official declaration of his death and sign the necessary papers. His family will no doubt wish to claim his remains for
burial as soon as possible. Bodies tend to rot fast in this
heat, as you well know."

"I'll try to look in on you later, Mrs. Tremaine," Evan
said formally, as though they were unacquainted. "Here is
a mild sedative to help you if you need it." He handed Rhea
a small packet.

Rhea turned her face to the wall. She just wanted to
block out everything—all of now, all of the past, even the future. Talmadge's words had shattered all her hopes. Logan
was dead. What could tomorrow bring for her now except
regret and emptiness? She wished she could die, too, even
though some small part of her wanted to hang onto the desperate hope that somehow Logan had accomplished his
plan and was still alive. But was she only torturing herself

more with such thinking? Evan would know, but he did not return. The hours of the afternoon passed slowly, agonizingly.

In the evening Ross Talmadge came to Rhea's cell. She didn't even look up from her cot as he had the guard unlock the cell door and let him in.

"And how is our distraught little widow this evening?" he inquired sarcastically. "The guard said you didn't eat any of your supper. We can't have that. You must keep up your strength, Miss Merrick. You will have your own day in court very soon, to answer the serious offenses with which you are charged."

Rhea made no response nor movement. Only her open eyes and the slow rise and fall of her chest told Talmadge that she was even still alive. It unnerved him somewhat.

"You will be glad to learn," he went on quickly, "that I have heard back from an inquiry I made to Philadelphia concerning you. My source could find no information linking you to the National Anti-Slavery Society or any other such radical abolitionist organizations. I had hoped to gain some incriminating evidence in your background to add to that which I already have to convict you. Of course, such things can be contrived easily enough, as you well know."

Rhea finally turned her head to look at him. "You never had any intention of keeping your part of the agreement you made with Logan, did you?" she asked listlessly.

"My dear woman, I feel no obligation to keep bargains with criminals, especially when they involve another criminal, namely yourself."

Rhea sat up on her cot, continuing to look toward him but showing no visible emotion.

"I expected as much from you, Captain Talmadge. You destroyed the man I loved. I am dead inside. You have done exactly what you wanted. Logan is dead. You will have my downfall also. It doesn't matter. What more do you want from me? If you have any decency in you, you will allow me some shred of dignity and let me grieve alone. Please get out."

Rhea had spoken in a monotone devoid of feeling. Her eyes stared at Talmadge yet were not focused clearly on him. There was no fire in their blueness. Talmadge had ex-

pected hysterics or weeping, perhaps even anger, outrage
from her. But not this. Rhea's eyes were dry, her manner
dazed yet comprehending.

Ross Talmadge shifted from one foot to the other, suddenly uncomfortable about being here. He didn't want to
push Rhea Merrick over the edge of sanity and have her go
to pieces on him. He still had use for her. Her trial would
draw almost as much attention and publicity as Tremaine's had if he played it right. Better to leave her alone
for now.

"I shall, of course, honor your wishes," Talmadge announced abruptly as he turned to leave. "Good night, Miss
Merrick."

No one came to Rhea's cell the next day except the same
sullen guard from the day before, bringing her luncheon
meal. Rhea didn't try to talk to him, and left the food un-
touched again. She didn't want to see anyone at all. Her
despondency was deepening with each long, dreary hour.

Rhea slept some in the afternoon, lulled to unconsciousness by Evan's medication. At supper Rhea forced herself
to eat some of the food that had been brought to her. She
knew Logan never would have wanted her to give up like
this. He had had courage, dignity, even hope right to the
very end. In his memory Rhea decided she could do no less.

And she had another reason for taking nourishment,
though she took no joy in knowing it now. While she'd convinced herself that the nausea she'd been feeling for days
now had been caused by all the terrible things that had
been happening, Rhea finally had to concede that they
were only part of the reason. She was certain now that she
was pregnant with Logan's child. Under any other circumstances she would have welcomed this news, but not now
with what she was facing—no Logan, no future except in
prison. Logan would never know that a part of him lived
on, not only in her heart and memory, but also within her
body as well.

Later in the evening a commotion in the alley drew
Rhea to the window of her cell.

"Meadows! Jackson! Captain says you're called off
guard here and ordered down to the Regency Hotel! It's on

fire and the governor's there! Every able man's being
called out!''

At almost the same moment the alarm bell in the nearest firehouse tower shattered the night with its loud
clanging, arousing all to the scene of the crisis. Rhea
caught a glimpse of people rushing down the main street
toward the big hotel. She could see the glow from red
flames licking the dark night sky just above the tops of the
buildings. The Regency was only four blocks away. Would
the fire spread this far?

Suddenly a movement at the other end of the alley
caught Rhea's eye. Was something lurking in the shadows
there? Something or some*one?*

Ross Talmadge strode hastily into his office in the same
headquarters, followed by Jake Stryker. He scowled as he
yanked open the bottom drawer of his desk and pulled out
a small box.

"Damn it! The Forsythes certainly picked a hell of a
time to have a slave uprising at their place! I'm up to my
neck helping to fight this blaze. The whole east side of
Richmond could go up in flames and that fop Forsythe asks
me for men to keep his niggers in line! Well, I can't spare
any. Take some of your men, Stryker, and get things under
control out there as quickly as you can, and then get back
here. Take these and consider yourselves deputized. Get
moving!''

"Right, captain. Leave it to me," Jake Stryker answered
as he grabbed a handful of the metal badges from the box
Talmadge was holding out and left the office.

Better make a quick check of things here before going
back to the fire, Talmadge decided as he walked out of his
office and turned down the corridor. He'd needed every
man at the fire and had only left a skeleton crew of guards
in the two cellblocks. He still had a valuable prisoner back
there. He should make sure someone was keeping an eye
on Rhea Merrick. He hadn't liked the way she'd been acting yesterday.

A sudden noise behind Rhea made her whirl around
away from the window in time to see the deputy who'd
been stationed outside her cell knocked unconscious by a

man with a mask over his face. Two other men with guns
drawn and masks covering the lower halves of their faces
rushed to Rhea's cell. One holstered his weapon and
jammed the key into the lock. Rhea gasped and backed
against the wall in fright. All three men came quickly into
her cell and one of them rushed toward Rhea. He stopped
just in front of her and pulled down his mask.

"Logan!" she cried as she rushed into his arms, laughing
and crying at the same time. "You're alive! You're alive!"

"Yes, love. That I am, thanks to you." Logan held her
close for a moment, then drew back so he could look at her.
"Are you all right?"

"Yes, oh, yes. I am now," Rhea assured him happily. "I
was so afraid."

"I know. I'm sorry there was no way to get word to you.
Evan tried, but he couldn't risk tipping his hand to Talmadge. But I'll explain everything later. Right now we
must get you out of here, and quickly."

"Dodd, Hitch, you know what to do," he called to the two
men who'd gone over to the far corner of the cell. "Don't
dally, boys."

The men had knelt down and were doing something with
a carpet satchel they'd carried in with them.

"Right, Logan. We'll need about five minutes here.
Then we'll have five minutes to get out."

"We'll check the outer corridor to make sure it's still
clear, then meet you in the alley," Logan said as he drew
his gun again and took Rhea's hand to lead her from the
cell.

Ross Talmadge had just found the unconscious body of
one of his guards. He drew his gun and glanced around, all
of his senses alert for danger. Then he crept along the
shadows against the brick wall toward where the corridor
took a right turn. Suddenly the sound of footsteps coming
at him from around the corner made Talmadge stop. He
pressed his back against the wall and waited, his finger
twitching on the trigger of his gun.

"Hold it right there!" he ordered as two figures came
cautiously around the corner into his range of vision. Both
froze at the sound of Talmadge's voice and Rhea gasped in
alarm.

"All right, drop your gun and get over there, both of you," Talmadge waved the barrel of his weapon toward an empty cell just to the left of them.

Logan let his pistol fall to the floor. Putting Rhea behind him, he started to walk slowly past Talmadge. As Logan stepped into the brighter circle of light thrown from the lamp overhead, Talmadge gasped at the face he saw reflected there.

"You!" Talmadge's jaw dropped open in shock.

It was exactly the reaction Logan was counting on. In the split second that Talmadge froze with surprise, Logan sprang. Catching Talmadge full in the stomach with a flying tackle, Logan took the police captain down, and the two of them grappled on the floor for possession of the gun.

Rhea frantically looked around for the gun Logan had dropped. Finally she spied it and dashed to pick it up. Holding the weapon with two hands, she tried to get a clear shot at Talmadge, but he and Logan were locked in close combat. Talmadge landed a jaw-cracking blow to Logan's chin which sent him reeling backward into the wall. But using that as leverage, Logan quickly thrust himself at his adversary again before Talmadge could swing his gun around and get a shot off. This time the impact of Logan's lunge caused Talmadge's gun to go flying out of his hand, into the darkness of the hallway. Their grappling continued for long minutes, with each man landing bone-rattling blows in turns. And still Rhea could not get a clear shot without risking hitting Logan.

Suddenly Logan was on his feet, pulling Talmadge up by the coat lapels. His right arm came back and like a shot went flying forward into Talmadge's jaw. Talmadge was hurled backward by the powerful blow. There was a terrible cracking of bone as he hit the brick wall hard with his neck and shoulders. His body slid limply down the wall toward the floor, stopping in a sitting position, his head cocked sharply to one side. He made no further sound or movement.

Logan was half bent over, clutching his midsection and breathing hard to catch his breath. Rhea ran to Talmadge and put her hand against the side of his neck, searching for a pulse.

"He's dead," she said in a hushed voice as she went then to Logan. "Are you all right?"

"Yes. Come on," he told her, taking the gun from her. "We have to get out of here before someone else shows up."

The two men who'd been in Rhea's cell came up then. One of them was carrying over his shoulder the unconscious guard that had been by Rhea's cell. They all moved quickly and quietly down the back corridor, stopping only long enough to pick up the other unconscious deputy whom Logan had knocked out before. They used the deserted alley to reach the back of a nearby building, then ducked behind a thick stone wall just as a thunderous explosion rocked the night. Flame and debris went flying from the jail in all directions.

The four of them watched the devastation for a few moments, then leaving the deputies behind the wall, they made their way to an old shed on a narrow street where horses awaited them. The man called Hitch left them. Following Logan, Rhea and the other man, Dodd, spurred their mounts into gallops, leaving Richmond in their wake.

Chapter 75

JUST BEYOND THE OUTSKIRTS OF THE CITY, Dodd pulled up to part company with Logan and Rhea. Rhea gave him her heartfelt thanks for his help, and then he was gone, swallowed up by the night shadows. Logan and Rhea went on, stopping only after an hour of hard riding. Logan reined in his mount and signaled for Rhea to do the same.

"I don't have Baron beneath me, nor Jade Wind for you. We'd better rest these animals and ourselves a little."

Logan seemed to know exactly where he was. Leading the horses on foot, he left the road and walked quickly across a small meadow to a stand of thick, tall pines. Rhea followed close on his heels. Logan tied their mounts to a sturdy bough and turned to find Rhea only too ready to hurry into the arms he held out to her.

"Oh, Logan, my darling," she murmured as she clung tightly to him. Her heart was filled to overflowing. Love, relief, gratitude tumbled together and spilled forth from the depths of her being. "Are we safe, really safe?" she marveled as she pulled back a little to look at him. There was no moon yet tonight and she couldn't see him clearly in the darkness. But her memory filled in the handsome features that her eyes could see only dimly.

"Safe for the moment at least, my love. How are you holding up?"

"Fine. I'm fine as long as I can be with you."

They sat down close together on the thick covering of pine needles on the ground. Logan kept his arm around Rhea's shoulders.

"Where do we go from here, darling?" Rhea asked then.

"I'll be glad to leave Virginia and all the terrible things that happened to us here far behind."

"We are leaving tonight, eventually to reach Canada," Logan assured her. "But we must wait here a little while. Some others are meeting us soon. There are yet a few things to be arranged before we can go."

They sat in silence holding each other for a time, listening to the sounds of the night and its woodland creatures, until finally Rhea spoke.

"Can you tell me now how you cheated the hangman yesterday? I tried so hard to believe you weren't really going to die, but when the lever was thrown and you were left there—left there . . ." She couldn't bring herself to say the words. The picture in her mind of Logan hanging suspended there on the gallows looking as though the life was being choked out of him was too horrible to frame into words. She heard Logan give a small laugh.

"I can tell you now I'm a little surprised myself that it worked. It was a risky plan at best but the only one we had. We used an old trick Miles and I devised as boys. We'd both forgotten about it all these years. I'd even forgotten that we'd had times like that as boys—good times, adventuresome times. They were buried in the bitter conflicts that grew between us, I suppose.

"I think it was the summer I was thirteen or so. There'd been a hanging in Richmond, a troublesome horse thief, and everyone in town was talking about it. Father hadn't let us attend the actual hanging so we decided to stage our own version from what we'd heard about it. Only neither one of us wanted to take the part of the thief with his head in the noose. But with Amos's help, we devised a beltlike harness for me to wear around my chest under my shirt. I remember our mother almost had heart failure when she saw me swinging from the big oak tree in the backyard. She thought Miles was trying to kill me.

"The one I wore yesterday was very similar to the one we'd made years ago. The wide belt went around my chest just under my arms. It had a piece of leather in the back that went between my shoulder blades. Sturdy hooks were attached to the leather. When the noose went around my neck, the hangman, who was a friend of mine, slipped the rope under the hooks. When the trap door dropped away, my weight was taken up by the hooks and distributed around my chest by the belt, instead of by the rope. That's why we needed the extra time your hysterical outburst gave us. You did that wonderfully."

"It wasn't hard to do," Rhea told him truthfully. "I simply let out everything I was really feeling inside. Had I been able to get to Miles, I might have killed him with my bare hands. I was certain he'd betrayed you."

The moon was rising over the horizon, touching its creamy glow to all within its vast range. Rhea could see Logan better now in its light, and her heart was filled with the love he'd awakened in her. He was shaking his head slightly as he spoke.

"No, he didn't betray me. The plan was mine, but Miles put it into operation. He arranged all of it and damned quickly, too. He risked everything to help me. If it weren't for him, I'd be dead now. He had Evan smuggle the harness in to me in his medical bag. He took care of the arrangements to have Tucker Corey stand in for the fellow who regularly does the hangman's task. The usual man lives in the next county and happened to be stricken with gout. He was very cooperative in letting another man take his place, especially when Tucker told him he hated me and wanted to be the one to put the noose around my neck, and he'd pay handsomely for the privilege of doing it. Tucker isn't known around Richmond. He told Talmadge he was a temporary replacement for the regular man and had a letter to prove it. That was the truth and Talmadge believed him."

"Why did he do it, Logan? Miles, I mean," Rhea asked then.

"Because he's my brother," came Logan's low reply. "I'd do the same for him." There was deep feeling in Logan's voice as he spoke. Rhea had heard it before when he'd told her he loved her. The old Logan never would have let such emotion tell in his tone or his face.

"But I must know more," Rhea perked up suddenly. "What happened after they cut you down? Surely Captain Talmadge checked to make certain you were dead. How did you fool him?"

Logan laughed again at her curiosity, but he understood and went on explaining.

"When Tucker stepped in front of me on the gallows to pull the hood over my face, he took an instant to slip a pill in my mouth. It was an opium-based drug that Evan uses to prepare patients for operations. It slows down your breathing and heartbeat drastically. I swallowed it immediately and by the time they cut me down, I was in such a deep sleep that I appeared dead. Evan is well respected for his medical skills. It wasn't difficult for him to arrange to be the one to examine my body and make the declaration of death."

"And all of this was devised in just these few days since we were captured?" Rhea asked in amazement.

"Believe me, they were the worst days of my life," Logan replied truthfully. "Not knowing what was happening to you was the hardest part."

The sound of approaching hoofbeats on the main road brought Rhea and Logan quickly to their feet then. Logan motioned for her to hold her horse's muzzle to keep it quiet as he did the same with his mount. Several riders galloped into the meadow just then. Rhea tensed with fear.

"It's all right, love," Logan told her. "They're the ones I was expecting."

Four riders trotted directly to the pines where Logan and Rhea were hidden. They quickly pulled up their horses and dismounted. One of them, the smallest, ran up to Logan.

"My God, it's true! You are alive!" Camille Tremaine gasped as she threw her arms around Logan's neck, hugging him tightly for a moment before she turned and hugged Rhea. "And Rhea, too! Oh, thank God, thank God!" Camille was crying with joy.

Miles stepped forward then. "I'm sorry, Logan. Camille insisted on seeing both of you. I had to tell her you were alive. She was so distraught with grief over your death that I feared for her health."

"It's all right, Miles," Logan assured his brother before he looked at his sister again. "I'm glad you know, little one. I was worried about how you would take all this."

"Oh, dearest Logan. I don't understand about all that's been happening, your being Mr. Exodus and everything else, but I am so glad you are alive and well. Both of you."

Camille smiled warmly at Rhea. "Your secret is safe with me forever, do not fear."

"I know it is, Camille," Logan told her.

"Well, now, ain't this a nice family gatherin'," a man Rhea didn't know said exuberantly as he stepped forward to shake Logan's hand. Evan VanHorn had also come with Camille and Miles.

"Rhea, this is Tucker Corey, my hangman," Logan explained.

"That was mighty fine hollerin' you did yesterday, ma'am. It sure made things easier." Corey flashed Rhea a friendly grin.

"Thank you, Mr. Corey. I'm so grateful for what you did."

"What's happening in Richmond?" Logan asked them seriously.

"No one was hurt in the Regency fire," Miles began to explain. "As you planned, most of the guests were out to supper or at the theater. The governor was nowhere near the hotel. Those few who remained were quickly evacuated. The fire was almost out before we left, though it served its purpose as a diversionary action.

"Nothing remains of the cellblock Rhea was in. No one was hurt in the explosion except Captain Talmadge. His body was found in the debris. Word has it the blast hurled him so badly he broke his neck in a fall. He won't be mourned by many. Hitch told us what really happened. The two deputies you dragged out couldn't make any identifications as to who hit them. It's a good thing you wore those masks."

"You got the letter to Babcock?" Logan asked. Miles nodded.

"He'll find it on his desk in the morning. It'll make front-page headlines. May even rival the story of your hanging, dear brother," Miles added with a slight smile. "It isn't everyday a Yankee insurrectionist is assassinated."

At Rhea's puzzled look, Logan explained.

"Calvin Babcock is the editor of *The Guardian* newspaper. A fictitious group that we call the "Southerners for the South and Slavery" delivered a letter to him tonight claiming credit for blowing you to kingdom come, my love.

If we make everyone think you're dead—that we're *both* dead—we won't have any bounty hunters like Stryker coming after us."

"I didn't think that crazy plan of yours had a chance in hell of succeeding, but somehow it did," Miles reflected, shaking his head.

"Thanks to you, Miles, and you, Evan and Tucker," Logan said gratefully as he moved his glance to each man in turn. "We both owe you our lives." Logan put an arm around Rhea's shoulders, drawing her closer against his side.

"Yes, thank you, with all my heart," she added.

"Well, just remember, Logan," Tucker Corey exclaimed with a broad grin as he mounted his horse. "That was for New Orleans. We're square now."

"Right, Tucker," Logan answered, smiling himself. "Try to keep out of trouble, old boy. I can't help you much from Canada."

"Reckon I'll just have to depend on my own wits, good looks, and devastatin' charm then," the big man shot back. "So long, Logan. Take care of this pretty little lady now, ya hear?" He touched the brim of his hat in a small salute to Rhea, then spurred his horse and rode away into the night.

"I've got to be going, too." Evan VanHorn spoke up then for the first time. "I have to look in on Jake Stryker. He won't be hunting for bounty ever again. He'll never ride a horse again, in fact. He had his leg broken in three places in a bad fall over at the Forsythe plantation tonight. Though we didn't plan it, some of Vanessa's slaves chose tonight to get riled up. Things have been very explosive over there ever since word got out among the Negroes about Vanessa's part in your capture, Logan. Mr. Exodus was like a savior to them. Losing you has made many of them lose their only hope of ever being free. Others are reacting violently." He paused to look at Logan before going on.

"They put Forsythe Hall to the torch, Logan. Wendall was down at the slave compound, but Vanessa was in the house. They say it went up so fast she didn't have a chance to get out in time."

Rhea gasped at his words. The others in the group were

somber. What Vanessa had done to Logan had been a terrible thing, but to die like that . . . to be burned alive . . .

Logan only nodded, saying nothing. He, too, was affected by Evan's grim news.

"I'm very glad everything worked out for you and Rhea, Logan, and that you're both all right," Evan went on then. He wouldn't meet Logan's look as he turned toward his horse.

"Evan . . ." Logan walked over to his friend and put a hand on his shoulder as he spoke. "My thanks for your help in making all these plans succeed these past few days. We've been a good team, you and I, but it's up to you to continue without me now."

"I can't begin to take your place, Logan," Evan protested. A frown marred his forehead as he faced his friend.

"No, not as Mr. Exodus, for he is no more. But what I've tried to do, what we and all the others in the network have been trying to do for the Negroes, that must go on, Evan. Every slave you help is one more free man. I will continue to do what I can in Canada. But you must lead them here now. Shut down the railroad for a few months until all this furor dies down. When things get back on keel again, you decide what to do next.

"I was forced to give Talmadge some information. Most of what I told him was false, but I had to give him some facts that were believable. I don't know if he had a chance to act on any of it or not, but just to be sure, perhaps you'd better shut down alternative routes D and Q."

Rhea sighed in relief at Logan's words, grateful to know he'd been able to trick Talmadge.

"Route K is just about complete," Evan offered then without hesitation. "We could finish recruiting the last two stationmasters for it over the next couple of months and put it into the network to replace D and Q."

"You'll do just fine, Evan," Logan told him confidently.

"Thanks, Logan. I'll miss you a lot, though. And you, too, Rhea. Godspeed to you both."

"And to you, Evan," Logan replied.

The two men shook hands. Rhea stepped forward to whisper a choked good-bye and put her arms around Evan in a farewell hug. Then Evan mounted his horse, reined him around, and rode away toward Richmond.

Logan turned to Miles. Now he felt a tightness suddenly constricting his throat. Miles, too, seemed somewhat uneasy when he spoke first.

"Well, don't get it into your head that I'm going to get involved with that damned underground of yours," he said, trying to sound stern, without success.

Logan smiled and shook his head. "No, big brother, you've done more than enough, believe me. All that I ask is that you forget anything you've learned about the network these past few days, especially about Evan."

"VanHorn?" Miles asked, pretending ignorance. "What's there to know about him other than that he's a fine doctor with much to offer the good citizens of Richmond?"

"Thanks, Miles," Logan began sincerely. "That word hardly seems adequate to express how I feel about all you've—"

"No need to say anything more," Miles interrupted, brushing aside Logan's words. "There aren't words for this, Logan, except perhaps to say I wish we could have all those years that we fought each other to do over again, this time differently."

"I know," Logan returned quietly.

The two brothers stood looking at each other for a long moment, speaking with their glances what words could not convey. Miles cleared his throat and dropped his gaze first.

"You're bound for Canada, then?" he asked hastily, changing the subject.

"Yes, probably Quebec," Logan replied. "It's certain we can't return to Fair Oaks ever again. It's yours now, Miles. Yours and Camille's and Drew's." He paused to glance at his sister, who stood quietly beside Rhea. "Guard it dearly for them. They need you and will require your intelligence and know-how even more now and in the times ahead. Change is coming, Miles. It's inevitable. Slavery will end someday. I'm certain of it. You'll have to find another way to work the land if the Tremaines and Fair Oaks are to survive. Start now. Give our slaves a stake in the land. Pay them, sell them shares of the planation for their own. It will give meaning to their lives and labor, and they'll work harder for you than any beating could ever spur them to do. Educate them, win their loyalty to Fair Oaks now, before it's too late. Make our family name and home something your son will be proud to inherit."

Miles was thoughtful a moment. "Maybe I could. The first thing I'm going to do at any rate is get rid of Dreed Jessup. He's no asset to us. I've been planning to dismiss him. I'll do it before another day is out. But you've laid a heavy task on my shoulders, Logan. I'll miss not having you around to keep my wits sharpened and help me think of new ways to keep our creditors at bay. You know we're heavily in debt." His brow knit into a worried frown.

"I may be able to help one more time in that," Logan offered. He pulled Rhea to him then and looked at her fondly in the moonlight as he went on to explain.

"One of the main reasons I drew Rhea into this intrigue of a false marriage was to stave off your plan to have Grandfather change control of Fair Oaks solely to you. I couldn't let that happen because I needed a few more months to see to fruition a plan of my own I've been working on for over two and a half years now." Logan looked at his brother levelly as he said his next words. "I was going to ruin you, Miles. Take control of Fair Oaks completely out of your hands. You would have been nothing more than a caretaker for me, had you chosen to stay on at the estate at all."

Miles's eyebrow went up in surprise. "That would have been quite a feat, had you been able to accomplish it. Truly the *pièce de résistance* of any scheme you and I have ever concocted against one another."

"I would have done it, all right," Logan assured him. "Those two large promissory notes issued by the Bank of Philadelphia are coming due the first of the year. Unless I'm mistaken, you won't have the money to pay them off. As of December, those notes will belong to me. Unknown to you, I have gotten into some very lucrative financial ventures the last few years—land speculation, a mining company, a shipping line. They have brought some high yields of return. In December I shall have the financial means to purchase those promissory notes from the bank. I was going to use them against you, Miles."

"And now?"

"Now all of that's changed. Instead of buying the notes, I shall pay them off. Do you remember Hugh Tennyson from

our youth?" Miles nodded. "He is a barrister in Philadelphia. I've been working closely with him in this and many
other things as well for several years now. Rhea and I will
go to Philadelphia en route north and take care of the necessary legal matters secretly with him. Fair Oaks will be
free of debt, Miles. My gift of thanks to you. You'll be able
to start with a clean slate and make our family estate what
you will. I know you'll do what's right, for you care about
Fair Oaks as much as I. I won't make any claim or interfere in any way again. You have my word."

"Oh, Logan—" Camille whispered, putting her fingers
to her lips as she wept. Rhea put an arm around her friend.

"I feel as though you've just saved my life, Logan,"
Miles admitted finally in a hushed tone.

"Then the debt I feel to you for these last few days is
met," Logan told him. The two men looked at each other
intently.

Hot tears welled up in Rhea's eyes as she watched this
midnight scene between two brothers who had been so
long lost to each other and who now were found.

"I'd like to tell Drew and Grandfather about all of this,
Logan, especially that you and Rhea are alive," Miles said
then, eyeing his brother carefully to see his reaction.

"Yes, Drew should be told, but give it a little time," Logan agreed thoughtfully. "And Grandfather, of course, if
you feel he would want to know . . ." He lowered his eyes
as a kind of sadness touched him.

Miles took courage from Logan's words to continue.
"You may find this hard to believe, but Grandfather's
been greatly upset by all this, and not because of the disgrace the family will be faced with for a while. We'll all
survive that. As you said, we've weathered worse."

There was an earnestness in his voice now as he went
on. "Logan, we may not be seeing you for a long time. We
don't know how much longer Silas will yet be with us. I
know you've always been at odds with him. But I think
perhaps the time has come for that to be mended between
you. I know he would want to be told of all this."

Miles paused briefly to let his words have their effect.
His eyes never wavered from Logan's face.

"Grandfather Silas is down by the main road in the carriage by now," he said then, a little apprehensively. "I told

Jubal to bring him to the crossroads on a matter of great importance. That was all. I know it is asking you and Rhea to take a further risk, so I shall leave it up to you to decide if you want Grandfather to know what has really happened with the two of you. If you choose not to see him now, I'll understand and can feign that having him brought here was a misunderstanding."

Rhea watched Logan as he stood silently in the moonlight.

"Oh, please go to him, Logan," Camille begged softly, stepping closer to her brother and putting a hand on his arm. "Make your peace with Grandfather."

Logan looked from Camille back to Miles.

"Come, Rhea," he said then, turning toward her and holding out a hand to take hers. "Let us see if he has arrived yet."

The black silhouette of the lone carriage was barely visible, outlined against the dense trees and overgrowth of weeds and bushes at the side of the road. The four riders approached cautiously from the meadow. Miles held up a hand to stop them, then dismounted, throwing his reins to Logan.

"Stay here where you're hidden. I'll make certain all is safe," he whispered just loudly enough for them to hear, then he moved away.

Rhea could tell by the way Logan sat in the saddle that he was alert to act at the first sign of danger. She felt nervous herself and listened intently for any sounds that might not be the usual noises of the breeze and the night creatures. She jumped when Miles reappeared from the shadows of the thick bushes a few moments later.

"Come ahead," he beckoned to them, still keeping his voice low.

The three of them dismounted. Miles and Camille stayed with the horses while Logan and Rhea went toward the enclosed carriage. No one else was on the road for the time being. Logan had just opened the carriage door to let Rhea climb in ahead of him when Silas Tremaine's acerbic voice broke the stillness.

"Confound it, Miles, having these leather window flaps down is going to suffocate me in this heat! Why—" The old man stopped abruptly and his jaw dropped open as Rhea came inside and Logan followed her. Two small lighted oil lamps attached to the inside wall just above the seat illuminated the inside of the large carriage.

"My God . . ." Silas murmured, his expression frozen in shock in the flickering light. "Logan . . . Rhea . . ." He put out a gnarled hand to touch them almost timidly, then he fell back against the leather seatback, hardly believing what his eyes beheld. "You're alive . . . ?"

"Yes, Grandfather," Logan assured him quickly, a note of alarm telling in his voice when he saw Silas's ashen features. "We are here, in the flesh. I hope the shock isn't too much for you."

"But how—how can this be?" Silas asked, his tone still incredulous. "I saw you hanged. And I was told of the explosion at police headquarters tonight." His blue eyes looked from Logan to Rhea in turn.

"We do not have much time to explain, Grandfather," Logan went on. "Miles, Rhea, and some others helped me escape the hangman. The explosion tonight was not what it appeared to be. Miles will tell you the details."

Logan lowered his eyes from Silas's direct gaze, and Rhea knew his next words would be difficult for him. She took hold of his right hand in both of hers and smiled encouragingly when he glanced over at her.

"Grandfather," he began slowly then, looking back at Silas across from him. "Rhea and I . . ." He'd been about to say that he was not really married to Rhea but quickly decided against it. To add that complicated story to the shock his grandfather had already suffered might prove too much. Miles could tell him all of that later, too.

"Rhea and I are going north to Canada. You understand that we can never come to Fair Oaks again? We may not see you after this night."

"Yes, of course, I understand," Silas easily comprehended, nodding his head and sitting up a little straighter in the seat now. He had recovered some from the initial shock of seeing them and was anxious to hear anything Logan was going to tell him.

"Grandfather, I want to explain. What I did as Exodus was something I was compelled by conscience to do. I do not regret any of it, save for the repercussions my actions have had on the family. I know you will not understand—"

"You are wrong, Logan," Silas interrupted then. His voice held a compassion Rhea had not heard from him before. He leaned forward. One hand rested on a silver-topped wooden cane for support. His other wizened hand he put over Logan's hand that Rhea was holding. "I understand that you did what you had to do, as you always have, no matter what the consequences. There was something different about you from the day you were born. I tried to change that over the years, but I could not do it. It has infuriated me endlessly all this time, perhaps because I saw myself in you in younger days that are long gone now." Silas's expression was gentle as he gazed at Logan.

"I have admired that steadfastness in you. For a man to stand against all others, even his own family, for what he believes is right, is an honorable thing to do. You nearly gave your life for those stubborn principles of yours—" Old Silas's voice caught then, and he had to clear his throat before he could continue. "And for that, I am proud of you, Logan, proud that Tremaine blood flows through your veins."

"Grandfather . . ." Logan murmured feelingly as he grasped Silas's hand in both of his and spoke his gratitude in the intense look he gave his grandfather.

Rhea was touched to the heart. Tears spilled down her cheeks as she watched the invisible wall of animosity that had been built so high between grandsire and grandson suddenly come tumbling down.

"But now you must go," Silas said then, some of his usual gruffness returning to his voice. "For there is danger of discover the longer you stay.

"Rhea . . ." He turned to her then. "I hope you realize what you are in for with this grandson of mine. But as I see it, you deserve each other. Now be gone, both of you. Make a good life together. Godspeed on your journey." He dismissed them with a wave of his hand as he leaned on his cane.

"Good-bye, Grandfather," Logan said, his eyes holding Silas's a moment longer. The old man nodded slightly.

"Good-bye, Grandfather Silas," Rhea added softly as she leaned over to kiss the gaunt cheek. Then she followed Logan through the door. They heard the carriage departing as they rejoined Miles and Camille off the road.

"All is well," Logan assured them, seeing their anxious looks. "Grandfather will have many questions for you, but we have buried our differences. Miles, thank you for that also." He looked intently at his older brother.

"I wish we had more time now that . . ." Logan's voice dropped off for a moment before he could continue. "Miles, I wish you and I . . ."

"I know, Logan," Miles said then, nodding. "I wish it could be otherwise, too. But the past cannot be changed, only the future. Now you and Rhea must be on your way. A long journey lies ahead of you.'

"We'll keep in touch through Hugh," Logan went on, knowing the time had come for them to leave.

"Yes, I'm certain that will work," Miles replied, turning then to Rhea and taking her into a hug. "Keep this brother of mine in line, will you, Rhea? Trouble seems to follow him. You'll have your work cut out for you."

"I shall try," she told him with a smile. "With all my heart I thank you, Miles, for giving Logan back to me, for everything you've done." She kissed him on the cheek before stepping back.

Miles put his hand out then and Logan took it in a strong grip, pulling his brother into a quick embrace. When they parted, Camille put her arms around both Logan and Rhea. Her eyes sparkled with tears in the moonlight.

"I shall miss you both terribly," she told them, her voice breaking with emotion. "But I can bear it knowing you are alive and safe. God bless you."

"And you, Camille," Logan and Rhea answered together.

Reluctantly Camille pulled away from them and walked to where Miles was holding her horse. They each mounted and looked back one last time.

"Good luck to both of you," Miles called to them. "And if you'll take some good advice from your older and wiser brother, Logan, you won't waste any time in *really* marrying Rhea!"

Logan smiled as he held Rhea against him by the waist.

"My exact intentions as soon as we're safe, big brother." He turned his head to look at Rhea and added, "If she'll have me."

"You and no other, my love," Rhea answered in a sure voice.

Miles and Camille called their good-byes then and disappeared into the darkness.

Chapter 76

RHEA AND LOGAN LAY NAKED IN EACH OTHER'S arms. Their bed was a soft quilt they had spread over a pile of sweet-smelling hay. They were in a corner of the huge loft in the main barn on Warren Laraby's plantation. High bales surrounded them, hiding them completely.

Rhea looked up through a hole in the roof at the sky overhead. The brightness of the moon almost obscured the stars. She sighed contently, thinking how wonderfully happy she was at this very moment.

"Is your wound hurting you?" she asked with concern, turning her head to look at him as she gently touched the bandage wrapped around his right shoulder. Her blue eyes wore a soft expression as she looked at Logan.

"No," he answered, smiling at her. "Don't worry, it won't hinder us tonight."

Rhea returned his smile and snuggled closer to his side.

"I'll have to tell Warren about that hole up there," Logan said then as he, too, looked at the stars above them. "The shingles must have blown off in the last storm."

"Or perhaps he leaves it that way so anyone who uses this loft can see the open sky," Rhea spoke her thoughts aloud.

"This may be the last soft bed we have for a while, so we'd better enjoy it." Logan looked over at her, and she felt her heart fill to overflowing with love for him.

"What will it be like in Quebec?" she asked suddenly.

"French," Logan answered teasingly, "very French. How's your command of the language?"

"I know it, but I'm rusty from lack of speaking it. I think it will come back to me, though."

"Good, because that is where our new life together will be, Rhea. To the world Logan Tremaine and Rhea Merrick are dead. We must build new lives. The past is gone and must be buried. But Canada is a good place to begin anew. Most of the slaves I've helped to escape have gone there. They need to be educated, taught skills so they can survive on their own. They've always been provided for by a master. They find freedom a strange and hard experience. There's much that we can do to help them." Logan's face was alive with hope and plans for better times to come.

"I ask only to be with you, my love, wherever you are," Rhea murmured in return, feeling the warmth of her love for him spread through her whole being. She was silent for a few moments as she let her fingers caress his chest.

"When we're in Philadelphia in a few days," she went on then, "I'd like to see my mother one last time, to try to explain what happened to Grayson . . . and to us. It's likely she will not comprehend what I will be trying to tell her. But still I must try."

"I understand," Logan replied, nodding. "I could have Hugh make arrangements for her care when I see him about the Fair Oaks debts."

"That would ease my mind greatly."

"Although we must take great care not to be seen in Philadelphia and cannot stay long, we must see one other person before we leave there," Logan told her then, his tone lighter now.

"Oh?" Rhea asked, looking up at him questioningly. "Who might that be?"

"An old friend of mine who runs a small mission for the poor near the wharf . . . Father Henry."

"And for what possible reason would we want a priest, pray tell?" Rhea asked playfully, raising up on one elbow to look at Logan. Her expression softened even more as their eyes met and held, and she read the same depth of feeling in Logan's pale blue gaze. How she loved him. Now was the time to tell him what their love had created. Her voice was hushed as she lowered her eyes and said the words, hoping she knew what his reaction would be.

"Will you finally do the honorable thing and make an honest woman of me, so our child can have a legitimate birth?"

"Our child . . . ?" Logan gazed at her in surprise. "You are with child?" The tenderness in his voice and expression spoke the answer to her question. But then his black brows knit into a slight frown.

"But are you all right?" He asked worriedly. "Is the child all right? You've been through so much."

Rhea smiled at him. "Yes. I can feel my body changing every day as your seed grows within me. He will be a strong and willful child like his father, I think," she teased, warmed by his concern.

"Or like *her mother,*" Logan added pointedly, returning her smile. "Now by all means we must have Father Henry make us husband and wife. No more pretending, Rhea." Logan's look touched Rhea to the depths. "I won't need Willy Scarsdale for this marriage certificate."

Rhea's joy over Logan's words faded at the mention of the ragged young man who had forged the marriage certificate that had begun everything between her and Logan.

"What is it, Rhea?"

"It's about Willy . . ." Her voice was hushed, and she couldn't meet his direct gaze. How she hated to have to tell Logan about his friend.

"He's dead, Logan. I'm sorry. Grayson was responsible for it. He bragged of it that day he attacked me in my cell. It was from Willy he learned that our marriage was a pretense, but I don't think Willy told them easily."

Rhea heard Logan sigh deeply. He was silent and Rhea was, too, as she lay back down at his side. She thought of the many things that had happened to them since their first fateful meeting back in Philadelphia outside Mrs. Wiggins's shop. But she and Logan had to put all that behind them now, except their love. None of the bad things could be changed. They must look to the future.

Logan and Rhea lay in silence for a long time, staring out at the summer night sky through the opening overhead. Finally Logan raised up to gaze at Rhea.

"What are you looking at?" she asked teasingly as she brought her arms up around his neck.

"You," Logan replied softly as he raised his hand to brush a wisp of hair away from her face. "How beautiful you are, my Rhea, with your hair touched by moonlight, your body so warm and inviting. How I dreamed of just such a moment during the long, agonizing days and nights we were apart. I dreamed of it many other times, too, even when I tried not to think of you back at Fair Oaks. In my mind and heart I made love to you again and again, longed to hold you, caress you, feel your body touching mine."

"Do that now, my darling," Rhea whispered. "Make love to me. You need dream of it no longer, for I am here with you now, where I shall always be, wanting you with all my heart and being."

Logan's hands moved over Rhea's body tenderly. His lips found her breasts and lingered there, savoring her and letting the smoldering embers of their love for each other slowly ignite into flame again. Rhea opened herself to him, coaxing him with her hands, her lips, and whispered words of love.

Heart spoke to heart. Touch inflamed desire until at last their overpowering longing for each other could not be held back and the two became one, lost in the sweet oblivion of their passion.

The crosswinds that had pulled Logan and Rhea apart had died away, never to return again. Another force, stronger and more all-consuming, overwhelmed them now—the love of a man and a woman for each other, enduring for a lifetime of tomorrows.

This is the special design logo
that will call your attention
to Avon authors who
show exceptional
promise in

THE AVON ROMANCE

the romance
area. Each
month a new novel
will be featured

SURRENDER THE HEART Jean Nash   89622-2/$2.95 US/$3.75 Can
Set in New York and Paris at the beginning of the twentieth century, beautiful
fashion designer Adrian Marlowe is threatened by bankruptcy and must turn
to the darkly handsome "Prince of Wall Street" for help.

Other Avon Romances by Jean Nash:

    FOREVER, MY LOVE   84780-9/$2.95

RIBBONS OF SILVER Katherine Myers   89602-8/$2.95 US/$3.75 Can
Kenna, a defiant young Scottish beauty, is married by proxy to a wealthy
American and is drawn into a plot of danger, jealousy and passion when the
stranger she married captures her heart.

Other Avon Romances by Katherine Myers:

    DARK SOLDIER   82214-8/$2.95
    WINTER FLAME   87148-3/$2.95

PASSION'S TORMENT Virginia Pade   89681-8/$2.95 US/$3.75 Can
In order to escape prosecution for a crime she didn't commit, a young English
beauty deceives an American sea captain into marriage—only to find his
tormented past has made him vow never to love again.

Other Avon Romances by Virginia Pade:

    WHEN LOVE REMAINS   82610-0/$2.95

Buy these books at your local bookstore or use this coupon for ordering:

Avon Books, Dept BP, Box 767, Rte 2, Dresden, TN 38225
Please send me the book(s) I have checked above. I am enclosing $_____
(please add $1.00 to cover postage and handling for each book ordered to a maximum of
three dollars). Send check or money order—no cash or C.O.D.'s please. Prices and numbers
are subject to change without notice. Please allow six to eight weeks for delivery.

Name _____

Address _____

City _____ State/Zip _____

Avon Rom 7 85